THE DARLING STRUMPET

Gillian Bagwell

WINDSOR
PARAGON

First published 2011
by HarperCollins*Publishers*
This Large Print edition published 2012
by AudioGO Ltd
by arrangement with
HarperCollins*Publishers*

Hardcover   ISBN: 978 1 445 87904 8
Softcover   ISBN: 978 1 445 87905 5

British Library Cataloguing in Publication Data available

Printed and bound in Great Britain by
MPG Books Group Limited

This book is dedicated to my family:
My sisters
Rachel Hope Crossman
and
Jennifer Juliet Walker
My father
Richard Herbold Bagwell
And the memory of my mother
Elizabeth Rosaria Loverde

She's now the darling strumpet of the crowd,
Forgets her state, and talks to them aloud,
Lays by her greatness and descends to prate
With those 'bove whom she's rais'd by
wond'rous fate.

From 'A Panegyrick Upon Nelly'
Anonymous, 1681

CAST OF CHARACTERS

NELL'S FAMILY

Eleanor Gwynn—Nell's mother.

Rose Gwynn—Nell's older sister.

Charles Beauclerk, Earl of Burford and Duke of St. Albans, referred to as Charlie—Nell's first son.

James, Lord Beauclerk, referred to as Jemmy—Nell's second son.

John Cassells—Rose's first husband.

Guy Foster—Rose's second husband.

Lily—Rose's baby girl.

MADAM ROSS'S

Madam Ross—keeper of a brothel in Lewkenor's Lane.

Jack—Madam Ross's lover and bouncer at the brothel.

Jane—one of Madam Ross's girls.

Ned—barman in the taproom.

Robbie Duncan—a regular client of Nell.

Jimmy Cade—an early regular client of Nell.

THE THEATRE

Charles Hart—leading actor, shareholder, and one of the managers of The King's Company. Nell's mentor and teacher.

John Lacy—leading actor, shareholder, and one of the managers of The King's Company. Nell's mentor and teacher.

Michael Mohun—leading actor, shareholder, and one of the managers of The King's Company.

Walter Clun, also known as Wat—leading actor and shareholder in the King's Company, specializing in character roles. Agrees to teach Nell to act.

Thomas Killigrew—founder and patent-holder of The King's Company and a supporter and intimate of King Charles.

Betsy Knepp—actress in the King's company. A friend of Nell and of Samuel Pepys.
Katherine Mitchell Corey, also referred to as Kate—actress in the King's Company, specialising in character roles.

Dicky One-Shank—old sailor and scenekeeper at

the Theatre Royal.

Harry Killigrew—son of Thomas Killigrew and lover of Rose Gwynn.

Aphra Behn—playwright with the Duke's Company and friend of Nell.

Anne Marshall—actress in the King's Company. Probably the first English woman to appear on the professional stage.

Rebecca Marshall, also referred to as Beck—actress in the King's Company.

Moll Davis—actress in the Duke's Company. Mistress of King Charles, and a rival of Nell's.

Mary Meggs, known as Orange Moll—holder of the concession to sell oranges and sweetmeats at the Theatre Royal.

Margaret Hughes, also referred to as Peg—actress in the King's Company and friend of Nell.

Edward Kynaston, also referred to as Ned—actor in the King's Company.

Elizabeth Barry, also referred to as Betty—actress with the Duke's Company and mistress of the Earl of Rochester.

Marmaduke Watson—young actor in the King's Company.

Theophilus Bird, referred to as Theo—young actor

in the King's Company, son of an actor by the same name.

Nicholas Burt—old actor in the King's Company.

William Cartwright—old actor in the King's Company.

Frances Davenport, also referred to as Franki—actress in the King's Company. Sister of Elizabeth.

Elizabeth Davenport, also referred to as Betty—actress in the King's Company. Sister of Frances.

Elizabeth Weaver—actress in the King's Company.

Betty Hall—actress in the King's Company.

Richard Bell—actor in the King's Company.

Anne Reeves—young actress in the King's Company and mistress of John Dryden.

Matt Kempton—scenekeeper at the Theatre Royal.

Willie Taimes—scenekeeper at the Theatre Royal.

Richard Baxter—scenekeeper at the Theatre Royal.

Sir Edward Howard—playwright.

THE COURT

Charles II—king of England. Succeeded to throne upon execution of his father Charles I in 1649. Restored to the throne 1660.

Catherine of Braganza—Charles II's queen, who had been the Infanta of Portugal.

James, the Duke of York—younger brother of Charles II and later King James II.

George Villiers, Duke of Buckingham—intimate of King Charles. Friend and advisor of Nell. Playwright, poet, politician.

John Wilmot, Earl of Rochester—intimate friend of King Charles and Nell. Poet and playwright.

Charles Sackville, Lord Buckhurst, Earl of Dorset and Middlesex—poet and playwright.

Sir Charles Sedley—playwright, and a friend of Dorset and Rochester. Known to his friends as 'Little Sid'.

Barbara Villiers Palmer, Lady Castlemaine, Duchess of Cleveland—longtime mistress of Charles II.

Louise de Keroualle, Duchess of Portsmouth—unpopular French mistress of Charles II.

Hortense Mancini, Duchess Mazarin—tempestuous mistress of Charles II, who he had wanted to marry as a young man.

James Crofts, Duke of Monmouth—illegitimate son and oldest child of Charles II. Friend of Nell. The namesake of Nell's little boy Jemmy.

Sir Henry Savile—courtier and friend of Nell's. Charles's Envoy Extraordinaire to France.

Anna Maria, Countess of Shrewsbury—mistress of the Duke of Buckingham and mother of his child, the Earl of Coventry, who died as an infant.

Lady Diana de Vere—Daughter of Aubrey de Vere, the twentieth and last Earl of Oxford.

NELL'S HOUSEHOLD

Meg—longtime servant of Nell.

Bridget—longtime servant of Nell.

Thomas Groundes—Nell's steward.

John—Nell's coachman.

Tom—Nell's chair man.

Fleetwood Shepard—courtier and poet. Tutor to Nell's boys.

Thomas Otway—playwright and tutor to Nell's boys.

OTHER FRIENDS AND ADVISORS

Samuel Pepys, also referred to as Sam—theatre aficionado, friend of Nell, and well acquainted with the king, Duke of York, and others at court through his position as Clerk of the Acts of the Navy Board.

Dr. Thomas Tenison—vicar of St. Martin-in-the-Fields and spiritual advisor to Nell.

Chapter One

London—Twenty-Ninth of May, 1660

The sun shone hot and bright in the glorious May sky, and the streets of London were rivers of joyous activity. Merchants and labourers, gentlemen and ladies, apprentices and servants, whores, thieves, and grimy urchins—all were out in their thousands. And all with the same thought shining in their minds and hearts and the same words on their tongues—the king comes back this day.

After ten years—nay, it was more—of England without a king. Ten years of the bleak and grey existence that life had been under the Protector—an odd title for one who had thrown the country into strife, had arrested and then beheaded King Charles. What a groan had gone up from the crowd that day at the final, fatal sound of the executioner's axe; what horror and black despair had filled their hearts as the bleeding head of the king was held aloft in triumph. And all upon the order of the Protector, who had savaged life as it had been, and then, after all, had thought to take the throne for himself.

But now he was gone. Oliver Cromwell was dead, his son had fled after a halfhearted attempt at governing, his partisans were scattered, and the king's son, Charles II, who had barely escaped with his life to years of impoverished exile, was approaching London to claim his crown, on this, his thirtieth birthday. And after so long a wait, such suffering and loss, what wrongs could there be that

1

the return of the king could not put right?

*   *   *

Ten-year-old Nell Gwynn awoke, the warmth of the sun on her back in contrast to the dank coolness of the straw on which she lay under the shelter of a rickety staircase. She rolled over, and the movement hurt. Her body ached from the beating her mother had given her the night before. Legs and backside remembered the blows of the broomstick, and her face was bruised and tender from the slaps. Tears had mingled on her cheeks with dust. She tried to wipe the dirt away, but her hands were just as bad, grimy and still smelling of oysters.

Oysters. That was the cause of all this pain. Yesterday evening, she'd stopped on her way home to watch as garlands of flowers were strung on one of the triumphal arches that had been erected in anticipation of the king's arrival. Caught up in the excitement, she had forgotten to be vigilant, and her oyster barrow had been stolen. She'd crept home unwillingly, hoped that the night would be one of the many when her mother had been drinking so heavily that she was already unconscious, or one of the few when the drink made her buoyant and forgiving. But no. Not even the festive mood taking hold of London had leavened her reaction to the loss of the barrow. Replacing it would cost five shillings, as much as Nell earned in a week. And her mother had seemed determined to beat into Nell's hide the understanding of that cost.

Nell had no tears today. She was only angry, and determined that she would not be beaten again. She sat up and brushed the straw out of her skirt,

2

clawed it out of the curls of her hair. And thought about what to do next. She wanted to find Rose, her dear older sister, with whom she'd planned so long for this day. And she was hungry. With no money and no prospect of getting any.

At home there would be food, but home would mean facing her mother again. Another beating, or at least more shouting and recriminations, and then more of what she had done for the past two years—up at dawn, the long walk to Billingsgate fish market to buy her daily stock, and an endless day pushing the barrow, heavy with the buckets of live oysters in their brine. Aching feet, aching arms, aching back, throat hoarse with her continual cry of 'Oysters, alive-o!' Hands raw and red from plunging into the salt water, and the fishy, salty smell always on her hands, pervading her hair and clothes.

It was better than the work she had done before that, almost since she was old enough to walk—going from door to door to collect the cinders and fragments of wood left from the previous day's fires, and then taking her pickings to the soap makers, who bought the charred bits for fuel and the ashes to make lye. Her skin and clothes had been always grey and gritty, a film of stinking ash ground into her pores. And not even a barrow to wheel, but heavy canvas sacks carried slung over her shoulders, their weight biting into her flesh.

Nell considered. What else could she do? What would buy freedom from her mother and keep food in her belly and a roof over her head? She could try to get work in some house, but that, too, would mean endless hours of hard and dirty work as a kitchen drudge or scouring floors and chamber pots, under the thumb of cook or steward as well as

3

at the mercy of the uncertain temper of the master and mistress. No.

And that left only the choice that Rose had made, and their mother, too. Whoredom. Rose, who was four years older than Nell, had gone a year earlier to Madam Ross's nearby establishment at the top of Drury Lane. It was not so bad, Rose said. A little room of her own, except of course when she'd a man there. And they were none of the rag, tag, and bobtail—it was gentlemen who were Madam Ross's trade, and Rose earned enough to get an occasional treat for Nell, and good clothes for herself.

What awe and craving Nell had felt upon seeing the first clothes Rose had bought—a pair of silk stays, a chemise of fine lawn, and a skirt and body in a vivid blue, almost the color of Rose's eyes, with ribbons to match. Secondhand, to be sure, but still beautiful. Nell had touched the stuff of the gown with a tentative finger—so smooth and clean. Best of all were the shoes—soft blue leather with an elegant high heel. She had wanted them so desperately. But you couldn't wear shoes like that carting ashes or oysters through the mud of London's streets.

Could she go to Madam Ross's? She was no longer a child, really. She had small buds of breasts, and already the lads at the Golden Fleece, where her mother kept bar, watched her with appreciation, and asked with coarse jests when she would join Mrs. Gwynn's gaggle of girls, who kept rooms upstairs or could be sent for from the nearby streets.

But before she could do anything about the future, she had to find Rose. Today, along with

4

everyone else in London, they would watch and rejoice as the king returned to take his throne.

Nell emerged from under the staircase and hurried down the narrow alley to the Strand. The street was already thronged with people, and all were in holiday humour. The windows were festooned with ribbons and flowers. A fiddler played outside an alehouse, to the accompaniment of a clapping crowd. The smell of food wafted on the morning breeze—meat pies, pastries, chickens roasting.

A joyful cacophony of church bells pealed from all directions, and in the distance Nell could hear the celebratory firing of cannons at the Tower.

She scanned the crowds. Rose had said she'd come to fetch her from home this morning. If Rose had found her gone, where would she look? Surely here, where the king would pass by.

'Ribbons! Fine silk ribbons!' Nell turned and was instantly entranced. The ribbon seller's staff was tied with rosettes of ribbons in all colours, and her clothes were pinned all over with knots of silken splendour. Nell stared at the most beautiful thing she had ever seen—a knot of ribbons the colours of periwinkles and daffodils, its streamers fluttering in the breeze. Wearing that, she would feel a grand lady.

'Only a penny, the finest ribbons,' the peddler cried. A penny. Nell could eat her fill for a penny. If she had one. And with that thought she realised how hungry she was. She'd had no supper the night before and now her empty belly grumbled. She must find Rose.

A voice called her name and she turned to see Molly and Deb, two of her mother's wenches. Nell

5

made her way across the road to where they stood. Molly was a country lass and Deb was a Londoner, but when she saw them together, which they almost always were, Nell could never help thinking of a matched team of horses. Both had straw-coloured hair and cheerful ruddy faces, and both were buxom, sturdy girls, packed into tight stays that thrust their bosoms into prominence. They seemed in high spirits and as they greeted Nell it was apparent that they had already had more than a little to drink.

'Have you seen Rose?' Nell asked.

'Nay, not since yesterday,' said Deb, and Molly chimed her agreement.

'Aye, not since last night.' She looked more closely at Nell.

'Is summat the matter?'

'No,' Nell lied. 'Only I was to meet her this morning and I've missed her.' She wondered if the girls' good spirits would extend to a loan. 'Tip me a dace, will you? I've not had a bite this morning and I'm fair clemmed.'

'Faith, if I had the tuppence, I would,' said Deb. 'But we've just spent the last of our rhino on drink and we've not worked yet today.'

'Not yet,' agreed Molly. 'But the day is like to prove a golden one. I've ne'er seen crowds like this.'

'Aye, there's plenty of darby to be made today,' Deb nodded. Her eyes flickered to a party of sailors moving down the opposite side of the road and with a nudge she drew Molly's attention to the prospect of business.

'We'd best be off,' Molly said, and she and Deb were already moving toward their prey.

6

'If you see Rose . . . ,' Nell cried after them.

'We'll tell her, poppet,' Molly called back, and they were gone.

The crowds were growing, and it was becoming harder by the minute for Nell to see beyond the bodies towering above her. What she needed was somewhere with a better view.

She looked around for a vantage point. A brewer's wagon stood on the side of the street, its bed packed with a crowd of lads, undoubtedly apprentices given liberty for the day. Surely it could accommodate another small body.

'Oy!' Nell called up. 'Room for one more?'

'Aye, love, the more the merrier,' called a dark-haired lad, and hands reached down to pull her up. The view from here was much better.

'Drink?'

Nell turned to see a red-haired boy holding out a mug. He was not more than fourteen or so, and freckles stood out in his pale, anxious face. She took the mug and drank, and he smiled shyly, his blue eyes shining.

'How long have you been here?' Nell asked, keeping an eye on the crowd.

'Since last night,' he answered. 'We brought my father's wagon and made merry 'til late, then slept 'til the sun woke us.'

Nell had been hearing music in the distance since she had neared the Strand. The fiddler's music floated on the air from the east, she could see a man with a tabor and pipe to the west, only the top notes of his tune reaching her ears, and now she saw a hurdy-gurdy player approaching, the keening drone of his instrument cutting through the noise of the crowd.

7

'Look!' she cried in delight. A tiny dark monkey capered along before the man, diminutive cap in hand. The crowds parted to make way for the pair, and as the boys beside her laughed and clapped, the man and his little partner stopped in front of the wagon. He waved a salute and began to play a jig. The monkey skipped and frolicked before him, to the vast entertainment of the crowd.

'Look at him! Just like a little man!' Nell cried. People were tossing coins into the man's hat, which he had thrown onto the ground before him, and Nell laughed as the monkey scampered after an errant farthing and popped it into the hat.

'Here,' the ginger-haired boy said. He fished in a pocket inside his coat. She watched with interest as he withdrew a small handful of coins and picked one out.

'You give it to him,' he said, holding out a coin as he pocketed the rest of the money. Nell could tell that he was proud for her to see that he had money to spend for an entertainment such as this.

'Hist!' she called to the monkey and held up the shiny coin, shrieking with laughter as the monkey clambered up a wheel of the wagon, took the coin from her fingers, and bobbed her a little bow before leaping back down and resuming its dance.

Laughing, she turned to the boy and found him staring at her, naked longing in his eyes. He wanted her. She had seen that look before from men and boys of late and had ignored it. But today was different. Her stomach was turning over from lack of food, and she had no money. Molly and Deb had spoken of the wealth to be had from the day's revelries. Maybe she could reap some of that wealth. Sixpence would buy food and drink, with

8

money left over.

She stepped nearer to the boy and felt him catch his breath as she looked up at him.

'I'll let you fuck me for sixpence,' she whispered. He gaped at her and for a moment she thought he was going to run away. But then, striving to look self-possessed, he nodded.

'I know where,' she said. 'Follow me.'

*   *   *

Half afraid that she would lose her prey and half wondering what had possessed her to speak so boldly, Nell darted through the crowds with the boy after her to the alley where she had spent the night. Slops from chamber pots emptied out of windows reeked in the sunshine, but the passage was deserted, save for a dead dog sprawled in the mud. Nell dodged under the staircase beneath which she had slept. The pile of straw was not very clean, but it would do. The boy glanced nervously behind him, then followed her.

With the boy so close, panting in anticipation, Nell felt a twinge of fear. For all the banter and jokes she had heard about the act, she had no real idea what it would be like. Would it hurt? Would she bleed? Could she get with child her first time? What if she did it so poorly that her ignorance showed? She wished she had considered the matter more carefully.

Her belly rumbled with hunger again. Why had she not simply asked the boy to buy her something to eat? But it was too late now, she thought. She pushed away her misgivings and flopped onto her back. The boy clambered on top of her, fumbling

9

with the flies of his breeches, and heaved himself between her legs, thrusting against her blindly. He didn't know what to do any more than she did, she realised. She reached down and grasped him, amazed at the aliveness of the hard member, like a puppy nosing desperately to nurse, and struggled to help him find the place.

The boy thrust hard, groaning like an animal in distress, and Nell gasped as he entered her. It hurt. Forcing too big a thing into too small a space, an edge of her skin pinched uncomfortably. Was this how it was meant to be? Surely not. Yet maybe to him it felt different.

She had little time to consider, as the boy's movements grew faster, and with a strangled moan, he bucked convulsively and then stopped, pushed as far into her as he could go. He stayed there a moment, gasping, and then Nell felt a trickle of wetness down the inside of her thigh, and knew that he must have spent.

The boy looked down at her, with an expression that mingled jubilation with shame and surprise. He withdrew and did not look at Nell as he buttoned up his breeches and straightened his clothes. She grabbed a handful of straw to wipe the stickiness from between her legs. The smell of it rose sharp and shameful to her nose, and she wanted to retch. The boy reached into his pocket and counted out six pennies.

'I must go,' he said, and almost hitting his head on the low stairs, he ducked out and scurried away.

Nell looked at the coins. Sixpence. She felt a surge of power and joy. She had done it. It had not been so bad. And now she had money. She could do as she liked. And she decided that first

10

and immediately, she would get something good to eat.

She used her shift to wipe as much of the remaining mess as she could from her thighs and hands, and then knotted the coins into its hem. She hurried back toward the Strand, her new wealth banging pleasantly against her calf.

The smell of food hung heavy in the air, and her stomach felt as if it was turning inside out with hunger. Earlier, she had noted with longing a man with a cart selling meat pies, and she sought him out, her nose leading the way. She extracted one of her pennies and received the golden half-moon, warm from its nest in the tin-lined cart. The man smiled at her rapturous expression as she took her prize in both hands, inhaling its heady aroma.

Voraciously, she bit into the pie, the crust breaking into tender shards that seemed to melt on her tongue. The rich warm gravy filled her mouth as she bit deeper, into the hearty filling of mutton and potatoes. She thought nothing had ever tasted so good. The pie seemed to be filling not only her belly, but crannies of longing and misery in her heart and soul. She sighed with pleasure, so hungry and intent on eating that she had not even moved from where she stood.

The old pie man, with a weathered face like a sun-dried apple, laughed as he watched her.

'I'd say you like it, then?'

Nell nodded, wiping gravy from her lips with the back of her hand and brushing a few crumbs from her chest. She was tempted to eat another pie right then, but decided to let the first settle. Besides, there were other things to spend money on, now that she had money to spend.

11

She again heard the call of 'Ribbons! Fine ribbons!' The rosette—her rosette—cornflower blue intertwined with sun gold, its silken streamers rippling in the breeze—was still pinned to the woman's staff. Waiting for her.

Nell raced to the woman, her face shining. 'That one. If you please.' The woman gave her a look of some doubt, but as Nell pulled up her skirt and produced a penny from her shift, she unpinned the rosette from the staff.

'Do you want me to pin it for you, duck?'

Nell nodded, feeling grown up and important as the ribbon peddler considered her.

'Here, I think, is best.' The woman pinned the rosette to the neckline of Nell's bodice and nodded approvingly. 'Very handsome. The colour brings out those eyes of yours.'

Nell looked down and stroked the streamers. Even hanging on the rough brown wool, the gleaming ribbons were beautiful, and she wished that she could see herself. At home she had a scrap of mirror that she had found in the street, but she would have to wait until she went home to have a look. If she went home.

That brought back to mind her next task—finding Rose. The street was becoming more crowded, and she would have a hard time seeing the king when he came by, let alone her sister. She needed to find a perch from which she could view the road. But not the wagon with the red-headed lad. Given his urgent flight, he might not relish her company. And in truth, she did not think she would relish his. He had served his purpose. Now, perhaps, there were bigger fish to fry.

She considered the possibilities. The carts,

wagons, barrels, and other vantage points at the sides of the road were packed. The windows of upper storeys would provide a superior view, if she could find a place in one.

She made her way eastward, searching windows for familiar faces but found none, and felt herself lost in a sea of strangers. She was almost at Fleet Street now. Surely Rose would not have come this far. She would go just as far as Temple Bar, she thought, and then turn back.

'Oy! Ginger!' The voice came from a window three floors up, where several lads were crowded. A stocky boy with close-cropped hair leaned out of the casement and regarded her with a wolflike grin.

Maybe she didn't need an old friend. Maybe new friends would do.

Nell put a hand on her hip and raked the lad with an exaggeratedly critical glance, drawing guffaws from his mates.

'Aye, it's ginger, and what of that?' she hollered. 'At least I've got hair. Unlike some.'

The lads howled with delight, one of them gleefully rubbing his friend's cropped poll and drawing a shove in response.

Playing to his audience, the boy took a deep swig from his mug and leered down at Nell. 'You have hair, do you? I'd have thought you was too young.'

'Too young be damned,' cried Nell. 'It's you who must be too old, bald-pated as you are.' The lads set up a raucous cry at that, thumping their friend from all sides. Nell grinned up at them, gratified at their reaction and the laughter from the crowd around her. In her years selling oysters, she had found that a little saucy humour helped her business, and made the time pass more quickly.

13

'Come up and join us!' shouted another of the lads, a cheerful-faced runt with bright blue eyes.

'Aye, come aloft! Let me get a look at you up close!' cried Nell's original sparring partner.

'And why should I?' Nell called back. 'What do I want with the likes of you?'

'Come up and I'll show you!'

'We've plenty to drink!' promised the thin lad, waving a mug. 'And a view better than any in London!'

'Well, I could use a bit to drink,' Nell twinkled up at her admirers. There was a scramble at the window, and a few moments later, the door to the street-level shop flew open and one of the lads beckoned. He was gangly and sandy haired, and he giggled as he ushered her inside. She hesitated a moment, wondering if she was courting danger. But she followed him up the narrow stairs, finally arriving at the room where the boys were gathered.

'Here's the little ginger wench!' The first lad swaggered over, chuckling as he eyed her. Behind him were the boy who had let her in, the scrawny lad, and a boy with dark brown hair and snapping dark eyes. They crowded around Nell, and she suddenly felt very small. But it would never do to seem shy, so she gave them a cheeky grin and chirped, 'Pleased to meet you, lads. I'm Nell.'

They were all about sixteen years old, probably nearing the end of their apprenticeships, and it looked as if their master was nowhere near, for a barrel had been tapped and stood on a table at one side of the room. Each of the boys held a mug, and from their red faces and boisterous laughs, Nell guessed they had been drinking for some time.

'I'm Nick,' said the first boy. 'This is my brother

14

Davy, and Kit and Toby.'

The boys nodded their greetings, and Nell took the mug Kit handed her and drank. The dark stout tasted full and bitter, much heavier than the small beer she was accustomed to drinking, but she swallowed it down as the boys looked on, grinning. Feeling their eyes on her a little too keenly, she went to the window.

From this height, the view stretched eastward down Fleet Street toward St. Paul's, and southwest past Charing Cross to Whitehall Palace. Across the road to the south, she could see over the walls of the grand houses along the Thames, their imposing fronts facing London and their capacious gardens sloping down behind to the river. Every wall, window, and rooftop was occupied, and the streets as far as she could see were aswarm. The noise of the crowd was growing louder. Nell heard drumbeats and the tramp of booted feet.

'Here they come!' Kit shouted, and the lads crowded to the windows around Nell. A shimmering wave of silver moved towards her, and she saw that it was a column of men marching. At the front was a rank of soldiers in buff coats with sleeves of cloth of silver, a row of drummers to the fore, rapping out a sharp tattoo as they swung along. Behind them marched hundreds of gentlemen in cloth of silver that flashed and shone.

Toby whistled. 'Lord. Never knew there was so many gentlemen.'

'There wasn't, a month since,' laughed Nick. 'They was all lying quiet in the country or somewheres. Only now the king is come and it's safe again. . . .'

The silver swarm was followed by a phalanx

15

of gentlemen in velvet coats, interspersed with footmen in plush new liveries of deep purple and sea green.

'I didn't know there was so many colours,' Nell breathed, awed by the beauty of the rich reds, greens, blues, and golds. 'I didn't know they could make cloth like that.'

'They can if you can pay for it,' said Davy.

'Aye,' Nick agreed. 'I'll wager Barbara Palmer has a gown of stuff like that.' He turned to Nell with a wink.

'Who's Barbara Palmer?' she asked, not wanting to seem ignorant, but desperate to know.

'Why, the king's whore!' Nick cried. 'They do say she's the most beautiful woman in England. Nought but the best for the king!'

Nell took this in with interest. The king's whore. Wearing fine clothes. The whores she knew made themselves as brave and showy as they could, but she had never seen anything like the finery on display today.

The Sheriff of London and his men, all in scarlet, passed and were succeeded by the gentlemen of the London companies—the goldsmiths, vintners, bakers, and other guilds that supplied the City, each with its fluttering banner.

'There he is!' cried Kit. 'Our master,' he explained, pointing to a beefy man in deep blue who strode along with his brothers in trade.

After the guilds came the aldermen of London, in scarlet gowns, and then more soldiers with tall pikes and halberds. But unlike the grim-faced soldiers who had patrolled the streets throughout her life, these men did not strike fear into Nell, for they couldn't help smiling at the ringing cheers.

16

The roaring of the crowd exploded into a frenzy. Nell scrabbled for a hold on the windowsill and craned to get a better view.

The king was coming. Three men on horseback rode through Temple Bar, but the king could only be the one in the middle, in a cloth-of-silver doublet trimmed in gold, his saddle and bridle richly worked in gold. He turned from side to side to wave as blossoms showered down upon him. The throngs pressed forward, waving, throwing their hats into the air, calling out to him—'God save the king,' 'God bless Your Majesty,' 'Thank God for this day!'

'Those are his brothers,' Toby shouted to Nell. 'The Duke of York and the Duke of Gloucester.' They were a dazzling sight, all in silver, riding side by side on three enormous dark stallions, radiant as angels in the noonday sun.

The king was close enough now that Nell could see him clearly. Big and broad shouldered, he sat tall in the gilded saddle, long booted legs straightening as he stood in the stirrups, as if he could not stay seated in the face of his people's adulation. His long dark curls cascaded over his shoulders as he swept his hat from his head and waved it, turning to either side to acknowledge the cheers.

He smiled broadly, laughing with exuberance at the tumultuous welcome. 'I thank you with all my heart,' he called, his deep voice ringing out amidst the clamour and cries.

'God save King Charles!' Nell realised it was her own voice. The king looked up, and Nell caught her breath as he looked her full in the face. He grinned, teeth showing beneath his dark moustache, eyes

17

twinkling in his swarthy face, and called back to her, 'I thank you, sweetheart!' Impulsively, Nell blew him a kiss and was immediately overcome with horror at the audacity of her act. But the king threw his head back and laughed, then blew a kiss to her, waving as he and his brothers rode on.

Nell giggled and bounced off the windowsill. 'Did you see? He blew me a kiss!'

'Aye, and from what I hear of him, he'd offer you more than a kiss, was you close enough for him to reach you!' Nick guffawed. 'He's got a mistress who's another man's wife, and two or three merry-begotten brats by other women, they say. For who will say nay to the king?'

Not I, thought Nell.

The procession continued below, but once the king had passed, Nell's attention was no longer focused exclusively on the street. Nick refilled her mug, and the other boys drifted away from the window to drink.

Nell was in high good humour, awed by the glamour of the procession and her exchange with the king. Her head swam a bit from the stout and from the excitement at being out on her own for the first time, in company with these older boys, almost men.

'What think you of the king, Nelly?' Kit asked.

'Oh,' she cooed, 'he's fine as hands can make him.'

'Not finer than me, surely?' cried Nick.

'Oh, no,' Nell shot back. 'No more than a diamond is finer than a dog turd.' The boys roared and moved in close around her. At the heart of this laughing group, she felt worldly and sophisticated. She had been silly to doubt that she could handle the lads. They were eating out of her hand.

'Ah, Nick, you're not good enough for Nell,' Toby chortled. 'Mayhap you'd have better luck with Barbara Palmer.'

'Well, Nell?' Davy laughed. 'Do you think she'd have him?'

'Aye, when hens make holy water,' Nell answered tartly.

'What?' Nick gawped at her in mock amazement. 'How can you say such a thing? When you've hardly met me! Why, I have qualities.'

'Aye, and a bumblebee in a cow turd thinks himself a king,' she retorted. 'Is there no end of your talking?'

'I'll leave off my talking and set you to moaning,' Nick leered, sidling closer. 'Once a mort is lucky enough to feel my quim-stake, she's not like to forget it.'

Nell gave him a shove in the belly.

'Enough of your bear-garden discourse.'

'Aye, speak that way to Barbara Palmer, and you're like to be taken out for air and exercise,' Toby grinned.

'No, you'd get worse than a whipping at the cart's arse for giving her the cutty eye,' Kit shook his head. 'Look the wrong way at the king's doxy and you'll piss when you can't whistle.'

'How say you, Nick?' Davy asked. 'Do you reckon there's a woman worth hanging for?'

'If there is,' Nick said, 'I've yet to clap eyes on her.'

'Don't lose hope yet.' Nell batted her eyes at him. 'The day is young.'

Eventually the last of the king's train passed, followed by a straggling tail of children and beggars, but the crowds in the street below did not disperse. Drink flowed and piles of wood were being stacked in preparation for celebratory bonfires. The party would continue through the night.

'Come on, who's for wandering?' Nick turned from the window. 'To Whitehall!' he bellowed, once they were in the street. 'I want to see this trull of the king's.'

Their progress was slow, as the way toward Whitehall was packed with others wending their way there, and there were constant diversions. Musicians, jugglers, stilt walkers, and rope dancers performed, as if Bartholomew Fair had come early.

Before the palace, the gang crowded with others around a roaring bonfire. The windows of the Banqueting House glowed from the light of hundreds of candles. Carriages clogged the street, the coachmen and footmen gathered in knots to talk as they waited for their masters.

'The king's having his supper now, before the whole court,' Nick said. 'I reckon he's got that Barbara Palmer with him.' He moved closer to Nell and she felt his eyes hot on her. He was quite big and the intensity of his gaze made her heart race.

'I know I'd have her,' he continued, 'wherever and whenever I wanted, was I king.' The boys hooted their agreement, but Nick's attention was on Nell now. He pulled her to him roughly and ran a hand heavily over her small breasts. She felt a surge of fear and tried to pull away.

Someone nearby cried out, the crowd stirred and buzzed, and Nell saw that the king had appeared at one of the windows of the Banqueting House. Nick loosened his hold on her and turned to gawk. The light blazing behind the king created a golden aura around him. The bonfires illuminated his face and made the silver of his doublet shine. He raised a hand to salute the crowds below, and they roared their approval and welcome.

Then a woman appeared next to him, and Nell knew that this must be the famous Barbara Palmer. She was darkly beautiful, her hair dressed in elaborate curls, and she wore a low-cut gown of deep red that set off the pale lushness of her bosom. As she leaned close to the king, sparkles and flashes of light from the jewels at her ears and throat cut through the shadows.

Nell had never seen a woman so stunning. She looked carefully, memorising every detail, and longed to be like her—gorgeously dressed, elegant, and at ease before the adoring crowds.

Barbara Palmer disappeared from view. The king gave a final wave to the crowds and followed her.

'Aye, just give me half an hour with her,' crowed Nick. 'I reckon she'd be worth the price.'

'You'll not earn the cost of her in your lifetime!' Davy gibed.

Nell felt a rush of envy. She didn't want to lose the delicious new sensation of feeling admired and special.

'She may be beautiful,' she announced, tossing her tangled curls, 'but she's not the only one worth her price.'

This pronouncement produced a ripple of some indefinable undercurrent and an exchange of meaningful glances among the lads. Nick moved close to her, and she could not breathe for the nearness of him and his size. The firelight flickered orange on his face, and on the faces of the other lads, who stood flanking him and regarding her

21

with new interest.

'Is that so?' Nick asked, taking a lazy drink. His eyes gleamed in the dark. 'And just what might your price be?'

Nell's stomach heaved with nervous excitement, but remembering Barbara Palmer's easy confidence, she managed an inviting smile as she looked up at him. She thought of what Deb and Molly had said—was it only this morning?—about the riches to be made this night.

'Sixpence,' she said to him. And then, taking in the others with a flicker of her eyes, 'Apiece.'

'Well, then. Time's a-wasting,' said Nick, with a canine grin. He glanced toward the blackness of St. James's Park, grabbed Nell by the wrist, and pulled her along, the other boys in tow.

The park was scattered with revellers, but there were secluded dens amidst the darkness of the spreading trees and tangled shrubbery, and in any case, no one was likely to ask questions, tonight of all nights. Nick drew Nell into a thicket of trees, and the others crowded in behind him.

This felt very different from the morning's hasty coupling with the red-haired apprentice, and facing the four lads, panic rose in Nell's throat. But there was nothing really to be afraid of, was there? A bit of mess and it would all be done. And she would be two shillings the richer. Best to get it over with. She turned to find the driest spot on which to lie, but before she could move further, Nick shoved her down and onto her back, pulled her skirt up to her waist, and was on top of her.

He leaned on one forearm as he unbuttoned his breeches, his weight taking Nell's breath away, then spit on his palm, guided himself between her legs and entered her hard. Her nether parts were tender, and his assault made her gasp in pain. She bit her lip and struggled not to whimper.

Nick lasted much longer than the young apprentice had, and finished with a low growl and a deep sustained thrust that made Nell cry out. He looked down at her for a moment, vulpine triumph in his eyes, then, grunting, heaved himself off her, put his cock back in his breeches, and buttoned his flies.

'Who's next?' he asked. There was a moment of hesitation, and he turned in irritation to his mates. 'What ails you? I said who's next?'

Toby came forward. He was faster than Nick, and Nick having spent within her made his entry easier, but still it was painful. Nell turned her head so that she would not have to look him in the eyes. The other boys needed no urging now. Davy and Kit hovered on either side of her, watching, eager for their turns, and Davy knelt between Nell's thighs as soon as Toby was done. He hooked his arms under her knees, and he looked down at her keenly as he moved inside her, snarling like an animal.

The other boys laughed and called out their encouragement. Nell shut her eyes. Rocks and twigs pressed into her back, and the damp earth was soaking through her clothes. She didn't feel elegant and enchanting, only uncomfortable and frightened. But it would soon be over. And the money would make it all worthwhile.

Kit nearly knocked Davy aside in his haste to get on top of Nell. She was so sore now that she could barely keep from crying, but managed not to let more than a stifled moan escape.

Finally, Kit finished, and sat back to fasten his breeches.

'Come on!' Nick ordered, yanking him to his feet.

'My money!' Nell cried, struggling to get up. 'Two shillings.' Nick shoved her onto her back with a foot.

'Two hogs?' he sneered. 'For that? We'll not pay a farthing. You're not only a whore, you're a stupid whore, at that.'

Nell scrambled to her feet and caught at him. They couldn't. After all she had suffered.

'You said—you agreed!' But Nick just flung her away, and she tripped sideways and fell to her knees as the boys ran, crashing away through the branches.

It was hopeless. She gulped, fighting back sobs. Every part of her ached; the insides of her bruised thighs were clammy; she was covered in mud. She tried to straighten her clothes, and cried out as she realised that her rosette was gone. In a panic, she looked and felt around her. And there it was. It must have come off when Nick first pushed her down and been crushed beneath her. It lay crumpled in the muck, its beautiful bright colours sodden grey.

The tears Nell had held back flowed now, and she wept, her body shaking, as she clutched the precious knot of ribbons in her hand. Nick was right. How stupid she had been, to think that she could ever be like the glorious Barbara Palmer. She was just a shabby little ragamuffin, fit for nothing better than selling oysters. Her dreams of freedom had been so much foolishness. She would have no choice but to go back to her mother, to endure the beating that she knew awaited her, and resume her life of drudgery.

When she had finally cried herself out, Nell pushed herself up, wincing in pain, and wiped her nose and eyes on her shift. Her fingers closed around the lump in the hem. Her remaining pennies were still there. One shred of consolation. But the money would not buy her lodging for the night, and she longed to lie herself down. She could go home. Or spend a second night on the street. Unless she could find Rose. That thought brought her to her feet. Rose would surely be at Madam Ross's.

She emerged from the trees. There were still crowds gathered around the bonfires before the palace. She hurried toward Charing Cross, spurred on by hunger and weariness and the hope of comfort. Fires burned in the Strand and music drifted towards her on the warm evening breeze. She turned into the warren of narrow lanes that lay to the north of Covent Garden. She was near home now, and it felt odd to bypass the familiar close. But, resolutely, she made toward Lewkenor's Lane.

'Nell!' Rose's voice called her name. Nell rushed toward Rose and clung to her.

'I've been looking for you all the day,' Rose exclaimed, and then took in Nell's state of dishevelment. 'Wherever have you been?'

Nell's tears burst forth again, and Rose guided her to a step, sat her down, and listened as the whole story came out in a rush. After she finished, Nell sat sobbing, overcome by humiliation and shame. Rose stroked her hair and kissed the top of her head.

'Oh, Nelly,' she said. 'I wish I had found you

25

this morning. If I had only known what was in your mind. . . .' She shook her head, considering, then put a finger under Nell's chin and tilted Nell's face to hers. Nell looked into her sister's eyes, and Rose's voice was gentle.

'I cannot make the world a different place than it is. But I can tell you this: Get the money first. Always.'

Chapter Two

Madam Ross pursed her rouged lips. Nell fidgeted under the examination and threw an anxious glance to Rose. The madam's red hair, unblinking gaze, and the quick tilt of her head made Nell think of a russet hen. She supposed Madam Ross must be as old as her mother, maybe even older. But she was a very handsome woman, and elegant in the dark green gown which showed off her buxom figure.

'Hmph,' Madam Ross mused. 'Good eyes, good skin. Hair not a bad colour, but monstrous wild.' Nell reached a hand up to try to smooth her curls and suffered Madam Ross to take her by the shoulders and turn her about.

'The beginnings of a nice little bosom,' Madam Ross commented. 'And I make no doubt you'll fill out more, like your sister. Yes, not bad at all. Lift your skirts.' Nell hesitantly pulled her skirt and shift to her knees.

'Higher, girl,' said Madam Ross, twitching Nell's skirts to waist height. 'Hmph. Very lovely little legs you have. And bit of feathering to the cuckoo's nest, I see. Do you have your courses yet?'

26

'Aye,' Nell stammered. 'Just.'

'Well, Rose can teach you what to do to keep yourself from getting with child.' She stepped back and regarded Nell for another moment, then nodded.

'Aye. You'll do well. Some of them like the look of a game pullet who's still but a child. We can sell you as a virgin for this day or two. And even without that, you're a pretty impish little thing.' She smiled at Nell and then turned to Rose.

'She can lie in the room next to yours. Get her things today. We're like to continue busy and we can use all hands.'

'Thank you, ma'am,' Rose said, and Nell echoed her, 'Aye, thank you very kindly, ma'am.'

Madam Ross nodded her acknowledgement. 'Rose, make sure she has a bath. And help her to do something about that hair.'

She sailed out the door in a rustle of skirts, and Nell and Rose were left alone in Rose's tiny room. Nell studied Rose, wishing as she frequently did that her own hair would fall in the smooth chestnut waves her sister had. Rose's blue eyes were intent on her with an expression Nell couldn't read, the colour standing out on her high cheekbones.

'Are you sure you want to do this?' Rose asked. ''Tis not . . . all ease. You could go back home.'

'No.' Nell shook her head. 'I'll never go back. Besides, you know Mam would have me working the same way afore long. I must earn my keep in some way. I had rather be with you.'

'Very well.' Rose gave Nell a squeeze and a smile. 'At least I can keep an eye on you here.'

27

That afternoon, Nell and Rose went to fetch Nell's few belongings from the Golden Fleece. Their mother, Eleanor, was behind the bar and scowled as they entered.

'I was wondering when you'd come creeping back. High time, too. There's work to be done.' She turned back to the keg she had been tapping.

Nell's heart pounded with fear, but knowing that Rose stood beside her, she found the courage to answer.

'I'm not coming back.'

Eleanor whirled to face her.

'What prating nonsense is that? Where else would you go?'

'With me,' Rose spoke up.

Eleanor shot from behind the bar with such violence that she sent a stool clattering to the floor, drawing the attention of the few tipplers who sat in a gloomy corner.

'With you? You talk hog-high. Are you so grand now that you've money to spare on the lazy little wretch?'

Rage overcame Nell's fear.

'Lazy? You've worked me day and night since I could scarce walk. I don't need you. I can get my own living!'

Eleanor's face flushed and she lunged for Nell, but Rose stepped between them.

'We've come to get Nell's things,' Rose said, toe to toe with their mother. 'Madam Ross has taken her on. Stand aside.'

Eleanor stood her ground for a moment, eyes blazing. But Rose did not back down, and all the

28

patrons of the tavern were watching now. With a snort of disgust, Eleanor moved away, and Nell followed Rose behind the bar to the stairs.

In the mousehole of a room she had shared with her mother for as long as she could recall, Nell gathered the few items of clothes she was not already wearing—her spare shift, a pair of woollen stockings, a ragged cloak and cap for winter. Her only other possessions were the precious shard of mirror wrapped in a bit of sacking, and a small doll, its body of stuffed cloth and its face a painted walnut. Nell had had the doll all her life, and Eleanor had told Nell that her father had made it for her. It was the only relic she had of his existence, the only evidence that he had once lived, and had loved her.

Eleanor looked up as Nell and Rose descended the stairs.

'You're an ungrateful little fool. And that Ross woman is an even greater fool if she thinks any man will pay to bed the likes of you.' The words hit Nell like a slap across the face, but Rose put a steadying hand on her shoulder and guided her past their mother.

'Goodbye, Mam,' Rose said.

*　　　*　　　*

Rose opened the door into what would be Nell's home and place of work. The room was tiny, scarce big enough for a bed, a chair, and a stand that held a basin and bowl for washing and a towel. There were three hooks on one wall, for hanging clothes, and a battered wooden box in which Nell could keep her belongings. Roughcast walls rose to the

29

dingy ceiling. Wide oak planks formed the floor, the grooves between them packed with ancient dust, the path from the door to the bed worn smooth from the passage of countless feet. A tallow candle stood in a bracket on the wall, but it was not lit, as the room's best feature, the southward-facing window overlooking Lewkenor's Lane, let in the noontime sun.

It was the most space that Nell had ever had to herself and she surveyed the little room with a sense of proprietorial delight. But the sudden change in her life was unsettling. She didn't want Rose to leave her, and turned to her sister.

'What must I do now?'

'We'll find you some better duds, and then you can sleep a bit before evening. 'Tis like to be busy tonight.'

'How will I know what to do?' Nell asked.

'Just chat as you're used to at the Fleece. Not everyone in the taproom is there to dance Moll Pratley's jig. If they want to go upstairs, they'll pay Madam direct. She'll tell you who to take next. Or Jack will.'

'Who's Jack?'

'Madam's man, who serves as bullyboy. Best to keep on his good side. He'll have his way with one of the wenches once in a while, but if you're lucky he'll leave you be.'

'How much do we get paid?'

'The house takes two shillings. We get sixpence. But regulars are more like to be generous and give you extra coin, or bring you fal-lals of some sort.'

'Like what?'

'Oh, garters, ribbons, maybe a fan or the like.'

Nell was pleased at the thought of owning such

30

fine things and determined that she would get herself some regular customers as soon as ever she could.

'There's more you need to know,' Rose continued. 'You don't want to get with child. You can't work once you're far along, and you're like to get flung out before then anyway.'

Nell had not thought about pregnancy, and wondered what other unexpected hazards lay ahead.

'Come,' Rose said. 'I'll show you what to do.'

In Rose's own little chamber, she produced a small lemon and a knife. She cut the lemon in two, squashed one half against a protruding knob in the bottom of a small wooden dish, and held up the resulting hollow little cup of rind and juiceless pulp.

'You put this up you, and set it so that it covers the entry to your womb.'

Nell goggled at her. 'How will I know where it is?'

'Lie on your bed or squat down and put your finger up inside you. You'll feel what I mean. A man's seed is what gets you with child, do you see, when it gets into your belly. This helps keep it out. A little sponge soaked in vinegar will work, too. And after a man spends inside you, get up as soon as you can, use the chamber pot, and squeeze the stuff out. And wash between men.' She hesitated, and her fair face flushed pink as she spoke.

'Since your mind is made up, I'd best tell you some other things. Some men will prefer your mouth to your belly. It can be bad but at least it will not get you with child. When you think a cull is about to come off, get his yard as far back in your mouth as possible so you need not taste his

31

spendings. Or have the necessary ready to hand so you can spit it out.'

Nell glanced at the chamber pot beneath the bed. It seemed that implement was quite an important tool of her new trade.

'What else?'

'Some will want to take you up the arse. It can hurt but you get accustomed. I'll give you some salve. If you put a bit onto him or yourself it will make the business easier no matter where he takes you.'

'Even in the mouth?'

'No, of course not.' Rose spoke brusquely, dismayed at the depth of Nell's innocence, and then continued more gently. 'That's different. The only difficulty there is breathing if he pushes in deep. You'll learn.'

In the alehouse and around the bawds from her earliest days, Nell had heard of these practices, but she had never given them any particular thought. Faced now with such stark descriptions of what she would shortly be called upon to do, she quailed a little. But surely, whatever came would be easier than her previous work? No hauling sacks of charred scraps of wood and ash, no pushing the unwieldy barrow of oysters, its rough wooden handles making her hands blister and callus, the weight of the load through the long day wearing her out until all she could do was drop to sleep, exhausted. Surely this would be better.

She squared her shoulders and looked at Rose.

'Aye. I'll learn.'

Rose stroked an errant curl out of Nell's eyes and smiled.

'Come, let's find you some rigging.'

This was a part of making ready that Nell thoroughly enjoyed. She watched in delight as Rose threw open the chest where Madam Ross kept a small store of clothes that had been left behind by girls who had been cast out or run away or died.

Rose rummaged through the brightly coloured garments, tossing flounced and ruffled articles into a heap on the floor. She pulled out a skirt and matching boned body in a blue that made Nell think of harebells. Its fabric was finer by far than any she had ever worn. She held the body against her chest and smoothed it so that the waist met hers. The fit seemed just right, the full skirt grazing the tops of her bare feet. In a moment Rose held up a pair of stays, their long laces trailing, and a shift of fine lawn.

'Perfect. Now all you need is shoes and stockings. You'll have to start with some of mine. It's best that way any road—you'll have to pay Madam Ross for these out of your earnings, and the less you have to work off, the better. But before you put any of that on, you need a bath. A real one, all over.'

Nell looked up at Rose, startled. She washed, using a bucket of water and rough lye soap to get the oyster brine and smell from her hands and arms and face. But bathing her whole body? She had never considered that.

A tub large enough to sit in stood in a small room off the kitchen, and Rose and Nell had only to carry enough buckets of hot water from the great kettle on the stove to fill it partway, and enough cold water to make the temperature bearable.

Nell looked at the steaming tub dubiously, but Rose was impatient.

'Come, off with your clothes. You'll feel better.

33

And you'll look better. Keep in mind, you're a good deal more bedraggled than what Madam is accustomed to taking in.'

Nell pulled off her dress and smock, lifted a leg over the rim of the tub, and waggled her toes in the warm water. It did feel good, and she climbed in and sat down so that the water rose above her waist.

'Wet your head. I'll wash your hair,' Rose directed. Nell closed her eyes and submerged herself. The water was already an opaque browny grey. Rose handed her a cloth and a pannikin of brown soap, and pulling a stool close to the tub, she rubbed soap briskly into Nell's hair. Nell submitted, enjoying the novel sensations.

'Well, wash yourself, goose,' Rose laughed.

Nell dutifully scrubbed herself. The water grew dingier, and her skin, flushed in the heat, got pinker. The ever-present feel of sweat and dirt was gone. She breathed in the steam and felt it clear her nose.

So far, her new life seemed more promising than the one she had left. She turned around and smiled up at Rose.

'I knew you would save me.'

Rose shook her head and grimaced wryly.

'I haven't saved thee, treacle. I'm afraid you've jumped out of the frying pan and into the fire. But in truth I don't know what else to do with you.'

After she was bathed and her old clothes set aside for washing, Nell returned to her little cubbyhole. The clean, soft stuff of her new shift clung to her damp skin and gave off a faint scent of lavender and beeswax. Her wet hair made her head pleasantly cool. The bath had helped ease the aches from her mother's beating and the scrapes and

34

bruises of the lads' brutal use of her in the park.

She climbed into the bed. It was far more comfortable than the little straw-stuffed pallet she had slept on for as long as she could remember, and had clean linen sheets, a pillow, and a wool coverlet. She curled into this new luxury and went immediately to sleep.

*　　　*　　　*

Nell woke to see Rose coming in with part of a cold meat pie and a mug of small beer.

'Feeling better?'

'Much.'

'Good. Eat, and then we'll get you dressed.'

Nell ate ravenously. Rose stopped her from wiping her hands and mouth on her shift, giving her a napkin instead.

When Nell had finished eating, Rose laced her into the stays. They were only covered in linen, not silk like Rose's, but pretty little tabs fluttered around the bottom. The stiff boning made her stand differently and forced her small breasts upward so that their swell showed above the scooping neckline.

'Here,' Rose said, handing her shoes and stockings, 'stampers and vampers.' Nell had only worn heavy grey woollen stockings, in the winter, and these were much finer, and a creamy white. The shoes were a revelation, too. Made of brown leather, they had a little heel that pitched her weight forward. She giggled as she took a tentative step. Walking in these would take some getting used to, especially as they were a bit too big for her, and Rose had stuffed the toes with rags.

Rose combed and parted Nell's hair as gently as she could, though her natural thicket of curls, not improved by having been slept on wet, was in a tangle. Then she scooped something sweet-smelling from a small pot and smoothed it into Nell's hair. Nell sat breathless as Rose formed ringlets on either side of her head and a fringe of tiny curls on her forehead. Rose viewed her creation.

'Would you like to see?'

Nell skipped along behind Rose to the little room where the chest of clothes was kept and approached the full-length mirror.

It seemed that it was the face of a stranger staring out at Nell. Her hair, usually matted and its colour dulled by dirt to an indifferent reddish brown, had altered into a glowing copper, with a shine and smoothness to the curls that danced around her head. Her skin had lost its greyish pallor, and her lips and cheeks glowed with a rosy flush. Her dark eyebrows and eyelashes stood out in contrast to the clean whiteness of her skin, and her hazel eyes sparkled.

The dress had transformed her into a young woman. The tightly laced body bared her shoulders, emphasized her bosom, and made her slender waist even smaller. The sleeves ended just below her elbows with a frill of lace, and the skirt fell in graceful folds. The blue of the fabric, like the depths of the ocean on a cloudy day, set off her colouring to perfection. Nell turned to Rose, no words coming to express her astonishment and gratitude.

Rose smiled. 'Aye, you'll do.'

Nell turned sharply at the sound of tapping footsteps. Madam Ross swept in, clad for the evening in a gown that alternated stripes of gleaming black and a colour like molten honey, which made Nell think of a tortoiseshell cat.

'Very fetching,' Madam Ross said. 'Indeed, much better than I would have thought, given what a wretched little thing she appeared this morning.'

Nell smiled shyly up at Madam Ross.

'Have you eaten, child?'

'Oh, yes, thankee, ma'am.'

'And your sister has told you what you must and must not do? Good. Then we shall very shortly set you loose upon the unsuspecting town.'

She gave a little chuckle and went, her heels clicking on the planks of the floor.

Nell turned to Rose. 'What did that mean?'

'I think it means, little sister, that Madam Ross thinks the gents will like you.'

*   *   *

The afternoon was lengthening into a warm summerlike evening as Nell followed Rose downstairs and into the large taproom for her first night of her new work. She felt self-conscious and apprehensive. Her initial foray with the red-headed boy had been impulsive, fuelled by hunger and desperation. With Nick and the others, any wariness she might have had was overcome by drink, and in the end she had had no choice. But this felt different. She was very sore from the previous night and wished that she could turn and run. But where was there to go?

The tables were crowded with men, and most of the girls were already present. As Nell watched their darting movements, the swirl and flounce of their brightly colored finery, and listened to their high-pitched raillery and chatter, they reminded her of the exotic songbirds she had seen for sale on the streets. And despite her new apparel, she felt like a small brown wren among them.

Rose went to a prosperous-looking man who called to her, and Nell was left on her own. She wanted to hang back unnoticed. Having spent so much of her childhood in similar surroundings, she drifted to where she felt most at home—near to the bar. The barman, of middle years and with a face as English and unexceptional as a crab apple, had a row of slipware mugs half filled and was topping off another. He looked friendly, Nell thought, as she peered at him, her head barely clearing the top of the bar.

'Do you want me to take these over?' she asked.

The barman gave her a lopsided grin.

'Aye, that'd be a right help,' he nodded. 'And who might you be?'

'Nell. I'm Rose's sister. I'm working here now.'

'Well, Mistress Nell,' he said, 'I'm Ned. And since you ask, you can take these to those lads, and bring back the dead men.' He nodded toward four young army officers at a table in a corner and the litter of empty vessels before them. Nell expertly grasped the handles of four full mugs and made her way across the room. One of the lads was just reaching the end of a story and the group broke into laughter as she set the mugs on the table.

'You're new,' one of them commented as he took up his drink. Four sets of eyes focused on her and it hit Nell with a sudden shock that she was there for their purchase. The first lad's dark eyes were intent. She flushed and then, annoyed with herself

38

at her shyness, tossed her head and gave the group a cocky smile. She recalled the line that Rose had instructed her to use.

'I'm Nell,' she said. 'It's a pleasure to make your acquaintance, gentlemen.' She dropped them a curtsy, gathered the empties, and hurried back to the bar. The place grew busier, so she continued to deliver drinks. It gave her something to occupy herself and made her feel less conspicuous, and after a lifetime of her mother harrying her not to be idle, she felt she should be doing something.

Madam Ross bustled into the room an hour or so after Nell had entered. In her wake came a man that Nell guessed must be Jack. He was above average height and muscular in a lean and catlike way, and though he did no more than amble to the bar, casually surveying the room and nodding at an acquaintance or two, he conveyed a sense of coiled danger. Nell could see why Rose had said that his mere presence was usually enough to discourage troublemakers. She remembered, too, what Rose had said about his occasionally requiring the services of one of the girls, and hoped that he would not find her to his liking.

Rose hurried up to Nell and leaned close to speak to her.

'The missus won't like it if she sees you back here. You've got to get out and speak to the men.'

'But what will I say?'

'It doesn't matter; you'll think of something. Ned—give me a cup of comfort for Nell, would you? Here—drink this down. It'll take the edge off and make things easier.'

Nell wrinkled her nose at the brandy but made herself swallow it in a gulp. She coughed, and

39

tears came to her eyes, but almost instantly she felt a warming sensation followed by a pleasant numbness.

'Better?' asked Rose. 'Good. Come with me.' She pulled Nell with her to the table where she had been sitting with her gentleman and his friend. 'Mr. Green, Mr. Cooper, this is my sister Nell.'

'The usual phrase is 'one of my cousins,' is it not?' asked Mr. Cooper with a leer, peering at Nell over spectacles. He was fat and greasy looking and Nell instantly hated him.

'Yes, sir, but I do not speak in jest or in cant. She really is my sister.'

'Pretty little thing,' Mr. Cooper commented to Mr. Green. Nell felt she might have been a doll on a shelf, the way he spoke as if she were not there to hear him. She thought of him touching her and wanted to run, but was stopped from further action by the arrival of Madam Ross at her side.

'I beg your pardon, gentlemen. Come, Nell. A gentleman is asking for you particularly.' She led Nell away and glanced at the table of officers in the corner. 'Mr. Cade. He says you've met. Take him upstairs. And treat him well. It will do us no harm to be in well with the army lads.'

Nell nodded, her heart suddenly in her throat. The young officer who had first spoken to her was making his way towards her. He was rather handsome, with dark curling hair and a face bronzed by the sun, and he had seemed friendly enough. Nevertheless, she was afraid. The brandy was making the noisy room echo around her and she felt rooted to the floor.

Madam Ross gave Cade a seductive smile and a half bow as he approached. 'Here she is, sir. Enjoy yourself, pray.'

Cade returned the bow and the smile.

'Of that I have no doubt, madam.'

With a flutter of her fan, Madam Ross drifted off, and Cade turned and looked down at Nell.

'Lead on, little one.'

His speech was casual, but his eyes were bright and she could sense the heat of his desire as he followed her out of the taproom and up the stairs to her room.

As soon as they were in the door, he shoved her against the wall, plunging one hand down her bodice and the other beneath her skirts, reaching between her legs and exploring her roughly. Nell caught her breath at the suddenness of his assault. Images of the previous night flooded her mind and she fought down panic.

Cade lifted her skirt and grasped her around the waist, thrusting against her backside. Nell could feel his hardness beneath his breeches. He pulled himself away and stood looking at her for a moment, his breathing rapid and his eyes like coals.

'Take your clothes off,' he commanded, pulling off his sword belt. She was frightened, but with his eyes on her she was more frightened not to obey, and she fumbled with the hooks of her bodice and skirt and dropped them to the floor. He ran his hands over her bare shoulders and throat, then unlaced her stays. When they were free he pulled her shift over her head. Standing there in nought but stockings and shoes, Nell felt more naked beneath his gaze than she would have if she had worn nothing.

'Come, wench. Onto your knees.'

So here it was, Nell thought. If this was her

chosen trade, this was a part of it, and she had better get used to it than fight it.

She knelt before Cade and unbuttoned his breeches. His cock sprang forth like a living thing. It seemed enormous, and was alarmingly ruddy and purple. Nell took it into her hand and tentatively licked the head. It felt velvety beneath her tongue, and tasted slightly salty, of sweat and something more, but was not vile, as she had feared it might be. Cade moaned and grasped a handful of her hair and thrust himself into her mouth. Nell felt her gorge rise and instinctively pushed him away. She turned from him, gagging and coughing. Fear rose in her. She was a failure at this, too, and would be turned out.

'I'm sorry, sir,' she said, her eyes fixed on his boots. 'Only I haven't—'

'You haven't had a prick in your mouth before?'

'No, sir.'

'Well, first time for everything, isn't there? Come, try again. I won't hurt you.'

Nell once again took him into her mouth, and he did not push so deep into her throat this time. She did nothing except let him move inside her, but that seemed to be all that was required.

After a few moments, he withdrew and pulled her onto the bed. His breeches around his knees and still wearing his boots, he nudged her thighs apart. Nell remembered the salve that Rose had left with her, but it was too late now.

Her nether parts were bruised, and Cade's entry hurt. She thought that if last night had been anything to go by, at least this would not last long. She was relieved to find that she was right. After only a few minutes, his thrusts sped up and Nell felt the spasm as he shoved hard and spent within her.

She felt his heartbeat slow along with his breathing before he rolled off her. She was unsure what she should do, but he seemed not to expect anything more. He gave her a brief smile and tousled her hair.

'That's a good girl.'

Evidently Nell had given satisfaction, for Cade gave her tuppence on his way out, and as she was washing herself, Madam Ross came to tell her not to bother dressing, as two of Cade's brother officers had paid for her services.

'Here's Lieutenant Dawkins,' she said. Dawkins, big and blonde, was out of his coat before Madam Ross had shut the door behind her, and without a word he pushed Nell onto the bed and settled himself between her legs.

'Oh, God, but you're tight,' he moaned in her ear. He moved slowly, lying heavy on top of her. Nell felt that she would smother under his weight and wrenched her head to the side, gasping for breath. Dawkins felt even bigger than Cade inside her, and she wondered how big a man's pego could be. She thought with alarm of the enormous member of a stallion. Surely no man could be as huge as that?

A fist thundered on the door.

'Hurry up, you poxy bastard. Are you going to take all night about it?'

'Piss off,' Hawkins answered, not interrupting his purposeful stroke.

The owner of the voice, Lieutenant Harper, was waiting outside the door and gave Dawkins a leering grin as they met in the doorway. He was a ruddy-faced young man with sandy red hair who reminded Nell of a fox.

'Give her a good one?' he asked, with a glance at Nell.

'Better than you could manage, mate,' Dawkins returned, and was gone.

Harper came to the edge of the bed where Nell sat naked and squeezed her small breasts in his hands, pinching her nipples until they stood erect and hard.

'Go on, open my breeches,' he said. She obeyed. 'Look what a star-gazer I've got. And it's going right down your gullet.'

He pulled Nell to her knees and shoved himself into her mouth, and she fought the urge to gag.

'Suck, wench.'

Nell did as he told her. Her lips hurt, stretched wide, and she wished he would stop. She felt his thrusts grow quicker but was not prepared for the sudden explosion of hot liquid into her mouth, and she choked and struggled as he held her head in place. When he withdrew, his mettle ran down Nell's chin and onto her bare chest. She scrambled for the pot under the bed and retched into it.

'What, wench, do you not like the taste of my buttermilk?' Harper laughed as he wiped himself with his shirt and buttoned his breeches. 'Well, you'll come to it with use. Still, here's tuppence for you. You'll do better next time.'

After Harper had left, Nell wanted nothing more than to sleep. But, afraid of being cast out if she failed to live up to Madam Ross's expectations, she washed herself, wincing as she did so, dressed, and went back downstairs. Rose beckoned and looked searchingly at her.

'How are you faring?' she asked. 'Not too bad?'

'Not too bad,' Nell responded, though she tottered on her feet with exhaustion. 'Will it always hurt so much?'

'No,' said Rose. 'You'll grow used to it by and by. Remember the salve.'

Madam Ross was approaching, an approving smile on her powdered face.

'You've done well. All the gentlemen were most pleased.' She looked at Nell's dishevelled hair and bleary eyes.

'That's enough for your first night. Go to bed now. Those lads and more will be back tomorrow.'

Chapter Three

As Madam Ross had predicted, the days following the king's arrival were busy. The town was crowded with Royalists returning from the years of exile at country homes, with village lads who had come to see the king's arrival and stayed to look for work, with sailors eager to ship once more under the proud flag of a monarch, and with huge numbers of soldiers glad to be done with fighting and hardship. London was mad with joy. Anything seemed possible now that King Charles was back, and Nell listened enthralled to the gossip and stories about the growing court at Whitehall. 'That Barbara Palmer doesn't trouble to hide from anyone, not even her husband, that she's the king's mistress!' Rose exclaimed. 'I've heard that he spent his first night at the palace in her arms.'

'Of course, he has no wife,' chimed in plump Jane, one of the girls who had taken a special liking to Nell. 'But still, he makes mighty bold with his dalliance.'

'And who's to stop him?' asked Rose. 'Harry Killigrew told me that the king has half a dozen bastards. He's got a boy that was born to him on Jersey afore he and his court moved to France, and he's brought the lad to live at the palace. Thirteen years old, and the spitting image of his father. Harry says the king so dotes on and dandles him the whisper goes he might be acknowledged a lawful son.'

When she heard bits of news about the king, Nell thought again of his darkly handsome face, jaunty carriage, and booming joyous laugh as he had ridden by, and the electric excitement she had felt when his eyes met hers. It was unbearably tantalizing to know that he was even now somewhere only a few miles away, doing—what? Whatever kings did, though what exactly that might be, she was not sure. Each piece of information she gained only made her long for more, and she added each new fact or story to the growing picture in her head of a life unimaginably different from hers.

Some of what Nell heard about the king and the goings-on at court fitted in some shadowy way with her own new observations about men. They seemed to be ruled by their desires in a way that she was not, and she realised that she held a kind of power over the men whose attention she caught. This was a novelty, and a mystery to be explored.

'They're like pups, these lads,' laughed Jane, 'tumbling all over themselves to get at you, their heads so full of cunt they can't think of aught else. Mr. Killigrew says his new young actors are so bad, he's going to hire me a-purpose so they can keep

46

their minds on their work.'

'Actors?' Nell asked.

'Aye,' said Jane. 'The playhouses are to open again. Tell her, Rose. I forgot all that Harry said.'

Nell had met Harry Killigrew a time or two. He was a wild young buck who had burst onto the scene in London recently, having fled from Heidelberg, where he had wounded a man in a duel. He ran with a rakish crowd of young bloods and visited Rose frequently. Nell thought his dark unruly hair and golden-hazel eyes were striking, but she was a little afraid of him.

'Harry's father, Tom Killigrew, was a theatre man in the old days,' Rose said. 'He fought for the king in the war, and now his loyalty is rewarded. His Majesty has given him one of the patents for the new playhouses.'

'That's it,' said Jane. 'It's to be the King's Company, and Mr. Davenant will run the other one.'

Never having been in a theatre or seen a play, Nell could not quite imagine what they might be like. Perhaps she would find out later. For the present, she had matters of more immediate interest.

Jimmy Cade, her client from that first night, had become a regular. Nell liked him well enough, and as Rose had said, there was a certain ease in bedding a man she was used to. She need not fear what the encounter would bring, and as she became more familiar with his preferences, she could better give him what pleased him, ensuring herself a steady source of money.

In contrast to the hot haste of their first encounter, Cade became more relaxed with Nell, not only stopping to take his boots off before he joined her in bed, but frequently chatting with her after. He was young, but he had seen action in the war, and she liked to hear his stories about battles and military life.

She watched him dress one hot afternoon, when they had dozed off after their bout and then awoken for a second round. His uniform made her think of her father, and she wondered if he had looked or moved as Cade did.

'My da was in the army,' she said.

'Was he? And where is he now?' Cade asked, struggling with his boots.

'He died,' Nell said softly. 'In prison in Oxford. He lost all in service of the king.'

'Long since?' Cade asked, looking at her more carefully.

'When I was but a baby. I never knew him.'

'I'm sorry for it, Nelly. There were too many died, too many babes left fatherless.'

Nell nodded silently. There was nothing to say, nothing that could express the pain that flooded her heart, the longing for something she had never known and would never know. Tears welled from her eyes, and she knuckled them away.

Cade buckled on his sword belt and picked up his hat, then gave Nell's damp cheek a gentle stroke. She wished he wouldn't leave her alone, but he was already at the door and spoke over his shoulder.

'I'll see you soon, little one.'

*   *   *

'What was our da like?' Nell asked Rose later. 'Why did he go to prison?'

48

Rose shook her head sadly. 'I don't remember much. I was very small myself. I remember him coming in the door and sweeping me up into his arms, laughing as he talked to me. Least, I think I do. Then he was gone. I remember Mam crying. It frightened me and I ran to her. But she pushed me away and shouted at me to leave her be.'

The sisters sat in silence for a few moments. The past was locked away, behind an impenetrable wall. Their mother was the only link to that distant time. But Nell found it impossible to think of her mother as other than she was now—bitter, blowsy, and hard. Was it possible that Eleanor Smith had once been young and happy, had brightened at the sound of her man's footsteps at the door, had had a tender smile for Rose and Nell or ever regarded them as other than a burden? If so, that woman was long dead. And Nell knew that Rose was her only ally in a harsh and unpredictable world.

* * *

The conversations with Cade and Rose seemed to have opened a rift in Nell's mind, a doorway to a rolling mist of fear and sadness. She could not shake off the dark shadows, and for the rest of the day she was weighted with a profound sense of loss and terror.

That night, Nell tossed fitfully before finally slipping into a dream. She was alone in a dark and narrow passageway. It might have been the lane outside her mother's home, or the alley where she had spent the night when she had run away, or perhaps it was a place dimly remembered from deeper in her memory. It was night, and a thick fog swirled, obliterating the moon and stars. The wintry wind bit into Nell's bare feet, penetrated the thin rags that covered her. Her teeth chattered in the cold, and she was so hungry that a pit seemed to gape at her very core. An aching loneliness seized her. She knew she would die if she did not find shelter and company.

The fog deepened. She crept forward, reaching out a hand to feel her way. Her fingers scraped along something clammy and hard, like the stone landing steps left bare when the river's tide receded, their surface greened over with the teeming life of the water. The slimy feel of the wall repulsed Nell, but a gust of air blew from the opposite side of the passageway and it seemed that some cliff yawned there. She feared that she would fall into oblivion and hugged close to the cold stone.

A shaft of light shot through the darkness. A door had opened ahead, and Nell knew that if she could just get through it, she would be safe. She stumbled forward, clawing at spectral cobwebs that drooped from above. Each step was a battle, and she despaired of getting to the door. But it was close now, the warmth and light beyond it a beacon to her soul, and she could hear voices and laughter within.

She reached the threshold, fingers scrabbling on the cold damp stone. Behind her loomed darkness, the icy and fetid reek of a tomb, and nameless terrors. Another few inches and she would be safe.

The door slammed shut with a reverberating thud.

'No!' The night enveloped Nell's cry. Her hands blindly sought a way to open the door, but its surface was smooth and heavy iron, with no knob, no keyhole, no way in. She beat against the door with her fists, but her hardest blows made no noise. Shrieking, begging, she pounded. But nothing happened and no one came.

In that moment of desperation and hopelessness Nell awoke and found herself alone in her bed. She was cold, and clutched the covers around her. She longed for someone to hold her and make all well. Her thoughts went to her mother, and she began to weep.

Erratic, frequently drunk, and occasionally violent though her mother might be, she was the only parent Nell had ever known, and she found that the loss of her mother terrified her even more than the unpredictability that living with her had meant.

She clung to her pillow and sobbed. All the bravery and cheer she had thought she had was hollow. She felt ashamed and an utter failure. In the endless watches of the night, with the world in cold blackness outside the window, she was only a frightened and wretched child.

She went from her room, pushed open the door of Rose's little chamber, and slipped to the side of the bed. Rose was alone, and Nell crept in beside her. She had shared a pallet bed with Rose for most of her life, until Rose had struck out on her own, and it was immeasurably comforting to feel the warmth of Rose's body and smell her scent. Rose stirred.

'What's amiss?'

'I was afeared. A dream.'

'All's well. Come to sleep now.' Rose drew Nell to her and draped a protective arm around her. Nell nestled closer. Safe in the snug cocoon of the shared bed, the demons receded and her shivering ceased, and soon she was asleep.

* * *

In the brightness of the morning sun, Nell's fears of the previous night lost their overwhelming power. She would not go back to live under her mother's thumb. She would see her mother when she could stand proudly, and prove that she had done well for herself. What that might mean, Nell had no clear idea. But she had a new determination. She would be someone to be reckoned with.

* * *

The summer brought brilliant blue skies, sunlit days, and balmy evenings. Although the long hours of daylight meant that the crowds at Madam Ross's stayed late, and the hours of sleep were fewer, Nell woke with the dawn. The house was quiet then and the glorious new mornings held the promise of adventure.

One sparkling August morning it occurred to her that she missed the river. She hadn't been near it since her daily sojourns to Billingsgate fish market to buy oysters, and she made her way towards London Bridge. She didn't mind the long walk into the City—she had made it often enough pushing the oyster barrow, and it was unutterable freedom to dance along unencumbered.

Shopkeepers were just opening for business, folding down the bulkheads that served as counters by day and shuttered up their shops by night. Street vendors were out in great numbers, their wares fresh and their spirits not yet worn down.

'A brass pot or an iron pot to mend!' called a man with a bag of tools slung on his back, beating the butt end of a hammer on the bottom of a pot.

'Knives or scissors to grind!'

'Delicate cowcumbers to pickle!'

'Fine ripe strawberries!'

The cries of the hawkers rose and mingled in pleasant chaos. A man and a boy sang out in harmony, 'Buy a white line! Or a jack line! Or a clothes line!' their words cascading in a catch.

'Buy a fine singing bird!' Nell stopped to admire the pretty little finches a small boy carried in a wicker cage. She was hungry and her attention was momentarily caught by a middle-aged woman balancing a great basket of green muskmelons atop her head, but instead she bought a dipper of milk from a milkmaid, whose buckets were suspended from a wooden yoke over her shoulders. Nell could imagine too well the weight and was grateful she had no buckets, baskets, or barrows weighing her down.

She made her way onto the bridge. She knew of a child-sized gap between two of the houses that crowded the bridge's span, and from this secret perch, she surveyed the scene. London stretched away to the west, its fringes fading into green countryside. The river surged beneath her, the high tide creating powerful eddies around the great starlings that supported the bridge. The boats travelling downstream glided easily, while the boatmen making their way upstream against the current pulled and strained mightily.

Nell watched the passengers in the crafts with a mixture of curiosity and envy. She had never been in a boat. Quite apart from the cost, she had never had reason to go anywhere that her own feet could not take her.

She watched two gentlemen getting into a wherry upriver at Three Cranes Stairs. Several more watermen waited for passengers, and Nell made up her mind that she would go down there, and perhaps even get into a boat.

As she made her way to the landing stairs, the scent of the river, fresh and alive, stirred her excitement. Three burly watermen were gathered on the stairs, their tethered boats bobbing in the current. A leaping fish broke the surface of the water and then disappeared once more into the greeny depths. The youngest of the men, his dark hair tied into a queue at the back of his head, squinted into the sunlight as he lounged on one of the steps. He cocked his head to the side as Nell approached, and the two others broke out of their conversation and turned.

'How much does it cost? To go in a boat?' she asked.

'That depends!' laughed one of the fellows, his face a deep red-brown from years of working in the sun. 'Where do you want to go?'

'I don't know,' Nell said. 'I've never been anywhere.'

'It's sixpence for a pair of oars,' he began.

'That's 'oars,' now, mind,' put in another of the men, 'not 'whores.' But perhaps you'd know better than I about the socket money for a brace of bobtails?' The others laughed, but the first waterman swatted the joker with his cap.

''Ere, leave the girl alone, Pete.' He turned back to Nell, his blue eyes startling against the mahogany of his skin. 'Pay no mind to 'im, sweeting, 'e has the manners of a dog. It's a twelver to Whitehall, eighteen shillings to Chelsea, three bull's-eyes to Windsor. Half again as much if the tide's against you.'

It seemed silly to spend money to get to the other side of the river or to the palace, and even if she had the five-shilling fare to Richmond, what would she do there?

'Another time,' she smiled. 'I'll take shank's mare today.'

'Another time then, sweeting,' the man grinned. 'When someone else is paying.'

Chapter Four

In October the executions of three of the men who had instigated the execution of the king's father, King Charles I, were to take place at Charing Cross. The king had spared the lives of dozens, but the few who had been directly responsible for his father's murder would die the terrible death reserved for traitors. A blood thirst seized London, and Nell listened to some lads in the street describing what would happen.

'They'll hang them first,' one said. 'But not until they're dead—only insensible, like. Then they'll cut them down, still breathing, and carve out their guts and hearts. And then they'll hack their carcasses into quarters, coat them in tar to make them keep, and post them on pikes at all the gates of the City.'

*　　　*　　　*

The day of death arrived, and Nell and Rose jostled for standing space around the scaffold. The crowds reminded Nell of the throngs that had welcomed the king only a few months earlier, but the mood was savage and sour. Packs of drunken lads roved, as they had on that spring day, but today they seemed like feral dogs.

Surrounded by tall strangers, Nell could not see anything but a patch of sky above, and suddenly she began to feel that she couldn't breathe. She clutched Rose's hand, fearful of losing her in the crush, and to her shame, she began to shake and cry.

'Let's go,' she pleaded. They threaded their way out of the seething mob. Nell fought down a rising sense of panic, and by the time they reached the edge of the crowd, her breath was coming in ragged gulps and her heart was pounding.

She sank to the ground and hugged her knees to her chest, trying to stop her shivering. Rose squatted and peered at her.

'What is it?'

'I don't know,' Nell gasped. 'I don't want to see it. I'm afraid. Do you mind?'

'No,' Rose shrugged. 'I've no great desire to watch anyone being butchered.'

There was a roar from the crowd. The condemned men must be arriving. It would begin soon. Nell struggled to her feet.

'Let's get away now.'

*   *   *

Madam Ross's establishment was full to bursting

that evening, and Nell had her first taste of the phenomenon of men who have felt the brush of violent death wanting to deaden the resultant chill by immersing themselves in warm flesh. The men she took to her bed that night were sodden with drink and unusually sombre, brutal, or even tearful. All wanted to erase the sights and sounds of the day and to remind themselves that they still lived and breathed.

Jimmy Cade and some of his officer friends came late in the evening, and after he had spent he lay with Nell, stroking her hair and face with unwonted tenderness.

'It had to be done,' he said. 'There must be severe punishment for a crime as foul as the murder of a king. But it's not a spectacle I'd want to see again. You can't help but feel the blade in your own gut as you watch it going into the poor bastards, imagine your own innards being wound out before your eyes, seeing your own blood sluicing over the scaffold.'

'Horrible.' Nell shuddered.

'And somehow it seemed to me that even worse than the pain was the loneliness.'

'How do you mean?' she asked.

'Well, it was the look in Harrison's eyes.' Cade paused, remembering. 'In the middle of a crowd that stretched as far as you could see. But not a friendly face among them. Voices shouting for his death, the slower the better. And he knew what he was in for. It seemed he tried not to cry out, not to give them the satisfaction.'

'But did he cry out?' Nell asked.

'Oh, yes,' Cade said. 'The fires of hell would have been a mercy after that death.'

57

Two more regicides were put to death a day or two later, and another ten within the next few days. The savagery of the executions seemed to have unleashed a wild mood in London.

'Death to all traitors,' Nell heard Jack snarl to one of his cronies. 'Too bad they didn't keep them another fortnight and do them on the Fifth of November.' The other man cackled his agreement.

The next afternoon Nell sat with Ned the barman and Harry Killigrew. It was too early for much business, and though it was freezing cold outside, the taproom was cosy, the flames in the fireplace chasing away the shadows in the corners and reflecting in the dark panes of the windows.

'What's the Fifth of November?' Nell asked Ned.

'Why, it's Guy Fawkes Day,' he said. 'Sure you've heard of him? A Papist. Tried to blow up King James and all the lords in the House of Parliament, he did. When was it, Harry?'

'Sixteen hundred and five,' Harry said. 'But they discovered the plot. 'Fawkes at midnight, and by torchlight there was found,"' he quoted. '"With long matches and devices, underground."'

'So the king and all were saved,' Ned continued, 'and Fawkes and the others that had intrigued with him were put to death. It used to be kept as a great holiday, but then you're too young to remember that. In the old days, it was a right party. A great rout of people in the streets, fireworks everywhere. And of course we young 'uns would always build a Guy to burn.'

'But not before we got our penny,' Harry chimed in. Ned laughed at Nell's blank expression.

'The Guy was a dummy, do you see, meant to be like Guy Fawkes. We would parade it through the

58

streets, crying out 'A penny for the Guy!' And then the Guy would be put into a bonfire. Fires all over London, there were, in them days.'

'I'll warrant there'll be a Guy or two this year again,' Harry said.

*   *   *

Harry was right, and on the Fifth of November bonfires lit the night sky and Guys of wood and straw and cloth blazed at the center of baying crowds. It was a busy night in Lewkenor's Lane, and Harry swaggered into the taproom in company with several other young men, whooping and in high spirits.

'We've done it!' he crowed to the room. 'We put the final nail in old Nol Cromwell's coffin tonight!'

'Aye,' laughed one of his mates. 'We've just given a show at the old Red Bull, with the blessing of the king himself! The theatre is back again, and no mistaking.'

'You couldn't have chosen a better day for it than Bonfire Night!' Ned called from behind the bar. 'Death to killjoys and traitors, and up with merriment!'

Cheers greeted this remark, and the lads were welcomed with slaps on the back and drink all around as they drew up stools and benches around a table. Their jubilation was contagious, and Nell worked her way through the admiring crowd that gathered around Harry and his crew. Rose and Jane had joined them, and Rose made room for Nell on the bench next to her.

'Here's to the King's Men!' Harry raised his tankard and all joined in the toast.

59

One of the company, a hulking man in his thirties with one squinted eye somewhat lower and larger than the other, who might have looked threatening were it not for the grin that split his face, banged his fist on the table for quiet.

'Here's to His Majesty, who brought us back. And may tonight be the first of many shows to come!' Voices joined in from all over the room. 'To His Majesty!'

Ned fought his way through the crowd and set a great jug of ale on the table before the squint-eyed man.

'Walter Clun!' he cried. 'I saw you play at the old Blackfriars when I was but a boy. I remember it still—I laughed 'til I came near to piss myself.'

'Aye, that's me,' Clun chortled. 'Not a dry seat in the house.'

'Wat!' Harry called across the table to him. 'Where are the others? I thought Charlie Hart was coming?'

Wat Clun threw up his hands and rolled his eyes heavenwards.

'Now there you have me, lad. I told Charlie not to be such a stick-in-the-mud, and to shepherd the old men here on this our night of triumph. But will he now? That is the question!'

'And here's me all this time thinking the question was 'To be or not to be'!'

The voice boomed from the door, and Wat surged to his feet, roaring with laughter.

'Charlie! My own true heart! You've come after all!'

The dark-haired newcomer enveloped Wat in a bear hug and kissed him loudly on both cheeks.

'Aye, I've come, and the other old men with me!'

60

Hart was indeed accompanied by several men who were noticeably greyer than the lads at the table, but there was nothing old about him, Nell thought. He was about thirty, tall and well built, and the grace and energy with which he moved made her think of the rope dancer she had seen at Bartholomew Fair. His dark eyes shone with happiness as he returned cries of greeting from all sides.

'Who's that?' Nell whispered to Rose and Jane.

'Charles Hart,' Rose answered. 'He's Mr. Killigrew's leading actor. Mighty fine, isn't he?'

'Fine as a fivepence,' Nell agreed.

Tables, stools, and benches were shuffled until all the actors were seated. Nell noticed that the younger men made way for the older, their deference tinged with admiration and affection. Wat Clun turned to Hart.

'Now then, Charlie, what do you say?'

'We've made a good start on it,' Hart said. 'And I raise my cup to each of you. To John Lacy and to Michael Mohun. Whose light shone through the long dark days. And without whom we'd not be here tonight.' The men on either side of Hart acknowledged the murmurs of agreement from their fellows.

Big John Lacy, sitting to Hart's left, surveyed the faces around him. 'Back onstage again. I didn't think I'd live to see the day. Here's to you, my old dear friend, and the lord of the dance, Charles Hart! And to His Majesty. God save the king!'

'God save the king!' The room echoed with the cry. Nell gazed at the solemn faces of the older actors around the table. For the first time she felt ashamed of her whoredom, and she wanted

61

desperately not to have to relate to the players as a whore. She felt sure that they embodied some mystery and wisdom, and she wanted only to be in their company and listen to them. She glanced around the room and was relieved that Madam Ross was nowhere to be seen and that Jack was engaged in a game of dice at a corner table and was paying her no mind.

Soon the spirit of the gathering lightened as the talk turned to the afternoon's performance.

'A good house, and a merry, especially considering the weather,' Lacy said.

'True enough,' Hart agreed. 'But then, considering how long some of them had been waiting to discover how it came out, perhaps they didn't mind braving the cold.'

Nell was puzzled by the laughter at this remark.

'Why were they waiting?' she ventured to ask. She felt self-conscious when all eyes turned to her, but Lacy answered her cheerfully.

'The theatres were outlawed under Old Nol, thou knowest that? Well, during that time, some of the old actors twice put up this same play at the Red Bull, and were twice stopped and arrested.'

'But now,' Nell ventured, 'now you can play again?'

'Yes, thanks be to God and to Charles Stuart,' Wat nodded. 'And after eighteen long years, here we sit before you, the King's Company, in business once again.'

Nell was chagrined that she had missed an event of such momentousness as the actors' triumphant return to the stage. Jimmy Cade and a few of his friends came in the door, and he caught her eye. She was usually happy to see him, but she lingered at the actors' table for a few minutes.

'This play you played today,' she queried, 'will you give it again?'

'We will,' Hart said. 'But we've other fare for the next few days.'

'And then'—Lacy grinned—'on Thursday, we move to better quarters, indoors, and give the first part of *King Henry the Fourth*.'

'I wish I could see it.' Nell looked up at him, hope shining in her eyes.

'And so you can,' Lacy said. 'Even better, come to our rehearsal tomorrow. Then you can say you saw it before any in London.'

Nell gave him a happy grin and danced off to find Jimmy Cade. By the time she returned downstairs, most of the actors had left. She longed to hear more about the theatre and couldn't wait until she could follow up on Lacy's invitation.

Chapter Five

The next morning, Nell woke to find that the insides of her thighs were streaked with blood, and she threw a fervent thank-you heavenward upon discovering that Rose had also started her monthly courses, and so they would both be excused from work and free to watch the King's Men rehearse.

Shortly before ten o'clock, they arrived at what had formerly been Gibbons's Tennis Court in Vere Street, only a few minutes' walk from Lewkenor's Lane. Nell had heard that the place, just off the southwestern corner of Lincoln's Inn Fields, had been for some time a resort of the gentry and nobility, offering not only tennis and bowls but the highest quality victuals and drink, sheltered gardens, and a large coach house.

Nell looked around excitedly as Harry welcomed them into the new playhouse. The high-ceilinged room was flooded with sunlight from the rows of windows at the backs of the galleries that lined the two long walls of the building. Knots of men and boys huddled and bustled in preparation for the morning's work, and with a thrill Nell recognised many of the actors she'd seen the previous evening.

'It will be the finest theatre that London has seen,' Harry said. 'Much better than the Red Bull.'

'Why?' Nell asked.

'It's a proper building, not just a yard open to the wind and rain. Less than fifty feet from the stage to the back of the house, so the actors will not have to shout to make themselves heard. It'll be more like playing at court in the old days.'

'Very fine,' Rose agreed.

'You're looking fine yourself this morning,' Harry said with a wink. 'Come, let's have a closer look.' He pulled her into the shadows under the gallery at the back of the theatre, and Nell took the opportunity to wander closer to the stage, where Wat Clun was in conference with one of the younger actors. He grinned as Nell approached.

'Well, I see you've come to join us. What do you think of the place?'

'It's grand,' Nell beamed. A raised stage at one end of the room sloped down a little from the darkly panelled back wall with its two doors, to within a few feet of the first row of green-upholstered benches. Candles in many-armed brackets were mounted along the galleries at the sides of the stage, reminding Nell of the light that had blazed forth from the Banqueting House on the night of the king's return.

'Come,' Harry called. 'It's about time.' A handful of people were seated on the benches in the pit before the stage, but Harry led Nell and Rose up narrow steps to the upper gallery at the back of the theater.

'Boxes for gentlemen,' he said. 'Much more comfortable than below.'

'To your beginners, please.' Nell looked down to where a man with a sheaf of papers before him on a table was calling to the actors. They disappeared through the doors at the back of the stage, and silence fell. Harry pulled Rose onto his lap and she giggled. Nell wondered how they could think of anything else when the play was about to begin.

A group of actors swept onto the stage with an air of regal gravity. They seemed to be wearing their own clothes, but had bits and pieces of what Nell thought must be their costumes. A grey-haired actor that she recognised from the previous night wore a heavy robe of red velvet and a crown, so he must be the king. Some of the others wore capes or had swords hanging at their sides.

The king glanced around at the men surrounding him, and spoke.

'So shaken as we are, so wan with care,
Find we a time for frighted peace to pant
And breathe short-winded accents of new broils
To be commenced in strands afar remote. . . .'

Nell was enthralled by the majestic words, and strove to understand them. To her relief the next

65

scene was much easier to follow, and funny. Wat lumbered onto the stage, a huge tankard in his paw, stretched luxuriously, scratched his arse, and demanded of the fair-haired young actor who followed him, '"Now, Hal, what time of day is it, lad?"'

'"What a devil hast thou to do with the time of day?"' the youth cried. '"Unless the blessed sun himself was a fair hot wench in flame-colored taffeta, I see no reason why thou shouldst be so superfluous to demand the time of day!"'

Nell thought she had never seen anything so funny as the picture of virtuous outrage on Wat's face.

'Look at him,' she chortled to Rose and Harry. 'Like a great round baby caught with stolen sweetmeats.'

Her heart skipped a beat when Charles Hart strode onto the stage in the next scene, his dark eyes full of snapping fire, and she feared for his safety when he raged at the king, his deep voice seeming to shake the walls as he cried, '"My liege, I did deny no prisoners!"'

When Harry Percy, in the person of Charles Hart, made ready to depart for the war and took tender leave of his wife, played by a young man, as true-to-the-life a woman as any that Nell had ever seen, she felt her own soul ache for his going.

When the rehearsal was done, Nell sat still for a few moments, not wanting to let go of what she had experienced. She felt drained and yet exhilarated, and as if she was changed in some way. In the course of the three hours she had felt herself consumed with the passions of the king, the prince, of Harry Percy and his wife, of fat Sir John Falstaff

66

and all the rest, had felt as though she herself had lived through all their griefs, their rages, and their joys. She did not want to leave the charmed atmosphere of the playhouse. She lingered to watch as the actors gathered on the benches below, and was overjoyed when Wat Clun waved at her. Dragging Rose after her, she bounded down to where he stood and beamed up at him.

'Well, sweeting, and what did you think of your first play?' he asked.

'It was a wonder! You were so funny!'

Clun grinned.

'Come to see *Beggars' Bush* tomorrow afternoon. It'll be our last show at the Bull.'

'Truly?' Nell cried. 'Can we, Rose?'

'Aye,' Rose nodded. 'We'll not miss such a kind offer.'

* * *

On the way home, Nell capered beside Rose, hopping on one leg in circles around her sister and then coming alongside.

'I thought the prince was wondrous,' she mused. 'Why should his father be displeased with him?'

'Why, for his mad freaks and roguerics with ruffians and low company such as Falstaff and the others. Bowsing, stealing, wenching.'

'But once the old king was dead could not Hal do as he pleased?'

'I suppose he could.'

'And why was Harry Percy so angry?'

'Lord, I don't know. I couldn't follow it all, in truth.'

'And why—'

''Fore God, Nell, you wear me out!' Rose cried in exasperation. 'Save your questions for Harry or the actors.'

Nell did not understand how Rose could not share her burning curiosity to know everything about the play, the players, and the theatre. She held her tongue, but her mind seethed with questions. Though she didn't have to work that night, she haunted the taproom, hoping that the actors might come in, and when Harry Killigrew strode in followed by two of the younger actors, she raced over to them.

'How can you remember all those words? What play did you play this afternoon? Where do the plays come from?'

Harry laughed. 'You'd best sit down if you've got so many questions.' Nell plopped herself on a bench facing the fair-haired young actor who had played Prince Hal.

'How many plays are there?' she demanded.

'What, how many plays in the world?' he laughed. 'That I cannot tell, but I can tell you what we've played over the past weeks, and what we'll give again. *The Traitor, Wit Without Money, The Silent Woman, Othello, Bartholomew Fair*—'

'Where do they come from?' Nell interrupted. 'And how can there be so many plays if there have been none for so long?'

'The two companies divided the plays from the old days,' said Harry. 'And my father got the best of those, as he did with the actors.'

'Is it all lads and men?' Nell asked. 'Are there no women players?'

'Up 'til now,' Harry said, 'it's always been boys acting the women's parts. But that's soon to change.

His Majesty saw women on the stage in Frankfurt and thought it a charming innovation.'

'Mr. Killigrew says he's going to try putting a woman on the stage in a few weeks,' the youngest of the lads said. 'My dad says it will cause rioting in the streets, either from outrage or from lust.'

Nell joined in the laughter, but was intrigued.

'Who are they, these women? Where do they come from?'

'Oh, they're pretty, likely-looking wenches my father has found somewhere,' Harry shrugged. 'Girls with a quick wit who are like to be able to learn their words.'

'Not married. And orphans, likely,' said the fair-haired actor. 'For who would want their wife or daughter on the stage?'

'Sir William Davenant at the Duke's Company has a couple of girls about your age in his care,' Harry said. 'Betty Barry and Moll Davis. Perhaps he'll make something of them.'

'But that's all to come,' said the fair-haired lad. 'Mr. Killigrew will not risk putting women on just yet. Certainly not when we play at court in a fortnight's time.'

'Is there a playhouse there?' Nell asked.

'There is,' Harry answered. 'The Cockpit. It's fallen into a sad state. But it'll soon be right again, eh, Marmaduke?'

'With not a penny spared,' the fair-haired young man agreed. 'My brother's a plasterer and he says there's night work as well as daytime labour. The king's in a tear to get the job finished, and when it's done, it'll be mighty fine.'

*　　*　　*

69

The next afternoon, Nell and Rose made their way up St. John Street to where the Red Bull stood near Clerkenwell Green. There was already a crowd at the door to the playhouse, and Nell was seized with fear that there would be no room for them. But when Rose told their names to the man with the box for the money, he nodded and waved them in with a smile.

The square yard was open to the winter sky, with enclosed galleries along three sides and a stage across the fourth. Despite the chill breeze, the benches in the galleries were quite full, and even the ground before the stage was crowded with men, women, and children, all eating, drinking, talking, and laughing. In the middle of this seething crowd, Nell could not even see the stage. Rose grasped her hand and they worked their way forward. The stage stood some five feet high from the ground, so that those standing at the back of the pit could see as well as those at the front, but its height meant that Nell had to look almost straight up to see it.

The play began and Nell was pleased to see Wat Clun, Charles Hart, and other actors from the previous day's rehearsal. The story rocked merrily along—everyone, it seemed, was in disguise, and at the end of the play all were revealed as their true selves. Charles Hart turned out to be a nobleman, and not only was he reunited with the girl he had been forced to forsake, but she proved to be the daughter of a duke, so all ended happily, if improbably.

Dusk was coming on when the play finished, with rain clouds lowering overhead, and Nell was shivering despite the heavy cloak she clasped

70

around herself and tired from standing for two hours. Yet she didn't want to go. The play had transported her, made her forget about Madam Ross's place. She had been in two playhouses now, and different though they were, they had both seemed to hold magic within them, to make her thrill with an excitement she had felt only once before—while watching the king's return to London.

*   *   *

The older actors did not return to Madam Ross's in the weeks after the King's Company moved to the Vere Street theater, but Harry and the younger actors were frequent visitors. When Harry went upstairs it was with Rose, and, as Jane had said, Tom Killigrew had retained her services for his lads. Nell was happy that matters had fallen out so. She desperately wanted to be thought well of by her new acquaintances, and though they must know she was part of Madam Ross's covey, she felt on more solid ground with them than she would have if she had to take them to her bed. When they came in of an evening, she always wanted to hear the particulars of the day's performance and begged them for news of the doings at the playhouse.

'Well,' said Marmaduke Watson one night in early December, 'Sir William Davenant has been training his women players, we hear, though they'll not be fit to send onstage for some time.'

'No,' Harry agreed. 'We'll beat him in that race, for we're putting a woman on the stage in a few days' time.'

'Who?' Nell asked. 'What will she play?'

71

'Anne Marshall,' Harry said. 'She's to play Desdemona in *Othello*.'

'And after that,' Ned Kynaston said glumly, 'who knows? Two weeks ago I played Arthiope in *The Bloody Brother*. But old Killigrew has told me that when we put it on again in a fortnight, I'm to play Otto instead, and Charlie Hart'll have a woman to his lover.'

A few days later Nell besieged the actors with questions about how the first performance by a woman had succeeded.

'Well, they didn't riot,' young Theo Bird said.

'Hardly,' Marmaduke put in. 'They ate it up.'

'I'd have been better,' said Kynaston. 'And prettier, too.' The lads laughed, but Marmaduke shook his head and winked at Nell.

'Can you not keep playing women's roles, too?' she asked. Kynaston stared into his tankard and didn't answer.

'No,' said Harry. 'Neddie's good, but when you put him next to the real thing, they're as different as chalk and cheese. Actresses. That's the future.'

Another question was on Nell's lips, but the words froze unspoken. Madam Ross's man Jack was making his way toward the table, scowling, his eyes fixed on her. She couldn't stand the thought of him bullying her before the actors, and she mumbled something to them as she scrambled off the bench and towards another table of men. Jack's big hand closed hard on her upper arm, and he yanked her to face him.

'You're not paid to take your ease,' he growled.

'I was just talking,' she answered, her throat constricted by fear and shame, knowing that the actors were surely watching.

'Less talking, and more time on your back or your knees.' Jack's fingers tightened around her arm. Obviously enjoying her discomfort, he reached his other hand under her skirt, and shoved his fingers hard inside her.

'That's your worth,' he said, his breath hot on her face, thrusting deeper into her. 'That and only that. Don't get above yourself, or I'll teach you a lesson you'll not forget.'

He gave a last vicious twist of his hand before letting Nell go, and she ran from the room, too mortified to face Harry and the other lads and too terrified to remain in Jack's presence.

*   *   *

After that, Nell no longer sat with the actors unless Jack was absent. When he was present, she kept quiet and out of his way, anxious not to give him any excuse to shame her further. She thought with longing of the theatre and begged Jane to tell her any news of the actors, but Jane had little interest in what the players did when they were not at Madam Ross's.

In late December, Jack disappeared without explanation. Madam Ross made herself scarce as well, disappearing into her rooms on the top floor of the house, and the girls whispered their conjectures about what had happened. On the second day of Jack's absence, Nell dared to hope that he had gone for good. The establishment was a much happier place with only Ned there to mind the shop.

Nell was overjoyed when Harry Killigrew came into the taproom one quiet afternoon a few days before Christmas. He ambled over to the table where Ned sat with Rose, and Nell joined them, happy at her unaccustomed freedom and the holiday mood that prevailed. Christmas under Cromwell had been kept as a day of fasting and atonement, but this year was different. Harry had been at court, where preparations for the festivities had been going on for days.

'You should see the palace,' Harry said. 'Holly and ivy everywhere, and a great Yule log. The king's mother and two sisters are visiting, and the king will keep the twelve days of Christmas as in old times, with masques, mummers, and banquets every day. We gave a show at the Cockpit last night, and the wine was flowing like water.'

Nell thought of what she had been doing the previous night. It had been a particularly unpleasant evening. The fat and revolting Mr. Cooper had fumbled with his limp prick, and struck her when even her sucking failed to rouse him. And then there had been a party of soldiers who were drunk and brutal. She had cried herself to sleep, despairing at the thought that she had no way out.

'Tell me more about the king and the court,' she begged.

'It's like a fairy land,' Harry said. 'There's music and dancing every night. The king has a consort of twenty-four violins, and musicians of every other kind as well. He outdances all the court and sings when he can dance no more.'

In her room alone that night, Nell wondered what the music of twenty-four violins would sound like, and tried to picture the king and his courtiers dancing, their finery sparkling in the gleam of

74

a thousand candles. She thought of the king's mistress Barbara Palmer, radiant at his side. She drew herself up straight, trying to feel the weight of a gown heavy with jewels, and danced, imagining herself partnered by the king, and watched by a host of onlookers at a great Christmas feast.

But on Christmas Eve, Nell heard that the king's sister Mary had died of the smallpox, and instead of revelry, Whitehall was sombre and still, the court dressed in purple mourning clothes instead of jewelled finery. Nell felt herself in mourning, too, as Jack returned to Lewkenor's Lane and resumed his rule.

The New Year of 1661 dawned cold and icy. The Thames froze, and Nell and Rose delighted in the frost fair that sprang up, with booths selling food and drink, and entertainments presented to joyous crowds. They ran and slid on the snow-covered ice, enjoying the novel view of London from the middle of the frozen river, then warmed themselves with hot wassail.

In February, coins bearing the king's face were minted and began to replace the old currency. The king's likeness was noted elsewhere, too, as Barbara Palmer bore a daughter that was rumoured to be Charles's child.

On St. George's Day, the twenty-third of April, the king's coronation brought celebratory throngs to the streets once more. The royal barge sailed down the river from Whitehall to the Tower, followed by a flotilla of craft bearing dignitaries, and then a flood of sightseers crammed onto any vessel that would float. The night sky blazed with fireworks, and London revelled until dawn.

One evening in early July Nell entered the taproom to find Harry, Marmaduke, and young Theo Bird slumped around a corner table, uncharacteristically subdued and glum.

'What's amiss?' she asked.

'We've been playing to scant houses all the week, and each day it gets worse,' Theo said. 'Davenant has opened his new playhouse, and everyone and his wife is going to see his opera.'

'Even the king has been,' added Marmaduke.

'But why?' Nell asked.

'Because he's built a much grander theater,' Marmaduke said. 'It's got painted scenery that moves, and machines—angels and gods coming down from the heavens and so on. Pageantry. Singing.'

'Don't forget Hester Davenport,' Theo said.

'Who's she?' Nell asked.

'One of Davenant's actresses,' Harry said. 'Toothsome. Bonnie and buxom. She's taken the fancy of everyone from the tom turd men to the Earl of Oxford.'

'And there are two parts to the poxed thing,' Marmaduke lamented. 'So everyone has to go twice.'

'*The Siege of Rhodes*,' Harry snorted. 'More like the siege of Lincoln's Inn Fields.'

'But things are bound to get better,' said Nell. 'People tire of a new thing soon enough, is what Rose always says.'

'Not this,' said Harry. 'We'll have to keep up with the Duke's Company or we're sunk.'

Not long after, Nell heard from the lads that

Tom Killigrew had leased a plot of land off Drury Lane and would build a fine new theatre that would accommodate the new fashion for moving scenery and machinery and would outshine Davenant's playhouse in style and grandeur. It was to be called the Theatre Royal.

*   *   *

Soon after Nell learned of Killigrew's plans for a new theatre, Harry became a page of honour to the king, as his father had been to the previous King Charles, and took up residence at Whitehall. He still came to see Rose, but not as frequently. Marmaduke Watson, Ned Kynaston, and the other younger actors of the King's Company continued to drink in the taproom, but when Jack was around, Nell avoided their company. She still ached with shame at their having witnessed Jack's humiliation of her, and wanted to be sure she gave him no reason to repeat the performance.

She longed to take part in the players' banter and jokes, but disciplined herself instead to cultivate regular customers and keep them happy. The more of them she had, the less she would be available for just any brute who might come in the door. One of her favorites was a young man by the name of Robbie Duncan, who seemed to seek her out for her company as much as for pleasure in bed. He worked with his brothers in their father's cloth exporting business, and on only his third visit he had brought her a length of soft brown wool that would serve to make a new cloak for the winter. And Jimmy Cade visited her frequently, always tipping her a few coins.

When Harry Killigrew did visit Lewkenor's Lane, he brought word of each story and scandal at Whitehall. In Nell's second autumn at Madam Ross's, London buzzed with the news that King Charles had ennobled Roger Palmer, the husband of his mistress, bestowing on him the titles of Baron Limerick and Earl of Castlemaine—with the shocking provision that the titles were to pass only to any children born by Barbara Palmer.

'In other words,' Harry explained, 'the king is granting titles to any bastards he should father on Mistress Palmer, and Roger Palmer is to stand by without complaint.'

*   *   *

The following spring, Nell saw people pushing close to the ballad singer near the Maypole in the Strand, shoving to buy his broadsheets.

'What's the news?' she asked a tired-looking woman with a small child in tow.

'The king is to marry! A princess from Portugal.'

Catherine of Braganza arrived in May, and Nell and Rose listened as Harry related the latest news from court.

'Barbara Palmer is seven months gone with child, and she'll not be budged from Hampton Court, queen or no queen, and has even been made a lady of the queen's bedchamber. I'm glad I won't be in the king's shoes when those two ladies meet.'

In August, Nell joined the throngs watching the water pageant in honour of the royal marriage.

Standing on a barrel, she craned her neck to catch a glimpse of the new queen and wondered what she must think about sharing her residence with the king's mistress and children.

The taproom was busy that night, and the patrons were more drunk and disorderly than usual. Jack broke up a fight, cudgelling the instigator into bloody insensibility before throwing him into the street. The tables were packed with drinkers and the girls didn't even bother to leave their rooms when they had done with one man, but took the next from the lines outside their doors.

It was well into the wee hours when the last man left Nell's room and no other appeared. She was exhausted, but put her head out the door of her room to be sure that no one was waiting. Jack was coming down the hallway, steady on his feet despite the half-empty bottle in his hand. His face was flushed and his eyes glinted dangerously as he bore down on Nell.

She ducked backwards but he blocked the door as she tried to close it. She retreated as he entered the room, kicking the door shut behind him. He reached her in two strides and pulled her by her hair onto her knees in front of him as he sat on the edge of the bed. He took a long pull from his bottle, set it on the floor, unbuttoned his breeches, and shoved himself into her mouth.

He smelled of piss and sweat and brandy, and Nell gagged as his flesh hit the back of her throat. She struggled against him, but he yanked her head up and down, his cock choking her. She pushed at him, desperate to draw a breath, but his iron grip would not release. She felt that she would faint or die unless she could free herself. Without thinking, she clamped her teeth down.

Jack gave a roar of rage and pain and let go of her. She scrabbled away from him, but he lifted her by her hair and smashed her across the face so hard she went sprawling face-first onto the bed, and he was on her before she could move, kneeing her legs apart. Nell heard him spit, and screamed as he forced himself into her arse. A filthy hand smelling of brandy was clamped over her mouth, stifling her cries. Another hand clutched her throat, fingers digging into her flesh.

It seemed to go on forever. Nell had never felt such searing pain. She sobbed into Jack's hand, her tears running down to mingle with snot as he slammed into her. At last he spent, giving a final deep thrust that Nell thought would split her. He left without a word, and Nell lay shivering and whimpering. After a time she crept into Rose's room, and Rose started awake at the sound of Nell's sobbing.

'Lord, what's happened?'

'Jack,' Nell whispered. 'He came for me and I didn't mean to, but I bit him. So he hurt me.'

'He hit you?' Rose pulled Nell into her arms.

'More than that. He—' Nell couldn't make herself say the words, but Rose understood her gesture.

'Let me see, honey.' Rose gently examined Nell. 'You're not bleeding, that's a mercy. Here, this will help.' Tears streaked Rose's face as she applied salve to Nell's battered flesh.

'Oh, Nell,' she whispered, 'truly I don't know what to do. It will do you no good to speak to the missus. And if you try to say him nay, it will only make him more determined to have what he wants.

Let me see can I think of something.'

*   *   *

The next day when Nell went into the taproom, Jack raked her with a look of triumph that made her sick to her stomach. She was powerless to stop him, and he knew it. That night he again forced his way into her room and brutalised her, enjoying her fear and pain.

Over the next weeks Nell avoided being on her own and tried not to cross Jack's path, but there were times when he appeared seemingly from thin air, and she had nowhere to run.

*   *   *

With the celebrations of the king's birthday on the twenty-ninth of May, Nell was amazed to realise that it had been two years since she had run away and embarked on her new life. She had gained freedom from her mother, as she had set out to do. She was better fed and clothed and she had several regulars whose money she could count on. But she did not like having to submit herself to the use of strangers, and Jack's visits were now almost nightly. She was always frightened, and despaired of finding a way out of the hell her days and nights had become.

As it happened, an escape presented itself that Nell could not have anticipated. Robbie Duncan noticed the bruises on her arms and throat and the livid blue-yellow patches on the insides of her thighs.

'What happened there?' he asked, his face darkening. 'Come, tell me,' he said gently when she didn't answer.

'It's Jack,' she whispered, clutching the sheet around her. 'Madam's man. He—he comes to me sometimes, and . . .' She could not finish the sentence, and could not bring herself to look at him. He squatted on his haunches before her.

'He hurts you? He means to hurt you?'

She nodded.

'He cannot do this to you. I will not allow it,' Robbie exclaimed, springing to his feet, but Nell knew that his slender frame was no match for Jack's sinewy muscularity.

She shrugged. 'But he can. There is nought I can do to stop him.'

Robbie paced and seethed, and finally stood before Nell.

'Come and live with me. He cannot come to you there. I will take care of you.'

Nell was astonished at the proposal, but Robbie was likeable enough and, given the choice, she would rather bed one man than many.

So, with a payment from Robbie to Madam Ross for the loss of one of her stable, Nell became his. She packed her few belongings in a sack and moved to Robbie's room at the Cock and Pie Tavern, at the top of Maypole Alley, only a few streets from the only homes she had known.

Chapter Six

Living with Robbie, Nell felt as if she were playing at being a wife. While he was at work at his father's business in the City during the day, she tidied their room and fetched food from a cookhouse so that she had supper ready for him when he came home, and Robbie told her of his day and any news.

'The king is to have bearbaiting at Hampton Court for Whitsuntide, as he did last year. Savagery. That's one old custom that would have been better left in the past. The playhouses are bad enough. Oh, and Lady Castlemaine is brought to bed of a boy. He's to be called Charles Palmer and Lord Limerick, as though he were the son of her husband, but no one believes that.'

'Barbara Palmer's husband had her son christened in the Popish church,' Robbie told Nell a week later over dinner. 'But today the king took the child and had him rechristened in the Church of England. He'll not have his son raised a Papist, bastard or no.'

'And how did Palmer take that?' Nell wondered.

'Not well,' said Robbie, chewing on a beef bone. 'He's broken from his wife at last and gone to France.'

That night, to Nell's surprise, Robbie went to sleep without touching her. She scarcely knew what to think and lay worrying. Was he tiring of her? Would he cast her out? But in the morning he seemed as usual, and she grew used to the novel idea that a man might not always want to couple.

Being free from Jack's attentions and serving

83

the needs of many men was a welcome change. Nell's body healed, and Robbie was gentle with her in bed. But before long, she found that the sameness of her days grew tedious. She missed the companionship of Rose and the other girls, but because she wanted to keep out of Jack's way and because Robbie did not like her going there, she stayed away from Lewkenor's Lane.

Rose joined her sometimes for little outings, to watch the river traffic from the bridge, or to walk as far abroad as the countryside of Moorfields or Islington. There was usually something of interest to be seen at Covent Garden—rope dancers, jugglers, or occasionally a display of prize fighting.

One brilliant summer day Nell and Rose set out on a pilgrimage to St. James's Park, near the palace.

'I hope we'll see the king,' Nell said.

'Perhaps we will,' Rose said. 'Harry says the king has laid out a mint of money making the park fine again and walks out most days.' Harry Killigrew had recently become groom of the bedchamber to the Duke of York.

The park, with its blooming flowers and trees, seemed a paradise to Nell, and a world away from the dark land of nightmare where she had last been with Nick and the other boys on the night of the king's return.

'Look!' cried Rose, clutching Nell's arm.

Not fifty paces from where they stood, King Charles strode along in earnest conversation with some puffing minister who struggled to match his pace, the royal retinue straggling along behind. Nell watched, entranced.

'He's even more handsome than I remembered

him.'

'He is that,' Rose agreed. A bevy of ladies strolled in the king's wake, decked in summer finery. The breeze caught their gowns and made Nell think of ships in full sail.

'Look, it's Lady Castlemaine!' cried Nell. 'I wonder where's her baby?'

'Why, ladies like that don't care for their own kinchins, but leave them to nurses. That's why she can look so fine so soon after birthing.'

'Look at that blue gown,' Nell sighed. 'Why, now it appears gold!'

'Changeable silk,' Rose said. 'You'd have to lay out a month's earnings to pay for that. But look at the patches now—those are cunning and would be easy enough to fashion.' Many of the ladies' faces were adorned with small black patches in the shapes of stars, moons, suns, and animals.

'That's the high kick, that is,' Rose said.

'I think it looks silly,' said Nell. 'Besides, they're like to itch most fearsome. I'd scratch them off in a minute.' She looked with longing at the pretty gloves, though, in a rainbow of shades of soft leather, and at the ladies' full-brimmed hats with ribbons rippling from them.

The weather was so fine and Nell's spirits so high, she didn't want the rare day of pleasure to end.

'Let's not go back yet,' she pleaded. 'I've heard tell there's an Italian puppet show at Covent Garden that would make a dog laugh. And I've a month's mind for some cherries.'

So it was evening before she climbed the stairs to Robbie's room, with the guilty recollection that the tuppence he had given her to buy candles had been spent during the day's outing.

'You spent it!' Robbie cried. 'And what are we to use for light?'

'It's not so dark,' Nell pleaded. 'I'll get candles tomorrow.'

'I'll get the candles myself,' he fumed, yanking the door open. 'Since I cannot trust you to do as you're told.'

Nell lay awake that night, chafing with resentment. It was only tuppence, after all, and the first money she had spent on herself since moving in with Robbie.

In the morning she strode into the taproom of the Cock and Pie downstairs. Cath, the barmaid, looked up from the jug she was washing and took in Nell's stormy face.

'You've a bee in your bonnet, I see.'

'Are you hiring?' Nell demanded. Cath laughed.

'Unhappy with Robbie, are you?'

'I've no money to spend but what he gives me and I cannot do anything but what he tells me,' Nell fretted. 'I spend my days alone and I'm so bored I don't know what to do with myself.'

'Best think twice afore you leave,' Cath cautioned. 'Bored and fed is better than free and hungry.'

Nell slumped onto the stool opposite Cath.

'You're right. I've nowhere to go. But please, to keep me from jumping in the river, have you no shred of gossip or excitement to share?'

'Well, that I do, now you mention it,' Cath smiled. 'Mr. Killigrew is to build his playhouse just across the road.'

*   *   *

86

As soon as the ground was thawed, the foundations of the theatre were laid in the old Rider's Yard. Now walls covered the framing, and acres of heavy oak planking and dark and gleaming hardwood disappeared into the maw of the growing theater. Each day Nell watched carpenters, masons, woodcarvers, and plasterworkers come and go, their tools slung in bags on their backs.

One summer day when the labourers had stopped work for their midday meal and were gathered outside to eat, sitting atop piles of lumber or leaning against the theatre's wall, she slipped in at the back door. Skeletal frames of timber stood in the hush of the midday sunlight that filtered through chinks in the unfinished ceiling. A mist of sawdust blanketed the rough-hewn floors.

Nell made her way through a doorway in a wall that was not yet built, and realised that she must be standing upon the stage. She crept silently forward, hardly daring to breathe. The centre of the space was a soaring emptiness. Like a cathedral, she thought. Galleries for spectators lined the walls. She wondered what it would be like to stand on that stage before an audience, and thought of how Lady Castlemaine had surveyed the crowds before Whitehall on the night of the king's return. She snapped open an imaginary fan and swished it languidly before her, her head held high, her chin tilted coquettishly.

'Lud, Your Majesty,' she trilled, batting her eyelashes, and gave the invisible king a pouting smile.

A harsh bark of laughter and the sound of clapping startled Nell so much that she almost cried

87

out. A figure stumped toward her from the shadows at the back of the theatre. It was a grizzled old man in a loose shirt and pantaloons, with a long pigtail, and Nell was amazed to see that he was missing the lower part of his left leg and walked on a wooden peg.

'I meant no harm,' Nell began. 'I'll go.'

'Don't go on my account,' the old man said with a grin. 'I was enjoying it. And any road, I'm just a harmless old carpenter.'

'You look like a sailor,' Nell said, staring at his weather-beaten face.

'And so I have been, since before I'd a beard to my face. But I'm too old for that now, and happy to have a berth ashore. A playhouse is much like a ship, you know—canvas, ropes, rigging—and needs a crew just as a ship does.'

'I wish I could work at the playhouse.'

The old sailor squinted at Nell and tapped a finger alongside his nose.

'And mayhap you can. I hear the king has ordered that from now it's only women are to act the parts of women.'

'No boys?' Nell asked.

'No boys. Not in petticoats, leastways. The Duke's Company sent little Moll Davis onto the stage but a month or two ago. A pretty little thing she is, and much cried up, too. About your years, I'd think.'

Nell had been so cut off from her theatre friends that she had not heard that bit of news. She felt a surge of jealousy towards pretty little Moll Davis.

'How came she to be in the Duke's Company?'

'I don't know,' the old man shrugged. 'But if there's call for one actress, there'll be call for more,

88

as sure as eggs is eggs.'

'What's your name?' Nell asked.

'Richard Tarbutton is the one my old mam gave me. But my mates call me Dicky One-Shank.'

'I'm Nell. Nell Gwynn.'

'Nell Gwynn,' said Dicky One-Shank, his blue eyes disappearing in the weathered folds of his face as he smiled. 'I'll remember that.'

*   *   *

'He said there are to be no more boys playing women's parts, but only girls,' Nell excitedly told Robbie that night over supper. 'Actresses.' She said the word reverently.

'Actresses!' Robbie spat, throwing down a chicken bone. 'Whores, more like. The only reason for putting women on the stage, mabbed up like slatterns, is so that men can look on them with lust.' He snorted again, tore a hunk of bread from the loaf, and furiously sopped it in the gravy on his plate.

Nell thought, but did not say, that he had had no objection to looking on her with lust when she was at Madam Ross's place. He seemed to have little sense of humour these days, and more and more she did not speak what was in her mind for fear of rousing his irritation.

*   *   *

The days shortened into winter darkness, and the Thames froze again. Nell and Rose walked onto the deep and shadowy ice, encrusted with sludgy snow, but Nell lacked the joy she had felt the previous

89

winter. And Rose was downcast.

'Is summat amiss?' Nell asked, and was surprised to see tears in Rose's eyes.

'Harry's got married. Lady Mary Savage.'

'Oh.' Nell hardly knew what to say. Of course Rose knew as well as she did that gentlemen like Harry would never marry girls like them, however much they enjoyed their sport and company. But knowing didn't stop the hurting.

'Hard luck, that is,' she ventured. Rose nodded, turning her head aside and wiping away tears.

'I was a fool to let myself care for him as I did,' Rose said.

'No,' said Nell. 'You can't help how you feel, Rose, any more than you can stop the rain from falling. He don't deserve you anyway. You'll soon find someone that treats you far better, I warrant.'

Rose tried to smile, and hugged Nell to her.

'Oh, sweet girl, what would I do without you?'

*　　　　*　　　　*

One morning in February, Nell and Robbie were awoken early by a pounding at their door. Jane, breathless and red faced, rushed in past Robbie.

'Oh, Nell! Rose has been taken up for theft!' She choked out her story between sobs. 'The shoulder clappers came at dawn. They had a gentry cove with them claimed she'd pinched his larum.'

'Oh, no,' Nell gasped. The punishment for the theft of something as valuable as a pocket watch was the gallows.

Nell was so terrified she could not think, but Robbie was cooler.

'Where stands the matter now? What's been

90

done?'

'Madam's gone to Whitehall to see can Harry help.'

'And Rose?'

'Clapped up in Newgate.'

Newgate. The name alone evoked darkness and despair. Nell knew that debtors rotted there in misery for years, as her father had languished in prison in Oxford. And all London knew of the regular pageant of death, when condemned prisoners were led from the prison to be driven in carts through jeering crowds and pelted with offal on their way to Tyburn Tree, the enormous three-sided gallows that could accommodate twenty-four nooses, and the resultant twenty-four swinging corpses.

'I must go to her!' Nell cried.

'No,' Robbie said harshly. 'You can do her no good.'

But Nell would not be deterred.

''Tis no place for a girl,' Robbie said, grim faced, shoving his hat onto his head.

'No, and no more is it a place for Rose than it is for me,' Nell retorted, stamping with impatience to be gone. Robbie had no answer to that, and they set off, Nell racing along in front of him.

The winter morning sky was leaden grey, the wind blew bitter cold, and a light shower of snow fell icy wet.

When they arrived at the gates of the prison, Nell's stomach tightened with fear. The ponderous stone walls towered before her, broken only by narrow slits. The enormous ironclad portals led into a cobbled courtyard, crowded with the morning's desperate traffic—prisoners in irons

91

shuffling through the doors that led into the depths of the prison; guards and soldiers, grim and armed; the usual London rabble of beggars and urchins; legions of wives, lovers, mothers, sisters, and friends. A foul stench permeated the air, a noxious mixture of human and animal waste, vomit, blood, rotting food, and the unmistakable odour of death. A grizzled guard stopped them.

'If she was shopped this morning, trial might be tomorrow,' the guard shrugged when Robbie explained their errand. 'Or mayhap the day after. No way of knowing.'

Robbie turned away, but Nell stayed where she was.

'Can I not see her?' she asked.

'That thou cannot.' The guard ran a tongue over his chapped lips and wiped his nose with the back of a dirty hand. Nell stared at him with hatred, taking in the broken and rotten teeth, the rough stubble on the heavy cheeks, the purple nose running in the cold air. She darted past him through the door. She was young and fast, but his stride and his reach were much longer than hers. He grabbed her by the hair and flung her down. She scrambled to her feet and, in a rage of humiliation and helplessness, ran at the man before Robbie could stop her. Disbelief and growing annoyance on his face, the guard caught her and held her from him at arm's length. He shook her hard, then lifted her so that her face was close to his. She smelled beer and onions and felt the moist warmth of his breath.

'Get yer arse out of here. And don't come back, unless you want summat worse.' He dropped her, and she cried out as she landed on the cobblestones. All the fight gone out of her, Nell

92

wanted only to flee before she shamed herself by crying. Robbie, grey faced and silent, helped her to her feet.

'Can you walk?' he asked.

Nell knew he was angry and nodded without meeting his eyes, hot tears falling onto her cheeks.

'We'll go to Madam Ross's,' Robbie said shortly. 'You can wait until there's news.'

At Lewkenor's Lane, Nell was relieved beyond measure that Ned was presiding over the bar and Jack was gone. The girls were gathered in the taproom like a flock of unsettled chickens, some crying, some railing against the cully who had turned Rose in, some taking a morbid enjoyment in the dramatic prospect of the execution of one of their own. They squawked and fluttered at the sight of Nell and Robbie.

'Nell!' Jane cried. 'Whatever's happened to you?'

'Nothing,' said Nell. 'We tried to see Rose, is all, and the bandog flung me out on my breech.'

'The brute!' cried Jane.

'Aye, for shame!' chimed black-haired Nan. 'What call had he to treat you so?'

'I tried to get past him. Came near to doing it, too,' Nell said, brightening.

'What a plucky thing you are,' said Jane. 'Come, let me bind your wounds, little warrior.' The other girls clucked with sympathy while Jane fetched a basin of water and a cloth and gently wiped the grit from the scrapes on Nell's hands and knees, crying out all over again at the red and purple blotches that already bloomed on her soft skin.

It was after noon when Madam Ross returned.

'Harry's gone to ask for the king's help,' she told the girls. 'He'll come here as soon as there's word.'

So there was nothing to do but wait. Robbie went on to the City. Exhausted by the strain of waiting, Nell went upstairs to Rose's room and climbed into bed. She could smell Rose's scent on the bedclothes and pulled them tightly around herself. Wrapped that way, she could close her eyes and believe that Rose lay next to her. Surely Rose was safe and would be back. But fear clutched at her, and she sobbed, finally falling asleep on the tear-dampened pillow.

* * *

The bleak afternoon had turned to wintry darkness when Nell awoke. She raised her head to see Rose coming through the door into the little bedchamber with Harry Killigrew. He was uncharacteristically subdued and stood by awkwardly as Rose flung herself into Nell's embrace and began to sob.

'Oh, Nelly,' Rose finally whispered, 'I was so frightened. I was afeared they was going to turn me off.'

'I tried to get you out,' Nell cried. 'But I couldn't. I'm so sorry.'

'Sorry?' Rose was half laughing and half crying. 'Oh, little one. You have the heart of a lion and nought to be sorry for. It took a pardon from the king himself to get me free.'

She nodded towards Harry and, reminded of how much she owed to his help, launched herself into his arms.

'I'll leave you to your sister,' he said. 'I'll come tomorrow to see how you're faring.'

When he had gone, Nell tucked Rose into bed and dashed out to the nearest cookhouse for a couple of hot pies. She and Rose sat together in the warm bed, the golden light of the candle in its wall bracket reflected in the black of the icy windowpane. Rose begged Nell to stay the night with her, and they nestled side by side in the darkness.

'When I went there today, it made me think of Da,' Nell whispered.

'Aye. I thought of him, too,' Rose answered. 'I cannot bear the thought that he died alone in such a place.'

She drew a shuddering breath.

'When they took me in, I could hear such awful moans and sobbing and screaming. Like souls in hell. And Nell . . .' She paused.

'They took me down this horrible passage, all dank and grey. And past this little room. And in it I could see arms and legs that had been chopped off, and heads and other parts. Like a butcher shop for men.'

Nell had no words for the horror of the image the words forced into her mind. She thought again of the traitors' deaths suffered by the men who had killed the first King Charles, and the black and featureless things she had seen on pikes on London Bridge and at the City gates, which she knew were the tarred heads and quarters of executed men. Like souls in hell, Rose had said. But Nell could not imagine a hell that could be any worse than a world in which such things were possible. She slept uneasily that night and dreamed again of the door slamming shut, of being left alone and terrified in a cold and hostile landscape.

It was not until morning that Nell asked Rose the question that had been gnawing at the back of her mind.

'Did you, Rose? Did you pinch the watch?'

'No,' Rose said. 'But I think Jack did.'

Chapter Seven

Rose came smiling into Nell's lodging one morning a few weeks after her deliverance from Newgate.

'Harry's got a way for me to get out of Madam Ross's!' she said. 'When the playhouse opens, there will be need of two wenches to sell oranges and sweetmeats. Harry says he can get me one of the situations, and you can have the other, if you want it.'

'When do we start?'

'Not 'til May,' Rose laughed. 'And Orange Moll has to give us the nod.'

'Who's she?'

'Mary Meggs is her proper name. She holds the licence to sell fruits and nuts and such. But Harry says he'll make it all come right.'

*   *   *

Nell stole a quick look at Robbie that night as he ate. 'Robbie,' she said, 'Rose has got me and her work at the playhouse. Selling oranges and so on.'

'You have no need of work.'

'But I could earn my keep. And perhaps I'd meet gentlemen who would want to do business with you.'

Robbie snorted. 'Who would want to do business with you, more like.'

96

Nell held her tongue. First she had to meet Orange Moll. If all went well and the job was hers—well, she'd cross that bridge when she came to it.

*   *   *

A few days later, she and Rose presented themselves at Will's, the fashionable coffeehouse in Russell Street at Covent Garden, to be inspected by the formidable Orange Moll. Harry was there with her, lounging against the bar. Nell surmised he must have made some impudent remark, for he roared with laughter, while Moll struggled to assume a look of dignified disapproval rather than the chuckle of flattered amusement that threatened to erupt.

Harry hailed the girls, and Moll turned to look at them. She was very round, billowing over the stool on which she sat, her capacious bosom overflowing the low neckline of her dress. Nell noted the shrewd evaluation in the quick glance. She felt like a heifer at Smithfield Market, but could tell that Moll was pleased with what she saw.

'Aye,' Moll said. 'They're comely-looked wenches, both of them. I'll warrant you've been peddling more than oysters, have you not?'

Before Nell could think how to respond, Rose, at an almost imperceptible nod from Harry, looked Orange Moll straight in the eye, and said, 'Yes, ma'am. I'm at Madam Ross's. And Nell was lately, too.'

'Well, that's all to the good,' said Moll. 'A pretty mab who know how to catch a gentleman's eye, and how to jest and flirt, will sell far more than a prim stick who thinks herself above it. Very well, we'll give you a try. The plays begin at three. You'll work from noon until the show is over and the folk have gone. Oranges are sixpence, and a ha'penny of that's yours to keep.' She gave the girls a knowing smile.

'And there's more of the ready to be made, for a girl who has her eyes open and her wits about her. Now. Have you ever et an orange? No? Well, here's your first, then.'

She gave Nell and Rose each an orange and showed them how to peel off the dappled skin to get at the pulp beneath. Nell inhaled the pungent scent and bit into a segment. The sweet tang of the juice was wonderful, different from anything she had tasted.

'Sweet Seville oranges,' said Moll. 'All the way from Spain, where it's warmer.'

The golden oranges, like little suns, conjured in Nell's mind images of a sultry land of constant languorous summer.

*　　　*　　　*

Robbie looked grim when Nell mentioned the playhouse again that night as they lay in bed. She had been bursting all day with the anxiety of talking to him and the fear of what he would say.

'Let me try it,' she begged. 'You'll see, no ill will come.'

'You may try it for a week,' he said finally. 'But I don't like it a whit. And if you come to any mischance in that time, you'll stop, and no argument.' He turned his back to her and pulled the covers over his head, and Nell reckoned she had best leave it at that.

98

*　　　*　　　*

The night before she was to begin at the playhouse, Nell's head was too full of thoughts of the next day for sleep to come. Robbie snored softly next to her in the dark. She slipped out of bed and padded to the window. The moon hung low and bright in the warm night sky. She regarded the stars in wonder. So many of them. She recognised some patterns that she knew—the Great Bear, the Small Bear, the Hen and Chickens—and wondered how many people had looked up at that same moon and stars since time began.

A watchman passed below, crying out, 'Two o'clock of a fair, clear night, and all is well.' All was well. Whatever the next day might bring, it must be good. The stars stood guard over her fortunes. And maybe somewhere, too, her father watched.

*　　　*　　　*

In the morning Nell dressed in the best clothes she had, a skirt and body in russet. She had washed her shift and it peeped out clean and white at her elbows and neckline. She took out her precious ribbon knot of blue and gold from the small box under the bed where she kept her few treasures—the shard of mirror; her little doll; a silk handkerchief left behind in her room at Madam Ross's by some man; a pink rose she had plucked and hung upside down by a thread to dry, its papery petals giving off a sweet scent, like memories of another day.

Rose arrived, flushed and smiling, her brown curls and blue eyes set off by a saffron-coloured

99

gown. As soon as she knew she had work at the playhouse, she had left Madam Ross's and moved into a room above the nearby Cat and Fiddle Tavern, and she looked happier than Nell remembered seeing her.

It wasn't far to the playhouse, but as Rose and Nell stepped into Bridges Street, the familiar thoroughfare seemed altogether different. A parade of fine carriages choked the way, and Nell realised with a start that their destination must be the theatre. She had not thought about so many people going to hear the play. But it stood to reason that everyone would want to be present for the first performance at the fine new Theatre Royal. And she would be a part of it! She felt a thrill, and then a stab of doubt. What made her so sure of herself? Maybe Moll would decide that she had made a mistake, that she wanted someone older, taller, fairer. Someone better. After all, who was she but a ragamuffin from the squalid streets?

'Have done with staring, chicken,' Rose chided her merrily. 'We've work to do.' The words brought Nell back to earth. She had worked more days than she could remember, and surely she could do this job, too.

* * *

'You'll find her right through there,' said the man at the stage door. As Nell and Rose followed where he pointed, Nell thought back to the day when she had crept into the unfinished playhouse and met Dicky One-Shank. Now she stood in a big room that must be just behind the stage. Charles Hart and a few other actors were lounging at a table, some of

100

them eating. A fair-haired girl sitting across from Hart was speaking to him in a low voice so that Nell could not catch her words. On the other side of the room were racks holding swords, and a table neatly laid out with cushions, books, wine bottles, cups, and other items Nell guessed must be for the play. Nearby a man was mending the torn seat of a chair. Nell thought she would burst from the excitement.

* * *

The girls found Orange Moll in a small cubbyhole built under a staircase, its shelves stacked with baskets of oranges, lemons, nuts, and brightly coloured sweetmeats. Moll gave them each a great round basket and showed them how to fill it with an array of goods.

'Look out sharp for pickpockets,' Moll warned. 'Now, then. There's three hours yet before the play begins. Until then, and in the intervals, you can cry your wares from the stage. During the show, you sell in the pit, and don't get so taken up by watching the actors that you forget that you're here to work. When the play has done, come back here so I can count your takings and give you your pay. And if you've any thought of trying to fleece me, put it out of your mind. I can smell a prigger at fifty paces.'

Rose flushed, and Nell wondered if Harry Killigrew had told Moll about Rose's confinement in Newgate.

'You can have an orange each today, gratis, and if you want them in future it'll cost you a ha'penny. Now, time to get to work.'

Nell followed Moll and Rose through a door and found herself in the public part of the playhouse.

101

She stopped and stared. She had never seen a place of such grandeur. Above a curtain of wine red at the back of the forestage, the royal coat of arms stood out proudly, supported by cherubs and surrounded by nude goddesses and billowing bunting, all worked in plaster. A glazed cupola high overhead let in the daylight, but the theatre blazed with dozens of candles, on huge wheel-like chandeliers, bathing the place in a warm and magical glow. Boxes flanked the stage, and two levels of horseshoe-shaped galleries ran all the way around the pit. Though it was a while until the play began, the theatre was quite full and echoed with voices and laughter.

Nell had thought the Red Bull exciting, and the Vere Street theater grand, but they were nothing compared to this. Ladies, some with their faces covered by black silk masks, preened and fanned themselves. Gentlemen took pinches of snuff from little jewelled boxes, posed languidly with tall gold-headed walking sticks, ran ringed fingers through the long curled locks of their wigs as they chatted and watched the crowd.

Music began—a sprightly dance tune. Nell turned and saw that a consort of about a dozen musicians was seated before and under the stage. The rich river of strings and woodwinds was something altogether different from anything she had ever heard, and thrilling. It must be to music like this that the king danced.

She was startled from her reverie by the realisation that two handsomely dressed young sparks were waving to get her attention. She went to them quickly and bobbed a curtsy.

'How much for your oranges, sweeting?' asked

the darker of the two, in a silk suit the color of honey.

'Sixpence, sir.'

'A sice for an orange?' asked the other, his fair ringlets cascading over his plum-colored coat.

'Aye, sir, but you may believe me that it'll be the second-best sixpence you're like to spend in your life.' She gave him an impish smile, and he laughed.

'Indeed! And what would the best-spent sixpence get me?' His eyebrows rose in challenge.

'Halfway to heaven, sir. But only a little more might get you through the pearly gates.'

The two men roared, and bought four oranges. Nell realised that if she wished, she could probably make a profitable assignation. But it was so much more pleasant to keep to an exchange of wit.

'Let's send her to George,' said the fair-wigged man.

''Sdeath! A most excellent notion,' agreed his friend. 'Do you see yon gentleman in blue? Here's another sixpence for you, if you go and say to him what you have said to us. Only you must tell him that his money will be wisely spent, because an orange will give him pleasure but not leave him pissing pins and needles.'

'He lately lay with a slattern who proved to be poxed,' explained the other, 'and he has laid out far more money on the cure than he spent to take a stroke in the first place.'

Nell carried out the jest as ordered and was sixpence the richer. She soon found that her customers were apt to make the same remarks, and began to develop stock lines that were sure to provoke a laugh and earn extra coin for her.

'I'll call thee Orange Blossom,' an old man

103

quavered, to which she replied, 'You may call me anything you will, sir, and you buy my oranges.'

When she noticed a gentleman surveying her bosom as well as her oranges, she said pertly, 'Sixpence for anything in the basket, sir, but the goods in the apple dumpling shop are not for sale.'

By the time an hour or two had passed, Nell felt that she was a dab at this business. Selling oranges was not much different from selling oysters, after all, and it was far easier to hold her basket of fruit, heavy as it was, than to trundle the oyster barrow through the streets. She sang out an occasional cry of 'Oranges to sell, who will have any oranges?'

Her old habit of raillery with her customers was good for business, as it had been when she sold oysters, and it was much more enjoyable now that she was bantering with richly dressed and handsome gentlemen. This felt much different from her interactions with men at Madam Ross's. There, she had had no choice. The bargain had been made and the end was known. But these men had no control over her, and the future held infinite possibilities.

*   *   *

By three o'clock, the pit, boxes, and galleries were filled to capacity. The expectant crowd fanned itself in the muggy warmth of the May afternoon and the combined body heat of five hundred people. The basket of fruit that had not seemed so heavy to begin with now felt burdensome, its supporting strap cutting into Nell's shoulders, and she longed for a chance to set it down.

There was a stir, and all eyes turned to one of the

lower boxes at the side of the stage. Nell realised with a surge of excitement that King Charles was entering, and that the small dark lady beside him must be Queen Catherine. They stood waving their reply to the cheers of welcome.

The audience turned its attention to the stage as a finely dressed grey-haired man entered through one of the two doors at its side. He strode to the front of the forestage and waited, a hint of a smile on his lips, as the hubbub subsided. Nell faded into a corner at the back of the pit, setting her basket down behind her, out of the way of thieves.

The man bowed deeply to the king and queen, then to the audience. He stood for a moment, his piercing dark eyes sweeping the packed playhouse.

'Your Majesties, my lords, ladies, and gentlemen. I am Thomas Killigrew, and it is with great pleasure, and very deep gratitude to His Majesty, that I welcome you to the Theatre Royal.'

The playhouse erupted into cries of 'God save the king.'

'This day has been many years a-coming,' Killigrew continued. 'Some of us thought it would never come. No doubt some of us thought so more than others.' He cast a puckish glance toward the royal box. The king laughed along with the rest of the crowd.

'I say again, welcome. We hope for the frequent pleasure of your company. And now, I give you *The Humorous Lieutenant*.'

Killigrew withdrew to resounding applause, and a girl pranced through one of the doors at the side of the stage and forward onto the apron. She was dark haired, her buxom prettiness enhanced perfectly by her golden gown. Illuminated by the candlelight against the deep red of the curtain behind her, she seemed to glow. Her eyes sparkled and her cheeks dimpled with amusement, and then she spoke, addressing the crowd directly.

Nell could not recall later what exactly it was that the girl had said. She knew only that it was charming and funny and that the wench held the audience in the palm of her hand, and that when she had done with her prologue she skipped off the stage to cheers and stamping and whistles. Nell felt she could hardly breathe, choked by a wrenching sense of longing to be able to accomplish such a thing of magic herself.

The great curtain rose as if by sorcery, revealing the grand hall of a palace. Theo Bird and Marmaduke Watson bustled onto the stage and began their scene. As the play went on, the decorous quiet that had reigned briefly was broken by a steady hum of chatter and laughter, by occasional outbursts of shouting from the top galleries, and by the calls of folk who wanted oranges.

Nell kept an eye on the play and followed the story as best she could. Charles Hart played a prince whose match with the girl he loved was hindered by his father's attempts to seduce her for himself. Nell was both entranced and consumed with envy as she watched the golden-haired actress playing Hart's love.

Wat Clun played a tough and taciturn soldier—the humorous lieutenant of the title—who somehow ended up drinking a love potion intended for the girl, and the audience roared with laughter at his giddy infatuation with the wicked king. Nell was pleased to see several other actors she knew.

The king appeared to be enjoying the play immensely, laughing with abandon and clapping his appreciation when actors left the stage after a particularly hilarious scene. But Nell was keenly aware that making a success as an orange seller was what would allow her to keep coming back to this place of enchantment, and zealously made the rounds of the pit.

The first interval came, and the musicians struck up. Nell gazed at the empty stage and longed to know what it felt like to stand there. Did she dare to try it? Moll had given her permission, so Nell clutched her basket to her and climbed the steps to the stage and surveyed the scene before her. She felt as if she were at the centre of the universe. The galleries rose to the ceiling, enwreathing the space, and the sloped floor of the pit made it seem as if its benches were marching towards her. The theatre was a swirling sea of movement. The king in his box was not ten paces away. She took a breath and sang out 'Oranges! Fine oranges! Who will buy my oranges, fine Seville oranges?'

The king smiled and beckoned. Nell went to him, her heart in her throat.

'Will you have an orange, Your Majesty? They're very sweet.'

'How could they be otherwise, with such a peddler? I'll take two.' She held out two oranges, but the king took only one.

'One for you and one for me,' he said with a wink.

Nell's scene with the king had been observed, and as she turned from him and sang her cry again, gentlemen pressed to the foot of the stage. By the end of the interval she had sold almost all that was in her basket.

*   *   *

When the play was done, the audience straggled out, pleasantly exhausted by the long, hot afternoon, and ready for real food and drink. Before Nell went to reckon up with Moll, she stood and looked around the emptying playhouse, breathing in the scent of perfume and the smell of hot wax and oranges and flowers and sweat. She imagined the gaze of hundreds of spectators watching her. Caught up in the fantasy, she dipped in a curtsy and was brought up short as she noticed two gentlemen watching her with amusement. She threw them a smile and scampered off to find Orange Moll, blushing and laughing with delight.

*   *   *

'You've done right well,' Orange Moll nodded as she counted Nell's takings. 'Here's four pigs for you.' She smiled as she put four sixpenny coins into Nell's hand. 'Only three for you!' she said to Rose. 'You'll have to show up your little sister tomorrow, eh?'

Nell was elated and ravenous. She and Rose went to an eating house and treated themselves to a dinner of fricasseed rabbit followed by apple tart and washed down with good ale.

The sky glowed pink and orange with the sunset as Nell headed toward the Cock and Pie. Her supreme happiness at the day dimmed when she thought of Robbie, waiting at home.

He looked up from the table as she entered their

room. He was eating cheese and the remainder of the wheat loaf from the previous evening's meal. Nell thought with a pang that she should have brought him something to eat.

'I thought you'd have been home before now,' he said. 'With my supper.'

'I'm sorry. I forgot, I was so excited.' She ran to him and kissed him. 'Oh, Robbie, you should have seen it. The king and queen were there! And ever so many grand ladies and gentlemen. There were painted scenes on the stage—it began with a great palace that moved and gave way to a street, as real as anything. And look—I've two whole shillings!'

Robbie seemed not angry but sad.

'I know I'll lose you to it, Nelly. When you came to me you were but a frightened little thing. But you'll have no need of me now, and if you're rubbing shoulders with the gallants of the town, you'll find me dull company.'

Nell threw her arms around Robbie, desperate to reassure him.

'I won't! Why do you not come tomorrow? Then you'll see how fine it all is.'

But Robbie said only, 'We'll see.' And that night it was he who lay awake long after Nell had fallen asleep. He did not come to the playhouse the next day, or the day after, and push came to shove at the end of the week.

'I still don't like it,' he said. 'And I want you to stop.'

'No!' Nell cried.

'Then you've a choice to make. You can stay with me and I'll gladly care for you. Or you can work at the playhouse. But you cannot do both.'

Nell was agonised at the thought of hurting

109

Robbie. He had taken her in and prevented her from further harm at Jack's hands. But her heart sank at the thought of endless days with no prospect of change or excitement. The playhouse, though—anything might happen there, and she could not bear to turn her back on its possibilities. So the next day she gathered her things and moved into Rose's room at the Cat and Fiddle.

Chapter Eight

June, 1663

'Well, if it ain't little Nell!'

Harry Killigrew's voice cut through the babble of the playhouse crowd. He lolled on a bench in the pit, flanked by a couple of richly dressed gentlemen Nell hadn't seen before.

'Not so little,' commented one of the men, eyeing Nell.

'Will you not introduce me to your friends, Harry?' Nell asked, meeting the stranger's gaze.

'Charles Sackville, Lord Buckhurst, first Earl of Middlesex and sixth Earl of Dorset, is the one drooling at the sight of your bubbies.'

A lord, and captivated by her. Nell was thrilled.

'And this'—Henry waved a hand at the other man—'is Sir Charles Sedley. Who, now I look, also appears to be salivating more than is common.'

Dorset laughed and stretched himself lazily. He was handsome and golden haired, and he reminded Nell of the young lion she had seen once when the menagerie at the Tower was open to the public.

Powerful and utterly assured.

'Damme, but the wench has the finest oranges I've ever seen,' he drawled. 'They positively set me to hungering.'

He picked up an orange and rolled it in his hand, squeezing it, then brought it to his nose and inhaled its scent, his eyes never leaving Nell's. He tossed the orange to Harry, trapped Nell's hand between his, and pressed sixpence into her palm. The touch of his skin made her heart race. To her annoyance, she felt herself blushing, and she slipped away, Harry's laughter in her ears.

That night, Nell remembered the pressure of Dorset's hand on hers and how his gaze had made her catch her breath and look away. He stirred something within her, and it was clear that she had excited his interest as well, but her experience at Madam Ross's had taught her that if she succumbed easily, even for a handsome price, he would lose interest and she would forfeit what power she had with him. She determined to keep her head when next she saw him and see what might befall.

The next day Nell watched Dorset as he stood with one booted foot on a bench, surrounded by Harry, Sedley, and a couple of other young bloods. The cut of his elegant clothes emphasized his well-muscled figure. The other men leaned in to listen to him, crowing with laughter and clapping him on the back. The leader of the pack, that's what he was, she thought. And yes, one who would relish a chase.

'So you're the dimber-damber, then?' she dimpled at him.

'I'm the what?' he asked, looking her over

languidly.

'Dimber-damber. Top man. King of the thieves. Chief rogue of the crew.'

Dorset laughed. 'Why, I suppose I am. And if I'm king,' he said, tracing a finger down Nell's throat, 'who's to be my queen?'

'Only time will tell, my lord,' she said, batting his hand away. 'Now, do you mean to buy any oranges of me today or am I to stand here all the afternoon listening to your fiddle-faddle?'

Nell was annoyed with herself that she was allowing Dorset to fascinate her, but she could not stop herself from thinking about him.

'What do you think of him?' she asked Rose one evening as they walked home. Rose blew out her cheeks and shook her head.

'A hellcat, born and bred. I swear I don't understand these gents. Harry Killigrew says Dorset and Sedley have just done a translation of a French tragedy that brings tears to his eyes for the beauty and grace of the poetry, and yet the pair of them near caused a riot the other night.'

'Really?' Nell giggled. 'What happened?'

'They were with Tom Ogle at the Cock Inn, drunk as dogs, and stood on the balcony, singing lewd verses. A crowd began to gather, and at length they stripped off their clothes, and Dorset and Ogle began to strike lascivious postures. When the people below cried out to them to behave decently, Sedley pissed on their heads. The folk in the street were so enraged that they started throwing stones, Harry said, and near tore down the house.'

Nell laughed, picturing Dorset and Sedley's antics, and Rose looked at her sharply.

'You'd do better to keep clear of that one, Nell,

112

is my opinion. He'll bring you nothing but hurt.'

*   *   *

The Humorous Lieutenant was a roaring success, and played day after day. After the first performance, it was John Lacy instead of Walter Clun who played the lieutenant, and as funny as Wat had been, Lacy was even better. Nell never tired of watching him in the part, marvelling at his transformation as the love potion took effect and the rangy, slow-moving lieutenant, inflamed with giddy passion, capered about the stage, long arms and legs a-spraddle with the ungainly appearance of a chicken in flight, howling, 'Oh, King, that thou knew'st I loved thee, how I lov'd thee!'

Nell learned that the girl playing Celia, Hart's lover in the play, was Anne Marshall, who had played Desdemona at the Vere Street theatre, thus becoming the first woman to act on an English stage. Nell admired Anne's blue eyes and porcelain skin, and wondered how she had been lucky enough to become an actress. She also wondered if the onstage love between Demetrius and Celia carried over into real life. She thought again of Charles Hart and Anne Marshall sitting together on the afternoon of the first performance. They had seemed comfortable, companionable. Because they were lovers? Or because they were not?

Nell watched Hart day after day, always finding something new to admire in his performance as the prince. Her feelings for him, she realised, were far more profound and confusing than the carnal rush of blood that Dorset induced in her. She held her breath as she awaited Hart's entrance, felt her heart quicken as he appeared. She loved the quick grace of his lean body, the play of his shoulders under his soldier's coat of red, the fall of his dark hair tied into a club at the back of his neck.

In his first scene, he stood silently by while the actor playing the king rhapsodised about him. There was an intense stillness within him, his eyes deep wells of emotion, and she found it impossible to look at anyone else when he was on the stage.

She mouthed Celia's lines along with Anne Marshall: "Now he speaks! O, I could dwell upon that tongue forever." Her skin broke out in gooseflesh at his deep growl of a voice—and she wished it was she that he crushed in his embrace for a last kiss. She thought he was the essence of perfection in a man—impassioned, witty, assured, but tempered with soulfulness—and by the tenth consecutive day that *The Humorous Lieutenant* was played, she found that she could think of little else but him. She lingered in the greenroom after the performance, bantering with Wat Clun and young Theo Bird as she settled with Moll and put her wares away, but her entire body was alert and listening for the sound of Hart's voice. When there was no longer any pretext for her to remain, she dragged herself home, thinking of Celia's words—'It was a kind of death, sir, I suffered in your absence.'

As she lay in bed his voice echoed in her head, and his image seemed printed on the inside of her eyelids. She slept fitfully, seeing his dark eyes in her dreams, her skin burning with his imagined touch.

She had never felt this way before, and it was all at once exciting and frightening and painful. She longed to speak to him, though she did not know what she wanted to say. She wanted to be caressed by him, to be devoured by him like tinder in a raging fire. She had taken many men to her bed as a matter of business, and had spent many nights in Robbie's arms. But she had never ached with desire, had never been consumed by thoughts of a man as she was now.

And she found herself increasingly anxious as each day passed. She had never seen Hart's eye upon her, and he had not spoken to her. Perhaps he had not noticed her, did not remember her. How awful it would be, to speak to this god and receive a cold and unknowing stare in response. Yet it would be absurd to ask someone to introduce her to him when they daily worked within feet of each other. And that course would be fraught with even worse peril—what if he remembered her well, as a child whore, beneath his dignity to converse with now? In any case, her feelings were far too tender to expose. She felt ashamed and helpless and hopeless.

And then a miracle happened. One evening when Rose had felt unwell and gone home immediately after the play was done, Nell was putting her basket in the little storage cubby, when someone behind her asked, 'And how is Nelly today?'

She turned, her insides contracting at the sound of his voice. Charles Hart, only a few feet away, smiling down at her. She had just been thinking of him, as she was always thinking of him now, and the surprise of him so solidly and suddenly there deprived her of all composure. The intensity of his dark eyes so close was almost more than she could bear.

'I'm very well,' she stammered. 'I'm Nell.' She

blushed at the idiocy of the remark, and Hart laughed good-naturedly.

'I know. And I'm Charles.' Nell tried desperately to think of something to say and was relieved when he spoke again.

'Do you like it here at the playhouse, then?'

'Yes,' Nell gulped. 'It's—I didn't know it would be so—so grand.'

Hart nodded at her as he turned to leave.

'Mr. Hart!' Nell continued in a rush. 'I watch you every day. I think you're wonderful. I thank you for—I thank you.'

Hart smiled gently. 'I thank you, Nelly. See you tomorrow.'

And he was gone. Nell exhaled heavily and leaned against the wall, giddy and light-headed. He did know who she was. He knew her name. He had spoken to her. She giggled at the joy of it and raced home, whooping, to tell Rose.

*   *   *

Once the ice had been broken, Nell found it easier to speak to Charles Hart, though she still held him in awe. She chatted more easily with the other actors she had met before, and was pleased that they remembered her.

'Look at you—our little wench is all grown up!' Wat Clun cried when he first saw her backstage.

'Could I watch a rehearsal again?' she asked him.

'I don't know why not,' he said, 'but best to ask Lacy. He and Hart and Mohun have the daily running of the company, you know.'

'To be sure you may,' said Lacy, to Nell's joy. 'Come tomorrow. We'll be getting *The Committee*

116

back on its feet.'

Nell arrived at the theatre at ten the next morning. It was the first time she had been there so early, when there was no one there but the actors and other playhouse people. With the bright morning light spilling through the windows of the greenroom, it felt homey and peaceful, and a completely different place than in the bustle just before a performance.

Beck Marshall, the darker-haired sister of Anne, who had spoken the prologue to *The Humorous Lieutenant*, sat at a table with a roll of papers before her, brow furrowed and lips moving as she muttered lines to herself. She glanced up as Nell came in and, though Beck said nothing, Nell saw appraisal and annoyance in her eyes.

Lacy, Wat, and other actors were already on the stage, so Nell took a seat in the pit near Hart. From the confidence with which the actors walked through their movements and spoke their lines, it was apparent that they knew the play already. Only occasionally did one of them call 'Line!' and the prompter read out what they were to say.

Nell laughed in delight at Lacy's personification of the well-meaning but intensely obtuse Irish footman named Teague.

'It's one of John's best parts,' Hart whispered to her. 'Never fails to bring down the house.'

Just as good as Lacy was Katherine Corey, the round-faced actress playing the overbearing rattle-mouth Mrs. Day. Nell had seen her only in smaller parts, and backstage, and had immediately been drawn to her sunny good humour and infectious laugh. This role allowed Katherine to make gloriously comic use of her ringing voice and ferocious energy. Nell observed her closely, trying to determine what made her performance so hilarious, and watched that afternoon's show with a newly analytical eye.

Nell was putting her basket away after the show when Hart greeted her and Orange Moll.

'Come and have supper with us,' he said. Nell's heart skipped, but then she realised that of course he must be speaking to Moll.

'Well?' he persisted, and she raised her eyes to see that he was looking at her.

'It's you he's speaking to, pet, not me,' Moll laughed. 'He's got no use for a homely old Joan like me.'

* * *

Many of the patrons at the Rose had just come from the play, and called out greetings and approval to Hart as Nell followed him to the table where Lacy, Mohun, and Clun sat. When supper arrived, talk turned to the afternoon's show.

'It's a bit rough in places, isn't it?' Lacy asked.

'A bit,' Mohun agreed. 'You're fine, but the girls still need some work.'

'Bad enough to need another rehearsal?'

'Oh, no,' Hart said. 'It'll settle. *The English Monsieur* needs more work.'

'What did you think, Nell?' Hart asked.

'It was very funny.' Nell struggled to think of something intelligent to say. 'Why are the women's parts so much better than in the other plays I've seen you give?'

'A very good question, indeed,' Lacy said. 'And with a simple answer. In the old days, the playwrights knew that young boys, without so much experience as the other players, would be playing the women's roles. But now they write knowing that the parts will be played by real women.'

'In fact,' Hart added, 'Sir Robert Howard wrote the part of Mrs. Day knowing that Kate Corey would be playing it, and suited it to her talents.'

It began to rain, and Nell listened to the drum of raindrops on the windows as the actors lingered over their meal. She felt at ease with them. They accepted her as she was, and seemed to enjoy her company. They did not regard her with the coolly predatory eyes of the cullies in Lewkenor's Lane or with the leering superiority of the gallants in the pit. They did not treat her like a whore. She studied Hart's face, noticed a tiny scar across one of his high cheekbones, the heaviness of his dark eyelashes, the fullness of his lips.

'How did you come to be actors?' she asked when there was a lull in their conversation.

'Well, Charlie and I were bred up as boys together at the old Blackfriars to play the women's roles.' Wat grinned. 'Can you see the pair of us in skirts? It's true, though. Charlie was apprenticed to Dick Robinson and made a name for himself as the Duchess in *The Cardinal*. A rare performance that was, heartbreaking and grand, and him only thirteen at the time. I can hear him yet—'There's not one little star in heaven will look on me!''

'He's hiding his own light under a bushel,' Hart told Nell. 'We played together in *Philaster*, and he near made me weep every day.'

'Did you apprentice, too?' Nell turned to Lacy.

'I did,' he replied, 'but as a dancer.' Nell found it comically incongruous to think of the great stocky man who sat before her, his deep voice rumbling with its thick Yorkshire accent, as a dancing boy, and she giggled.

'Truly?' she asked.

'Aye, truly,' he laughed. 'I was apprenticed to John Ogilby and played at the old Cockpit, not two hundred paces from here.'

'Tonight's on me, lads,' Wat said, drawing out his purse as the serving man presented the reckoning. Hart shook his head as Wat counted out coins from a handful of glinting gold and silver.

'You shouldn't carry so much money, Wat,' he murmured, giving a glance about the room. 'You never know who's taking more of an interest than is comfortable.'

Wat waved him away with a bearlike paw. 'Charlie, I've spent too much of my life without two pennies to rub together. Now that I'm a bit more flush in the pocket, thanks to the success of the King's Company, I like to know that I've got enough of the ready about me to lay out on my friends.' He grinned around the table, his broad lopsided face alight with wine and happiness.

The rain had stopped by the time Nell and the actors left the tavern, and a full moon hung in the watery night sky. As the other men took their leave, Hart looked up to the heavens and breathed in the scent of the summer evening.

'Shall we walk a bit, as it's so fine?' he asked, and Nell nodded, happy to prolong her time in his company.

They ambled north to Holborn and then east. The sky was still light, and others were out enjoying their leisure at the end of the day.

'What did Wat mean about having so much

money because of the company's success?' Nell asked.

'He was a sharer in the building,' Hart said. 'Ten of us put in money to build the playhouse. Tom Killigrew and Sir Robert Howard own the greatest part, but Wat bought two of the thirty-six shares for about a hundred and twenty-five pounds. He sold them a few months ago for near four times that much, and he and some of the others put the money into the building of three houses to be let, so he hopes to keep making money.'

'Was that wise?' Nell asked.

Hart shrugged. 'Who can say? I've got two shares in the building myself, as well as a share and a quarter of the twelve and three-quarter shares of the company and its profit.'

'Twelve and three-quarter shares?' Nell giggled. 'That's a funny number.'

'Aye, don't ask; it's not worth the trouble of explaining it,' Hart said. 'But if the company lasts I should do well, and I've no mind to sell my shares anytime soon. But as we know to our cost, anything can happen, and theatre is even more chancy a business than most.'

The clouds were clearing, and stars glimmered above in the blackening sky.

'What did you do when the theatres were closed and you could act no more?' Nell asked.

'Went to war,' Hart said. 'Many of us who were King's Men as players came to serve him as soldiers. I was in Prince Rupert's regiment of horse. Mohun served in Flanders. There was nothing for us here, and the king's return was our only hope.'

'What was it like?' Nell asked. 'The war?' A shadow seemed to pass over Hart's face.

121

'Like hell itself,' he said, and walked silently for some time before speaking again. 'Not like in the plays. There's nothing grand about seeing your fellows bleeding and screaming in the mud.'

'Were you a hero?' Nell asked. Hart's mouth twisted in a bleakly ironic smile.

'I did my duty. Like many more who did not come back. My old master Robinson was captured, and though he gave up his arms readily, I watched him shot like a dog.'

They had turned south toward the river. A bunch of boys ran in the narrow lane, shouting and laughing as they kicked a ball along between them. Hart stopped before some houses, and gazed at them before looking down at Nell.

'This is where it stood,' he said. 'The Blackfriars, where I acted as a boy.'

'What happened to it?' Nell asked.

'Pulled down to the ground by Cromwell's men,' he said. 'On a beautiful summer's day. I wept to see it, as I had not wept at all the horrors I saw in the war.'

Chapter Nine

Nell and Rose were leaving the theatre after a performance when a familiar voice hailed them.

'Rose! Nelly!' Jane, their friend from Madam Ross's, bustled toward the stage door. 'I hoped as how I'd catch you.' Her straw-blonde hair was dishevelled, and her eyes were dark with worry.

'Jane! What's the trouble?' Rose asked.

'Remember you thought it were Jack that had

122

taken that watch and set you up for the pinch? Well, I think you were right. This morning poor Nan was taken off by the bums to Newgate. They said one of her gents claimed she'd took his gold snuffbox. She swore she didn't, but they were having none of it, and Jack was standing by all the while, looking like the cat that ate the canary bird.'

'What knavery!' cried Nell.

'Aye,' said Jane. 'But I ran after the gent and told him about Jack and the time before. He said that if we could prove it weren't Nan that took his money, he'd withdraw the charge.'

'But how will you do that?' Rose asked.

'Me and Emily have got a plan.' Jane's eyes shone with excitement. 'One of her regulars who's an alright sort will help us. He'll stand and chat with Emily near Jack tonight, flash his watch, let on that he's more drunk than he really is, and drop the watch in his pocket so Jack can't miss it. If the watch turns up missing, he'll go and send the bailiffs round.'

'It sounds a dangerous game, Jane,' Nell said. 'You're as good as take a bear by the tooth.'

'But what else can we do?' Jane asked. 'Madam won't help, of course. She'll stand by him no matter what he's done. And if this works, we've got him. The biter bit, do you see?'

'Oh, Lord, have a care, Jane,' Rose worried. 'That Jack is a right bad 'un. He'd stop at nothing, him.'

'Do this for me,' Nell said. 'Will you come round tomorrow and let us know what happened?'

'I will,' Jane agreed. 'Right on this spot I'll be tomorrow same time, and tell you we've sent the villain away.'

123

But Jane was nowhere to be seen the next afternoon. Nell and Rose waited for nearly an hour, long past when all the actors, scenekeepers, and others of the playhouse had gone and the stage door was locked. Each time a woman passed on the street they looked up hopefully, but no Jane appeared.

'What now?' Nell asked.

'It looks bad, doesn't it?' Rose said. 'Let's go to Madam Ross's. We can go in the taproom, same as anyone else, as if we're only there to wet our whistles, and see what we can learn.'

Ned was at the bar when they entered, and from his face it was apparent that there was awful news.

'What's amiss, Ned?' Rose whispered. He looked around and answered in a low voice.

'I'm sorry to tell you, but poor Em was found dead in her bed this morning,' he said, his eyes reddening with tears. 'Strangled, by the look of it.'

'Dear God, no!' Rose cried. 'Ned, where's Jane? Where's Jack?'

'Jane?' He looked at them in confusion. 'Why, she went out but a bit ago, saying she needed some air to calm her down. And now that I think on it, Jack went out, too, almost on her heels.'

'We've got to find Jane!' Nell cried. 'It was Jack! He killed Emily, and now he's after Jane! Help us, Ned!'

*   *   *

The summer evening was long, but even so, the light was fading, and Nell despaired of finding Jane before nightfall. She sank to her haunches and leaned her back against a brick wall still warm from

124

the sun, trying to catch her breath and think. Jane could be anywhere. Maybe Ned or Rose had found her, and she was safe, but she could just as easily be lying dead. Nell felt the tightness in her chest that presaged her fall into panic. Don't think like that, she told herself. It's just as like that Jane is with some friend, or sitting down by the river. But she felt cold with fear and decided she must press on. She was a little west of Covent Garden and decided to go up to Long Acre and make her way back to Lewkenor's Lane. If she hadn't found Jane before dark fell, she'd go back to Madam Ross's and see if there was any news.

Nell suddenly recalled that Jane was friendly with one of the barmen at the Lamb and Flag. Perhaps she'd gone there for a visit. She headed for Rose Street, the short and winding passage where the alehouse lay. She had always disliked the blind curve of the little street, with brick walls rising on either side. One man at each end easily turned it into a trap, and it was a favourite haunt of footpads.

She entered the street, and joyfully saw Jane ahead. And then everything seemed to happen in a flash. Jack stepped from the door of the alehouse, clapped a hand over Jane's mouth, and dragged her a few feet. She had been taken completely by surprise, and Nell saw the blind terror in her eyes as Jack shoved her against the wall and wrenched her head back. Nell saw the knife in his hand as he drew it back, saw the blade plunge into Jane's bared throat, saw the shower of blood.

She cried out as Jane slumped to the ground in a widening pool of crimson. Jack turned and saw her. For a second that seemed to last a century, his eyes held hers as he hefted the knife in his hand. Nell felt rooted to the spot. Then Jack moved swiftly toward her, and she turned and ran, not making a sound, so profound was her terror. She raced for her life, not knowing where she was headed, as long as it was away from Jack and certain death.

It was dark now, and Nell scrambled her way toward Covent Garden. Perhaps even now there would be boys finishing a game of football, or costermongers packing up the last of their goods. She stole a glance over her shoulder. She could see Jack's shape, but she had put some distance between them. And then she heard a crash and a curse. He had fallen over something. She had precious seconds to make her escape, and willed herself to run faster, but she knew she couldn't run much longer.

The Church of St. Paul's Covent Garden rose before her. She sprinted into the black emptiness of its portico and threw herself to the ground, flattening herself against the wall of the church. She heard Jack's heavy footsteps. Too late to do anything but stay where she was and pray that he would not think to look there. She covered her face with her arm, held her breath, and willed her thudding heart to be silent. She heard Jack run past, stop, return to the front of the church. He had surely seen her. And then, miraculously, with an exhalation of fury, he left.

Nell lay motionless. Church bells rang the hour of nine. Ten. Finally she dared to move, barely able to stand, her body stiff and painful from lying so long on the cold stone. She did not dare go anywhere near Lewkenor's Lane and instead made her way south to the Strand. There were people abroad there, but still she looked over her shoulder fearfully until she reached the Cat and Fiddle and the safety of her room.

*　　　*　　　*

The next day, even in the crowded playhouse, Nell felt she could not stop shaking. The image of Jane's terrified eyes haunted her, and she could not shake the feeling that Jack could be nearby, watching her and waiting. Rose had sought out Harry Killigrew and begged for his help, and he met them in the greenroom after the performance had done. The word of the murders had spread, and other members of the company clustered near to hear the news.

'I went to Madam Ross's with a couple of bailiffs,' Harry reported. 'Ned says Jack never went back last night and if Madam knows where he is, she isn't saying. The watch will be looking for him, but unless they catch him, Nell, the best I can say is you should watch your back.'

'And we'll be watching, too, Nell,' Clun assured her. 'You're safe here with us.'

'Don't go anywhere on your own, will you?' Rose asked anxiously. 'Will you promise me that?'

Nell was happy to promise. She felt terrified at the thought of finding herself alone and face-to-face with Jack, and for weeks, she left the Cat and Fiddle only to go to the playhouse, always in Rose's company and always keeping to the well-travelled Drury Lane, and made sure she was never abroad when it was dark. Only when two months had gone by, and Harry's inquiries confirmed that Jack had disappeared, did she begin to feel less fearful.

127

Chapter Ten

Third of August, 1664

Nell had never heard an audience laugh so loudly. Walter Clun had set the house on a roar again. His performance as Subtle in *The Alchemist* had packed the theatre though the audience was sweltering in the heat of the summer afternoon. Nell looked around the pit. Orange Moll was using her apron to wipe tears of laughter from her eyes. Sir Charles Sedley's guffaws had turned into a cough and Henry Savile was striking him on the back. Dorset was pounding his walking stick on the floor in approval. The crowded galleries shook.

I want to do that, Nell thought. I want to make them love me like that.

*   *   *

After the performance, Nell spotted Clun in the greenroom, towelling off his face as he spoke with Kate Corey.

'Truly the best show ever, Wat,' Kate said, kissing Clun's ruddy cheek. 'Ain't life grand sometimes?'

'It is, Kate, it is. And the best thing is—we get to do it all again tomorrow.' Kate's hearty chuckle floated behind her as she left, and Nell judged she had better speak to Wat now while he was alone for a moment.

'Will you teach me to act?'

Wat raised his eyebrows in surprise, and Nell was

afraid he was going to tell her not to be silly, and to run along. But he gave her an appraising look.

'Why do you ask me?'

'Because you can do what I want to do,' Nell said. 'You can make people laugh.'

'I'm not the only one can make folks laugh,' Clun said.

'No, but you do it better than anyone. You know how to make them laugh, and you know what you have to do differently if what you did at first doesn't work. I've watched you. I want you to show me. Please.'

Wat threw the towel over his shoulder and sat. 'Can you give me any of the lines from the play today? Say, where Doll Common says—'

'"'Sdeath, you abominable pair of stinkards!"' Nell cried. '"Leave off your barking and grow one again, or by the light that shines, I'll cut your throats!"'

'That's Kate to the life!' Wat chortled.

'I pay her close mind,' Nell said. 'And I know all of that scene.'

'That's well and good,' Wat said. 'A talent for mimicry will help, but there's more to it than that. You've a strong voice and great energy for such a little mite, and those are good things, too, for an actor.'

'So will you teach me?' Nell repeated, her eyes pleading.

'Aye, we'll have a go,' Wat smiled. 'I'll tell you what. I've no rehearsal tomorrow. Come at eleven, and we'll see what we can do in an hour.'

*   *   *

Nell was so excited she could scarcely keep from dancing her way back to the Cat and Fiddle, and she kept having to stop and wait for Rose's slower pace.

'He said yes! He said yes!' she cried again.

'I'm happy for you, Nelly, if it's what you want. But have a care and don't get your hopes too high.'

'Why?' Nell was suddenly brought to earth. 'Do you not think I can be an actress?'

'I think you have the makings to be as good as any I've seen,' Rose said. 'But many things fall out between the cup and the lip, and I'd not have you disappointed should things not come about as you want.' She looked at Nell, now walking instead of dancing, and hugged her little sister to her.

'Wat would not have said yes did he not think you showed promise. It's a great compliment to you that he'd take his time to teach you.' Nell's step was jaunty again, and Rose smiled to see it. 'Do you really know that whole scene of Doll Common's?'

*　　　*　　　*

Nell breezed into the greenroom in high spirits the next morning but knew from the moment she entered that something terrible had happened. Kate Corey was sobbing in John Lacy's arms, and tears streaked Lacy's face as well. It was rare that Tom Killigrew was at the playhouse early, but he stood with Mohun and Hart, and when they looked up at Nell's approach their faces were stricken. Her heart stopped in her throat.

'What is it? What's happened?' she cried.

'Wat Clun,' said Hart, his voice breaking. 'He's murdered.'

130

*   *   *

The play was long over, but the actors of the King's Company remained in the greenroom, unwilling to be alone in their grief. Outside thunder shattered the sky and lightning flashed, and the downpour of rain mirrored the fall of tears.

'On his way home. Accosted by footpads, it would seem. Bound and robbed.' Lacy spoke the words again, as if the repetition would help to give them sense.

'If his wound was not so great, I cannot see how he died,' Kate sobbed.

'With the struggling, they said,' replied Mohun, his face grey. 'So that he bled to death.'

Nell thought of Lacy's warning to Wat about showing his money so carelessly among strangers, and wished she could go back and make him heed. What a senseless loss, to die over a few pounds. Was that the price of a life, then?

*   *   *

The rain was still lashing down when Hart and Nell arrived before the door of her lodgings, but rather than hurry off as he usually did, Hart stood silently, his head bowed. Nell thought again of Wat's great bulk struggling against his bonds and him dying alone and helpless in a ditch.

'A mighty heart he had,' Hart said, and he began to weep, great wrenching sobs. Nell pulled him to her, murmuring love and comfort against his chest, noting how slender he felt in her arms. In all the times he had walked her home that summer, he

131

had never tried to bed her, never asked to come in, never asked her into his lodgings in Henrietta Street nearby, and she had been afraid to wonder about the reasons or to tell him how she felt about him. But tonight was different.

'My Hart,' she said. 'My heart. Come.'

*   *   *

It was cold in Nell's room, and bed was the only place to keep warm. Hart stood in his shirt and breeches, the moonlight falling silvery across his pale skin. Nell went to him. She had been with so many men, but tonight all felt new. He kissed her softly, and unfastened her bodice and skirt. They fell to the floor in a soft pool around her feet. His eyes on hers, he lifted her shift and pulled it off, then kissed her again, and his hands were warm and gentle on her skin as he drew her with him into bed, his dark hair falling over her face as he kissed her throat.

Despite how she had burned for him, she felt shy. But under his touch, she caught fire. She had never been with a man who cared for her pleasure as well as his own. For all the countless men who had spent inside her, she had never come off herself. But tonight she did, her heart and soul seeming to coalesce in a molten pool in the pit of her belly.

After, Hart held her. His tears had stopped and soon his breathing told her he was asleep. Wat's face came again into Nell's mind. But despite the horror of his death, with her head upon Hart's chest and his arms encircling her, Nell felt safe as she had never felt before.

* * *

The show went on the next day, as it must if the playhouse was to survive. One of Clun's murderers had been apprehended, an Irishman who refused to give up the names of his accomplices. But the news was little comfort. Wat was gone, and his absence seemed to echo throughout the playhouse.

'He was going to teach me,' Nell said to Hart, watching over his shoulder in the mirror as he wiped the makeup from his face.

John Lacy was nearby, brushing the lint from his coat. 'If Wat was going to teach you, then we shall have to do it instead, eh, Charlie?'

'Certainly,' said Hart. 'And if you work hard, I'll put you on in *Thomaso*. It's a comedy of Killigrew's, in two parts. There's just the role for you, a saucy young doxy. Just a few scenes, so you can get your feet wet.'

'I cannot read,' Nell blurted, ashamed.

'No more did I think you could,' Hart said. 'I'll read your words to you, and you can learn them by repeating them back until you have them down. And for the rest'—he waved his arm to indicate all else that his twenty years upon the stage had taught him—'Lacy and I can teach you.'

* * *

'"'Tis the humor of most men, they love difficulty and riches. Slight them, they are yours forever,"' Nell recited.

'Again,' said Hart. 'From the gut, and think of your voice bouncing off the back wall of the theatre. Remember what a racket you're fighting

133

against onstage. Just use your orange-selling voice.' That helped, and Nell was proud to get Hart's smile of approval when she repeated the line.

She ran through her whole first speech again, trying to remember everything at once—to address her lines to the actors onstage and yet keep her face forward so the audience could see her well; to keep her feet planted firm and stand straight; to speak her words clearly and loudly without shouting.

'Good,' said Hart. 'Good. You would have done Wat proud.'

*　　　*　　　*

Nell was nervous on the morning of the first rehearsal for *Thomaso*. The stage door keeper, Eddie Gibbs, greeted her as usual, but today she felt different. Today she was entering the playhouse as an actress. She paused a moment outside the greenroom door, her heart pumping in her throat. Much of the cast had already assembled around the big table, and Nell felt curious and appraising glances as she entered. Killigrew was using the play as an opportunity to try the talents of several new girls, and among the established members of the company were the newcomers Elizabeth Weaver, Betty Hall, Betsy Knepp, and the sisters Frances and Elizabeth Davenport, eyeing each other and Anne Marshall, who was playing the lead.

Nell smiled at the group, wondering if the new girls all knew that Hart was her lover, and whether they were predisposed to resent her for it, or whether they perhaps regarded her as safely out of the running for the bigger fish they might

134

be angling for. Hester Davenport, formerly of the Duke's Company, had just given birth to a son by the Earl of Oxford, with whom she was living in luxury as a wife in all but name.

Nell was grateful to see Kate Corey and slipped into the empty seat next to her.

'You'll be fine,' Kate whispered to her. 'And just you stick with me if any of these cats start to hiss.'

Nell looked at the actresses and thought of the girls at Madam Ross's jealously guarding their regulars. She was glad that Hart had drilled her in her part so well, and that she had repeated the words to herself in bed each night before she fell asleep so that they now came to her without thinking. When it came to rehearsals, she would not have to worry about her lines and would only have to learn her movements.

Killigrew had written *Thomaso* during the long closure of the theatres, and it had not yet been performed, so everyone was new to their parts. Killigrew read the script aloud to the assembled cast. He took on each of the characters as he read the play, to Nell's delight, and she remembered that he had been an actor himself in the old days. Hart had told her that the boy Killigrew had got his start in the theatre by going on as a little devil at the Red Bull so that he could see the other plays free. As he read the lines of the mountebank Lopus, she thought she could picture him as a mischievous round-faced lad dressed up with tail and horns. The company laughed heartily at his performance, and Nell yearned to begin rehearsals in earnest.

When Killigrew had done reading, the prompter handed around the sides—each actor's lines and cues, copied from the precious fair copy that

135

would be kept at the theatre and turned into a promptbook. Killigrew appointed rehearsal times for the rest of the week, and the work for the day was over.

Nell was to be at the rehearsal the next morning, and she was so elated at being finally counted among the company's actresses that she didn't even mind selling oranges during the afternoon's performance of *The General*, a tragedy that she found dull. Dorset and Sedley were there, apparently enjoying the play more by making sport of it than by watching it, and she bantered happily with them during the interval.

'What a bacon-faced fool that general is,' Sedley said. '"My rival do but possess her,' says he. Why, pox, what is there more to be had of a woman than the possessing her?' Though Nell's interest in Dorset had dimmed to no more than a slight flicker since Hart had become her lover, Sedley's remark reminded her that she had promised herself not to be too much in Dorset's company, so she gave a full-throated cry of 'Oranges! Fine oranges!' and turned her back on the laughing duo.

*   *   *

When the day of the first performance of *Thomaso* came, it seemed very strange to Nell to listen to the buzz and laughter of the audience from the women's tiring room instead of being in the thick of things with her basket of oranges. But it was a feeling she could happily get used to, she thought. She thanked the tire-woman, Rachel Brown, for lacing her bodice, and checked her reflection in the mirror. She loved the gold-coloured dress that she

136

wore as Paulina, and turned this way and that to admire it. Its skirt fell in heavy folds, and she felt like she stood in the centre of some great blooming flower.

'Here, a little more red to your cheeks,' Kate Corey said, helping her. 'Just so. Now don't forget to piss afore you go on. That was the mistake I made the first day I went onstage. Oliver's skull is right back there.'

'Oliver's skull?'

Kate indicated the chamber pot tucked behind a screen, and Nell giggled in delight at the thought that Cromwell's hated name had come to mean a lowly pisspot.

Nell's first scene was the second scene of the play, and when she and Betty Hall made their entrance as the courtesans Paulina and Saretta, in their wildly colourful gowns and accoutrements, she was electrified by the feeling of all eyes turned upon her.

'"Would the army were drawn into garrison,"' Betty lamented. '"I long for some fresh lovers to dress our house."'

Their wry bantering commentary on the foibles of men was well calculated to get the crowd in a laughing mood at the start of the play, and by a few lines into the scene, describing ladies whose beauty was made up of cosmetics and accessories, Nell could feel that the audience was primed and with her.

'"Death,"' she trilled. '"They'll make love to petticoats! One that never goes to bed all, nor sleeps in a whole skin, one whose teeth, eyes, and hair rest all night in a box, and her chamber lies strewed with her loose members, high shoes, false back and breasts, while he hugs a dismembered carcass!"' The audience howled, and Nell felt the scene was over entirely too soon.

She thrilled as she took her bow before the packed house and to the applause that continued to resound as she left the stage. Lacy pulled her into a bear hug and kissed her on both cheeks.

'Look at her glow,' he laughed, turning to Hart and Mick Mohun. 'Ready for more already, she is.'

'And so she should be,' Mohun agreed. 'Well done, Nell.'

She blushed happily at the praise as Hart swept her off her feet.

'You were the best of the new girls,' he said, kissing her before setting her down. 'No question. You've got true presence and a great gift for comedy. And Killigrew's agreed—we'll put you on in *The Siege of Urbin* next. You'll have four or five quite nice little comic scenes that will let you stretch your wings a bit.'

*   *   *

'I'm really to wear these, am I?' Nell asked Hart, holding up the breeches that were part of her costume as Malina, a girl who disguises herself as a boy.

'You are. And I don't know whether I'll be more proud that those sleek little legs of yours are mine to touch, or ready to kill anyone for looking at them.'

Nell loved playing in *The Siege of Urbin* even more than she liked *Thomaso*. She had the second-largest female role, after Anne Marshall as Celestina, and their first scene opened the

138

play. Later, disguised as a young man, she flirted outrageously with Betty Davenport as Clara, and her terrified reaction when Hart as the Duke drew his sword against her always got shouts of laughter.

Nell also relished the opportunity to work with Michael Mohun and Nicholas Burt, always learning as she watched and played with them, and grateful for their compliments and words of advice.

Looking over at Hart at supper one evening after the play, she laughed to remember how she had been jealous of him and Anne Marshall. She adored him with her soul, and he had never given her a moment's reason to think that he did not feel the same.

*   *   *

The end of the year was almost come, and soon it would be 1665. Nell and Hart had stayed up late and come to Tower Hill to get a good view of the comet that had illuminated the sky for several nights. They stood together in the dark, looking heavenward. There was a chill wind biting, and clouds scudded across the icy face of the moon, waxing toward fullness.

'There!' Hart cried.

'Oh!' Nell sighed. 'Magnificent.'

The comet shone bright, trailing a sparkle of stars in its wake. It must be a harbinger of glorious things to come, Nell thought. This year had been one of supreme happiness, and the coming year promised more joy, with Hart at her side and her first leading role.

'When will the comet come again?' she whispered.

'Not until you and I are long gone from this earth, sweeting,' Hart said into her ear, holding her close. 'So look well upon it, that we may always hold this moment in our hearts.'

* * *

Nell was so caught up in the excitement of the playhouse that she cared little for what was happening in the world beyond. But it was becoming impossible to ignore the talk of war with the Dutch that was looming on the horizon. Many of the scenekeepers at the playhouse were sailors, like Dicky One-Shank, and Nell found a knot of them gathered in angry discussion outside the stage door one morning.

'What's happened?' she asked Dicky.

'The press-gangs are out,' he said, 'and they've taken up Bill Edwards and John Gilbert.'

'Press-gangs?' Nell asked, looking in confusion at the agitated faces around her 'What's that?' A babble of voices broke out in explanation.

'The king is readying for war, and needs sailors to build up the navy,' said Matt Kempton, a young red-headed giant. 'And if he cannot get enough sailors who are willing, he gets them any way he can. The press-gangs pluck men off the street and press them into service, whether they will or no.'

'But that's terrible!' Nell said. 'Is there nothing to be done?'

'Nothing, once they've been taken off by force,' Dicky said. 'The only thing is to avoid capture in the first place.'

* * *

John Dryden's new play, *The Indian Emperor*, was a grand tragedy in verse. The part of Cydaria, a noble lady, was far more challenging than Nell's first two roles, and she needed much training before she would be ready. Lacy was undertaking her lessons in carriage and movement.

'Slow down,' he exhorted her. 'Cydaria has no need to hurry and bustle like that. And don't fidget and shift when you're not speaking. Stand straight and proud. Stillness draws more eyes and lends more regal grace than any movement.'

And though she would not dance in this play, Lacy was looking further ahead.

'You'll need the dancing soon enough. And when you do, you'll not want to have it all to learn on top of your words and everything else.'

So he worked with her daily, teaching her court dances, from the stately pavane to the lively galliard and coranto. Nell was surprised at the delicacy and liveliness with which he moved.

'You have to think yourself light,' he explained. 'Picture yourself like a puppet, your head suspended by a thread dropping down from heaven. That's it. You've got it now.'

Nell had far more lines than she'd had in her previous parts. Hart read them to her and she repeated them back until she had them pat. He was astonished at how quickly she learned the words. She heeded his advice and repeated them over to herself whenever she could.

'You'll need that discipline,' Hart said. 'You may need to keep a score of parts in your head so that you can perform with not much more than a run-through.'

'A score of parts?' Nell asked, horrified.

'Easily, if you do well. I know forty or more.'

* * *

Remembering the words was one thing. Understanding them was quite another. With a frequency she found embarrassing, Nell had to ask Hart to explain the meaning of a word or a whole string of words—each of which she understood on its own, but which when put together seemed incomprehensible.

'What does it mean, 'My feeble hopes in her deserts are lost?"'

'It means Cydaria fears Cortez can never love her. She thinks he loves Almeria, you see.'

'Oh,' said Nell. 'Well, why don't she say that, then?'

'Try it again,' said Hart. 'And remember the verse. If you're speaking it right you can feel the metre, and it will help you both to remember the lines and to speak them so they will be understood.' Nell gave the line once more.

'That's it!' Hart cried. 'Now do it again. And this time you must make it seem as if you are thinking and speaking the words for the first time. Listen:

'Make me not doubt, fair soul, your constancy,
You would have died for love, and so would I.'

'Do you see?'

Nell did see, and as she listened to Hart repeat the words over to her, she was struck by the thought that her own speech placed her upbringing squarely and undeniably in the maze of filthy streets and

142

alleys around Covent Garden.

'You've no need to make big changes,' Hart assured her. 'Your voice is pleasing and strong. Pronounce a few words differently and you'll be fine. In this speech, for instance, remember there's an 'h' sound at the beginning of 'heaving,' 'heart,' and 'here,' but not of 'injuries.'''

Each day Hart and Lacy worked Nell rigorously, prompting, correcting, and praising. Each day she felt that she knew a world more than she had known the previous day, and yet became more keenly aware of how much more there was to know about the business of acting. Her head was full of the lines she was learning. Her body ached from the unaccustomed dancing. She found that she was hungry all the time and ate ravenously. She could not easily get to sleep at night, though once asleep she slept like the dead.

*   *   *

At last came the day of the first performance of *The Indian Emperor*. Nell's stomach had been churning with nervous excitement since she had woken, and now, pacing backstage as she waited to go on, she was terrified. Why, oh, why had she ever wanted to be an actress?

Her cue came. She launched herself onto the stage, conscious of the hundreds of eyes upon her. Her throat tightened, and she could barely speak her first line, an aside. Then she looked to Hart, found safety in his eyes, and to her surprise, her voice came out clear and strong.

143

'"Thick breath, quick pulse, and heaving of my heart,
All signs of some unwonted change appear . . ."'

The symptoms required no acting—her heart felt as if it would leap from her chest. Hart moved closer to Nell, taking her hands in his. She looked up into his eyes. He smiled. She felt her body relax in the warmth of his presence and her fear melted away.

*   *   *

Later, Nell sat next to Hart as the company supped, her head pleasurably abuzz from wine. In the flickering candlelight, she looked at the faces around her, laughing at some jest of Lacy's. It was dark and cold outside, but here all was warm and snug, and she was among friends. She heard once more in her head the opening lines of the play, and thought how apt they seemed.

On what new happy climate are we thrown,
So long kept secret, and so lately known?

The day after the first performance, Nell went to the stage to check her props and found Dicky and several of the other scenekeepers gathered in the wings, some with tears on their weather-roughened faces. Matt Kempton turned as she approached.

'It's the *London*,' he said. 'The ship that Bill and John were pressed to. It's blown up, with great loss of life.'

'They were my shipmates,' Dicky said, wiping his

144

ruddy cheeks. 'And my captain, Robert Lawson. We all served in the *Fairfax* at Goodwin Sands. Where I lost my leg.'

'How many are lost?' Nell asked. 'Are Bill and John killed?'

'No one knows yet,' Matt said, 'but the crew numbered more than three hundred, and they say but few survived.'

Chapter Eleven

Third of April, 1665

'You should learn however you can,' Hart said. 'Watch other actors. Observe what works and what does not, and why.' So today Nell sat with Beck Marshall in an upper gallery at the Duke's Playhouse, to see their rival company perform Lord Orrery's new play, *Mustapha*. Nell didn't think much of the play, but the day was a success anyway, because the king was there.

Barbara Palmer sat beside him, preening and fanning herself, obviously aware that she was being watched as closely as the actors. Nell thought how magnificently beautiful she looked, but there was something cold and hard about her. The flashing eyes she turned on the king were proud and triumphant. Did she love him? Nell wondered. She saw little tenderness in Lady Castlemaine's gaze.

To Nell's shock, she realised that the king was looking up at her. He smiled, and bowed his head in greeting. Thoroughly flustered, Nell inclined her own head. Barbara Palmer had seen, and there were thunderclouds behind her gaze.

'Brr,' said Beck. 'Those are icicles, not eyes! Well done, Nell. You've not only got the king's attention but put Lady Castlemaine's nose out of joint, too. Not a bad afternoon's work!'

Though all had congratulated Nell on her success in *The Indian Emperor*, she felt awkward in the serious part and begged Hart to let her play in another comedy.

'It's already in hand,' he said. 'I'm meeting with Killigrew and Mohun and Lacy tomorrow, and we'll find something for you to get your teeth into.'

But when she saw the men in conversation the next afternoon, their faces were grim.

'Pray that it does not get any worse,' Killigrew said, shaking his head as he walked away.

'Pray that what does not get worse?' Nell asked. Lacy glanced around and lowered his voice.

'The plague. I saw two houses closed up today. If it gets bad, the playhouses will be shut to stop it spreading.'

Nell's heart sank. Not now, she pleaded to whatever power might be listening. Not when complete happiness is so close at hand.

But the plague showed no signs of abating, and before long Killigrew gathered the company and told them that the king had ordered the theatres closed until the plague should pass.

The weather grew hotter as spring turned to summer, and soon there were few streets that did not have a house shut up. Even if the playhouses had been open, there would have been no one to come, for the court had fled to Oxford, followed by much of the town. In the last week of June, Nell listened in horror as Hart told her of the week's

146

bills of mortality.

'Two hundred and sixty-seven dead of the plague,' he said. 'That's ninety more than last week.'

But those numbers soon paled. The plague's toll doubled the following week, doubled again the next week, and then again.

A pall of terror settled over London. The plague came upon its victims so suddenly that a person might wake feeling fine and be dead by nightfall. The grotesque black swellings in the armpits and groin bloomed quickly and agonisingly, the putrid pus within seeping into the body or oozing forth when the buboes burst. No one knew how the contagion spread, but it was impossible not to look with fear upon anyone who came near, for they might be carrying the seeds of death.

*   *   *

'We're taking the company to Oxford,' Hart told her. 'We can play there to the court. You can learn some more parts, in readiness for when the playhouse is open again.'

'I can't leave Rose.'

'We'll make room for her, too. We'll need a tire-woman, and Rachel's gone to her family, so Rose can take her place.'

That night, Nell thought about her mother. She had not laid eyes on Eleanor since the day she had left home, now five years ago, and when thoughts of her mother had come to mind she had pushed them down. There was no good to be had from revisiting the painful past. But tonight the memories pushed forward, jostling with the thought that her mother

147

might die of the plague while she was gone, could already be dead.

An image from the distant past flashed into Nell's mind—her mother's face, smiling and laughing as she bounced Nell on her knee. Rose stood beside them. They were outdoors, and sunlight fell upon them through the green foliage of a tree. Nell looked up at the sound of a bird's cry and saw a flitting brown shape splashed with red.

'Robin Red Breast,' Eleanor said. 'Robin.'

'Wobbin.' Little Nell tried out the word, and Rose and Eleanor laughed in delight.

Nell found that tears were running down her face at the memory. She had forgotten the moments of love and tenderness, and the fleeting glimpse of her mother's warmth awoke intense feelings of longing. Perhaps she should go to see her mother before she and Rose left London. Or would it be a fool's errand, putting herself in the path of rejection and pain?

*   *   *

The next day, Nell and Rose went to the Golden Fleece. Coming in from the sunshine, it took Nell's eyes a moment to adjust to the dim light. The smell of the place, that distinct mingling of ale, food, sawdust, sweat, dirt, and urine, flooded her mind with memories, and for a moment, it felt as though she had never been away, that Hart and the playhouse and all that had happened since the day of the king's return to London were only a dream.

Eleanor was behind the bar, and turned at the sound of footsteps. From the ingratiating smile that fleeted across her lips before it died, Nell could tell that her mother had not at first recognised her daughters. But then Eleanor's mouth flattened into a hard line, and she jutted her chin at them belligerently.

'Well, look what the cat dragged in. And what might the two of you want?'

'We were worried about you, Mam,' said Rose. 'Because of the plague.'

Eleanor snorted.

'Well, I'm aboveground, as you can see.'

We shouldn't have come, Nell thought. She's just the same as ever, and would give me a kicking just the same as before. She turned to leave, but Rose laid a gentle hand on her arm and faced their mother steadily.

'We're glad you're well. We're going to Oxford, Nell and I, with the playhouse. Is there aught we can do for you?'

Eleanor had been caught off guard, and for a minute Nell saw beyond the defensive mask of her mother's face to the bottomless well of pain and self-loathing. It was not a frightening witch who stood before her, but a pathetic old woman, beaten by the world. Nell felt tears welling up and sobs choking her chest.

'Will you come with us?'

As soon as she had said the words, she knew that they were folly. She had no money to keep herself, much less her mother. And she cringed at the thought of Hart, of Killigrew, of the Marshall sisters—everyone—knowing that this creature was her mother. And then she felt ashamed at the thought, and began to cry.

Eleanor stood uncertainly. Finally she shook her head.

'Oxford has naught for me but black memories. If I'm to die, I'll do it here.'

Rose handed her a knotted handkerchief containing a few shillings. Eleanor looked as if she would give it back, but then clenched it in her work-roughened hands, as if afraid that someone would snatch it away.

'Then we'll be off,' Rose said. 'We'll come to see you when we're back. God keep you.'

Eleanor nodded slowly. 'And both of you.'

*   *   *

A few days later, the King's Company left London. As the coach jolted towards the road to Oxford, Nell had never seen the town so empty. A few scrawny dogs stared out from the shadows, hopeless in their heat and hunger. Shops were shuttered and houses silent and watchful. And here and there that dreadful sight—a house with red letters painted stark against the boards. 'God Have Mercy on Us' was what it said, Hart had told her.

At Tyburn Tree, the gallows stood empty, the dirt beneath turned to dust. No crowds gathered there this day. Death as entertainment had lost its appeal, for now death hung unseen behind every shoulder. It lay in wait, breathless, watching for its chance. This day might be your last.

On the seat opposite, Betsy Knepp gasped, and turning to see what had provoked it, Nell, too, caught her breath. A little way off the road, men were labouring at a gaping trench. The stench of rot was heavy in the heat and Nell gagged and snatched at her skirt to cover her nose. But nothing could cover the horror of the knowledge of what

150

lay within, and as the coach passed, the men tipped barrows of quicklime into the pit. Friends and lovers, strangers and enemies lay all together now, all pride and dignity gone, all hopes and dreams and smiles forever lost.

Nell moved closer to Hart and put her hand in his, and his touch and solid presence made her feel safer.

The sun shone bright and as city gave way to country and fields stretched off on either side of the road, Nell breathed again and felt a lifting of the shadows covering her soul. A troop of butterflies swooped and soared, a yellow blur against the blue of summer sky. Trees hung heavy with fruit sweetly scented the air. A village appeared in the distance, a few houses clustered amid the golden fields. What must it be like, Nell marvelled, to live in such a place? No theatres, no shops, no court. Excitement took hold of her at the thought of what lay ahead. Performances for the king and court by night, and a new world to explore by day.

*   *   *

Away from the grimness of plague-ridden London and spending her time learning the part of Celia in *The Humorous Lieutenant*, Nell's spirits rose. She was never happier than in Hart's company, and together they strolled the town, the parks, the mossy banks of the river. She was amazed at the range of subjects on which he was knowledgeable, and he delighted in her eagerness to see and to learn. He laughed as she exclaimed in astonishment when he explained to her as they walked in the park one afternoon that it was not the sun that was rolling higher in the sky, but the earth that was moving around the sun.

'"O brave new world!"' he exclaimed, smiling.

'What?'

'It's from *The Tempest*,' he explained. 'You're like Miranda, who has lived on a small island all her life, and is enraptured by what is new. Though now I come to think about it, it was a young man she was speaking of, as she had never seen another man besides her father. So I can only hope that the sun and earth are enough for you today.'

He said it lightly, but Nell saw a shadow of sadness pass over his face. She squeezed his hand and looked anxiously up at him. In an instant, his mood turned playful, and he cried, 'Come—mount and ride!'

Giggling, Nell hopped onto his back, clasped her legs around him, and held on tight as he whooped and galloped. Faster and faster he went, swooping in circles and looping around a towering oak tree as Nell shrieked with laughter. A dog's sharp bark answered her, and suddenly a small pack of yapping spaniels was converging on them.

From her bouncing perch, Nell was astonished to see that the king and Barbara Palmer stood not twenty paces away, watching her and Hart with evident interest.

'Hart! Charlie!' Nell beat on Hart's shoulders with her hands. He finally took in the royal presence and came to a halt, Nell still clinging to his back.

'Mr. Hart,' said the king, inclining his head. An ironic smile twitched the corners of his mouth, and Lady Castlemaine was regarding Hart and Nell with amusement.

'Good afternoon, Your Majesty,' Hart said, setting Nell on the grass beside him and bowing. 'May I present Nell Gwynn? You've seen her in our performances in town.'

'So we have,' said the king. 'How could I forget that charming face, with or without her oranges?'

*   *   *

The hot summer days stretched on. At the end of August, Michael Mohun rode alone to London and returned with cold comfort.

'All who can flee have done so. The rest just wait. The weekly bills showed more than six thousand dead last week, but people murmur that it must be nearer ten thousand. The night is not long enough to bury the dead, so the corpses are buried by day as well, and the tolling of the bells never stops.'

Nell looked at Mohun's haggard face in the flickering firelight, his eyes weary and shadowed, his mouth grim. He passed a hand over his forehead, as if he could wipe away the lines of exhaustion and tension.

'It would be folly to return to London. It would be death.'

*   *   *

That night Nell lay awake and thought again of her mother, alone in the grey streets of Covent Garden, where the plague raged most fiercely. If Eleanor died, no one would know to tell her. Would she at length go home to find her mother gone, buried nameless in some pit? Nell buried her face in her pillow and, trying not to wake Hart next to her,

153

sobbed herself to sleep.

*   *   *

Like the ripples of a pebble thrown into a pond, fear spread outward in widening circles. The court moved to Salisbury. And then to Wilton, when a royal groom at Salisbury dropped dead of the plague.

With the king and his retinue gone from Oxford, Killigrew departed for France to find musicians for the court. The players tightened their belts, gave performances in college halls, and rehearsed the plays they would present when it was safe to go back to London.

*   *   *

'We ought to use this time to teach you to read,' Hart urged Nell. 'It will make learning lines much easier for you.' He wrote the letters of the alphabet out for her and taught her the sounds that each should make. But once they were strung together into words, and the words into lines, and the lines into endless pages, the task of deciphering them seemed overwhelming to Nell.

'You know this word,' Hart urged, pointing at the page. Nell stared at it. It began with one of the two letters that looked like little fat men, their bellies sticking out before them. But which one was it?

'Bog?' She looked up to him for confirmation.

'No! Dog. Dog. You just read that same word up here.' He stabbed his finger at the book. Nell turned away in shame and frustration at the irritation in his voice. He sat down beside her and

154

stroked her head.

'I'm sorry, honey. I don't mean to grow impatient with you. Remember—when the little fat man is coming onto the stage from the right, he's a 'b.' And when he's entering from the left, he's a 'd.'''

'Please can we stop for now?' Nell begged. 'The letters just jumble together and make my head hurt something fierce.'

*   *   *

By the end of September, it finally seemed that the worst was over, and the King's Company packed up for the trip back to town. A third of the population of London was dead of the plague.

*   *   *

The coach rumbled along the Oxford Road and past Tyburn Tree, and Nell knew she was almost home. The air was oppressive, the muggy afternoon sky clouded over and brooding. As they turned south toward Drury Lane, there was a searing bolt of lightning, and a clap of thunder exploded overhead, seeming to shake the earth itself. Rose started in shock beside Nell, and then laughed self-consciously. But Nell felt uneasy, too, and sensed from the others who rode with her that she was not alone.

Nell and Rose had given up their lodgings when they went to Oxford, as had Hart, and Nell realised that she had no home. The thought brought with it a stab of longing, a deeply animal instinct to seek a safe place to burrow.

'We'll go to the Cock and Pie for tonight,' Hart

said, watching the downpour. 'And then see what's what.'

As it happened, they took Nell's old room. She felt somewhat comforted to be back in the same place, and the familiar cracks in the walls and the dusty bubbled windowpanes seemed like old friends. Worn out from the journey, she climbed into bed and was lulled to sleep by the gentle sound of the rain pattering on the roof.

*　　　*　　　*

It was still raining when Nell woke, and from the bed she could see the grey sky and dark clouds. She looked at Hart beside her and ran her fingers over the scratchy stubble of his cheek. He stirred and pulled her closer to him. Nell felt safe as she always did when next to him, but worries about the future crowded into her mind. They were back in London, but what now? How long would Hart continue to support her? How long could he continue? She thought about the other girls who had been in Killigrew's company. Where were the Davenport sisters, Franki and Betty? Where were Margaret Rutter and Elizabeth Weaver? Had they found a safe port in the storm, or were they on the streets whoring or begging, or were they dead?

She thought back to those heady days when she had played in *The Indian Emperor*, reveling in the excitement of being an actress, glorying at sharing the stage with Hart. It had been too good to be true, that brief glimpse into heaven. Ease and happiness were not to be her lot in life. Why should she be different from Rose, who would like as not have to return to whoring; different from her mother; than any other of the thousands upon thousands of women in London, who had no choice but to earn their bread how they could, like it or not? The world was a hard place, and wishing it to be otherwise was a waste of time.

Hart stirred, and turned toward Nell with drowsy eyes. He saw the worry in her face and pulled her close.

'What's amiss, little one?'

Nell hesitated. She was afraid. Afraid to be too needy, to burden him with her fears.

'Hmm?' Hart prompted her, and leaned up on an elbow. She noted the faintest spray of freckles across the bridge of his nose, how his cheeks were bronzed from spending so much time outdoors in Oxford.

'It's just—I do not know how I will keep myself if the playhouse is not open. Unless I—' She stopped, unwilling to speak out loud what she still did not know if he knew. Unable to face him, she turned away and hugged her knees to her chest. Hart gently pulled her to face him.

'You will not have to sell yourself, honey. I have yet some money put by, thank God. Wheresoever I go, you will go, too. If you wish it. You'll not lack for food or drink or a roof over your head, or shoes for your pretty little feet.'

Nell burst into tears, angry at herself for the loss of control, for such transparent terror and dependence. But she was grateful. And held tight to Hart.

*   *   *

The next day, Nell and Rose sought out their

157

mother. The day was cold, and Nell pulled her cloak close around her as they neared the Golden Fleece. Only a few tipplers sat within, and Eleanor was nowhere in sight. Nell felt a clutch of fear at her stomach, then saw her mother ascending through the open hatch from the cellar, a keg in her arms.

'Mam!'

Eleanor turned at the sound of Nell's voice. At the sight of her daughters, her face crumpled and she began to weep, slumping to the floor.

'I thought I'd never see you more.'

Nell rushed to her mother and buried her face in her skirt. Eleanor's hands stroked her hair. Five years of buried pain surged to the surface, and Nell sobbed like a small child.

'We're back,' Rose said. 'We're all together now.'

*   *   *

London was changed. The ghosts of those who were gone walked the streets, hovered in the shadows, drew breath through the breaths of the living. Nell had gone to buy shoes to replace the pair she had worn since the previous year, now split and ragged. She found a used pair in fine condition at a stall, but the thought struck her that they might have belonged to some girl dead of the plague, and she left without buying them and headed back to Drury Lane.

The mounds of earth heaped over the graves and plague pits were still raw and grassless. Like new scars, Nell thought, as she passed by the churchyard of St. Giles. This parish had been one of the hardest hit, and the ground around the church was an ugly welter of trenches and heaps, damp greeny brown

158

stains marring the walls of the church, dirt spilling out through the churchyard fence, as though the dead had been packed in so tightly that the bounds of the churchyard could not hold them, and a hand or knee might burst through the blanket of sod.

An ancient and evil smell of rot rose from the soil, and Nell pinched her nostrils closed and covered her mouth with her hand as she hurried by. Night was coming on, and she quickened her pace, loath to be out of doors when dark engulfed the remaining light in the autumn sky.

The weather was growing colder. That was a blessing, as it seemed to lessen the effect of the plague. But Nell dreaded the darkness of winter, when the sun came up late and sank again too soon. Her spirits ebbed with the daylight, and she felt hemmed in and fearful in the grey bleakness. Christmas came, and the New Year. Nell was glad to see the back of 1665. It had begun promisingly enough, to be sure, but it had grown poor and meagre soon enough. Surely next year would bring better.

1666 began auspiciously. The king and court returned to Hampton Court. It was not London, but it was a step closer. Barbara Palmer had another baby by the king, and it was said the queen was finally with child.

Then came the news that France had declared war against England. Nell wished that both nations would go to the devil, if their warring delayed the long-awaited opening of the theatres.

The end of January brought a violent storm. Heavy rain battered the town, and the winds ripped tiles and bricks from their places, toppled chimneys, and wrought destruction among the ships and boats in the river, tearing vessels loose from their moorings and driving them against each other and blowing one ship completely over, so that its keel rose from the water like the fin of a great fish.

The spirit of the country mirrored the ravages of the storm when word came that the queen had miscarried.

*   *   *

On Candlemas, the second day of February, came Nell's sixteenth birthday, and with it the glad news that the court had returned to London.

'It won't be long now before we can open again,' Hart assured her. 'I met with Killigrew, Lacy, and Mohun today, and we've decided to use this idle time to make some improvements to the playhouse. We'll widen the stage, add some room for storage. God knows we need it, and we'll not get such a chance again.'

Nell finally let herself believe that the theatres would be open again soon when she went with Hart to inspect the progress of the work a couple of weeks later. Everything was in chaos and dirt, but it cheered her mightily, for out of the sawdust and plaster would emerge a bigger and more elegant stage, on which she would soon be acting.

'Nelly!' The familiar gravelly voice rang out from the stage as Dicky One-Shank stumped toward Nell.

'Dicky! I've thought of you often. How happy I am to see you well!'

'Aye, I'm aboveground and breathing, and that's enough in these times, we may say. I'm pleased to see you, pigsnie.' He pinched Nell's cheek and then turned to Hart. 'And right pleased to see you, too,

160

sir, and looking forward to the pleasure of watching you act again.'

'I'm going to act again, too!' Nell cried. 'In *The Humorous Lieutenant*! Remember? It played the day this theatre opened.'

'I remember it well.' Dicky nodded. 'And it'll be better than ever with you in it, sweeting.'

*   *   *

Nell was overjoyed to begin rehearsals for *The Humorous Lieutenant* and to be gathered once more at the playhouse with the other members of the company, with work before them.

'It seems an age since last we were here,' Kate Corey said.

'It has been an age,' Nell said. 'Truly, I never thought I'd play again.'

'Nor I,' agreed Betsy Knepp.

'Look how fine it all is here now,' Beck Marshall marvelled. 'I like this bigger stage, and it's so much better now everything is not all jumbled together in here with us.'

Sunshine flooded the greenroom, and the other actresses seemed to share Nell's high spirits. Talk turned to the latest gossip from court.

'They say Lady Castlemaine's newest baby looks as much like the king as if he'd spit him out of his mouth,' Betsy said.

'That's five babies in five years she's had,' laughed Kate. 'The king's obviously not put off by a breeding woman.'

'No,' said Beck. 'But he treats her like a mere wife. Visits her before breakfast and then goes off to see the beauteous Frances Stuart, I hear.'

161

'And the queen?' Nell asked.

'Keeps her mouth shut and prays for a baby of her own, I warrant,' Betsy said.

*   *   *

May the twenty-ninth, the king's birthday and the sixth anniversary of his return, was marked as it was each year with a day of public celebration. But that happy day was followed by a tremendous four-day battle at sea with the Dutch. The first wild reports of a great English victory were soon contradicted by the sombre news of a terrible defeat, with appalling loss of ships and men. Then came panicked rumours that the French were about to invade England. With no standing army and the navy woefully inadequate to defend against such a breach, hundreds of foot soldiers set sail from Blackwall to join the battle, and the navy began to press men into service once more.

'It's not right,' Dicky One-Shank growled. 'The press-gangs are seizing men off the streets. Labourers, merchants, artisans, men with no fitness for the sea, shipped against their will. They've not even been paid the press money they're due. How are their families to live?' Nell pitied the poor men and their families, and despaired at the knowledge that the war would further delay the opening of the playhouse.

Spring turned to high summer. There had been no rain since winter. The unpaved streets cracked and the hot wind threw up choking clouds of dust. Rain barrels and troughs went dry. The marshy slopes of the river turned from mud to baked clay. And as the weather grew hotter, the spectre of

162

the plague loomed. Nell knew well that the king would not reopen the theaters now, with the risk of contagion so great, and fought down her rising fears of what would become of her.

With Lammas Day, July passed into August. The plague had not erupted into the terror that it had been the previous summer, but the threat of it hung in the air.

The sun was barely up on the morning of Sunday, the second of September, when Nell and Hart were awakened by a clamorous alarm of bells. A knot of people gathered in the street below, fingers pointed east. Hart opened the window.

'What's amiss?' he called.

'A great fire,' a man shouted back. 'Near Fish Street.'

'That's a long way off,' Hart said, turning back to Nell. 'Near two miles. No need to fear, I think.'

But by late morning, plumes of smoke billowed into the eastern sky and cast a pall over the sun. Nell and Hart went across the road to the theatre and found Lacy, Mohun, and others of the company gathered there.

'It began in a baker's shop in Pudding Lane,' Lacy said, mopping his brow with a handkerchief. 'Whole streets of houses are gone—three hundred already, they reckon. St. Magnus's Church has burned, and the flames have spread to houses on the bridge.'

'Worse than that,' said Killigrew, coming in. 'The winds are whipping it on. It's got to Thames Street.'

'Christ,' said Hart. 'All those warehouses . . .'

'Standing cheek by jowl, and packed full of pitch, oil, wine, brandy,' Mohun said.

'Aye,' said Killigrew. 'It's like the fires of hell.'

163

Fear clutched at Nell's heart. What if the theatre should burn? What then?

'What will they do?' she asked, trying to keep her voice steady.

'The king has given orders to blow up houses in the fire's path, to create a break. It's the only way to hope to stop it leaping from building to building.'

'And us?'

'Wait and see,' Killigrew said.

But by afternoon, the fire was worse. More and more people of the company came to the theatre, and all the news was that the fire was burning rapidly westward.

'Folk who removed their goods this morning in hopes of safety have removed again,' Rose said.

'They say it was the French that set the fire to burning,' said young Richard Baxter, one of the scenekeepers. 'And now they've started another, further east.'

Night came, and from the street Nell could see that the eastern sky burned orange. She and Rose went down to the river and saw a flaming arc of fire a mile long, a vibrant golden corona shading upward into angry red. The whole of the City was engulfed in flames, and smoke clouded the night sky. The river was crowded with every kind of vessel. Boats crammed with people and laden with furniture, chests, barrels, musical instruments, and animals collided with jetsam that floated in the black water. Showers of hot ash and flaming bits of debris rained from the sky, hissing as they hit the river. Even at this distance, Nell could hear the roar and crackle of the fire. The horror of what was happening seemed in odd contrast to the beauty of the summer night, with the moon hanging bright in the balmy sky.

She tried to tell herself that all would be well, that surely the fire would be stopped before it reached Drury Lane. The magnitude of its destruction was too awful to face, and, exhausted, she went to sleep curled on a pile of cloaks in a corner of the greenroom, comforted by the rise and fall of voices nearby. She woke after a few hours to find the theatre was crowded with more people, not only actors and others from the playhouse, but their friends and families with nowhere to go. A sound like thunder reverberated in the distance, followed shortly by a second explosion.

'What was that?' she asked Hart.

'They're blowing up houses in Tower Street.'

'Tower Street? But that's east of Pudding Lane. Has the fire changed course?'

Hart shook his head. 'It's burning in all directions now. The Duke of York is patrolling the City with guardsmen, trying to keep some kind of order. I'm going out to see if I can get more news or be of any use.' He was buttoning up a buff coat, and the sight of him armouring himself with the thickly padded suede made Nell realise what peril he could be facing.

'I'm coming with you.'

'No, it's too dangerous.' His face was grim.

'I care not what happens to me if anything happens to you or to the playhouse,' Nell pleaded. 'If there's aught I can do I must do it.'

Hart shook his head in exasperation. 'Then at least put on some boots and breeches. You'll go up like a haystack if a cinder lands on your skirts.'

*   *   *

165

Nell hurried behind Hart down the southeastward curve of Drury Lane and Wych Street, fighting through the heaving crowds that streamed in the opposite direction, carrying with them what they could in carts and barrows and on their backs. Panicked people and animals shrieked, brayed, and shouted as they struggled their way westward.

The churchyard of St. Clement Danes was mobbed, its portico stacked with barrels and furniture. Hart stopped short as they came abreast of the church, where they had an unobstructed view down Fleet Street. Nell cried out in terror. A wall of flame spread over the eastern horizon as far as she could see, angry tongues lashing the sky. The fire was roaring toward them. A torrent of embers bounced and skipped along the ground like a river of fire. A pigeon shot past, its singed wings working furiously. The street seemed to be seething, and Nell realised with a shudder of revulsion that the movement was hundreds of rats scurrying away from the fire. Hart pulled her flat against a wall to prevent her from being run over by a wagon.

'Mr. Hart!' Dicky One-Shank's gravelly voice cut through the confusion as the old sailor stumped toward them. 'The king has called for help on the fire lines. I was on course for the playhouse to raise a crew.'

Hart turned to Nell before she could speak. 'No. I'll not hear of it. Go back to Drury Lane. You'll be of more use there. Tell Killigrew to send what lads he can spare—actors, scenekeepers, whoever is there—with buckets. And tell him to make ready to fly.'

166

Back at the theatre, Nell and Rose and the other women folded the best of the company's costumes into great chests while Killigrew packed the precious play scripts and promptbooks in a strongbox and went in search of a wagon. The frantic activity kept Nell's mind from dwelling on the fear of what danger Hart would be in so near to the fire and what would become of her if the theatre burned. Would she have to return to whoring? Only hope for the future had sustained her through the long wait in plague time. If the playhouse went up in smoke, her dreams with it, she didn't think she would have the strength to continue.

*   *   *

As darkness fell, Hart staggered into the greenroom, his face and clothes black with soot. Nell ran to him and threw her arms around him, not minding the reek of smoke in her relief to have him back. Then she cried out at the sight of his hands, scorched and blistered.

'Water,' he coughed, and he gulped it down when she brought it to him. The company gathered around and he stared at them, his haunted eyes bright in his sweat-streaked face.

'St. Paul's has fallen,' he said, his voice flat and hoarse.

'And Cheapside?' someone asked, and other voices chimed in.

'Newgate Market?'

'Thames Street?'

'The great houses by the river?'

167

'The theatre in Salisbury Court?'

'Gone,' he said. 'All gone.'

*   *   *

Nell slathered Hart's hands with grease and bandaged them in strips of linen.

'Are you hurting?' she asked.

'Not so much now,' he said. 'Only I wonder will I be able to play the fiddle when my hands have healed.'

Nell stared at him in horror and his lips twitched in a smile.

'It would be a miracle, indeed, as I could never play before.'

Nell began to laugh but it came near to turning into a sob. 'Don't frighten me so.'

'I'm sorry. Never fear. We'll come through it.'

'Will we?' Nell's fears were too enormous to voice. She looked into those dark eyes that had reassured and sustained her so often.

'Take heart, my little love. I'll not leave you to the wide world. While I have a home, you have one, too.'

*   *   *

An hour or so after Hart had returned, a tall stranger, hatless, his face swathed in a filthy kerchief, limped through the stage door. He cradled his bloody right hand against his chest, and Nell saw with shock that the sleeve of his long coat and the thigh of his breeches above his tall boots were soaked through with blood. He collapsed onto a bench, unwound the cloth from around his face,

168

and pressed it to his hand.

'Dear God,' Rose exclaimed, as the cloth bloomed crimson.

'Bene darkmans,' the man said in greeting, looking up at the alarmed faces around him. 'I'm sorry to intrude. I was struck by falling timbers. Crushed my arm and gashed my leg, and I'm losing blood that fast that I thought it best to get indoors before I fell in a swoon, though I feel like a cow-hearted granny to say it.' He gave a wry smile, but his face was deathly pale and he slumped back against the wall, his eyes closed.

'Don't move, sir, I'll tend to you,' Rose murmured, and she hastened back with a basin of water, a sponge, and clean linen strips. Nell helped her to remove the man's coat and waistcoat. He shuddered and set his jaw as Rose rolled up his bloody sleeve. He looked down at his limp forearm and hand and when he tried to move the fingers, he went even more pale.

'Broken, and badly at that,' he said. Rose, kneeling before him as she gently swabbed away the blood, looked with concern into his face, and he smiled down at her. 'Good thing heaven's sent me an angel to care for me, though I've little deserved it.' He was very handsome, Nell thought, or would be when his long dark hair was not soaked with sweat and dirt and his face was not caked with grime, and from Rose's blush she knew her sister agreed.

*　　　*　　　*

Late that night, Nell sat numb with exhaustion. It seemed centuries since Sunday morning, when she and Hart had woken to hear of the fire. What day was it now? Wednesday. She lay down and slept fitfully, uncomfortable on the hard floor, her dreams filled with fire.

She was awakened by excited voices. At first the words did not penetrate her sleepy haze, but suddenly she heard what was being said and sat up abruptly.

'It's out,' Lacy said again.

'It's out?' Nell asked, scrambling up.

'Aye,' he said. 'By the grace of God. And the hard work of the king and the Duke of York, among many others. His Majesty stood in the bucket brigade himself, working like a horse through the night.'

*   *   *

In the days following the fire, everyone was hungry for news, and stories and rumours flew.

'The king is calling for proposals for a new plan for the City,' Killigrew said. 'And to rebuild the churches. Eighty and more we lost.'

'Buildings can be replaced,' Hart said. 'I mourn for poor old James Shirley and his wife. It was his play *The Cardinal* that gave me my first great role. And now the pair of them are dead of fright and exposure for that their house burned and they had nowhere to go. It breaks my heart. Why did they not come to the playhouse?'

'There's to be a monument to those who died,' said Richard Baxter. 'And it will be graven in stone what all do know—it was the Papists that started it.'

'No one knows that,' Lacy said. 'And they say that by a miracle fewer than a dozen were killed.

170

But the City . . .' Nell felt an overwhelming need to see for herself.

'Come with me, Hart,' she begged. 'I want to know that something is still left.'

*　　　*　　　*

The air hung hazy and oppressive, dampening the sounds and the spirits of the City. The blood-red sun cowered behind curtains of grey, and black flecks of ash rose in listless eddies, as a sudden gust of dry wind drew them up and then spat them out, so that they drifted into and became part of the wash of grit and mud that fouled the streets even as far west as the Strand. Nell felt the foul air choking her and held a handkerchief over her nose and mouth.

As they made their way eastward, she felt a sense of dread and sadness, as if she were approaching a home in which there had been a death. As Fleet Street rose to Ludgate Hill, she clutched Hart's elbow and gasped. It was not so much what she saw as what she did not see that produced that sensation of a blow to the stomach, for the towering front of St. Paul's, as much a part of the landscape as the sky and the clouds, was gone. Its absence was palpable; the emptiness of where it should have stood was shocking in its blankness.

To the north, familiar streets and houses remained. But down to the river and eastward as far as Nell could see lay a rubble of stone and charred wood. What had been the bustling streets of the City were unrecognizable, buried in debris and impassable except by foot.

Nell and Hart skirted the desolate skeleton of

St. Paul's. Its ancient walls, which had seemed eternal, had fallen; its very stones had cracked and shattered in the heat. The lead of its roof had melted in the inferno and run into pools, now hardened into freakish frozen puddles. Curls of smoke rose and met the grey mist that hung over all—even now, fire still smouldered in the depths of the vast ruin.

They picked their way through what had been St. Paul's Churchyard, where London's booksellers had stood, and here and there Nell could discern the remains of books, their leather bindings charred black, the creamy purity of their pages sodden and smeared. An orange cat streaked by, yowling, its eyes wild, its fur blackened.

In Cheapside, parties of men with kerchiefs over their faces against the foul air were already at work at the unfathomable task of clearing the wreckage, heaping stones into piles, and loading into wagons what was beyond hope. Here and there others picked through the rubble or simply stood and stared at the emptiness that surrounded them.

Nell felt lost as she looked around her. She turned in desperation, striving to find some identifying marker that would provide connection between the streets of her memory and what lay before her.

'Oh!' She stopped short and pointed, realising that the shambles of stone on their right was what remained of St. Mary-le-Bow, and that most of the higher outcroppings that dotted the landscape were the remnants of churches, their stones having survived the fire better than the timber, plaster, and thatching of the surrounding houses.

Terror welled within Nell. Her heart raced and

her palms sweated. So much of what she had known was gone, and the realisation seemed to open a deep chasm that yawned before her. If so much that had seemed eternal could vanish overnight, what safety or certainty could there be in anything? The faces of Nick and the boys in the flickering firelight before the palace and in the shafts of moonlight in the park on the night of the king's return to London flashed into her mind like a nightmare. She felt once more Jack's rough hands seizing her, his rank smell smothering her as he pressed her to the bed.

Wild panic seized her and she began to run blindly towards the river. Hart called to her to wait, to stop, that she would harm herself in the treacherous ruins through which she plunged. But she could not, and she came to a halt only when she stood in the middle of what had been Thames Street. She had not known until that moment what it was she sought, but as she looked to the east, she knew. London Bridge and the Tower. Both still stood. She realised that if she had found that they, too, had been swept away, it would have been more than she could bear.

Her strength left her and, gasping, she sank to her knees. Hart caught up to her as she burst into tears of loss, of rage, of loneliness, of fear, and of relief. He knelt and held her close, stroking her hair, murmuring softly to her as she clung to him and wept. When her sobs subsided she drew away from him a little to wipe her eyes and nose on her sleeve. She tried to find the words for what she felt, but none came. She wept again and Hart pulled her to him.

'I understand,' he said. 'The loss of so much. Like a friend you do not pay enough mind to, and

173

then is gone, without warning.'

'Aye,' Nell said. 'Something like that. Let's go to the bridge. I need to feel it beneath me.'

They made their way arm in arm to the bridge and stood at the centre of its span, the sweep of London before them. A brutal swathe had been cut through it, from east to west along the river for more than two miles, and northward as far as the old City walls in places. This had been the ancient heart of London—the first tracks trampled into the riverside meadows by the Romans, and those same streets trodden every day in the centuries since. And now it was gone.

The wind whipped their clothes and hair. It smelled of the sea, and blew away the acrid reek of burning. Nell felt her heart beat within her, and the warmth of Hart next to her. And knew that she would go on, that he would go on, and that London, somehow, would go on.

Chapter Twelve

January, 1667

Audiences flocked to the playhouses once they were finally in business again, and Nell was giddily busy, performing Lady Wealthy opposite Hart's Mr. Wellbred in *The English Monsieur*, Celia in *The Humorous Lieutenant*, and Cydaria in *The Indian Emperor*. She watched the company's shows when she was not in them, and a new girl was now selling oranges alongside Rose. She had even won the grudging approval of her mother for her

174

advancement at the playhouse. And she had moved with Hart into lodgings in Bridges Street, just across from the playhouse.

The happiness of her life was beyond what she could have dreamed, Nell thought, as she and Betsy Knepp climbed the stairs to the women's tiring room. Betsy had taken Nell to her favourite frippery, where fashionable secondhand clothes could be found, and Nell clutched to her the precious package containing a bodice richly embroidered with flowers. She wore her newly purchased velvet cloak, and a black rabbit-fur muff hung from a ribbon around her neck.

'Why, there you are, Betsy!' a voice cried from the top of the steps. 'I was about to give you up as lost.'

'Good afternoon, Sam,' Betsy said. 'We've been shopping and we're behind our time. Nell, this is Mr. Pepys.'

'Your servant, Mrs. Nelly,' said Pepys, grinning. 'Delighted to make your acquaintance. I enjoyed you most heartily as Lady Wealthy. Your scenes with Hart are beyond compare. I won't detain you now, but perhaps you'll both join me for supper after the show?'

In the tiring room, Beck Marshall was already putting on her makeup. 'Sam found you, did he?' she asked. 'Good. He's been following me around like a tantony pig, 'til I was near to lose my patience. Oh, what tackle have you there?'

Nell and Betsy unwrapped their purchases for Beck's admiration.

'There were the most cunning shoes,' Nell said. 'Black with a red heel. And I truly have need of a good petticoat or two. But I was too short of

175

gingerbread to buy more than this.'

'Get you a gent who's flush in the pocket,' Beck advised.

'Like that Sam Pepys, now,' laughed Betsy. 'He runs the Navy Office and has dealings with the king and the Duke of York all the time, and always seems to be rhinocerical. You need a few like him, Nell, to smooth the way a bit.'

'I'd never. I'm happy with Hart.'

'Happy only goes so far,' said Beck. 'Hart's a duck, but give me a man with plenty of chink.'

*　　*　　*

Officially, no backstage visitors were permitted, but the women's tiring room was crowded each day with gentlemen on the prowl. Nell watched Anne Marshall, surrounded by a knot of admirers, and thought of the lines from a recent play: ''Tis as hard a matter for a pretty woman to keep herself honest in a theatre as 'tis for an apothecary to keep his treacle from the flies in hot weather, for every libertine in the audience will be buzzing about her honeypot.'

A newcomer entered the room and though he joined the knot of men near Anne, Nell saw him glance at her and immediately look away, and she sensed that he was watching her from the corner of his eye. Making a show of powdering her face and arranging her hair, she studied his reflection in the mirror. She knew she had not seen him before. The elegant cut and fine cloth of his coat, the delicate lace at his throat and cuffs, the gloss of the curling wig that cascaded over his shoulders, the arrogance and assurance of his carriage all proclaimed that here was a man who knew without doubt that he rested at the pinnacle of society and that what he wanted he would have.

The stranger glanced her way again for a fleeting moment and though his eyes had not met hers, she sensed that he was as keenly aware of her as a hound of its prey, his nostrils trembling with the scent of her. She found that her belly was surging with excitement.

'Nelly!' Sir Charles Sedley called to her from where he stood near Anne. 'Come out with us? Johnny, do you know Nell?'

The stranger shook his head.

'Mistress Nell Gwynn,' Sedley said, as they moved to join her. 'John Wilmot, Earl of Rochester.'

'Your humble servant, madam.' Rochester's eyes did not leave her as he bowed. He was tall, standing head and shoulders above her, and the intensity of his gaze made her catch her breath. There was a leonine glint in the golden brown eyes that raked her from head to toe. She could almost feel the quickening of his heartbeat as he looked down at her and felt her own pulse throbbing in her temple as she returned his bow.

And then she saw Hart at the door of the tiring room, and the expression of fear on his face hit her like cold water.

'Not tonight, I thank you, Sir Charles,' she faltered. 'I'm already engaged.'

*   *   *

'I'm sure I've not seen him before,' Nell said to Betsy later.

'No, he's been in Adderbury with his wife.'

'His wife?' Nell found herself unreasonably disappointed to learn that Rochester was married.

'Oh, aye,' said Betsy. 'I'm surprised you've not heard the story. Quite the roaring boy he is, and her family objected to his wooing, but he'll buckle to no man, so he kidnapped her.'

'Go shoe the goose!' Nell was incredulous, and yet it fitted entirely with her first impression of him.

'Truly,' Betsy said. 'Waylaid her carriage at Charing Cross with a coach and a gang of armed men and bundled her away. By the time the family tracked them down it was too late—they were married.'

'I'll warrant all the fat was in the fire then,' Nell said.

'Well and truly,' Betsy agreed. 'The king was in a rage. It was only because Rochester's father had been one of his bosom friends that Rochester didn't end up in the Tower. But apparently all is forgiven now. He's taken his seat in the House of Lords and moreover he's a groom of the bedchamber to the king.'

*   *   *

Nell was eager to begin rehearsals for *Secret Love*, the new play Dryden had written for her and Hart, and could scarce wait to learn her lines.

'This is priceless,' Hart laughed, flourishing the script. 'Dryden's got you to perfection. Listen, this is how Celadon describes Florimel. 'A turned up nose, that gives an air to your face . . . a full nether lip, an out-mouth, that makes mine water at it; the bottom of your cheeks a little blub, and two

178

dimples when you smile.' And let me read you the last scene, where we agree upon how we shall live as man and wife. Oh, this part will be the making of you, Nell.'

* * *

Nell loved every minute of playing Florimel, especially the scenes when she disguised herself as a young man in order to follow the lover whose fidelity she doubted. She always got an enormous laugh when she strode onto the stage in the character of an arrogant young spark, and the audience, well aware of her liaison with Hart, roared with laughter as Celadon and Florimel negotiated the terms of their marriage.

'"As for the first year,"' Hart led off, '"According to the laudable custom of new-married people, we shall follow one another up into chambers, and down into gardens, and think we shall never have enough of one another."'

'"But after that, when we begin to live like husband and wife, and never come near one another—what then, sir?"'

* * *

Nell was giddy with the resounding cheers and whistles that greeted her at the end of the play. The applause went on and on, drawing her back for curtain call after curtain call, and *Secret Love* ran for days.

It seemed that all of London flocked to see the show. When Nell looked out at the house as she delivered her lines, she always saw faces she knew

179

from her days as an orange seller, from Lewkenor's Lane, from the Golden Fleece. At Rose's insistence, even her mother came.

*　　　*　　　*

One afternoon after an especially riotous performance, Tom Killigrew intercepted Nell as she was headed to the tiring room.

'The Duke of Buckingham was in the house today. He has particularly asked me to present his compliments, and asks if you would be good enough to allow him to wait upon you in a few moments.'

Killigrew's normally expressive face was impassive. Nell had seen Buckingham at the playhouse, when he'd read his adaptation of *The Chances* to the assembled cast at its first rehearsal, but had never passed a word with him. Why had he chosen to send a formal request, instead of simply turning up in the tiring room like everyone else? And why was the manager of the King's Company acting as his messenger? Nell was mystified. But Buckingham, close friend and adviser to the king, was one of the most powerful men in England. And reputed to be the richest, Nell remembered.

'Of course,' she said. She turned away, then realised that she did not want to have this meeting, whatever it was, before the other members of the company.

'Mr. Killigrew,' she called. 'Would you ask His Grace to give me a few minutes? So that I may make myself presentable?'

*　　　*　　　*

Nell picked up her already-damp handkerchief and blotted it across her forehead and chest, then dusted powder across her face, hoping that it would dull the sheen of sweat without caking. She glanced in the mirror. Her hair was as good as it was like to get, the ringlets and curls pagan-wild in the damp heat of the tiring room.

Well. He had asked to see her, not she him. He had just had as good a view of her as anyone could desire, and she had been at her best today, she knew, carrying the house to wave after wave of laughter. So she had nothing to fear.

Lords were nothing new to her now, she reflected. And yet—the Duke of Buckingham. A duke was only one step below a prince, and some said this duke was less than that step, having been raised almost as brother to the king when his own father died. What was it Hart had said once? 'Like one of the royal pups.'

To counter her nervousness, she leaned back in her chair and breathed deeply of the familiar mixture of smells—sawdust, paint, tallow candles, gunpowder, dirt, and sweat, overlaid with the sweetness of face powder and perfume. Motes of dust drifted in the rays of summer evening sunlight that came through the high window.

She heard a footstep in the hall and half rose, then forced herself to sit again. She'd meet him like a lady. Or as close to that as she could manage. She turned as she heard the rap of his stick against the door, and then found herself rising, unable to keep her seat in his overwhelming presence.

He was very big, this duke—tall and broad, and his height and breadth emphasized by the fullness

181

of his wig and the feathered broad-brimmed hat that topped his finery. The richness of the burgundy fabric of his coat and breeches, the fall of soft lace at his throat and wrists, the gold buttons, and the gloss of the fine leather of his high boots overshadowed any show of wealth the gaudy costumes of the theater had to offer.

His eyes met Nell's and she felt her stomach lurch. With fear? Desire? For what? Surely not a carnal craving, but a coursing flame of longing to possess that assurance, that unquestioning belonging in the world. Though she'd bed him right enough, Nell thought, and think it no drudgery.

'Mistress Nelly.' His voice was deep, the accent not striking in any particular way except that it was somehow free of the cramped quarters of London.

'Your Grace.' Nell dropped her eyes and swept him a low curtsy, taking the opportunity of the break in eye contact to compose herself, to will her heart to slow and her damp palms to dry. As she met his eyes again, Nell found that he was smiling faintly and it steadied her.

'Will you not join me for supper?' So she was to be fed, at least. 'You must be famished after your labours.'

Was he mocking her? This man who had never known a moment's labour in his life? Perhaps he caught a flash of something behind her eyes, for he bowed again and gave her a smile that seemed to light the room. 'After your enchanting labours, which so deliciously relieve the daily dreariness of our lives.'

Nell suddenly felt that she stood on more solid ground than she had a few moments before, and

182

smiled back at him. 'It would be my great pleasure, Your Grace.'

* * *

Hart was in his shirt and breeches with a worn gown over them to keep warm when Nell crept in the door of his rooms.

'And so? What brings you down from Olympus so soon? Surely you didn't refuse His Grace the pleasure of your continued company?'

Nell felt flustered at the mockery in his words.

'I tried to find you,' she said. 'I asked Mr. Killigrew to tell you where I'd gone.'

'And so he did,' Hart said. 'And I'm sure everyone else in the company heard, as well.'

'Nothing happened,' she said. 'He took me to supper. We talked. And that was all. I wanted to come home to you, and here I am.' She knelt and laid her head on his lap. 'Don't be angry.'

Hart stroked her hair and sighed.

'I'm not angry. I just see what will come. So he didn't try to bed you tonight. But he will. You know it.'

'And if he does?' Nell asked, looking up into his eyes. 'Do you think it will change how I feel for you?'

'You will not mean it to,' he said after a moment. 'But yes. In time it will change you.'

March, 1667

The king had ordered a command performance of *Secret Love*. Nell was at Whitehall Palace and could scarce believe it. She recalled the night she had first

183

met the actors, how she had listened to Marmaduke Watson and Harry Killigrew talk about the theatre at court and longed to see it. And now she would be acting there, wearing a new costume constructed for her by the royal tailors. The rhinegraves breeches she wore when in disguise as a young man were slashed to the thigh, so that they flew open to show her legs, especially when she danced.

*   *   *

The performance was the best they had given. The king roared with laughter at Nell's personification of a cocky young gallant, and the audience clapped along as she danced the jig that had made her famous. Offstage, Hart swept her into his arms, beaming.

'You've never been better,' he cried. 'I'm so proud of you, my Nell.'

A sudden flurry of movement caught Nell's eye. The king had entered the room and was making his way straight to them. Nell dropped into a deep curtsy and flushed as she raised her head to find the king's eyes intently on her, his teeth showing in a broad grin. Despite his elegance, she could not help thinking there was something piratical about him.

'Mistress Nell,' the king said, ''od's my life, I scarce know where to begin. You captured the carriage and manner of a spark to perfection. I was thinking I would tell you that I had never been more entertained by anything in all my life than to see you as a blade, when you topped all in that final scene. 'Love until we no longer can,' forsooth!'

He turned to Hart. 'And you, sir. You never disappoint, and you are a prince among players, but by God, I think you've met your match in the wench!'

'You speak the truth, Your Majesty,' Hart laughed. 'I try to hold my own against her, but it would take a better man than I to steal a scene from Nell.'

*   *   *

Everything seemed wrong the next day as Nell worked with Hart to learn lines for their new play, *All Mistaken*.

'Your wits are woolgathering.' Hart spoke sharply. 'Pay attention if you want to get through this scene. I have to get ready in half an hour.'

He was right. Nell's mind had been on the excitement of the performance at court, and the fact that not only the king but both Buckingham and Rochester had been there and had come back to pay their addresses after the show. Hart's voice, reading her next line, had penetrated somewhere at the back of her mind, but she could not have repeated the words if her life depended on it. And she had so many lines to learn.

'I'm sorry, Hart,' she said. 'Read it to me again.'

'"I tell the fat man I cannot marry him till he's leaner, and the lean man I cannot marry him till he's fat. So one of them purges and runs heats every morning to pull down his sides, and the other makes the tailor stuff his clothes to make him show fatter,"' he read, and she repeated it. She did love the part of Mirida. James Howard had written the play for her and Hart, capitalising on their success in *Secret Love*. Once more Nell disguised herself as a young man, providing the opportunity to display

185

her legs, and once more she and Hart jousted and sparred wittily, but ended up happily together at the end. The theatre was almost counting the ticket sales already.

*   *   *

The play banned?' Nell asked, stunned. 'The theatre closed? Lacy locked up? But why?' Hart had just come home from the first performance of Edward Howard's new play, *The Change of Crowns*.

'Because the king was there and flew into a towering rage.'

'For what cause?'

'The play sails mighty close to the wind in making light of the court,' Hart said. 'And Lacy was so flown with his own wit that he threw in a handful of extra jests at the expense of the king, in the presence of not only His Majesty, but the queen, the Duke and Duchess of York, and half the court.'

Nell threw up her hands in frustration. 'What are we to do? How long will we be closed?'

'I don't know.' Hart sank onto the bed, his head in his hands. 'Pray God not long. Mohun's gone to beg of the king that he might relent.'

'Will you run my lines with me as you're home?' Nell asked.

'Not now. My head is so full of this I cannot think.'

Nell's heart melted to see him so troubled, and she went to him. 'Come. Your neck and shoulders are in knots. Lie down and let me knead them for you. It will all come right, I'm sure.'

A couple of hours later, Mohun knocked on Hart's door.

'His Majesty has agreed we can play tomorrow, but not *Change of Crowns*, of course. What'll it be instead? *Secret Love*?'

'Pox on it,' Hart said. 'No, not that, we've played it too much lately. We have *Epicene* on for next week. I suppose we can throw that up instead. But not with John. Nick Burt will have to go on as Otter.'

'Right,' said Mohun. 'Rehearsal in the morning then. I'll send someone round to let the actors know.'

*　　*　　*

The company was to perform *Secret Love* at the palace three days later, but Nell did not look forward to it as she had her first command performance of the play only a few weeks earlier. Lacy was still locked up, and she felt as if she were venturing into the lion's den to play.

The actors usually enjoyed their performances at court, but the rest of the cast seemed to share her feelings, and they were uncharacteristically subdued as they arrived at Whitehall. As she made herself ready, Nell glanced down the table. Betsy Knepp, Kate Corey, Beck and Anne Marshall, Franki and Elizabeth Davenport, and Margaret Rutter sat in a row, silently focused on their images in the mirrors set up to face them.

'It'll be like pulling teeth to get laughs tonight,' Nell murmured to Betsy.

'You're right there,' Betsy agreed. 'Feels like we're getting ready for a hanging, not a comedy.'

'Don't even say that,' Nell said, putting down her powder puff. 'Not with John Lacy under lock and

187

key.'

'Oh, the king won't go that far,' Betsy said. 'Though I thought he'd have a fit right enough on Monday, with Lacy throwing out lines extempore right in his face, practically calling him a thief and a cheat for the selling of places at court.'

Nell struggled to be comfortable on the stage that night, and for the first time her usually triumphant scene with Hart at the end failed to get its usual laughs. The mood at the playhouse was grim the next morning when she and Hart arrived for a rehearsal of *All Mistaken*, and the afternoon's performance of *The Surprisal* felt leaden. More than ever, she hated having to play a serious part, although, she considered as she sat in the tiring room after the show taking her makeup off, at least in a tragedy she wasn't waiting for laughter that didn't come.

Angry voices rose from the greenroom below. Kate Corey looked at Nell.

'That sounds like Lacy.'

No doubt about it, it was Lacy's voice, now raised in a shout. Nell and Kate sprang to their feet and rushed down the stairs.

John Lacy, his clothes dirty and rumpled, his round face red and sweaty, stood faced off against Sir Edward Howard, the playwright of *The Change of Crowns*.

'Because of your poxy play I've been locked up for three days!' Lacy shouted.

'In the porter's lodge at the palace! Drinking wine and taking your ease, no doubt,' Howard scoffed. 'Don't make out as if you were in Newgate with the cutpurses and whores!'

'By God, then you try how you like it!' Lacy

188

retorted, shaking his walking stick at Howard. 'Locked up is locked up. No change of shirt, let alone wine to drink.' Actors, scenekeepers, and behind-the-scenes visitors were crowding into the room, drawn by the sound of the argument.

'Don't cry to me, sir,' Howard said, drawing himself up. 'It's not my play that's got you in trouble but your confounded additions. No wonder the king was in a rage. Damned impertinence!'

Lacy appeared ready to swallow his tongue with rage, and took a step toward Howard, towering over the little playwright.

'Impertinence! True enough that my family be not high like yours, yet I'll have you remember that I'm a shareholder and manager of this company, sir, and I am no hireling to do your bidding.' There were mutterings of agreement from the gathered actors.

'I am a gentleman, sir, and a poet!' Howard cried. He looked like a bantam rooster taking on a yard dog, Nell thought.

'Poet!' Lacy shouted. 'You're more a fool than a poet!' Someone laughed out loud at that, and the sound seemed to push Howard over the edge. With one of his beribboned gloves, he slapped Lacy across the face.

'That, sir, is the action of a gentleman. Do you dare acknowledge the insult?'

'I'll acknowledge it right enough,' Lacy roared, 'like the honest common Yorkshireman that I am.' He thumped Howard over the head with his walking stick, and Howard fell back, appearing more shocked than hurt. Hart was at Lacy's side, pulling him away, and Mohun rushed to restrain Howard.

''Fore God, John, get hold of yourself, man,' Hart begged.

'Did you hear what he said?'

'I heard, but let it go, or you'll only make things worse for yourself. You're free now and all's well.'

'And what are you all looking at?' Lacy roared at a knot of gentlemen who had stood watching the argument like a tennis match. 'Get out! Go home!' Taken aback, the gawkers departed.

Howard picked his hat up from the floor and jammed it onto his head. Nell thought she could practically see steam coming out of his ears.

'You have not heard the last of this, I vow,' he said. 'I'll to the king, and he shall teach you your lesson.' He stumped off toward the stage door. Once he was gone, the air seemed to go out of Lacy, and he sagged onto a bench.

'I'm sorry, Charlie. Sorry, Mick.'

'Never mind,' said Hart. 'It'll pass.'

'Yes,' said Mohun. 'I'll to the king again. But I don't think we'll be playing tomorrow.'

As Nell left, the scenekeeper Richard Baxter was tearing down the playbill that had been posted outside the theatre, announcing the next day's play.

'A bad business.' He shook his head. 'How are we to eat if we cannot play?'

*   *   *

Despite Mohun's entreaties, the king insisted that the playhouse would remain closed. But he knew the entire company suffered hardship if they could not play, and Lacy was a great favorite of his. So, having made his point, he relented after a week, and the next Saturday the playhouse put on

190

Bartholomew Fair. A week after that, Lacy was back onstage and charming the crowds once more, in his famous role as the country fool Thump in *The Changes*.

*   *   *

Shortly after the hubbub over *The Change of Crowns* came the first performance of *All Mistaken*. Nell's role of Mirida, another saucy, gamesome wench, fell solidly in the mould of the parts in which audiences so loved her.

'"I'll lay my head,"' she began, '"ne'er a girl in Christendom of my age can say what I can. I'm now but five years i' the teens, and I have fooled five several men. My humour is to love no man, but to have as many love me as they please, come cut or long tail!"'

After her first scene, Nell saw Dicky One-Shank and several of the scenekeepers gathered in the wings.

''Fore the devil, I doubt I've ever laughed so hard,' Dicky said, giving her a slap on the back. 'Keep it up, Nell, and I'll go to my grave with a smile on my face.'

'He's right,' Richard Baxter agreed, grinning. 'This one'll play for a while, and no mistaking.'

'That's our girl!' Matt Kempton laughed. 'Our own Nell!'

The laughter built with each successive scene. Nell and Hart were on fire, and Nell knew it.

At the end of the play, Nell came offstage elated, the applause still echoing in the house. Hart kissed her as soon as they were in the wings, his eyes shining with love and pride. Lacy stood there, beaming, but seeming on the verge of tears. He pulled her into his arms and kissed the top of her head.

'What a show you gave today!' he cried. 'Wat would be right proud of you. There is not one thing I'd tell you to do different, sweetheart. You've taken all we've taught you to heart and put it to work with the gifts God gave you and what no one could teach you.'

Rose rushed toward them, nearly dropping her basket in her haste to crush Nell in a hug. 'Oh, Nell, I'm that proud of you!' she cried. 'You were born for the stage, wasn't she, Mr. Lacy?'

'Indeed,' Lacy agreed. 'Our girl's done right by us, hasn't she, Charlie?'

'She has,' Hart said. 'I knew all the world would be in love with her, and so they are.' His smile was affectionate and proud, but there was a shadow of sadness behind his eyes. Nell put her hand in his, and he raised it to his lips and kissed it. 'Our own Nell, with the world at her feet.'

The next day, Dorset, Sir Charles Sedley, and Harry Killigrew ambled into the tiring room before the performance.

'Need any help dressing?' Harry leered.

'Shoo,' Nell laughed, flicking a powder puff at him. 'How can I be expected to concentrate with the likes of you running about underfoot?'

'I could concentrate your mind wonderfully,' Dorset drawled, leaning against the dressing table, where he had a view down Nell's bosom.

'I could do it better,' Sedley argued, coming to her other side.

'Mayhap we should all have a go, and see who succeeds best,' Harry said, moving close behind her and sliding his hands over her shoulders.

Nell looked from one to the other. 'I think the three of you are mighty full of talk,' she laughed up at them.

'Nelly—' Hart's voice broke off as he took in the scene, Harry's hands on Nell's bosom, Dorset and Sedley lounging on either side of her. Nell slapped Harry's hands away and jumped to her feet. Harry chuckled and Nell rounded on him.

'Get out, the three of you,' she snapped. 'Could you not have heeded me before?'

The three men exchanged glances and made for the door where Hart stood, thunder in his face.

'Hart,' said Harry, smirking as he passed. 'Always a pleasure.'

*   *   *

'It's coming, Nell,' said Hart, later that night. 'You won't admit it even to yourself yet, but one day not long from now you'll find you've come to hate me because of what I cannot be and what I cannot give you, when you're offered such temptation as daily parades itself before you.'

'My Hart, my heart, I could never hate you,' Nell whispered. 'Harry's a fool.'

'It's not just Harry,' Hart said. 'It's all of them. With their money and power and youth. I've loved you so, Nell. It would be more than I could bear to see contempt for me in those bright eyes of yours.'

'But I love you!' Nell cried.

'Do you? Then do this for me. Take your freedom. Move to your own rooms. And if at the end of three months you still want me, I'll be here.'

193

Chapter Thirteen

May Day. Nell had heard the fiddle from her room upstairs at the Cock and Pie and run down half dressed, in her skirt and smock, to see the milkmaids dancing. Their pails were decked with little nosegays of flowers and their sleeves were adorned with ribbon garters.

'Mistress Nelly!' Sam Pepys was waving his hat as he made his way grinning across the road toward her. 'A splendid day, is it not?'

'It is indeed,' Nell answered, smiling at his good humour.

'I'm seeing the play this afternoon, but I believe you are not in it, alas?'

'No,' Nell said. 'A rare day off for me.'

'Indeed.' Pepys seemed not to want to leave. 'A well-earned rest, I make no doubt. Though my pleasure in any play is always less when it lacks your talents. I hope you have no thought of quitting the stage?' He'd heard, Nell thought. Damnation. Did all London know that she and Hart had split?

'You're too kind, Mr. Pepys. But no, I assure you, you'll find me back on the boards tomorrow.'

She watched Pepys hurry off down Drury Lane, and sadness gripped her. It would be a wonderful day for a walk out to Islington or by the river, and many such a day she had enjoyed with Hart, needing only his company to make her happy. His lodging was within sight, just across Catherine Street. But she feared he would not welcome her knock at his door. Another lonely day to face.

It was ironic, Nell thought, swabbing the makeup off her face after another uproarious performance, that at the very time that she and Hart were no longer lovers in real life, they were a resounding success as a couple onstage. London could not get enough of them. The playhouse was doing so well with *Secret Love* that Killigrew had revived Dryden's earlier comedy *The Wild Gallants* and an addition had been written into *The Knight of the Burning Pestle* parodying *Secret Love*, and Nell was also to give a specially written new prologue. The Duke's house, in an effort to ride on the coattails of Nell and Hart's success, had hastily put up a play in which Moll Davis dressed as a boy and danced, but it faltered in the face of the new sensation produced by Nell and Hart in *All Mistaken*.

Nell smiled to remember how she had burned with jealousy when Dicky One-Shank had told her about Moll's first appearance on the stage. Five years ago that had been. A lifetime, it seemed.

A movement at the door caught her eye. The Earl of Rochester stood there. He moved forward until he stood directly behind her, his tigerlike eyes holding hers in their reflection. She found that she could hardly breathe. Without having spoken a word, he grasped her around the waist with both hands and pulled her close against him. He pulled aside the curls at the back of her head, and softly bit the nape of her neck. Nell gasped and found herself arching against him.

Finally, he spoke.

'Come.'

Nell only nodded. He took her by the elbow and

195

led her out the stage door, then handed her into the carriage that waited there. As the carriage started forward, he regarded her with a languid smile.

'Are you hungry?'

The question was so incongruous that Nell laughed.

'I am, but damned if this is not the most abrupt invitation I've ever had, my lord.'

'Call me Johnny.'

The carriage was moving through Lincoln's Inn Fields, and in a few moments it drew up before an imposing house next to the Duke's Playhouse in Portugal Street. The door was opened by a liveried servant, and as Rochester led Nell upstairs, he called over his shoulder, 'Bring up supper and leave it in the outer room.'

Upstairs, he pulled Nell into the bedroom, kicking the door shut behind him.

'Undress yourself,' he commanded, and watched while she obeyed. His eyes on her lit fires deep within her belly. He threw off his coat and waistcoat as she knelt and opened the flies of his breeches. She took him into her mouth hungrily, devouring him. His gasps told her that he was as inflamed as she, but after a few moments he withdrew, positioned her on hands and knees on the bed, and took her from behind, pulling her to him as he thrust deep inside her. He spent quickly, then let go and lay beside her, panting.

'Supper,' he said. 'And then we'll do it again properly.'

*   *   *

'Maybe it's good,' Rose said. 'Think of it—you've

196

been with men for money, and then only with Robbie and Hart. You're under obligation to no one. He has a wife, but that's his lookout. As long as you keep your eyes open and your wits about you, what's the harm? Does he please you?'

'Yes,' Nell said with a shiver. 'I can scarce keep from laying my hands on his tackle the moment I see him.'

'I feel the same about my Johnny,' said Rose. 'He's a rogue, but I can't help myself.' Ever since the night of the fire, she had been keeping company with John Cassells, the handsome stranger who had stumbled into the playhouse, and had lately moved into his lodgings.

* * *

Nell lay with Rochester beside her in the tangled bed linen. She was utterly spent, yet felt more alive than she had ever been. Her nether regions were still humming from Rochester's attentions. She had not known it was possible to experience a sensation quite like that his tongue had produced in her. 'Tipping the velvet,' he had called it. Certainly she had never imagined anything like that inexorable build to the shattering release that had had her gasping, bucking, pulling his head to her, never wanting it to end.

Rochester brought her back to the present with a squeeze of her right breast.

'Fetch the wine.'

Nell turned her head. The wine lay on the table several feet away.

'Why me fetch it?'

'Because I told you to.'

She padded naked across to the table, returned with the bottle, and filled the glasses they had abandoned. Propped against the enormous down-filled pillows, she surveyed the bed and its trappings.

'I love this bed. It's so . . .'

'This bed is your stage,' Rochester said. 'From such a stage you could do anything.'

Nell set the glass down and moved on her knees closer to him. He kissed her deeply, his tongue probing her mouth. He seized first one breast and then both of them, his fingers playing on her nipples, teasing and then pinching until she gasped.

He looked intently into her eyes, and pinched harder.

'Give me drink.' She held the glass to his lips and then to her own.

'You've spilled.' He used a finger to wipe a drop from her breast, touched it to her lips, and then thrust it into her mouth.

'Suck. Now use your tongue, too.' He watched her. 'Good. Now stop.'

He withdrew his finger slowly from her mouth and pulled her head back so that she had to look at him, then released her and gestured for his wine. Nell felt a curious excitement and anticipation.

'You look pleased with yourself,' he said.

'Should I not?' she replied. 'You liked it. See, I've made you hard again.' She reached for his cock, but he stayed her hand.

'Yes. But I can make you better. So good that you can leave the feel of your tongue and throat on a man's tarse for days.'

Nell smiled at him, catlike. 'Very well, my lord. What would you?'

She knelt between his thighs, her hand still moving lightly, her eyes looking up at him.

Rochester shook his head, impatient. 'Do you not understand? What power there is in that mouth, these sumptuous tits, that tight cunny of yours?'

'Power to do what?'

'Almost anything. Now you can give a man a quick ride that leaves him happy or a night of play that tires him. But there is more to learn. You can give a man such pleasure, not just in his body but in his mind, his soul, that you become a drug. So that he will crave you. So that his bollocks will ache and give him no peace until his prick is once more master of that smooth warmth. And I can train you, pretty pet. Do you want that?'

Nell found that her heart was beating and her loins were on fire. She looked up at Rochester and found that she could hardly breathe.

'Yes, my lord.'

'Good. On your knees. No, off the bed. For this is your god, and you must worship it.'

He moved to the edge of the bed and stood, and she knelt at his feet. She took his cock in her hands and kissed it, then took him into her mouth slowly.

'Look at me.' Nell didn't lift her eyes but took him further into her mouth. Rochester grasped a handful of her hair and yanked her head back.

'Look at me. So that I know that my pleasure is all your world.' Nell, breathless now, nodded, and kept her eyes on his.

'Now a little harder. Good. Use your tongue. Delicately. Ah, yes, so good. The desperate softness of your tongue, and the insistent sucking of your mouth. Now a hand on the cods. Gently, gently.

They are spun of pure silk, of cloud.'

For all the times that Nell had performed this act, she felt as if she had never before truly noticed the feel of a prick in her mouth, of bollocks in her hand. Her tongue slid voluptuously around him, feeling the velvet softness.

'Now,' said Rochester, his breath faster, 'the other hand on the shaft. First lightly, then a firmer grip. Up and down. Meeting your mouth on its downward journey. Good. A little harder now. Now think of your tongue again. Look at me. Yes, and use your hand to keep the foreskin pulled back. Don't forget the bollocks.'

His head was thrown back, his breathing heavy. Nell marveled how she could be giving him pleasure in so many ways at once and sought to feel each individual sensation at the same time. He looked down at her again and slowed his movements.

'Now put a finger in my arse. Look at me. Let me see the promise of what is to come. Yes, gently, slowly. Now, take all of it in, show me you're hungry for it. Your mouth moving, sucking hard, tongue caressing, hand on the cods. Yes. Good. Remember—I am your god. Take me as far down your throat as you can.'

He guided her with a hand grasped in her hair, the other hand rolling and squeezing one of her nipples, which were hard as pebbles.

'Do you love my cock?'

Nell found that she did.

'Do you worship it, my *arbor vitae*, my tree of life?'

Yes, that, too.

'And do you now wish for holy communion?'

Here it was, the culminating inevitability, and

Nell did wish for it.

'Then you shall have it.' Rochester came deep in her throat, holding her head fast with one hand, the other hand pinching her nipple hard.

'Swallow. Waste not a precious drop. Now look at me. Let me see it in your eyes. It's the nectar of life. Sweeter than honey, more potent than brandywine. And what you crave above all else. Yes. Now, a kiss to finish. Obeisance to your lord.'

Nell did as he told her, her lips and nose grazing the damp and delicate flesh.

'Eyes on mine.' She looked up at him, mouth still nuzzling. He stroked her hair, smoothing the tangled curls from her flushed forehead, and nodded.

'Do that, and there is nothing that you cannot do.'

Nell felt overwhelmed by physical sensations—a tingling mixture of pleasure and pain, the feel of him in her mouth, and the caustic warmth of his spend still at the back of her throat—and a tumult of feelings—joyful submission, exultation, astonishment at the newness of it all. She stared up at Rochester and shook her head in amazement.

'How ever did you learn all this?'

Rochester gave a lazy smile as he sat on the edge of the bed and leaned back against the pillows. 'That's what Europe is for.'

*　　　*　　　*

Nell was both elated and exhausted. She was playing most days, in *All Mistaken*, *Secret Love*, *The Surprisal*, *The Committee*, *The Knight of the Burning Pestle*. And most nights were fevered bouts in

Rochester's bed.

Whether anyone knew of the affair or no, Rochester's rough and implacable wooing seemed to have sounded an inaudible chime, an alarum of desire that drew men to her as never before.

Dorset had been several times to see *All Mistaken*, and each time he visited her backstage. Today, his eyes were hot as he gazed down at her, and she felt a tremor of excitement as he took her hand. Rochester had awakened in her an intense and bestial desire that would now not be quieted.

But she forcefully thrust these sensations away. Rochester's words had opened her eyes. Dorset, and all like him, could be her making or her ruin. All depended on how she played her hand. So she coolly accepted Dorset's compliments. She was cordial, but no more. She gave him no special mark of favour among the other sparks who pressed around her, though inwardly she was comparing him and found that he far exceeded anyone she had ever met, except Rochester, in every quality that shouted his wealth, power, advantages, and the nobility of his birth and upbringing. All the features, she realised, that made every instinct in her incline to be intimidated by him, to want to please him, to fear the loss of his favour.

But she resisted these impulses and refused his invitation to dine. She was still standing by herself, shaking with the effort of the part she had just played, and resolutely pushing thoughts of Charles Hart from her mind, when Betsy Knepp popped her head in at the tiring room door.

'What's amiss?' Betsy asked. 'You look as though you've seen the ghost of Hamlet's father.'

'No. Only the Earl of Dorset.'

'Oh, aye?' Betsy raised her eyebrows. 'And?'

'And nothing.' Nell shrugged, aiming for nonchalance. 'I think he's—interested.'

'Good on you,' Betsy breathed.

'I must consider what to do. I've sent him away.'

'You sent him away?' Betsy giggled incredulously.

'Yes.'

'Well played, Nell. Excellently well played.'

*   *   *

Nell was preoccupied with the world of the theatre and took little notice of talk about troubles abroad. There was always some difficulty, it seemed, with France or Holland or someone else, and it had little to do with the here and now. But on the twelfth day of June, she arrived at the playhouse to find the greenroom packed with a chattering and nervous crowd, as it had been during the days of the fire.

'Is there trouble?' she asked Lacy.

'Trouble and plenty of it,' he said, distractedly running his hands through his hair. 'The Dutch slipped up the river during the night. They've burned two ships that were at anchor near the Tower and captured the *Royal Charles*. It's war. And we're closed again, until the king says we're not.'

A cold knot formed at the pit of Nell's stomach. Not now! Not when life was finally going her way. She had no Hart to save her now, and she had no way of riding out a long period with no work. She felt herself possessed by fear that was near to panic. She must do something, must find shelter and safety from the gathering clouds.

Nell looked over at Rochester. She'd learned his lessons well, and that night she had drawn out his pleasure until he could bear it no more and finished with an explosive climax deep within her arse, driving hard, his desire fuelled by her cries of ecstatic pain.

'Johnny, you've heard the theatres are to be closed?' He grunted, eyes closed.

'Would you not like it if I were with you more?' He was near to snoring. Pox, he was not going to take the hint, and she would have to be blunt.

'Johnny. I need money. It would cost you little to keep me.'

Rochester opened his eyes, reached across her to retrieve the wine bottle, and chuckled.

'What?' Nell prodded. 'Why are you laughing?'

'At the irony, my darling strumpet. It would be perfect but for the fact that my wife has grown tired of being alone in the country and is shortly to join me here in London. Which is not an insurmountable problem, I grant you, but it makes it less convenient for me to swive you day and night.'

Nell waited, hoping. It had not occurred to her that he might say no.

'What about Dorset?' Rochester said. 'I know he's been nosing around your honeypot of late. And he's good for more ready cash than I've got right now, I'd be willing to wager.' Nell had not been prepared for this suggestion. A memory flashed to her mind of Dorset's eyes hot on her and the desire it had roused in her.

'Perhaps,' she said slowly. 'But I can't skip up to his front gate and offer myself to him.'

'No.' Rochester considered. He had been absentmindedly playing with Nell's right breast and now heaved himself on top of her, positioning himself between her thighs. 'He's a bullheaded fool, and would only balk and bridle if I spoke to him directly. But we have many friends in common, Charlie and I, and he'll seize the bait like a good 'un if he but hears you're looking for a keeper and he thinks it's his own idea. Ask him for fifty pounds a year.'

He grunted with enjoyment as he entered Nell, and moved slowly, his eyes closed and his head thrown back. Nell thrust up to meet him, enjoying both the sensation of him inside her and the knowledge of what pleasure she was giving him.

Rochester opened his eyes and looked down at her intently, moving harder and faster now. She clasped him to her and tightened the muscles inside her. Rochester drew in a sharp breath, grasped a handful of her hair, and thrust deeper. He leaned in and growled into her ear.

'No. Ask him for a hundred pounds a year.'

*   *   *

As if on cue, the next day Dorset sent word to the playhouse that he would be gratified if he might wait on Nell that evening.

He arrived on the stroke of seven, as the bells from St. Martin-in-the-Fields, St. Giles, and churches farther away sounded in the fading light of the summer evening. He was outwardly self-assured, but beneath the ease of manner, Nell

205

could sense his desire, and that he had come with a purpose. He had taken Rochester's hook, and it now remained only for her to pull him in gently.

Dorset directed his carriage to the Swan Tavern in the palace yard, which was so crowded with gallants of the town that Nell felt as conspicuous as if she were onstage when they entered.

'I've taken a house in Epsom for the summer,' Dorset said, eyeing her over his wineglass. 'Charles Sedley's coming. It promises to be a delightful holiday.'

Nell smiled, her heart pounding.

'I hope,' Dorset continued, 'that the unfortunate news that the playhouse has been closed means that you might be at leisure to join us. I know that your absence from the stage would mean the loss of your livelihood, and of course I would be pleased to find a way to compensate you.'

And now we've got down to brass tacks, thought Nell, watching his eyes.

'I am prepared to offer you seventy-five pounds,' he said easily. 'Which I hope will make up what you will lack from employment.'

It was a lot of money. Far more than she had ever had the promise of. But Nell willed herself to be calm.

'One hundred pounds, my lord,' she said, 'would be nearer the mark.'

Dorset's eyebrows shot up in surprise.

'Indeed?'

'Yes, sir,' said Nell. 'I should not want to find myself having to return to town should the playhouse reopen of a sudden, for lack of means to keep myself.' She looked him in the eye and gave him a smile freighted with promise. 'But for one hundred pounds, my lord, I shall be entirely at your disposal.'

*   *   *

Even as she had been striking her bargain with Dorset, at the back of Nell's mind lay thoughts of Charles Hart. Her feelings for him were entirely different from those she had for Dorset, so much so that he seemed to exist almost in a different world, but now those worlds could not be kept apart. He had no claim on her, it was true, but still she felt a pang at the thought of telling him outright that she was now Dorset's mistress.

Dorset had taken possession of his new property the previous night after supper, after laying out a down payment of ten pounds. And in the morning, as his coach left Nell at the door of the Cock and Pie, Hart was heavy on her mind. Best to get it over with, she thought, and instead of going up to her room she went to find him.

Hart was home and as soon as he opened the door, Nell knew that she was already too late. He looked weary, and his handsome face wore an ironic half smile as he waved her in and shut the door behind her.

'I know, I've heard,' he said. 'You've gotten a good price, I hope?'

There was no use trying to put any kind of a false face on it.

'A hundred pounds a year.'

'Then you've done well for yourself. Much better than I could give you.'

The blow hit Nell in the heart.

'Don't say that,' she pleaded. 'You know that

with you it was different.'

Hart looked at her steadily. 'Was it?'

'Yes. I loved you. I love you still. But . . .' She trailed off.

'I know,' he said. 'You must look to your future.'

They were both silent for a moment. Nell heard the cry of an oyster peddler outside on the street, and the briny smell of the barrels and heaviness of the barrow handles in her hands came vividly back.

'Yes,' she said. 'I must look to my future. We're to go to Epsom in a few days, but I'll see you—' She didn't know when she would see him again, and her heart felt as though it were constricted in a wire cage. She went to him and tried to put her arms around him, but he pushed her away.

'Go now,' he said. 'And I wish you luck.'

Chapter Fourteen

The bed dominated the room. It stood like its own little kingdom—high from the floor, with a little step stool to climb into its soft embrace. Huge posts rose at the corners, dark wood ornately carved with acorns and oak leaves, fading into the shadows of the canopy above. The heavy bed curtains were of damask, gold flowers woven into the deep red of the silk. Closed, they would make the bed a little room of its own, a private world of secrets and games. But now they were drawn back, held by heavy silken cords.

Nell climbed onto the bed and bounced, sinking into the soft caress of the feather bed. There was a bank of pillows, plump with down. She laid her head against them and felt the exhalation of air.

She looked around the room with satisfaction. Candles flickered on little tables at either side of the bed and from brackets in the walls. The warm and mysterious glow played over the Turkey carpet on the floor and the tapestry hangings on the walls, the corners and ceiling of the room receding into deep brown depths of shadow.

A little off from the bed stood three chairs around a small round table, set with wine and goblets, bread, cheese, roasted chicken, strawberries, and grapes, the fruit spilling in artless profusion from a pewter bowl and onto the linen tablecloth.

The window casements were open, and a whisper of warm breeze brought with it the smell of honeysuckle and the fields beyond. Crickets chirped in the distance and a bird called from a tree outside, the rustling branches reaching almost to the bright white moon that hung in the summer night, the diamond glimmer of stars scattering over the black velvet of the sky.

The tension drained from Nell's body. She wanted to lie there forever, she thought. But her bladder had been full for some time, and she longed to peel off her dusty clothes.

She found the pot under the bed and made use of it, noting with relief that a steaming pitcher of water and basin stood on a side table. She unlaced her bodice and pulled it off, gratefully scratching her breasts as they were freed from the constriction of her stays. Her skirt, shoes, stockings, and shift followed. It felt blissful to sponge away the grit of the road. She rubbed herself dry with a linen towel, luxuriating in the feel of the air on her still-damp skin.

The warm night outside called to her, and she went to the window. Then—voices. The door opened. There was no time to even move towards something with which to cover herself, and she simply stood there, naked, as Dorset and Sedley entered and stopped at the sight of her.

'I was—dressing,' she said, and couldn't help a giggle of amusement at her predicament. Sedley turned to leave, but Dorset stopped him.

'No need to leave, Charlie. Nell don't mind. Do you, Nell?'

She took in their faces—Sedley slightly awkward, but interest growing in his face; Dorset, obviously enjoying himself. He wanted her to show herself, she saw. To let Sedley see his new toy. She felt a surge of power at their rapt attention and stood for a moment, bold and unashamed, and then crossed unhurriedly to the trunk where her clothes were, drew out a clean shift, and pulled it on before joining Dorset and Sedley at the table.

The food was good, and they ate ravenously, tired and hungry after the long trip from London. The wine went down smoothly, dulling the aches of travelling, and Nell's mind was pleasantly blurred. She felt free and light in nothing but her shift, and the men were at their ease, too, in shirtsleeves. The meal refreshed all of their spirits, and as the drink flowed, Dorset and Sedley became voluble, debating the relative merits of Epsom and Tunbridge Wells as places of entertainment and retreat.

Nell listened to them with amusement. She had nothing to contribute to the argument, having never been anywhere but London and Oxford, but she enjoyed their sallies of wit, so she climbed into the big bed and drifted off to delicious sleep.

*   *   *

Two horses stood saddled and waiting outside the house by the time Nell and the Charlies had dressed and gone downstairs in the morning. A groom hoisted Nell up behind Dorset on a dappled grey stallion while Sedley climbed into the saddle of his roan-coloured mount.

The town was not large, and soon the road was flanked by green fields dotted with sheep and cattle. Suddenly Sedley spurred his horse into a gallop, and Dorset followed, so that they were flying along, dust rising in their wake. Nell clung to Dorset, finding the speed exhilarating, and laughed with him as they shot past Sedley. With a whoop, Sedley took the lead again, and the race was on.

The horses turned into open country, heading for a dark line of trees that marked the sloping banks of a stream. The Charlies slowed their pace and rode to the water's edge to let the horses drink before following the creek's flow downstream. Shortly, they came to a place where the water formed a clear pool, flanked on either side by velvet grass starred with clover and shaded by the overhanging branches of willows.

They dismounted and tethered the horses to a fallen log, and Sedley tossed a rug onto the grass beside the river.

'A perfect place for bathing,' he said with satisfaction, and began to undress. Dorset was halfway out of his clothes, too. The crystal water looked appealing, and soon Nell waded to where

211

the Charlies were already splashing. Dorset watched her appreciatively.

'Does she not look like a water nymph of some kind, Little Sid?'

'She does,' Sedley agreed. 'Waiting to catch unwary travelers and lure them to a watery death while they gaze in stupefaction at her beauty.'

Nell giggled and splashed water at Sedley, and soon they were all three sending arcs of water at each other and into the air.

Eventually they emerged, and Nell squeezed the water out of her hair before flopping onto the rug to dry herself in the sun. Dorset, still naked, was unpacking food and drink from his saddlebags, and she watched the play of his muscles under the smooth white skin. The daily riding, tennis, and fencing made him taut and lean, despite the nightly drinking, and with his wet golden hair hanging onto his shoulders Nell thought he looked like some kind of woodland creature himself. She glanced at Sedley, who was towelling himself off with his shirt, and he grinned at her, his hazel eyes flashing. He looked even more like some mischievous mythical being. A faun, perhaps, like those she had seen painted on theatre scenery.

The meal and wine went down well. Nell listened to a bird calling in a nearby tree. When it ceased its song, the only sounds were the gentle whisper of the breeze in the treetops and a honeybee buzzing in the clover. Otherwise, silence. Nell had never heard such quiet before. London was a constant din—the rattle and creaking of traffic, the cackle of poultry and sharp squealing of pigs, dogs barking, the raucous shouts of tradesmen, children crying. But here, on this sun-dappled bank, was blissful silence, and Nell realised that such peace was another privilege that came with money. She wished Rose could be there to share it. She had never been separated from her sister for so long, and missed her intensely.

Nell finished eating and lay on her side, her hair curling softly in the breeze. Her eyes met Dorset's, and he beckoned her. From the look in his eye she knew what would follow, and she hesitated for a moment, but she was alone in this Eden with the Charlies, so she went to Dorset and did not protest when he pulled her down beside him. He cupped one of her breasts, running his thumb over her stiffening nipple as he slipped a hand between her thighs. She was conscious of Sedley watching, close enough to touch her, close enough to hear the tiny moan that escaped her as Dorset caressed her.

Dorset guided her so that she knelt between his legs and she took him in her mouth. His smooth skin tasted pleasantly of the cool river water, and the curly hair she caressed with one hand was still damp. She knew that Sedley, behind her, had a clear and inviting view of her rump.

'Go ahead, Sid,' Dorset said, in a low voice. 'Touch her.'

A mild protest formed at the back of Nell's mind, but was overridden by the wave of desire that overcame her. She felt Sedley's hand slide over her buttocks, then into the cleft between her legs, his strokes matching the movements of her head. Nell found that she liked surrendering herself to the two men. And although it was a surrender, there was power in it, too, for both of them were in her spell.

Sedley was working magic with his hands, simultaneously penetrating her and caressing her

213

most tender part, and she exploded in a climax just as Dorset spent. He stroked her hair, turned her toward Sedley, and sat back to watch as she took Sedley in her mouth. After, the men dropped off to sleep, but Nell immersed herself once more in the cool green of the pool before lying down in the sun.

*   *   *

That evening, after another supper in the bedchamber, the three of them, well lubricated by wine, repaired to the big bed, and this time Dorset and Sedley enjoyed Nell at the same time, one in her belly and one in her mouth. They woke about the middle of the night and sported again, then slept until late morning, Nell nestled companionably between them.

*   *   *

Three or four weeks into their stay in Epsom, Nell and the Charlies received a visit from Sam Pepys, who was staying next door at the King's Head with his wife.

'The greatest news,' Pepys said, 'is that a peace has been reached with the Dutch.' Nell thought with a pang that that meant the theatres were likely to open again soon.

'The worser news,' Pepys reported, 'is that my Lord Buckingham is in great peril. He's been accused of having the king's horoscope cast.'

'Why, what's the harm in a horoscope?' Nell asked.

'It could be construed as predicting or wishing for the king's death,' Sedley explained.

214

'And it's a capital offence,' Dorset said.

'Aye,' said Pepys. 'His Majesty has not only turned him out of the Privy Council and his place as groom of the bedchamber, but Buckingham is sent to the Tower.'

'A gentleman of three inns,' Sedley commented, and then, seeing Nell's blank look, 'In jail, indicted, and in danger of being hanged.'

'But surely the king cannot think Buckingham wishes him dead?' Nell cried.

'Likely not,' Pepys said. 'Buckingham turned himself in, though not until he'd stopped to sup with Rochester and other friends at the Sun, making a triumphant appearance on the balcony and waving to the cheering crowds below. Just like a celebrated highwayman on his way to Tyburn. And my Lady Castlemaine is working to have him freed. He's her cousin, you know.'

'Yes, and it's to her advantage to have him at liberty,' Dorset said, 'as they've long been plotting the downfall of Clarendon.'

'Who?' Nell asked.

'Edward Hyde, the Earl of Clarendon,' Sedley said. 'He's been the king's closest adviser since he was in exile. He and Buckingham hate each other like poison.'

'With Clarendon out,' Dorset said, 'there would be no limit to Buckingham's power.'

*   *   *

The next day a messenger came from Killigrew, and Dorset read the note aloud to Nell. The theatres were to be opened again. Nell must return to London or return her parts to the playhouse.

Somehow, she had not anticipated such an explicit moment of reckoning. She had thought that perhaps she and Dorset would have returned to London by the time the summons came, and that she could return to the stage and continue as his mistress. Or—what? That he would be content to drop his plans and take her back to town? She had not thought it through clearly. And now Dorset was watching her, and the messenger stood waiting for her answer. And she knew she must choose.

'You had not considered returning to town soon, had you, Charlie?' she ventured. He shook his head. She imagined the company reassembling without her, and her parts being handed out to others. Her prized parts, which she had worked so hard to get, and which had brought her such joy. But if she left Dorset to go back to London, she would lose the security his money would bring her. He might keep her for years. Who knew when the theatres could be closed again or for how long?

She climbed the stairs to the bedroom and retrieved the precious bundle of her parts. Florimel, Mirida, Celia, Cydaria, and the rest. They were all here. She held on to the packet for a moment before handing it over to the messenger.

*   *   *

In the following weeks, Nell tried not to think about the playhouse, and there was much to distract her. Epsom was crowded with London holidaymakers. Between them, Dorset and Sedley knew almost everyone, and evenings were filled with suppers, cards, music, talking, and drinking. Dorset and Sedley were both prodigious drinkers, and Nell

216

found that in their company she was drinking more than she ever had in her life; she frequently rose with the ill effects of the previous night or did not rise at all, but slept until late, only to begin it all again.

*   *   *

One warm August night, another familiar face appeared—Rochester. Dorset and Sedley welcomed him like a long-lost brother, and they chewed over the latest news from court.

'Yes, of course Buckingham's freed,' Rochester said. 'Though he cannot seem to go a day without some new scrape. Harry Killigrew picked a fight with him at the Duke's Theatre, whither Buckingham had repaired with both wife and mistress. It ended with Buckingham giving Killigrew a kicking and taking away his sword, and Killigrew running like a dog. The king declares he'll clap him in the Tower if he's found.'

'That Harry's become nothing but a roaring damme boy,' Dorset sneered.

'Then the playhouses are open again?' Nell asked. She wondered with a stab to her heart whether her shows were soon to be presented and who had been given her parts.

'Yes, both houses are open again for the first time in some month or six weeks,' Rochester said. 'Though most no one is in town. And here's more news,' he grinned. 'Lady Castlemaine is with child again. By Henry Jermyn, they say.'

'Jermyn!' cried Sedley. 'The ugliest man in London.'

'But with a prick like a cudgel, the rumour goes,'

Rochester smiled. 'The king swore the brat could not be his, as he'd not lain with Barbara these six months and more, and that set her in a rage. 'God damn me, but you shall own it!' she shrieked, for all the court to hear. But the king will none, and Jermyn's hightailed it for some safer country.'

'And if His Majesty's not making feet for children's stockings with Barbara, where is he planting the royal sceptre?' Dorset mused.

'Twixt the nimble legs of Moll Davis,' said Rochester. 'You know the king's taken the queen to Tunbridge Wells in hopes the waters will help her conceive, and of course to refute the usual rumours of divorce. And both the King's and Duke's players are there to add to the sport.'

As the evening wore on, the party moved from the dining room to the more comfortable confines of the bedroom. Rochester and Sedley lounged in chairs near the table, and Dorset propped himself against the pillows on the bed, with Nell at his side. He had given no indication that he knew of her past relations with Rochester, and Nell was grateful that Rochester had said nothing to give them away. It was unusually restrained behaviour for him, she thought.

Suddenly she realised that Dorset was speaking of her. 'The best,' he repeated to Rochester. 'And obedient, with it.' Nell didn't like the note of triumph and challenge in his voice. She knew Rochester too well.

'Indeed?' Rochester said, raising his eyebrows. Nell's heart sank. Nothing good could come of this discussion. '"The best" is quite a claim, Charlie. Perhaps you'd let me judge for myself?'

Dorset held Rochester's gaze for some seconds

218

without responding.

'No,' he said at length, smiling complacently. 'I don't think so.'

Nell inwardly breathed a sigh of relief. But then Dorset spoke again.

'But I've no objection to letting you watch.'

Rochester smiled back at him, a wicked glint in his golden eyes.

'I'd relish that, Charlie,' he said, taking a swallow of his wine.

'Nell.' Dorset didn't even look at her. Eyes still meeting Rochester's, he simply beckoned her to him as he sat up on the edge of the bed. Nell felt that she would be wading into a disaster, but to refuse him seemed the worse option.

She knelt before Dorset and opened his flies. She had never felt him so hard. She knew that Rochester and Sedley must be able to see all, and knew that Dorset knew it, too, and was enjoying his mastery over her.

She worked for some minutes. There was no sound but that made by her mouth, and Dorset's occasional exhalation of pleasure. He was holding back, she could tell, prolonging his triumph. Finally he spoke.

'As I said, Johnny. And as you can see. She gives the best.'

'She ought to,' said Rochester lazily. 'I taught her.'

Nell felt Dorset's cock wilt in her mouth.

219

Chapter Fifteen

Killigrew, Lacy, and Mohun regarded Nell silently. Hart sat next to them but would not even meet her eyes. Finally Killigrew spoke.

'And why should I take you back, pray?'

'Because I have nowhere else to go. Because I never should have left. Because I promise you that I will work hard and be no trouble.' None of them said anything and Nell knew that there was only one real reason they would give her a second chance.

'Because I brought in crowds before, and you know I'll do it again.'

*   *   *

How could she have fallen so fast? Nell asked herself as she left Killigrew's little office. Six weeks earlier she had been the darling of the playhouses, with a dozen parts that were hers alone, and the knowledge that whenever she put foot onstage there would be a crowd clamouring to see her. Now she was back to where she had been so long ago, hoping she might be given a part, and she felt keenly that when the chance did come, she must do very well to regain her place in the good graces of Killigrew, Mohun, Lacy, and Hart.

Hart. He had stalked out of the meeting without a word to her. His love and approval had shone on her as steadily as the sun, and she had turned her back on him. For what? For foolish visions of grandeur that had crumbled to dust. To be sent packing by Dorset with the insulting sum of five pounds and have to come crawling back to the theatre. The other actresses—she had thought them her friends—had not been happy to see her walk in the door that day, were no doubt loath to relinquish the parts they'd inherited from her.

Nell went to the women's tiring room to retrieve some shoes she had forgotten that summer. Anne Marshall had the one private dressing room, with its fireplace. The door stood ajar, and Nell could hear Anne and her sister Beck giggling inside.

'Lord Dorset's whore.' It was Beck's voice. Nell didn't hear the rest of the sentence, but that was enough. She flung the door open.

'I was but one man's mistress,' she bellowed, resisting the urge to slap Beck, 'though I was brought up in a brothel. You,' she sneered, her outrage at Beck's hypocrisy overwhelming her, 'are mistress to three or four, though a Presbyter's praying daughter.'

'One man's mistress?' Beck's eyebrows shot up. 'That's not what I heard. Three to a bed is the story round the town. Was his lordship paying you by the hour or by the yard?' Anne broke into giggles at the play on words.

Nell felt her face burning in humiliation. Her frolics with Dorset and Sedley in Epsom had seemed the natural course of events in the trio's holidaymaking, merely an extension of their rambles in the countryside, their merry meals alone or with other company. But the thought of the two Charlies recounting their sport to leering cronies cast it all in another light. She felt dirty, and foolish to have thought that they regarded her as anything but a whore, bought and paid for.

And for such treatment she had cast off all that she had worked so hard to gain at the theatre. Had she valued it so little? Her soul ached with such despair that she had not the heart to find any retort to Beck's taunts. Suppressing her tears, she retreated without a word and fled the theatre.

*   *   *

Summer was gone. Each afternoon the sun sank earlier and rose later, and Nell felt enveloped by the chilly darkness. Rose tried to coax her into going walking or to see the plays at the Duke's, but she wished to do nothing but stay abed and keep warm. After two weeks when she had barely left her room at the Cock and Pie, John Lacy came to see her.

'Come,' he said. 'You can't lie here forever. Time for you to get back onstage.'

'I can't face it,' Nell said. 'Everyone is laughing at me.'

'Not true,' Lacy said, sitting on the edge of her bed. 'You know any one of the women in the company would have done the same in your shoes. If Dorset had made the same offer to Beck, she would have been out of the theatre so fast she'd have left her petticoat standing.'

He held up a roll of papers. 'A new part for you. Panthea in *A King and No King*. No time to waste— we'll open at the end of September. I'll help you learn it.'

'But that's one of Hart's plays!' Nell cried. 'He won't even look at me. How are we to play together?'

'You'll have to face each other again sooner or later.'

222

'Will he forgive me?' Nell asked.

'Firstly, he'll do what's good for the company,' Lacy said. 'And that means getting back onstage with you. And secondly, he loves you still. He'll come around.'

*   *   *

Lacy came to see Nell daily, and by the time of the first rehearsal for *A King and No King* she was word perfect in her part. She was thankful that though she had several scenes with Hart, she was playing his sister and not his lover. She couldn't bear the thought of playing one of the witty love scenes they had so enjoyed and seeing contempt and coolness in his eyes.

'Nelly! So good to see you!' Kate Corey bustled over.

'Thanks, Kate,' Nell said, hugging her. 'You're a sight for sore eyes.'

'Come sit with me,' Kate said, leading Nell to the benches around the greenroom table. 'You look as nervous as you did when you walked in for your first rehearsal of *Thomaso*—when was it? Three years and more ago.'

Nell felt comforted to be taken under Kate's wing, and smiled blithely at each new arrival.

'Glad you're back, love,' said old William Cartwright, lowering his bulk onto a bench across the table from her. 'You'll be good as Panthea.' Hart was the last of the cast to arrive.

Because he doesn't want to see me, Nell thought. He can't stand to be in the same room with me.

The rest of the actors all suddenly seemed to be busy looking at their scripts or anywhere but at

Hart as he came to the table. Get it over with, Nell thought, and lifted her head. His eyes met hers, and she saw sadness, but no hatred.

'Nell.' He nodded and then looked around the table. 'Right, everyone, let's get to work.'

*   *   *

Though the part of Panthea had too many serious scenes for Nell to truly enjoy, she was cheered by the smiling faces and applause that greeted her at the first performance. It felt wonderful to know that the audiences had missed her, and moreover, the company's managers could not help but see that she had been missed. Maybe it wouldn't be so long before she got her old parts back after all.

Sure enough, only a few days later, Michael Mohun approached her after a performance.

'We've got a couple of new parts for you, Nell. The king's mistress in *The Black Prince*, and a new little comedy, *Flora's Vagaries*. Better get someone to start working on your lines with you—you've got a lot of words.' He smiled over his shoulder as he walked away, and Nell realised how tense with anticipation and hope she had been since her return.

I'm back, she thought. They've taken me back.

Not only had she been taken back, but she seemed to have resumed her place at the top of the heap. She was once more playing with Hart, Kate Corey, and William Cartwright in *The Black Prince*, though she thought her part as the king's mistress Alizia weepy and disliked the plodding rhymed couplets. Better, she had the title role in *Flora*, a part well suited to her comic talents. She

224

and Betsy Knepp had several funny scenes. They enjoyed working together, and spending so much time in each other's company on- and offstage, they became closer friends.

One afternoon in October, Betsy arrived in the tiring room with Sam and Elizabeth Pepys and their maid in tow. Mrs. Pepys greeted Nell, then departed to do some shopping, leaving Sam to visit on his own.

'What's the house like today?' Betsy asked when Lacy stopped by.

Lacy shook his head. 'Less than two hundred. Everyone's gone to the Duke's to see *The Coffee House*.'

'Hell and the devil!' Nell exclaimed in irritation. 'Nothing worse than trying to get a laugh when the pit's so empty they're rattling around like peas out there.'

Pepys chortled in amusement. 'I vow I'll laugh enough to make up for the lack of all the others, Nelly.'

'If you're going to sit here, Sam, be a dear and run lines with me,' Betsy asked, handing him the sheaf of paper on which her part was written. 'I didn't get a chance this morning and my head is full of *The Traitor*.'

*   *   *

Nell was relieved to be back onstage, earning her own living, once more part of the family of the playhouse. But she would not be truly back at home, truly comfortable, until she felt right again with Charles Hart. He had been cordial enough, but had not spoken to her alone, had not gone out with

225

members of the company after shows when Nell went with them. She could hardly blame him, Nell thought. She had walked away from him and all that he had given her, and he could not know what a hole had been left in her heart at his loss.

She sought him out in the men's tiring room after a performance of *A King and No King*. Only Lacy was with Hart, and he smiled at her and found reason to leave almost as soon as she had come in. Nell hadn't known what she would say to Hart, how to approach him, but seeing him sitting there at the dressing table before the mirror, his makeup and brushes laid out before him just so, as she had seen him so many times when they were a couple, her fear left her.

'Will you take a walk with me?' she asked, and was relieved when he nodded.

It was near dark, and they kept to Drury Lane and the Strand, where lights shone from within taverns and coffeehouses and made the way easy.

'I'm sorry,' Nell said, wishing she dared to put her hand in his. 'I never meant to hurt you. I was foolish to leave.'

Two stout chair men carrying a brightly painted sedan chair hustled past them, their breath huffing clouds in the chill air.

'Not foolish,' Hart said. 'Yes, it hurt, but I've come to see that the picture I had, of us going on forever as we were, was not like to happen. You're only seventeen, after all. You have so much life before you, so many opportunities that I can't give you.'

'Can we try again?' Nell asked.

'I don't know,' he said, and they walked in silence for a few moments. 'I've heard it said that you can never step in the same river twice. And the current has carried each of us on from where we stood before. But we can care for each other, and find our way anew, as friends, if you're willing.'

'Yes,' Nell said. 'I'd like that.'

'We were at our best together onstage,' Hart said. 'I've never felt like that with anyone, man, woman, or boy, in all the time I've been acting. I've missed it. Shall we try that, too? Maybe *All Mistaken*, and see how we do?'

'I'd like that, too,' Nell said. 'Above all things.'

*   *   *

Nine times out of ten backstage visitors were gentlemen. But it was a lady that Tom Killigrew ushered into the tiring room one evening in November. She was tall and dark haired, handsome and well dressed, but Nell could tell at a glance that she was no mere mistress nor yet a lady of the court. She carried herself with a sense of ease and confidence, Nell thought. Not a person who sought approval from anyone. Yet not vain or haughty.

'Nell,' Killigrew said, 'allow me the honour of presenting my friend Mrs. Aphra Behn.'

'Mrs. Gwynn,' the lady said, and Nell felt that in her gaze was admiration, curiosity, humour. 'What enjoyment you gave me with your charming performance. You will know how long I've been away from London when I tell you that I hadn't had the privilege of seeing you onstage before today.' She laughed a throaty laugh that made Nell like her instantly. 'But I certainly hope to make up for lost time.'

'With pleasure, Mrs. Behn,' Nell said. 'I shall
227

be happy to see you in the audience and would be honoured if you would call on me at home sometime.'

'Then we shall make it so,' said Aphra, the deep violet of her eyes shining with warmth.

*　　*　　*

'She means to be a playwright!' Nell exclaimed to Rose. They stood near the Maypole in the Strand, among a crowd who had gathered to watch two rope dancers performing.

'I've never heard of such a thing—a woman who writes. And Killigrew says he's all for it and will help her as he can.'

One of the dancers, lithe and wiry, was making his way slow footfall by slow footfall across the slack rope that was strung between the maypole and a tree. Nell watched the play of the muscles of his bare calves and idly thought that his thighs and buttocks must be a marvel.

'And where has she been all this time,' Rose asked, 'that she hasn't seen you onstage?'

'That's even more odd,' Nell said. 'According to Killigrew, she's been in Antwerp, spying for His Majesty.' The acrobat reached the far end of the rope, swung himself down in a flip, and took a graceful bow to the applause of the crowd.

'What was she like?' Rose asked.

'Sterling,' Nell answered. 'She's a lady. But feet on the ground and more pleasant and companionable to me than any other woman I've met. Excepting you, of course.'

'Of course,' Rose twinkled. 'I'm glad for you, Nell. And I've some news. My Johnny has asked me

228

to marry him.'

'Oh, Rose!' Nell cried. 'That's wonderful. He treats you so well, and your eyes shine with happiness when you're with him. What did Mam say?'

Rose laughed. 'She just shook her head, and snorted 'Love and a cough can't be hid.' But I think she's well pleased.'

*   *   *

A few weeks after her first meeting with Aphra Behn, Nell arrived at the theatre to find a message that the Duke of Buckingham would be pleased if she would join him for supper after the performance. From the stage, she could make out Buckingham in the pit, and she threw him a smile at the curtain call.

*   *   *

At supper, Nell watched Buckingham over the rim of her wineglass. The fire glowed behind him, creating a golden halo around his fair wig. He was a handsome man, Nell thought. Not pretty, not in the least foppish, for all his elegance. No, he had a rugged maleness, a sense of coiled danger beneath the good manners. She was a little baffled by his conversation so far. If he wanted to bed her, he was taking his time about getting to the point.

'You've met the king,' he said.

'I have,' Nell agreed, puzzled.

'Could you like him?' The image of her first sight of the king flashed into her mind—astride his horse, standing in his stirrups to acknowledge the cheers of the crowd, unabashedly grinning. And blowing her a kiss. She felt again those eyes on her and the breathless joy she had felt at that moment.

'How could I not?' she asked with a laugh. 'He's—the king.'

'Good. Listen to me now. The time is ripe to put a new mistress in his bed. Barbara's angered him too often to be certain of keeping her place and her influence. Oh, to be sure, there's never a shortage of willing females, and Old Rowley's not one to let an opportunity for minge go by. But I don't mean just for a night or two. I mean a woman who will appeal to his heart and mind as well as his prick. That takes spirit and charm and brains as well as looks and skill in bed.'

Nell's head was spinning. A new mistress for the king? Could he really mean—

'He likes you,' Buckingham said simply. 'Not only onstage. He told me he remembered the first time he ever spoke to you, over your basket of oranges. And he laughed out loud in recalling how he saw you riding pig-a-back on Charles Hart in Oxford.'

Nell stared at Buckingham. 'He remembered that?'

'He remembered it well. Said he knew you'd be a terror onstage when you got there. And that he envied Hart that it was he who was keeping you warm at night.'

'But why?' Nell asked.

'Why put you in his bed, you mean? I won't pretend there's not self-interest in it. Charles is led by his pintle, to a degree greater even than most men. It would be useful to me to have a friend with her hand firmly cupped around the royal whirligigs. Someone who can put in a gentle word when needed, when he's drowsing off and in an indulgent mood after a good gallop. And from what I know of you and your talents, I think you're just the wench that can do it. Don't look surprised,' he added, catching Nell's glance. 'We have friends in common, you and I.'

Nell laughed. 'But you make it sound so easy.'

Buckingham shrugged. 'As Otway says, 'Give but an Englishman his whore and ease, beef and a sea-coal fire, he's yours forever.'''

Chapter Sixteen

Nell's first impression of the king's privy chamber was that it was like a chessboard filled with clocks. The floor was in squares of black and white marble, and a row of timepieces stood along the shining black mantel atop the enormous fireplace. Others dotted tables and shelves, and a tall case clock emitted a steady tock. The vast bed was surmounted by a canopy with great eagles above it, its curtains supported by cherubs that appeared to be in flight towards the elaborately painted ceiling high above. Paintings in heavy gold frames were mounted on the walls. The life-sized portraits of ladies and gentlemen in stiff finery seemed to Nell to look down on her as she passed.

It took Nell a moment to spot the king. He was seated at a writing desk, his back to the door, evidently engrossed in whatever he was studying. Three spaniels lay curled near his feet, and they lifted their heads to regard the visitors.

'Your Majesty,' Buckingham began, but as he spoke, the tall clock began to tell the hour with a series of deep bongs. Another clock sounded, and then, as if they had been caught napping and were guiltily snapping to their work, the others chimed in one by one on their own notes and rhythms, creating a cacophonous jangle.

'George.' The king stood and came smiling towards them, embraced Buckingham, and turned to Nell as the last of the bells faded to silence, pulling her up from her curtsy.

'Mistress Nelly. May I call you Nelly? I always think of you like that, you know, and calling you anything else would seem amiss.'

'Of course, Your Majesty,' Nell dimpled at him, pleased beyond measure that he 'always' thought of her in any way at all.

'I've just been looking at Wren's plans for some of the new churches—come and see.' The king led them toward the desk, where a large drawing was unfurled.

'St. Paul's,' he said. 'Is it not splendid?'

'Magnificent,' Buckingham agreed. 'But what about some wine?'

Charles laughed. 'Of course. Forgive me, Nelly, for being such a poor host. Faith, you grow more beautiful each time I see you.'

'If it be so, Your Majesty, then I hope that you shall see me frequently, so that both of us may benefit,' Nell laughed.

'And witty as well,' Charles said over Nell's head to Buckingham. 'Pretty, witty Nell.'

*   *   *

232

Save for the servant who brought in the food and poured the wine, and the dogs, the three of them were alone. Charles and Buckingham were in jovial spirits, and chaffed with each other like the brothers they almost were.

They lingered over wine and sweetmeats, but as the clocks set up their clamour on the hour of ten, Buckingham declared that it was time for him to be gone.

'And you, Nelly?' asked Charles. 'Must you run away? Or will you stay to keep me company a little while yet?'

'Gladly, sir,' Nell said, 'if it will give you pleasure.'

Buckingham's footsteps faded, and Nell felt momentarily awkward—what should she do or say? But Charles poured more wine, silently raised his glass to her with a smile, and she felt at ease.

'Why do you have so many clocks, Your Majesty?' Nell wondered.

'I have a great interest in all things mechanical, not to mention chemical, astronomical, and philosophical. I find clocks and watches in particular to be wonderful things, and so my collection grows. The one in the antechamber not only tells time but also the direction of the wind.'

Nell laughed in surprise and delight. Every surface seemed to be cluttered with books and curious objects, and she pointed to an item that had been puzzling her all evening.

'What is that?'

'A lunar globe,' Charles beamed. 'With all the hills, valleys, and other features of the moon.' He laughed at Nell's look of astonishment. 'It's true, I vow.'

He pulled a morsel of meat from the pullet carcass on the table and held it out to one of his spaniels, who wolfed it down. Nell giggled as the dog licked its chops and cocked its head expectantly, clearly hoping for more. Charles gently pulled one of the dog's ears and scratched it under the chin.

'I had one of these beasts with me in France,' he said. 'Sometimes I thought he was my only true friend in the world.'

'I have never had a dog, Your Majesty, but have often wondered if I had a true friend. He must have been a comfort to you.'

Charles leaned forward and brushed a tendril of hair from Nell's cheek, letting his hand trail down her face, her throat, her breast. Nell felt a twinge in her belly—the involuntary contraction of arousal. She had fully expected the king to bed her. She had not expected to desire him as intensely as she suddenly found she did.

He stood and drew her to her feet, took her head in his hands as he bent and kissed her deeply. Her arms went around him and her mouth welcomed his, her body responding with a wave of fire as his tongue caressed and probed. He moved his mouth to her throat, his moustache tickling as his lips moved down her skin. Nell gasped, and she arched to meet him as he reached within her stays, lifting one of her breasts free. His tongue flicked across her nipple as he suckled her and she felt she had never wanted anything more urgently in the world than she wanted him inside her.

He placed her on the bed, lifting her skirts as his knees coaxed her legs apart. He thrust against her, and through his breeches she felt the hardness of him—and his size. Rochester's witticism that 'his sceptre and his prick are of a length' flashed into her mind.

He knelt upright to remove his waistcoat and open his breeches. He shuddered as Nell grasped his cock with firm but delicate fingers. She looked up at him as she extended her tongue to delicately caress him—soft, so soft, warm, teasing—just enough to set him on fire for more. She paused, reaching down to lift her breasts toward him. Seizing her with both hands, he plunged himself into the valley of her cleavage, so that the length of him slid between her breasts as she sucked.

His breeches were hindering her from giving him all the pleasure she knew she could and she worked them down and slid one hand between his thighs so she could caress his bollocks and move a butterfly-light finger over the cleft of his arse. She grasped him tightly now, sliding her hand over the silky skin, her fingers meeting her lips as her mouth settled into a steady and insistent rhythm.

He pushed her onto her back and straddled her, thrusting deep into her throat, filling her, possessing her utterly. Nell breathed on his outstrokes and opened her gullet to receive him as he spent.

He collapsed beside her on the bed, and she rolled to her side to look at him, trailing a finger down the dark line of hair on his belly. What fantasy this seemed, and yet it was true. It was the king's bed in which she lay, and his mettle that tasted yet in her throat. The king—and yet a man like any other.

Charles looked at her and laughed softly, caressing her hair.

'I must thank George when next I see him.'

She laughed, too, and gently touched his now-soft cock. 'And I as well.'

'You've not had much yet to thank him for,' he said. 'But wait but a bit. The lad will be back, and able to last longer the second time.'

*　　　*　　　*

Long after Charles had fallen asleep, Nell lay awake. She was tired, but her mind would not be still. She was kept awake by the snuffling and restless movement of the spaniels that sprawled on the floor near the bed. And every time she was near to drifting off, the clocks would fall to striking the hour, each in its own time. But at last she slept, curled in the secure warmth of the royal bed.

Charles sent for Nell twice more in quick succession, and she began to feel at home as old William Chiffinch, the keeper of the privy closet, lantern in hand, ushered her up the shadowy staircase to the king's bedchamber and later helped her into the waiting boat in the grey light of dawn. Each time he sent her homeward with a gift of money, offered matter-of-factly as His Majesty's thanks for her company. Nell was well pleased, but Buckingham wanted more.

'A night here and there keeps you in the place of a common drab. He likes you, I know, and God knows he's crowing about your talents. We must strike while the iron is hot. Ask him for five hundred pounds a year.'

So Nell did. But like a horse brought to the edge of a river to board a ferry, the king balked.

'This is Buckingham at work, I can smell it,' he

236

said. 'You can tell George from me that I'll manage my own affairs.'

'He'll come around,' Buckingham said. 'He's stubborn as a mule when he thinks a thing is not his own idea. You should see him with his mother. Wait a bit and he'll change his tune.'

But weeks passed, and no summons came. The old year went and the new year of 1668 arrived. Nell played in *The Maid's Tragedy*, hating its grandiose turgidity. And worried. Once more she had seemed on the brink of something wonderful. And once more her dreams had receded even as she tried to touch them. Backstage, she fretted to Betsy.

'I've heard nothing even from Buckingham. Perhaps he's forgotten me, too.'

'He has more on his mind than you just now, Nell,' Betsy said. 'Or have you not heard about Lord Shrewsbury?'

'Of course,' Nell said. 'That was weeks ago.' There couldn't be anyone in London who had not heard that Lord Shrewsbury, the husband of Buckingham's mistress, had challenged him. They had met, with two seconds each, and fought three on a side at Barn Elms. One of Buckingham's seconds was killed outright, and Buckingham had run Shrewsbury through the breast. But he was recovering, and the king had pardoned everyone involved.

'Shrewsbury died yesterday,' Betsy said. 'That changes everything. Buckingham's in no position to help you now.'

*   *   *

237

Nell sought to lose herself in work and was pleased to play once more in *The English Monsieur*. It was like old times, working opposite Hart again. He seemed to have forgiven her for Dorset, and they played to packed houses that braved a bitter cold snap to see them.

Sam Pepys came backstage one day, no wife in sight, and he responded readily when Nell artlessly asked him what was the news at court.

'There was a rare scene a couple of evenings ago,' he laughed. 'Some of the players from the Duke's gave a show at the palace. The high point of the evening was Moll Davis's dance. You've seen it?'

'No,' said Nell, forcing a smile, 'do tell.'

'It'll get a man's attention, I'll just say that. And it got the king's. Of course you know he's been bedding her?'

Nell's stomach heaved, and she managed a nod.

'Well, Moll was wiggling and flinging away, those bold eyes of hers right on the king's, with the queen to one side of him and Lady Castlemaine on the other, the queen near tears and Barbara breathing fire. Comes the end of the dance, and Moll curtsies low before the king, looking up at him, and he looking down at her as though he would devour her. And just as he starts to clap, the queen springs to her feet and stalks for the door. And damn me if Castlemaine don't rise with icy majesty and sweep out after her, leaving the room agog.'

'Did he go after her—them—the queen, I mean?' Nell asked, dreading the answer.

'No, by God, that's the best of it,' Samuel chortled. 'He never turned a hair. Just clapped, which got the crowd applauding, then went straight

238

to Mistress Moll, picked her up out of her curtsy, kissed her most freely, and led her straight off to his chamber for a private dance that went on all the night, or so I'm told.'

*   *   *

'The king has bought Moll a house in Suffolk Street!' Betsy Knepp cried to Nell in the tiring room the next afternoon. 'And a ring worth six hundred pounds. And she's sent her parts back to the theatre and says she'll act no more!'

Over the next few days, it was all Nell could do to keep from screaming. It seemed everyone she met wanted to tell the news. There were numerous variations of the tale. Sometimes the ring was worth seven hundred pounds. Sometimes the king had sworn his love to Moll. Sometimes it was said that Mr. Betterton had begged Moll not to leave the Duke's, had offered to double her wages. But whatever embroidery the story gained, the essentials remained the same.

There was nothing for it but to get on with life, Nell realised. Candlemas came, and she celebrated her eighteenth birthday with Rose and her new husband, their mother awkwardly joining them. She slogged her way through another of the tragedies she hated so much, *The Duke of Lerma*. Only the humorous prologue she spoke with Betsy made the show tolerable.

Even that equanimity was shattered when she overheard a group of the scenekeepers sharing a raucous laugh one cold dark afternoon.

'What d'ye say to that, Nell?' Richard Baxter called out.

'To what?'

'To the news that my Lady Castlemaine has taken our very own Charles Hart to her bed. Can't get enough of him, apparently, and heaps him with gewgaws and gifts.'

Nell turned away, tears stinging her eyes. Not only did the king prefer Moll Davis's company to hers, but Hart had taken up with the woman who all England considered to be the epitome of beauty and glamour. She had never felt more defeated.

*   *   *

The furious winter cold of February seeped into Nell's bones, and her heart felt as frozen as the river. With the first days of March came a thaw. Each day brought a few more minutes of sunshine, and Nell gradually felt her spirits begin to lift. By late March there were the first hints of spring. Delicate green shoots braved their way through patches of bare earth, and tight blossoms clung to the tree branches, holding their breath until it should be safe to open.

As always, Nell's mood lifted as the days began to lengthen and the weather grew warmer. By April, with a promising slate of roles ahead of her, she had almost convinced herself that it was just as well she had not heard from the king. But when Buckingham appeared at the door of the tiring room, her hopes soared.

'Aye, His Majesty was angry about the duel,' Buckingham agreed over dinner. 'But a prince's anger is like the thunder—it clears the air a great while after. I hear that Moll Davis has lost some of her charm for him. I think he'd welcome your company, if we do but remind him he misses you. He and the Duke of York will be at the Duke's Playhouse tomorrow for *She Would if She Could.* And so will you be.'

'And then what?' Nell asked in exasperation. 'Am I to throw an orange at him to get his attention?'

'Nothing so obvious. Though it might work, at that. I've a cousin who'll accompany you, and ensure that you're seated conveniently near to the king.'

'I'd rather it was you.'

'Not this time. He must not know he's being led. And he'll bridle if he gets any whiff that I'm involved.'

*   *   *

The scheme seemed so far-fetched that Nell could scarce believe it when the king and the Duke of York took their places in the royal box next to where she sat with Buckingham's cousin. And she found it still more astonishing when a royal page bowed before her a moment later with the king's request that they join him and the duke at supper after the show.

'"If this were played upon a stage now,"' she muttered, '"I could condemn it as an improbable fiction."' Mr. Villiers, a rabbit-faced gentleman whose innocuous personality was ideally suited to the evening's plot, gave her a quizzical look but did not question her.

*   *   *

'We'll slip in somewhere for a bite and I can leave the watchdogs behind,' the king said after the play was over. So servants and carriage waited near the playhouse, and Nell found herself entering the White Hart behind Mr. Villiers, with the king and the Duke of York in tow, their hats pulled low over their brows.

Soon the party was laughing as they tucked into a fricassee of rabbit and chicken, and when the king squeezed Nell's leg under the table, she had no doubts about the success of the evening.

An hour later, after a plentiful feast, the landlord, innocent of the identity of his patrons, presented the bill. The king felt his pockets.

'By God,' he said. 'But I've forgotten—I have no money. Jimmy, I'd be obliged if you'd help me out.'

Now it was the duke's turn to clap his hands to the skirts of his coat, looking sheepish.

'I would if I could,' he said, 'but I've nothing either.'

''Od's fish!' cried Nell, in a creditable imitation of the king. 'But this is the poorest company I ever was in!' The red-faced landlord exhaled in irritation and turned to poor Mr. Villiers, who gamely drew out his purse.

In the street outside, Nell whooped with amusement.

'I thought the man would have an apoplexy,' she crowed. 'And poor bastard, if he'd only known who he was about to take to task.'

*   *   *

'By God, but I've missed you, Nelly,' the king said an hour later, smiling down as he moved on top of

242

her. 'Don't let it happen again, will you, that you deprive me of your company for so long?'

*   *   *

May Day dawned clear and fine. Nell awoke to the sound of music in the street below, and, from her window, watched milkmaids dance their way down Drury Lane to a fiddler's tune. What changes in her life a twelvemonth had wrought. Last year at this time she had been debating the wisdom of leaving the stage for Dorset's bed. This year, she had spent more nights in the past fortnight in the king's bed than in her own. She had no thoughts of giving up the playhouse this time, though. She could go to the king as often as he called her, and the experience with Dorset had made her cautious about casting off her only source of steady income.

Besides, such an array of roles stretched before her that she had no mind to leave. Charles Sedley's comedy *The Mulberry Garden* would be followed by *Philaster*, another breeches role that put her legs on display and once more paired her and Hart as battling lovers. Then would come *The Virgin Martyr* and further performances of the perennial favorite *The Humorous Lieutenant*.

Buckingham was, miraculously, back in favour with the king and, having dispatched Lord Shrewsbury, was now unrestrained in enjoying the company of his widow, the beautiful Anna Maria, Countess of Shrewsbury. Perhaps conscious of having overplayed his hand in advising Nell to ask Charles for an allowance so soon, and relieved at having succeeded in getting her back into the royal bed again, he was cautious in his counsel to Nell.

'It's more than just a matter of keeping him happy in bed, Nelly. Never be a burden. There's a never-ending queue of people making demands upon the king. You must be a welcome respite from all that. Make him laugh. Make him forget his cares. Make him believe you care for him.'

Buckingham's advice was given in cynicism, but Nell found that she could follow it without dissembling. She did care for Charles. Behind his laughter there lay a deep sadness that touched her heart.

*   *   *

'I'm sorry I've not seen you these last days,' the king apologised, as Nell lay in his bed for the first time in more than a week. 'The queen has miscarried again.'

'Oh, Charles, what a grief for you!' Nell passed her hand over his brow, the lines there seeming more deep-set than usual. 'I wish that I could ease your pain.'

'You do, sweetheart. You do.'

Nell put her arms around him and held him to her, rocking. Though he was twenty years older than she, she could see in him the vestiges of the boy scarred by war and years in exile, the losses of his father and his crown, and now this new loss, and she felt as tenderly towards him as she might toward a child.

*   *   *

Nell felt oddly private about her feelings for Charles. But it was impossible to ignore the fact that

244

the liaison was widely known. She received more callers than ever after performances, but there was a deference now that had been lacking before. 'Meat for my master, she cries.' The line from *The Humorous Lieutenant* sprang into her mind as the Earl of Mulgrave bowed over her hand. He was one of a dozen gentlemen who were crowding the tiring room, and they were not seeking to bed her now, but to keep her good opinion.

'I declare, you grow prettier every day,' Sam Pepys grinned, kissing her cheeks. He held her out at arm's length to admire her. Her costume for the role of the page boy Angelo consisted of breeches that displayed her calves in their silk stockings, and a neatly cut jacket that did nothing to disguise the fact that she was in truth a girl.

Pepys cast a glance at Beck Marshall, who was halfway out of her gown, her shoulders and a dangerous amount of bosom bare as she bantered with Rochester and George Etherege.

Sometime that summer, Nell's name in the playbill at the theatre was transformed from mere Nell Gwynn to Mrs. Eleanor Gwynn. She snorted with derision when Betsy told her about the change, but within, her reaction was more complicated. Though it was the name bestowed on her at birth, she had never been addressed as Eleanor in her life. Eleanor was her mother. There was an element of fear that lurked, too. What would become of Nelly if Mrs. Eleanor Gwynn now inhabited her form?

Even people at the playhouse treated her differently. Though Nell was sure her conduct had not changed, the other actresses kept more aloof.

'I fear they hate me,' she confided in Aphra.

245

'You great goose,' Aphra chided. 'You can have no conception of how winning and cheerful your company is, else you would stop your fretting. You're a sunny soul who brings light wherever you go. If they stand off, it's only because they wish they were in your shoes. Sure the king likes you well enough, else he would not send for you. And that's all that matters, isn't it?'

Nell was warmed by Aphra's encouragement, but the one person that could truly bring her comfort, and in whose presence she felt wholly at home, was Rose. Rose was happy these days. Although Rose would never quite say so, Nell thought the rumours that her husband John got his living from highway robbery were probably true. He certainly had more flash than most labouring men. Whatever the case, he was often gone at night, and Nell spent frequent evenings with her sister.

Summer brought five or six new roles for Nell, and of course the plays already in the repertoire were revived regularly. As Hart had long ago predicted, she now carried almost twenty parts in her head, ready to perform with only a little dusting off.

Sam Pepys visited Nell backstage one evening in October, burning to tell the latest gossip.

'The story is all over Whitehall,' he said, plopping himself down beside her at the dressing table. 'The king lent Lady Castlemaine the crown jewels to wear in a performance of *Horace* at court last night. He made for her apartments this morning to collect the jewels and spied a man— John Churchill, they say—coming out of her bedchamber, and far too early for a mere social call it was. The poor man froze at the sight and bowed nearly to the ground. But the king only laughed and said, 'I forgive you, for I know you do it for your bread!"' Pepys laughed nearly till he cried at his own story. 'Oh, and did you hear the latest story of your old friend Lord Dorset?'

'You mean my Charles the Second?' Nell asked archly. Pepys chuckled.

'Indeed. And your other friend Charles, as well. Sedley, that is. High flown in drink, they stripped off most of their clothes and tore through the streets with their arses bare, singing and shouting, and at last fell to brawling with the watch.'

The picture of the two Charlies engaged in near-naked horseplay came readily to Nell's imagination, and brought back vivid memories of the previous summer. She wondered how much Pepys had guessed about the sleeping arrangements in the house in Epsom.

'No one was wounded, I hope?'

'Oh, no,' said Pepys. 'They were taken up before they could do much damage, and were clapped up all night, but the king took their parts and the Lord Chief Justice hath chid and imprisoned the poor constable, who was only doing his duty.'

As Nell walked home that evening, her cloak pulled tight against the chill wind, she thought again of Dorset, and she realised that for the first time since the intense pain and shame of the previous summer, she could think of him without bitterness. She had thought that his casting her off was the death of her hopes. But it had not fallen out so. She reigned supreme at the playhouse and as Dorset himself had acknowledged with a rueful smile, she had gone from the bed of an earl to the bed of the king.

Chapter Seventeen

December, 1668

The king's bedchamber was cosy, the blazing fire and dancing candlelight driving the shadows into the corners. Nell and Charles were propped against the pillows in the big bed.

'What was France like?' Nell asked.

'Like a sewer filled with vipers,' Charles snorted. 'I barely got out of England with my life, you know, after the Battle of Worcester. I was a pauper, dependent for my very food on my cousin kings. And of course it was not only my mouth there was to feed, but my mother, my brothers and youngest sister, my loyal friends. My beggar's court.'

'And Mr. Killigrew was there?' Nell asked, stroking the hair on his belly lazily.

'He was. And Buckingham, Clarendon, Rochester—the father of Johnny Wilmot, that is. And many other great friends who'd put their lives at risk for me, left home and country behind. And I had not the price of their bread.'

'What did you do?' Nell asked.

'We cooled our heels and waited. By God, I hate the French. The Dauphin waited a month before he received me. Precious little cunt. Then had the cheek to turn up his delicate nose at the rags I wore.'

'You? In rags?' Nell pulled back to look into Charles's face for a sign that he was jesting.

'After Worcester, when all was lost, I had to go

in disguise. I was fortunate that someone had an ungodly big servant with clothes to give for king and country, but there aren't many with feet as big as these.'

He stuck his bare foot out from under the sheet and wiggled his toes. Nell giggled and slid her hand down to his cock.

'There aren't many with one of these as big, either.'

Charles laughed and kissed her. 'That's what they tell me, and who would lie to a king? But not a whoreson could be found with shoes would fit me. I walked in boots too small, slit about the edges to let my toes out, bleeding every step. By the time we reached the coast, my clothes—' He broke off at the sound of a female voice outside the door.

'Christ! The queen!' He bolted to his feet and Nell scrambled out of bed.

'Behind there!' He thrust his finger at a tapestry, and Nell darted behind it, snatching up her gown, as she heard the door open.

'Why, Catherine!' Charles managed a tone of pleased surprise.

'I came to see if you were feeling better.' The queen's soft voice was heavily accented, despite her six years in England.

'Oh, much. Taking my rest, as you see.'

'Have you a fever?' Nell heard the rustle of skirts, and guessed that the queen must be sitting beside Charles. From her hiding place, she could see the foot of the bed. And then she saw something else that almost made her gasp aloud— one of her shoes lay in plain sight on the floor. The queen must have seen it at the same moment.

'Oh.'

249

'Hmm?' Charles had not seen it yet. Then he did. 'Ah.'

There was another rustle as the queen stood. 'I will not stay, for fear the pretty fool who owns that little slipper might take cold. I am glad you are well.' The door closed, but Nell still waited.

'You can come out now, Nelly,' Charles said.

'Shall I leave?' she asked, emerging.

'No, no,' he said. 'The damage is done. Poor soul, I try not to rub her nose in it. But it's sweet of you to ask.'

*   *   *

After that night, everyone was more careful. The queen stayed away from the king's bedchamber. The king's attendants took care to ensure that no one entered unannounced, and Charles, wishing to avoid any unpleasant scenes, emphasised that this precaution also applied to the Countess of Castlemaine. For it was no longer Barbara Palmer but Nell who was his frequent companion at night.

She grew accustomed to the morning ritual—the arrival of the king's breakfast, the barber's coming to shave him, the attendance of the groom and gentleman of the bedchamber to help him bathe and dress, and the appearance of various ministers to report about the matters requiring his attention.

After Buckingham and Lady Castlemaine brought down the hated Earl of Clarendon the previous summer, Buckingham had succeeded Clarendon as Charles's first minister, and he was almost always the first visitor of the day. Nell enjoyed listening to them confer as she ate breakfast in bed. It was fascinating, the variety of subjects in which Charles was interested and over which he had sway.

'Wren is making great progress on the plans for the new churches,' Buckingham reported one morning, consulting his notes. 'He proposes to begin with St. Bride's and St. Lawrence Jewry, and is ready to show you drawings when convenient.'

'Excellent,' Charles said, biting into a piece of bread.

'There is to be a committee meeting on Tangiers tomorrow, again. And the Duke of York has proposals for victualling the navy.'

'God, yes, the ships must be provisioned, but must I hear the details of every cask of beef and barrel of ale that is put aboard?'

'Rochester had his clothes taken the other day while he was tiffing some Covent Garden nun,' Buckingham smiled. 'Perhaps news more to your liking?'

'More entertaining, at any rate,' Charles said, wiping coffee from his moustache. 'Did he get them back?'

'The clothes, yes,' said Buckingham. 'They were found stuffed into a mattress. His gold, however, was gone.'

'Poor Johnny,' Charles said. 'Never learns, does he? What else?'

'Only the usual wranglings. My Lady Castlemaine—'

'Oh, spare me!' Charles cried.

But though Charles was spared the telling of Lady Castlemaine's complaint on that morning, it was played out very publicly, to the delight of the town, and Nell found herself on the battlefield.

After an absence of a few weeks from the stage,

she was to speak the prologue and epilogue to Ben Jonson's *Catiline His Conspiracy*. On the afternoon of the first performance, she strode forward onto the apron of the stage. Her Amazon costume, a short feathered skirt and Roman sandals, with a diaphanous drapery that bared most of one breast and some of the other, was greeted with whoops. She raised her short sword in salute, and addressed the packed house.

'Since you expect a prologue, we submit!'

When she came to the end of her speech, she bowed, thus baring both breasts in their entirety, and made her exit to cheers. Lacy was in the wings, and she stood with him to watch the play. Kate Corey, in all her Roman finery as Sempronia, sailed onto the stage. Her initial speech was getting laughs much bigger than usual, and Nell cocked a curious ear.

'Why on earth is she lisping like that?' she whispered to Lacy. He listened, a quizzical expression on his face.

'By God,' he gasped. 'She's doing Lady Harvey.'

'What?'

'Lady Elizabeth Harvey. Her husband's the ambassador to Turkey. Her cousin's the Lord Chamberlain. That's her to the life.'

The audience had obviously also recognised who Kate was personating, for they were roaring with laughter. Nell and Lacy watched in silence. Kate pursed her lips in a way that made Nell think of a thoughtful duck, and rolled her eyes dreadfully. She appeared to be enjoying her own performance immensely, and with every knowing cackle from the pit, her mannerisms became more pronounced and her lisp more ridiculous.

'Hang virtue! Where there ith no blood tith vithe,
And in him thauthineth!'

'What a devil is she up to?' Lacy asked. 'She's getting laughs, so no harm, I suppose, but it's damned odd.'

'A new attack on an old part?' Betsy Knepp asked when Kate came giggling into the tiring room.

'Just a little jest,' Kate shrugged. 'Lady Castlemaine has fallen out with Lady Harvey and paid me to lampoon her.'

'You take your life into your hands, girl,' Betsy said, shaking her head.

The response from the audience grew more uproarious in Kate's subsequent scenes, but the other shoe seemed to drop at the end of the climactic conspiracy scene just after she left the stage.

Young Theo Bird as Sanga turned to Nicholas Burt, as Cicero, and asked, '"But what'll you do with Sempronia?"'

Burt drew his breath to answer, but before he could speak, a lisping voice rang from the house, 'Thend her to Conthtantinople!'

It was Lady Castlemaine who had shouted out the answer. She stood in her box, triumphant, as the auditorium dissolved into pandemonium— howls of laughter, raucous shouts approving and disapproving the improvisation, the pounding of walking sticks, nuts and apple cores sailing through the air.

The final act was interrupted repeatedly by

253

cheers, catcalls, and further remonstrances from the audience, but the extent of the reaction to the performance did not become clear until the following day.

'Kate Corey has been arrested for her little mockery yesterday,' Michael Mohun fumed to the assembled company. 'Lady Harvey went crying to her cousin the Earl of Manchester, and he went straight to the king. So now we shall have to put on something else tomorrow, unless we can get this sorted out by then.'

'But why did Lady Castlemaine want to mock Lady Harvey, anyway?' Nell whispered to Betsy. Betsy raised her eyebrows significantly.

'A lovers' quarrel, so I hear. Apparently Castlemaine took comfort in Lady Harvey's arms when the king was in a rage over her going to bed with Ralph Montagu.'

'And why Constantinople?' Nell pressed.

'Why, because both ladies got the king to send their husbands far away, so they could do as they pleased. But their intrigue soured, as these things do. I fear me Kate has got herself in deeper than she knew.'

*   *   *

Nell spent that night with Charles. She did not dare raise the subject of the arrest of her fellow player, but it lay heavy on her mind. It was Charles who mentioned the play, saying that he would be at the next day's performance.

'But I thought—' Nell stopped. This could be dangerous territory.

'No, no, it's all settled. It's a command

performance, in fact, and I'm looking forward to it immensely.'

It seemed that Charles was not the only one eagerly anticipating the afternoon's entertainment. The theatre doors opened at noon to a mob of patrons, and when Nell made her entrance for the prologue, she had rarely seen the theatre as crowded. The seats in the pit were full, and men stood shoulder to shoulder in the aisles. The upper galleries seethed with bodies. She curtsied to Charles in the royal box, with Barbara Palmer preening at his side, and waited for the hubbub to subside before she spoke her prologue. When she had finished her speech and made her exit, she found the entire cast watching from the wings.

'I've heard murmurs that Lady Harvey has got people in the house today to cause trouble,' Lacy said. 'Have a care.'

Kate Corey appeared none the worse for her time in jail. She made her entrance to loud cheers, and if anything, her mimicry of Lady Harvey was even more pronounced than in the first performance.

"There are three competitorth," she lisped broadly. "Caiuth Antoniuth, Publiuth Galba . . ."

The audience howled in glee as she continued the list of Romans with their 'S'-laden names.

'"Luthiuth Cathiuth Longinuth, Quintuth Cornifithius, Caiuth Lithiniuth"'—Kate paused masterfully before finishing—"'and that talker, Thithero."'

The level of excitement and tension in the house mounted as the play progressed to the scene into which Barbara had thrown her verbal gauntlet during the previous day's performance. Kate fought the rising tide of voices, almost shouting to make herself heard above a chorus of hisses, but she carried gamely on.

She swept offstage at the conclusion of her scene, leaving Nicholas Burt and Theo Bird. They seemed to visibly brace themselves as they came to the infamous line.

'"But what'll you do with Sempronia?"' A fusillade of oranges pelted the stage, hitting the actors, smashing against the scenery, rolling back down to the audience. Theo ducked an orange and tried again to speak, but jeering shouts and stamping rose to such a level that he and the other actors gave up, held their places in silence until they could make themselves heard, and then simply got through to the end as quickly as they could.

'Don't go out,' Hart said, as Nell stood ready to make her entrance for the epilogue. 'Let's just end it.'

In the tiring room afterward, Kate looked shaken but defiant.

'It was worth it,' she claimed, stripping off her gown. 'Lady Castlemaine was so happy about yesterday that she got the king to let me out and spent all the morning with me coaching me to better mock Lady Harvey. And paid me twice what she had before, knowing that we should have a bigger audience for the jest today.'

'Lady Castlemaine's still got quite a hold on the royal cods, apparently,' Beck Marshall said, with a sidelong glance at Nell, 'despite rumours to the contrary.'

*   *   *

256

But Barbara's hold was weakening. Charles made no secret of his exasperation with her, and during his breakfast briefings, he vented his growing exasperation with her political machinations, extravagant spending, constant requests for money, and endless parade of lovers.

'I've had enough,' Charles announced to Nell soon after the New Year. '"Madam,' I told her, 'All that I ask of you for your own sake is, live so for the future as to make the least noise you can, and I care not who you love."'

'What did she say?' Nell asked.

'She threw a clock at me. But she'll be out of the palace within a fortnight. Don't worry for her,' he said, seeing the look on Nell's face. 'She and the children are well provided for. And while I'm thinking of it, Buckingham tells me there's a pretty little house available at Lincoln's Inn Fields.'

'For Barbara?' Nell asked.

'Barbara?' said Charles. 'No, she has houses enough. For you, Nelly, for you.'

Nell could scarcely draw breath to thank him she was so stunned, so she kissed him instead.

'Quite fashionable that area's become,' Charles said. 'And it's close by the theatre but near enough to here that we can see each other easily.'

*   *   *

Soon after that promise, Nell sat happily in an upper box at the King's Playhouse with Peg Hughes, who had joined the company that season. She was Sedley's mistress, which had made Nell initially wary of her, but she liked Peg's straightforward humour and even enjoyed watching her onstage.

257

Today they were watching the new tragicomedy *The Island Princess*, and Nell was in great spirits. She had just moved into her house in Newman's Row and could hardly believe that she was living in such grandeur.

'It's got two whole storeys,' she told Peg. 'Parlour, dining room, kitchen, bedchambers, garden at the back. Only steps from Lincoln's Inn Fields!'

'And servants?'

'A cookmaid, a maid of all work, and a porter,' Nell said. 'Think of that! You'll have to come and visit.'

'I wish Charlie would take a house for me,' Peg said. 'He keeps saying he hasn't the money. I like him, but I can only wait so long.' Her dark curls bounced as she giggled, and Nell thought she was a pretty wench indeed, and Charlie Sedley had better look sharp if he wasn't to lose her.

'Look,' Nell said. 'There's Moll Davis down there. She's looking a bit fat, don't you think?'

'If you ask me, there's always a bit of the piglet about her,' Peg said, and they both broke into laughter.

'Why, Mrs. Nelly!' The voice came from the next box, and Nell saw that Sam Pepys was there with his wife.

'Good afternoon, Sam. A pleasure to see you again, Mrs. Pepys. You know Margaret Hughes?'

'Yes, indeed,' Pepys smiled. 'It would be hard to forget such a charming face as hers is. Of course,' he hastened to add, 'not quite so charming a face as that of Mrs. Pepys, if you'll forgive me, Mrs. Peg.'

A couple of weeks later Peg came to call, and Nell showed her around the house.

'I can scarce believe it,' she said. 'All my life I've lived in wretched little dog holes. And now so much room, just for me.' She guided Peg to a window on the upper storey that looked out over Lincoln's Inn Fields.

'That's the Duke of Buckingham's house, and the Earl of Sandwich lives there, the Earl of Bristol there, and the Countess of Sunderland there. It's a bit noisy at night, is the only trouble. Whetstone Park is just there, you see, and of an evening the street is full of bingo boys drinking and roaring.'

'Did you hear about Ned Kynaston?' Peg asked, as they sat down to chocolate and cakes.

'No, what?' Nell asked in alarm at the worried look in Peg's eyes.

'He was set upon and beaten last night by two or three bravos and was hurt so bad he had to keep his bed today. Will Beeston had to go on in his part with book in hand.'

'Who would have reason to hurt poor Ned?' Nell asked. Peg looked down at her lap, tears welling in her eyes.

'They're saying it was Sedley did it, because Ned mocked him in his playing of *The Heiress*, but I'll not believe it.'

Nell wondered. Sedley was certainly a wild one, but would he go so far as that? She thought of poor Kate Corey spending a night locked up for her mockery of Lady Harvey and Lacy jailed for *The Change of Crowns*. The highborn might enjoy the playhouse and its pleasures, but there was no question that they thought actors were creatures far below them, to be taught a lesson if they got above their place.

259

Nell was going to celebrate her nineteenth birthday by having Charles to supper at her new house. She surveyed the table, its pewter dishes gleaming in the firelight, and breathed in the scent of pigeon pie and lamb with onions. It was perfect.

Charles arrived by sedan chair, anonymous and unnoticed in the wintry dark.

'Your birthday gift, sweetheart.' He brought a squirming something from beneath his cloak. A little black spaniel puppy, its laughing eyes looking up at Nell as she took him into her arms.

'His name is Tutty.'

'What a little heartbreaker!' she cried. 'I'll cherish his company when I can't have yours.'

* * *

Nell watched happily as Charles ate. It was wonderful to sit with him in her home, truly alone for the first time. She smiled, thinking about the night before them. With the security of her own house, she had decided she would no longer use the little lemon rind cups or sponges soaked in vinegar that had prevented unwanted conception, and she hoped that tonight Charles would give her the start of a baby.

After supper, she led him to the bedroom. Her maid, Bridget, had folded the linens into chests and scattered them with dried lavender, and the bedding gave off a pungent, honeylike smell. Taking Charles into her bed like this, with only one candle burning in the small chamber and the sounds of the street outside, was so different from

260

spending the night in the palace, knowing that attendants lay in the next room and would burst in at dawn. It felt like he was truly her lover. And it was so much more peaceful without those infernal clocks and dogs, Nell thought, drifting off to sleep curled against her king.

Chapter Eighteen

June, 1669

Nell was not happy with *Tyrannick Love*. She had barely been onstage over the past few months and had been longing to return, but this was another of Dryden's grand tragedies, and Valeria was the kind of serious role that always made her feel awkward. Worse, the play centred around the life of Saint Catherine and was intended as a tribute to Queen Catherine. Nell couldn't help but wonder how the queen would feel about watching her onstage, knowing how frequently the king was in her bed. And Hart, Lacy, and Mohun were wrangling with the painter Isaac Fuller about his commission to paint the elaborate scenery.

She arrived at the theatre for a rehearsal a few days before the play was to open to find the greenroom abuzz. What new calamity had befallen now? she wondered.

'The queen has miscarried again,' Beck Marshall hissed at her. 'The king's pet fox jumped on her bed and frighted her half to death.' Poor queen, Nell thought. And poor Charles, his hopes for an heir disappointed once more.

'Will the play go on?' she asked.

'Don't know,' Beck said. 'I reckon we'll find out soon enough.'

* * *

The play did go on. And despite her misgivings, Nell thought that the first night was going well. The house was packed, with the king, queen, and half the court there, and they sat rapt while angelic Peg Hughes as Saint Catherine ascended in her bed past Isaac Fuller's painted clouds to heaven.

The play drew to its close. Nell stabbed herself and died her best stage death. She lay there trying not to breathe visibly and looking forward to the epilogue that Dryden had written for her. Hart stepped forward and declaimed the solemn final speech of the play.

A funereal silence filled the theatre, and Richard Bell as the lead centurion bent to lift Nell's lifeless body. But up she popped and cried, ' "Hold, are you mad, you damned confounded dog? I am to rise, and speak the epilogue!" ' A wave of laughter went up.

She skipped forward onto the apron, and continued.

' *"I come, kind gentlemen, strange news to tell ye:*
I am the ghost of poor departed Nelly . . ." '

She gazed out over the pit, a sea of smiling faces, all eyes on her, hanging on her every word.

262

> *'"Gallants, look to't, you say there are no sprites,*
> *But I'll come dance about your beds at*
> *nights . . ."'*

Such a roar of laughter went up that she had to pause before she could go on. This was so much better than tragedy! Nell grinned with delight as she cried out the final lines of her speech.

> *'"Here Nelly lies, who, though she lived a slattern,*
> *Yet died a princess, acting in Saint Cather'n."'*

The crowd shouted their approval, clapping and stamping, and Nell curtsied deeply to the royal box, to the pit, to the packed galleries. It was good to be back.

*   *   *   *

James, Duke of Monmouth, was strikingly beautiful, Nell thought. There was no doubt he was the king's son, but the full lips, fair skin, and green eyes were evidence that his mother, Lucy Walter, must have been stunning. He had an engaging charm, and Nell liked him immediately and understood why Charles adored him.

They sat in the house in Newmarket that Charles had taken for her while he was attending the races. She had met Monmouth the previous day and invited him to come to visit. He was less than a year older than she was, and she felt an affinity with him despite the vast difference of their circumstances.

'I lived with my mother in Brussels until I was nine, you know,' Monmouth said, stretching his

263

long legs out before him in their silken stockings.

'Did you know who your father was?' she asked.

'Oh, yes. Of course he had no kingdom then. But my mother always told me my father was King of England, and I told it to my friends. They laughed,' he said, 'as well they might, for I ran barefoot in the streets with them and looked more like a beggar than the son of a king, albeit a bastard. I couldn't even read.'

'Really?' Perhaps this not-quite-prince had more in common with Nell than she had thought.

'Not a word, nor had I need. No school for me, only drudgery at home. My mother was little better than a whore, you know.' He said it abruptly and looked to Nell. What did she read in his eyes? Challenge? Shame? The desire for pity?

'Mine was no different,' she said, and he smiled at her, a shameful secret shared and accepted.

'But still I loved her,' Monmouth continued. 'When I was taken from her to be sent to the queen, my grandmother, in Paris to be brought up like a gentleman, I fought like a wolf, and cried to stay with her. The king's men took me from her by a trick. I didn't know until later that she had followed and begged to see me. But they kept her away.'

'How monstrous!' Nell cried. 'Did they never allow you a visit?'

Monmouth shook his head. 'She died. I never saw her more.' Tears glistened in his eyes. Nell felt a rush of maternal affection and pulled him to her, letting his head rest on her shoulder and stroking his hair like a child's.

Fingers crept onto her bosom. Nell thrust Monmouth away and smacked his hand.

'That's the last time you'll do that, or we will not speak again. I love your father, and am for him alone. Do you understand?'

Monmouth nodded sheepishly.

'Good. I would like us to be friends.'

*   *   *

That summer, with Parliament dismissed, Charles and the court escaped to Windsor, and he established Nell in a house only steps from the castle gate. The ancient castle with its ponderous walls looked like the Tower, a fortress rather than a home.

'That's why I like it,' Charles said. 'It can be properly garrisoned.' His mouth took on a grim set, and Nell thought of his father, helpless to defend himself as he was handed over to Cromwell's forces.

'But see,' he said, pointing towards the royal park, 'how many new trees are planted now, to replace those destroyed during the war. And how peaceful the gardens here within the walls.'

*   *   *

Nell was glad to have Rose's company again when the court returned to town in September. Her maid Bridget brought them cakes and ale as they sat enjoying the sun in Nell's little back garden, but Nell took only a bite before pushing her food aside with a grimace.

'What's the matter?' Rose asked.

'I don't know. I just don't seem to have an appetite for it. My belly's a bit off.'

'And how long has this been going on?'

'A few days. I feel out of sorts.'

Rose looked at Nell searchingly.

'Could it be you're with child?'

She was a few days late for her courses, and now she came to think about it, her breasts were tender, and everything about her body felt somehow different than ever before. She laughed out loud.

'Of course! What a fool I am!'

'Will the king be happy?' Rose asked.

'Yes,' said Nell. 'Oh, yes.'

*　　　*　　　*

Charles caught Nell up in his arms and stroked her belly as though he could feel the child within her already.

'He will be beautiful,' he told her. 'And with your spirit, he will be loved by all.'

*　　　*　　　*

Nell was supremely happy over the next weeks. Charles's joy over the child seemed to bind him more closely to her. He spent most evenings and many nights with her and even conducted business from the little house in Newman's Row. The French ambassador, Colbert de Croissy, seemed taken aback when he arrived as directed from the palace, but bowed low and kissed Nell's hand, and she strove to put him at his ease. She made small talk with the elegantly dressed Frenchman for a few minutes, but left him and Charles on their own when they got down to the purpose of the meeting, a treaty between England and France against

266

Holland.

Croissy appeared again a few days later, but his mood was sombre, and he sorrowfully conveyed the news that Charles's mother, Queen Henrietta Maria, had died at her house at Colombes, outside Paris.

'She was sixty and had been ill for some time,' Charles told Nell later that evening. 'I've known it was coming. But I fear for Minette.' His beloved youngest sister had just given birth. 'Croissy tells me she's beside herself with grief, and she's always been delicate.'

'When did you last see your mother?' Nell asked.

'Four years ago. Don't think me heartless that I do not weep for her. Try as I might, I cannot think of her without feeling myself back in those long and bitter years when I sometimes had not enough to eat, let alone a crown or a country. She held the purse strings and made things quite difficult. And all my life, it seemed that I could never meet with her approval, never be what she wished.'

'I understand,' Nell said. 'All too well.'

*   *   *

By the time Christmas came, Nell's swelling belly made her feel unfit to appear in public, and much of the time she kept to home. But she had frequent visits from Rose, Aphra, Buckingham, Monmouth, Rochester, and friends from the playhouse.

Charles seemed to be hers alone. Barbara had gone from the palace. The queen, apparently resigned to childlessness, had moved to Somerset House. If there were other women, they could not be taking much of his time, as he was so frequently

267

with her.

Spring came, and this year Nell felt a kindred spirit to the lambing ewes and calving cows. On May Day, a line of milkmaids stopped before Nell's door to dance and she had Bridget distribute coins to them.

'Thank you, ma'am,' they chorused. 'Thank you, my lady.'

My lady? Nell thought. It's only me, only Nell. But she could read awe in their faces and knew that a vast chasm now yawned between her and girls like them.

*　　　*　　　*

A week later, Nell's pains began. Rose, Bridget, and a midwife attended her, sponging the sweat from her face and body, holding her hand, murmuring their encouragement through the long hours when the torment seemed to go on and on and to be too great to bear. But finally, Nell gave a last push and felt the baby leave her, and a moment later, the afterbirth. The midwife cut the writhing cord and wiped the mucus from the baby's eyes. It coughed and began to cry.

'A fine and perfect boy,' the midwife said, wrapping the baby in a blanket and laying him in Nell's arms. She stared in amazement at the tiny wrinkled face, the dark damp curls, the rosebud lips that opened into a toothless cavern and let forth a furious yowl. She brought him to her breast, and thought there had never been anything so miraculous as the little bundle that sucked and cooed and gurgled.

Though the king already had three sons bearing his name, the baby could not be called other than Charles. So Charles he was, but from the day of his birth he was Charlie to Nell. His father visited that night, and held his newest son proudly.

'He looks just like you,' he said.

'No, just like you.'

'Well. The best of both, let's hope.'

*   *   *

During Nell's upsitting in the days following Charlie's birth, a stream of callers came bearing gifts and good wishes for the health and happiness of baby and mother. Peg Hughes had left the stage and Charles Sedley both to become the mistress of the king's cousin Prince Rupert, and she came with yards of fine French lace for the baby's gowns.

'Such a beautiful boy, Nell,' she cooed over little Charlie. 'And a surety for your future, too,' she added, with a flash of diamond hardness in her azure eyes. 'I hope that I may give my Rupert such a sign of my love for him.'

'I am so pleased for you,' Aphra said, when she called a few days later. 'But I do hope you'll get back onstage as soon as you are able. The theatre is the poorer for your absence.'

'We'll see,' Nell said. The world of the theatre seemed far off, its importance fallen away since Charlie's advent. What miraculous changes a baby wrought, she considered, observing her own mother hold her first grandchild, with a look of tenderness Nell had never seen before.

*   *   *

Less than a week after Charlie's birth, Charles took leave of Nell and journeyed toward Dover, where he was to meet his sister. As the Duchess d'Orléans and wife of the French king's brother, she was representing the French court, and the formal occasion was the signing of the treaty that had been so long in the works. But Nell knew that what gladdened Charles's heart was the prospect of being reunited with his adored baby sister Minette, whom he had not seen in many years, since she was almost a child.

With the court gone, it was only playhouse friends who visited. Hart came, and he and Nell sat quietly together.

'I'm happy for you, Nell,' he said. 'Happy to see you happy.'

'I am happy,' she said. 'But I wish . . .' It was only as the words left her mouth that she realised what she had been about to say. That some part of her wished it was his child that lay in the cradle nearby, and that it was for his footstep on the stair that she listened. Hart looked away and shook his head.

'It's for the best, Nelly. I could never have given you all this.' He gestured at the room and its furnishings, the piles of gifts.

'You gave me—everything,' Nell said softly. 'The playhouse. Where my life began. And in return . . .' Her voice caught, and Hart took her hand.

'You gave me your love,' said Hart. 'And that was enough.'

'You have it still. You always will.'

'And you mine, my little Nell.'

*　　　*　　　*

270

Charles returned from Dover with tales of banquets and dancing, hawking and hunting, and especially his joy at seeing his sister. He brought gifts for Nell from Minette—a magnificent necklace of pearl and gold, perfumed gloves of fine soft leather, and a silver cup and rattle for the baby.

'She sends her love, and regrets she could not meet you on this visit,' Charles said. 'She longs to meet you and knows you will be great friends.'

'The next time,' Nell said. 'I would be honoured to meet her.'

But less than a month later, shortly after her return to the French court, Minette died in agonised convulsions. Charles retreated alone to his bedchamber and wept for days. Nell, frightened by the lack of contact, summoned Buckingham.

'He loved her unreasoningly,' Buckingham said. 'She was but a baby when the war began, and he knew her only as a sweet and loving child who could do no wrong. And he was not the only one—she was the sweetheart of the French court. It's well known that her husband forsook her bed and preferred his lover the Chevalier de Lorraine, and that betrayal only made her seem the more virtuous.'

'But what was it killed her?' Nell asked.

'There are rumours of poison, of course, but then there always are. I'm going to France, to thank Louis for his condolences. I'll sniff around to see what I can learn, but I doubt anything but time will bring Charles to himself. Don't worry, he'll soon be back in your arms.'

Charles was back in Nell's arms within a week, but it was clear that his soul still ached. His humour was supplanted with an air of sadness. Nell did all she could to pet and comfort him, and he found solace in company with her and little Charlie.

'You are my family now,' he told her, bending over the baby's cradle. 'She was the last of my brothers and sisters but James, you know. There were two little girls who died as babies. Little Elizabeth died in captivity during the war, and the bastards told our poor brother Henry she'd died of a broken heart because I'd signed the Covenant. I lost Henry and Mary to smallpox not long after I came back to England. But Minette was the best of us.'

* * *

Charles sought the serenity of Windsor, and Nell was just recovered enough from little Charlie's birth to accompany him. But only a day or two after their arrival, she was disturbed to hear shouts from the street outside her house. Rushing to the window, she saw a scene below that looked like the opening of *Romeo and Juliet*. Liveried servants, some in the red of the king's household and some in the green of Prince Rupert's, were engaged in battle. Fists and kicking feet were flying, but two of the combatants had drawn knives. The young king's man faced off with a lad in green, while two or three others from each side tried to keep them apart. It looked for a moment as if they would succeed, and the fight was all over. But suddenly Prince Rupert's man called out, 'And a whore, to boot!'

The king's servant broke free from the grasp of his fellows, rushed at the other lad, and, to Nell's horror, thrust his dagger into his belly. The boy

272

staggered with the impact and looked down in disbelief at the bloom of blood darkening his livery. Then he fell, dropping to the dirt like a rag doll.

'A surgeon! A surgeon!' The cry went up from the servants in the street. Below, the front door of Nell's house flew open. Her page went pelting toward the castle, while Joe, her porter, helped a bawling crowd of liveried servants carry the wounded lad into the house.

Nell ran down the stairs, her stomach heaving in fear. The boy lay on the floor of the hallway, his blood already pooling on the planks, his face a sickly white. He wasn't moving. Joe straightened up and shook his head.

'I'm afraid he's dead, madam.'

'Dear God.' Nell felt her knees give way and just managed to slump onto a chair. 'Send someone to Prince Rupert's house.'

*   *   *

That evening Nell lay in her bed, her head still reeling from the shock of the fight and the murder. Bridget came in with her supper.

'I'm not hungry,' Nell said.

'You have to eat, madam,' Bridget said, setting out a bowl of broth and some bread. 'Awful though it is, you're still here, and you have to care for yourself for the sake of the baby, if nothing else.'

Nell knew she was right, and reluctantly sipped a spoonful of soup. It tasted good, and the warmth was comforting.

'Did they find out who he was? Why they were fighting?' Bridget didn't answer immediately, but busied herself tending the fire. 'Bridget?'

'Yes, madam.' Bridget spoke reluctantly. 'He was the brother of that player friend of yours, Mrs. Peg Hughes.'

'Oh, no!' Nell cried. Poor Peg. 'But what was the cause of such a terrible fight?'

'I hate to say it, madam, but it was you and Mrs. Peg.'

'What!'

'Yes, madam. Somehow the king's lads and Prince Rupert's lads got to arguing over who was the most handsome, you or Mrs. Peg. And that was the cause of all.'

'Oh, no.' It couldn't be. Nell thought of the boy's pale face, his head lolling to the side, smeared with blood. What a waste. What a senseless waste.

The next day Nell dictated a note to Peg Hughes, expressing her condolences, but the circumstances scarce seemed real. Could young men truly work themselves into a murderous rage over the respective charms of two actresses? The death of young Hughes hung over Nell, and she was relieved when the court left Windsor in the autumn to return to town.

Chapter Nineteen

September, 1670

'She's here,' someone hissed, and Nell turned, with the rest of the gathered company, to the doors of the Banqueting House. The newcomer had paused with exquisite timing so that she was framed in the doorway. Her gown, of cloth of gold, embroidered with pearls and jewels, caught and reflected the light of the candles so that it seemed to shimmer with fire, and she stood as some fairy queen stepping from the realm of the shadows. Dark ringlets cascaded over her white shoulders and reposed on the luxurious curve of her bosom, thrust high by the tightly laced bodice. From her tiny waist the skirt of her gown billowed gracefully, swaying slightly in a breath of warm evening breeze.

Her face was doll-like, Nell thought. Luminous dark eyes with lush lashes and arching brows. A delicate flush over the rounded cheeks, pouting lips that managed to be simultaneously sensual and childlike, inviting thoughts of acts which seemed both promised and forbidden.

Nell glanced to the dais where Charles sat, and felt a twinge in her heart. His lips curved into a catlike smile as he watched the girl, who now curtsied to the floor, casting her eyes demurely down and then raising them to meet his eyes. The look in his eyes—hot, predatory—sent a cold wave through Nell's stomach.

The interloper was making similar impressions around the room. The queen sat silently, but the compression of her lips and the hovering presence of her ladies gave an unmistakeable aura of tension. Barbara Palmer stood still but visibly agitated, her nostrils flaring and her eyes afire. Her little black boy, Mustapha, dutifully flapped his large fan of blue ostrich feathers toward her, but she slapped him away, and he retreated awkwardly, as if trying to become invisible.

*　　　*　　　*

'Louise de Keroualle,' Buckingham had told Nell earlier. 'She was one of Minette's ladies. Louis insisted I bring her back, said her presence might console Charles for the loss of his sister.' He'd caught Nell's sharp glance. 'No need to worry. She's famously a virgin, and on the hunt for a noble husband.'

*   *   *

Charles stood and went forward to meet Louise, still prostrated in a pool of gold silk, and extended his hand. She brought his ring to her mouth and kissed it. As her lips met the stone she raised her eyes, fixing him for a fleeting second with a bold and inviting glance, and then looked down again, as if the king's power had overwhelmed her.

Virgin, my arse, Nell thought. Or if so, she's been in training for her debut. Nell was glad that Charles's voluminous petticoat breeches hid the hardness she was sure was there. It would have been too humiliating to have to be made so unmistakeably aware of his reaction to this French baggage.

She glanced around. The eyes of every man present were focused intently on Louise.

*   *   *

'She may turn the king's head for a few weeks, but she'll not last,' Buckingham predicted over supper at Nell's house a few days later. 'Wenches are like fruits—only dear at their first coming in; their price falls apace after. She's already made herself heartily disliked. Even the queen and Barbara are united in

276

their mutual hatred of her.'

'Now there's an unholy alliance,' Rochester grinned.

'Besides, he dotes on little Charlie,' Buckingham said. 'That strengthens your hand. Charles has never abandoned the mother of one of his children.' Except poor Lucy Walter, Nell thought. Dying desperate and alone in Paris, denied even the chance to see her royal son.

*   *   *

Nell found herself fretting with worry about Louise de Keroualle. She was the talk of the court. Her beauty, her ancient and noble lineage, her fierce defence of her virginity until a suitable match should present itself, and of course her connection with the tragic and beloved Minette all made her fascinating.

'I've had enough of this,' Nell said to Rose one evening. 'Killigrew and Dryden keep trying to tempt me back to the stage, and mayhap I should go.'

'I think it's an excellent idea,' Rose agreed. 'It will give you something to occupy your time, and you won't look as if you're just waiting for the king's attention. What's the part?'

Nell made a face. 'Queen Almahide. Virtuous and stuffy. I hate these tragedies so. And the damned thing has two parts to it, each of them endless. But at least Dryden's agreed to write me an amusing prologue.'

So Nell set to work, hiring young Anne Reeves, a newcomer to the playhouse, to help her learn her innumerable lines. Dryden had written the part of

Almahide's servant, Esperanza, just for Anne, and Nell guessed that the wench either was or would shortly become his mistress. But she was a smart and likeable girl, happy to have the work, and gratifyingly in awe of Nell, so they got on well.

'You're perfect in that scene now,' Anne said after Nell repeated back her speech once more.

'Good. I don't think my head can hold any more today. And I'm hungry, aren't you?'

Rose was at the house that afternoon, and the three girls ate supper in the kitchen, with baby Charlie cooing in a basket next to Nell. The main rooms of the house were drafty, but the kitchen was cosy, and the homely surroundings and unpretentious company cheered Nell. Bridget fussed at her to eat more.

'You need your nourishment for your milk, madam,' she clucked. 'He's got such an appetite, the little lamb.'

Charlie did have an appetite, and though it was unfashionable to do so, Nell nursed him herself rather than giving him over to the care of a wet nurse. She brought the baby along to the playhouse so she could feed him during rehearsals, and Bridget watched over him in the greenroom while she worked. She was determined to make sure he knew he had a mother who loved and cared for him.

December, 1670

The first performance of *The Conquest of Granada* packed the theatre. Nell listened to the buzz of the audience, impatient to make her entrance

278

for the prologue. She knew her costume alone, an outsized cartwheel hat and ridiculously broad belt that mocked the fashions of the French court, would bring down the house. She enjoyed speaking prologues and epilogues more than almost anything else she did onstage. She did not have to put on the character of some dignified and highborn lady, but could be herself, or at least those aspects of herself that audiences most adored and responded to. She was speaking lines written for her, directly to the audience, picking out familiar faces to address. It was during prologues and epilogues that she most truly felt she was loved, and she had missed that love.

At last the musicians stopped, the prompter waved her on, and she entered.

'Nelly!' Cries of her name and cheers rang throughout the house. Yes, she thought, this is where I belong.

The play, pairing Hart and Nell once more, was wildly popular, and the performances stretched into mid-December. Despite her misgivings, Nell was enjoying herself. It felt like she was home again. She bantered backstage with Sam Pepys one afternoon, amused as always by his cheerful humour and lively interest in the life of the playhouse and court.

'The Duke of York simply hates that Mrs. Carwell,' he grinned, using the Anglicised butchery of Louise de Keroualle's name that had become common.

'Dismal Jimmy?' Nell laughed. 'There's precious little he takes pleasure in.'

'He'll be a sorry sight at the ball, I'll warrant,' Pepys chuckled. 'Or as it's to be masked, perhaps he'll send a servant in his place.'

'What ball?'

'The Christmas ball at court.'

'Oh, of course,' Nell faltered. She felt suddenly sick and wanted only to be alone. She had not been told of any ball, and that meant only one thing. She had not been invited.

On the night of the ball, Nell sat at home with Rose and baby Charlie, listening to the church bells sound the passing hours. The wind whistled, rattling the window casements. The streets outside seemed deserted, and Nell wondered if there was anyone in London who felt as alone as she that night.

*   *   *

The Conquest of Granada was such a success that Charles ordered a command performance in January. Nell thought how she used to look forward to shows at Whitehall. But her heart was no longer in it, and from her first entrance, the evening confirmed her apprehensions. Her outlandish French costume failed to get the laugh it always did at the playhouse, and even her prologue fell flat.

The rest of the play went no better. She could not find it in herself to rise to the heights of drama the part required, and felt foolish mouthing Dryden's bombastic verse.

> *". . . As you are noble, sir, protect me then*
> *From the rude outrage of insulting men."*

She noticed Louise giggle and whisper to a neighbour, hiding a smirk behind her fan. Nell had a sudden view of herself as Louise must see her—

an upstart oyster wench in tawdry worn-out finery, playing at being a noble lady. A beat too late, she realised that it was her cue and came in with her line just as Hart was going on with his to cover her lapse. She was sure she had never had a more disastrous performance.

*   *   *

A few days later, Nell sat at home with Aphra. Despite the roaring fire, the parlour was cold, and Nell pulled her shawl tighter about her.

'Truly I don't know what to do,' she said again.

'If you want my advice, Nell, keep up with your work. Not *Conquest* or any of these other tragedies—you hate them and they don't suit you. Get Killigrew to revive *All Mistaken*. Or let me write something for you. I'd love to, you know.'

Nell turned to Aphra and squeezed her hand. 'You're too good to me.'

'It's not a question of being good to you. You're a delight onstage and my treasured friend. It would be a joy to write you a good part.'

Alone in bed that night, Nell thought about what Aphra had said. A return to a favourite part or a new one might be just the thing. But could she go back? In this last show, her fellow players had treated her with deference and even awkwardness. She was no longer the girl she had been when she first stepped onto the stage. Nor was she a lady, and she never would be. What was she then? Neither fish nor fowl, she thought. Neither fish nor fowl.

Rose was practical as usual.

'What do you want, Nell? To be the king's wife? Impossible. To go back to the stage? You're no longer at home there, and in any case you could never earn enough from the playhouse to live as you do now. There is no one else you care for, and if there were, how should it fall out? No man of wealth and position would marry you. And no man of our sort either, now. Could you live above a shop and bed the king's son down on a pallet? No. So where does that leave you? In the king's bed. And what did I tell you all those years ago? Get the money first. Always.'

February, 1671

Charles was coming to supper for Nell's twenty-first birthday and was due at any moment. She surveyed the room with satisfaction. The fire crackled in the big fireplace, and she had had the table moved close to the hearth to counter the drafts. It was draped with a snowy damask cloth, and the pewter and glasses gleamed in the firelight. Candles were expensive, and she had waited until the last minute to have Bridget light them, but now they burned in brackets on the walls and on the table itself. The room looked as elegant as she could make it. And if anything was lacking, well, that was part of the point of the evening.

She heard the rumble of carriage wheels in the street below and checked her reflection in the mirror. She had taken special care over her hair and the application of colour on her cheeks and lips. The candlelight gave her skin a warm glow, and she was satisfied that she looked her best.

Charles smiled down at her as he embraced her. 'You're looking very handsome tonight, Mrs. Nelly.'

He pulled a small flat package from inside his coat.

'A little something in honour of your birthday. But you may not open it until after supper. And before anything else, I wish to see this son of mine.'

Little Charlie wore a fresh white gown and had fortunately managed not to soil it while waiting to make his appearance. Charles took him from Bridget's arms, and the baby reached up a small fat hand and tried to grasp Charles's moustache.

'Pluck thy father by the beard, wilt thou?' he laughed. He hefted the child in his arms. 'He's growing fast.'

*   *   *

As they lingered over wine, Charles was in a good humour. Nell felt that the time had come to make her request, but she was afraid to ask of him so bluntly what she wanted. She found her opening when he picked up the packet he had brought and placed it before her. She hesitated, and then looked him in the face.

'I am most grateful,' she began.

'You haven't seen what it is yet,' Charles laughed.

'You're always generous and thoughtful in your gifts, Your Majesty.'

He glanced at her, surprised at her unaccustomed formality.

'You give me beautiful things, and you provide for me this house to live in, and all that it contains.'

'But?' Charles prompted.

'But I never know when your presents will come. I cannot live on silks and jewels, without I pawn them. Your son must be fed and clothed, and I am

283

in constant doubt and anxiety about money.'

Charles was idly turning his wineglass back and forth, watching the play of the firelight upon it. He looked stern, but he frequently looked so when he was merely thoughtful. Go like the bear to the stake or hang an arse, Nell thought.

'This house is cold and drafty. I'm always in fear that your son will take cold. I do not mean to complain. I am most grateful for your protection and kindness. But I cannot go on as I am.'

A sharp gust of wind rattled the shutters and a cold breath of winter made the fire and candles gutter. Nell lifted her head to look at Charles, and his eyes met hers.

'I am your whore, Your Majesty. And whores must be paid.'

Charles looked at her in astonishment for a second, and then broke into hearty laughter.

''Od's fish! And so you shall be paid, sweetheart. You're right. My son must be well cared for, and you must live in comfort. You don't ask for much, God knows. You shall have a regular allowance. Four thousand pounds a year, let us say. And a better house.'

Nell hardly dared ask, but, flush with her success so far, ventured on.

'Oh, Charles, I know the perfect house. Just down Pall Mall, with a great garden at the back, that abuts the park.'

Charles laughed again and came around the table to take Nell into his arms.

'Very well,' he said. 'It shall be so. And now, won't you open your birthday present?'

Nell did, and it took her breath away—a heavy rope of shimmering pearls. She was even more

284

stunned when Buckingham told her the next day that Charles had paid four thousand pounds for them, and she knew she would never have had the courage to ask for a house if she had known what an extravagant treasure lay in the little packet.

*   *   *

The house was a wonder. All the morning Nell had kept walking from one room to another, scarcely able to believe that it was hers for life, as Charles had said. It sat smugly on the west end of Pall Mall, its brick façade rising tall and proud three storeys above the street. And seventeen fireplaces! She would no longer have to worry about little Charlie catching cold or bundle herself against the winter drafts.

She went again to the window of her bedroom and marvelled at the view—St. James's Park, the palace, the river. The garden was filled with fruit trees, barren now, but before long they would be laden with blossoms, sweetening the house with their scent.

*   *   *

'Why,' Charles raged, 'must my brother be the greatest blockhead in England?' Nell, weary of the tirade, which had broken out at intervals throughout the week, varied only by the pitch of the king's irritation, could only shake her head.

The Duke of York's wife, Anne, the daughter of the Earl of Clarendon, had died suddenly. Though outwardly the court was hushed in seemly mourning, behind closed doors there was urgent

285

whispered speculation about who the duke would marry.

'It's the perfect chance to counter the people's fear of his being a Papist,' Charles continued. 'Every Protestant lady in England is making sheep's eyes at him, and he has no thought beyond that squinting, pale-faced trollop Catherine Sedley!'

Nell winced at the cruelty of the comment. The duke's mistress, Charles Sedley's sixteen-year-old daughter, was not a beauty, but Nell could not help remembering her as the shy little girl who had visited the house in Epsom one afternoon during her riotous summer there with the two Charlies.

'I swear by my soul,' Charles ranted, 'his mistresses are so plain, I vow his confessors must give them to him as penance.'

'He could not marry Catherine Sedley, I suppose?' Nell asked.

'No!' Charles shouted. 'He must marry well. A lady of unquestionable virtue and most certainly not a Roman Catholic. Someone who could be queen if—' He faltered to a stop, his face red, and Nell saw the despair and sadness behind the anger. 'Someone who could be queen if he is king. For it may come to that in the end.'

*   *   *

Shortly after the death of the Duchess of York, Buckingham's mistress Anna Maria gave birth to his child, and the king stood as godfather as the baby was christened in Westminster Abbey. Despite the child's bastardy, Buckingham bestowed on him one of his own hereditary titles, Earl of Coventry. Nell wondered if Monmouth believed a precedent

286

had been set.

At the reception following the christening, Nell thought she had never seen Buckingham so happy, and Anna Maria glowed as she hovered over the tiny earl in his gilded cradle. Nell congratulated them sincerely, and resolved that if Anna Maria could accept that Buckingham had a wife, and yet live contentedly with him, she would make her mind up to be as happy with Charles and to put away her fears and discontents.

*　　　*　　　*

By May Nell's garden was adrift in clouds of white and pink blossoms, and from her bedroom windows she could see signs of spring—nesting sparrows, flowers sprouting in the green grass of the park, the bright flash of butterflies' wings. She felt a quickening of life within her, too, and knew that she was with child again.

Charles was jubilant at the news. Nell felt a twinge of sadness that as much as he adored his children, it was becoming apparent that the next king would be no son of his. It had been a year and a half since the queen had miscarried for the fourth time. She was now thirty-two, and there had been no word or even rumour of another pregnancy. Nell's new baby would be Charles's eleventh child, but none were legitimate, and Nell sensed his growing worry that his brother might succeed him, and what it would mean to the country.

*　　　*　　　*

The terrace at the back of Nell's garden overlooked

287

St. James's Park, and she could see Charles approaching, in conversation with a dour figure in black. John Evelyn, Charles's fellow enthusiast in scientific inquiry, always radiated disapproval, no matter how pleasant Nell tried to be to him. He bowed stiffly as the king stopped at the foot of the garden wall.

'Will you come to supper tonight?' Nell asked.

'I will,' Charles said. 'Kiss Charlie for me and tell him his da will see him soon. It's been too many days since I've held my bonny boy.'

'And too many days since you've held his bonny mother,' Nell teased.

'I'll soon put that right.' Nell leaned over the wall to receive a kiss from Charles. Evelyn looked pained.

''Fore God, you're positively glowing,' Charles said, stepping back to look at her. 'I think I'll have Lely paint you, so I can admire you even when you're not with me.'

Nell watched Charles and Evelyn walk on and realised that they were headed for Barbara Palmer's house. But that put no fear into her now. Charles had told her, almost with relief, she thought, that Barbara was now Dryden's mistress. Bound perhaps by their long history or their children, Charles and Barbara had settled into an amicable truce, but the fire of passion had burned out.

*   *   *

Nell lounged against a pile of pillows, naked but for a gossamer piece of white silk draped across her lap and her hair flowing over her shoulders. She had been sitting so for an hour, and could not stop herself from moving her head to release the tension. Sir Peter Lely looked up from his canvas.

'Not much longer today. It's coming splendidly.'

'I should hope so. Why, Charles!'

Lely stood and bowed as the king entered and advanced, grinning, to examine the canvas and then the original posed before him.

'Gorgeous. Both of them.'

Nell laughed. She didn't know whether Charles meant both her and the portrait, or both of her breasts, grown fuller and rounder in her pregnancy, but she was happy all the same. Charles tossed his hat onto a table, helped himself to a glass of wine, and straddled a stool.

'Where's the little one?' he wanted to know. Charlie was to be in the painting, as a little cherub.

'We do not need him today, Your Majesty,' said Lely. 'When I have Mrs. Nelly well set, then I will paint him in. Too tiring for a baby to sit still for so long.'

'And for me!' Nell said.

'Here,' said Charles. 'Revive your flagging spirits.' He squatted and tilted his wineglass to her lips. A drop splashed onto her nipple, and he put his mouth to her breast and sucked it clean.

'I think I'll hang the picture in the Banqueting House,' he said. 'So it will be the first thing that foreign ambassadors see when they present themselves.'

Nell giggled. 'So you'd share me with them, then?'

'Share, no. Let them have a peek, so they can envy what I've got, yes.'

289

In August, Buckingham and Anna Maria's little son died suddenly. Under her veil, Anna Maria's face was a mask of devastation, and Buckingham's pallor stood out from his clothes of solid black. The little earl was laid to rest in the Villiers family vault in the Henry VII Chapel of Westminster Abbey, as the stones echoed with Anna Maria's sobs. Nell ached for her and longed to get home to hold little Charlie in her arms and know that he was safe. She would not survive such a loss, she thought.

Chapter Twenty

Third of September, 1671

Charles loved his sojourns to Newmarket, which had become regular excursions each spring and fall, and Nell loved to be with him there. He was so much more relaxed than in town. He lived for the races, and went early each morning to consult with his trainers and jockeys about how his beloved horses were coming on and to be sure that the great sleek animals were being fed their particular mix of soaked bread and eggs. During the day he delighted in strolling the town, chatting to whoever approached him, jesting with blacksmiths and dairymaids as easily as he did with dukes and earls.

So pleased had Charles been by his first visit to Newmarket that he had commissioned Christopher Wren to build him a house in town. It was finally finished, and Nell and Charles had retreated there after a glorious day, summer's warmth just beginning to hint at the fade to autumn. It was pleasant to have had a quiet supper alone, and now Nell lay in bed with her swelling belly and breasts pressed against Charles's back. Their breathing was quiet and slow, in time with each other. Outside, rain pattered on the trees. Nell thought that there was no place in the world she would rather be.

Through the window, the moon was just coming into view. The stars were banked with clouds, the twinkle of their fire only intermittently visible.

Nell had thought Charles was asleep, but he stirred, bringing her hand to his lips and kissing her fingers. He sighed deeply and Nell kissed his shoulder.

'What, my love?'

'Nothing. Just—memories.'

'Of what?'

Charles was silent for a moment before answering. 'It was on this day twenty years ago that we lost the battle at Worcester.'

'Tell me.'

'Have I not told you the story?'

'No.'

He rolled to face her, stroking the curls tumbled about her face. His eyes were sad and tired. She took his hand and kissed it, then pressed it to her cheek. He pulled her to him so that her head was cradled on his chest.

'I was in Scotland. In Perth, godforsaken Perth, reduced to depending on the Scots. Cromwell and his army were to the north and began to advance on us, and the time seemed right to push into England. The people would rally to us, it was said; would send Oliver's troops scurrying like rats. So we set forth, and I was proclaimed king in Penrith and Rokeby. But as we drew further south, it was the Scots soldiers who scurried from our ranks, and none came to take their place.'

As though a dam had broken, the words now poured from Charles, and Nell saw written on his face long-banished memories.

'There were spies among us who betrayed our positions and plans, and hundreds—nay, thousands—were arrested. And seeing this, those who might have come lost heart and stayed away. We pressed on, and limped into Worcester.'

He paused, staring intently into the darkness, as if planning again his strategy.

'Cromwell soon came with a vast army. And seasoned men, not the weakened rabble that we were. I was glad of the chance to fight instead of waiting and running, and we charged upon them with the fury of despair and rage. But they captured Fort Royal and turned our own guns upon us; our losses were heavy, and we had no choice but to retreat. Many of my men threw down their arms, aweary of the fight. I urged them on, cajoled, threatened, wept. But it was no use.'

He covered his eyes with his hand, as if to block out the sights in his mind's eye. Nell stroked his cheek.

'I would that I had been there,' she said. 'I would gladly have died with you a hundred times before I would have left you to fight alone.'

'I know you would. You've a stouter heart than many a soldier.'

Nell poured him wine, and he drank absently, his mind still in the past.

'What then?' Nell prompted.

'Dark was coming on. The city was surrounded, and Cromwell's men were searching for me. Although I had no great wish to live, I could not let myself be taken captive, and so become the pawn of the enemy. And so I flew, and not a moment before time. As I was leaving by the back door of the house where I had been staying, the troops were at the front.'

'And so you went to France?' Nell asked.

'Aye, after six weeks of hiding and terror and hunger, my feet bloody with walking. But that's a story for another time. Truly I do not know how or why I was preserved, except by the hand of providence. And I live every day with the thought of the thousands who were lost.'

He gave a choking sound. Nell stroked the stubble of his cropped head.

'Oh, my love. You did all you could, and no man could have done more. And your salvation has meant the salvation of so many.' She pulled him close to her breast as she did their son, murmuring consolation and love, until his sobs ceased.

*   *   *

In the morning, Nell woke feeling wretched. Her burgeoning belly, aching back, and swelling feet made her constantly uncomfortable, and she craved the cosy familiarity of her own house.

'You will not mind if I go back to London a few days early, will you?' she asked Charles. 'I'm not fit to be seen in public, and I had rather be at home with Rose's company than sit here while you spend your days at the races and your nights dancing.'

'No, lambkin,' he assured her. 'You go, and I'll

293

be back in town by the end of the week.'

So Nell went home, but a fortnight passed, and still Charles remained at Newmarket.

*   *   *

Laughter poured from the open windows of Euston Hall, breaking the calm of the warm autumn evening and the steady chirp of crickets. The light from hundreds of candles spilled forth, too, making the grand house a beacon in the warm darkness of the surrounding grounds.

The musicians struck up a dance tune, and rhythmic clapping accompanied the clatter of heels on the wooden floor of the great hall and the swish and rustle of silks as the dancing couples paraded.

On the terrace outside, Lady Arlington and the French ambassador Colbert de Croissy watched the merrymaking through one of the tall windows. Lady Arlington smiled. The king headed the dancers, leading Louise de Keroualle down the length of the room, a crowd of revellers flanking them. Louise was flushed with wine, the heat of the dance, and, unmistakeably, erotic excitement tinged with pride at her public triumph in capturing the king's attentions so wholly. For there was no doubt about the intensity of his gaze at Louise's dimpled smirk and heaving décolletage.

Lady Arlington turned to Croissy, who was also watching the king and Louise with a knowing smile.

'It will be tonight,' she purred. 'At last.'

'Yes,' he agreed. 'And she does not need a throne to rule. Only a bed.'

*   *   *

Nell could not seem to sit still. She started as the bell of a nearby church struck ten, and Rose looked at her sharply.

'You're not yourself tonight.'

They had sat for some time in silence in front of the hearth. Nell's thoughts had been racing, anxiety clawing at her mind.

'Oh, Rose. I'm afraid. Charles is still at Newmarket, and so is that little French wagtail. I've left him a clear path to her bed.'

'Well, and what then?' Rose asked. 'How many other beds has he graced these past years? Yet he comes back to you.'

'True. But this one feels different. The queen, Barbara—they were here before me. It irked me to share him with Moll Davis and the others who've passed his way, but I never felt as I do now. That I might lose him.'

Rose came to stand behind Nell's chair, stroking the russet curls, and bent to kiss the top of her sister's head.

'You'll not lose him. He cares for you, Nell. He adores little Charlie, and he'll adore the second child. Louise may have his eye at the moment, but not forever. You feel it more because you're with child.'

Nell nodded, and reached up to hold her sister's hand.

'No doubt. But it's real enough. And as I am now, I can do nothing. Just sit and wait. While she triumphs. And everyone laughs.'

Rose shook her head. 'This I promise you, Nell. No one is laughing at you. There's nothing you can do for the moment. But soon you'll have another royal baby. And eventually he'll grow tired of Louise and see her for what she is—vain, shallow, and with her own interests first and always in her heart. But your heart is good, and full of love for the king. And he knows it.'

Nell cradled her sister's hand to her cheek. 'I pray you're right. Why are you so good to me, Rose?'

Rose laughed. 'I'm only telling you the truth, pigwidgeon. You'll see.'

*   *   *

Charles and Louise kissed, to the applause and raucous calls of the crowd. To the delight of all, Lady Arlington had arranged that the evening should culminate in the mock marriage of the couple. Croissy had given away the bride, leading her forward and giving her hand into the hand of the king with a pride and triumphant excitement that almost eclipsed Louise's. With Lord John Vaughan serving as Lord of Misrule and priest in proxy, Charles and Louise had stood before the rapt congregation and exchanged vows—in voices too low to be heard, but of an unmistakeable fervour.

Dancing followed, and when everyone was heated to a fever pitch, Charles had hoisted Louise's skirts to reveal her shining white silk stockings and the creamy smoothness of the thighs above, and removed one of her blue ribbon garters. Raising it above his head, a trophy of his conquest to come, he had thrown it to the throng of men, who had jostled and shoved to be the one to catch the prize. Triumphant and catlike, the Earl of Mulgrave had caught it and pinned it to the breast of his waistcoat like the favour of a lover.

And now, as the candles burned to their nubs and the guests were sodden with liquor and the evening's increasingly erotic undertones, the public rites were drawing to a close and the wedding night approached.

'It is late,' Charles remarked, yawning ostentatiously for the benefit of his grinning audience, 'and time for bed.'

'Your Majesty?' Lord Arlington was at the king's elbow, bowing and smiling. Charles offered Louise his arm. She simpered and lowered her eyes with a maidenly blush, and allowed him to lead her behind Arlington up the broad staircase.

The musicians and guests followed, the fiddles keeping up a jaunty country dance tune as if the nuptials celebrated were those of some farmer lad and his milkmaid bride.

The crowd halted as Arlington threw open the doors of Louise's bedchamber. Red rose petals were scattered over the snowy damask of the sheets and pillows on the huge bed and their perfume mingled with the honey-sweetness of the candles. The bedroom glowed with a soft and magical light, enhanced by the silver moonlight cascading through the leaves of the trees rustling outside the open windows.

The revellers surged in behind as Charles and Louise followed Arlington into the room. But as if unexpectedly ushered into a sanctuary, the musicians faltered into silence and the chattering and laughter died away. All eyes were on the king, who stood to the side of the bed, burning eyes on Louise, who stood hardly breathing only a few inches from him. Slowly and deliberately, he removed his coat and held it out. Someone rushed forward to receive it, and others stepped forward to unbutton his waistcoat, remove his shoes, disencumber him from his stockings, garters, sashes, and sword belt.

A crowd of ladies engulfed Louise. The layers of satin and brocade were peeled away until she stood in only a shift of the most delicate lawn and a pair of stays in an exquisitely pale blue silk, embroidered in gold. Her dark hair tumbled onto her shoulders, her dark eyes glowing as she faced her lord.

Charles, now clad in only his long shirt and breeches, took Louise in with a hungry glance.

'Out,' he commanded, and there was a surge toward the door.

Alone with his long-sought prize, Charles grasped a handful of her hair, pulled her head back, and devoured her mouth, his other arm grappling her body to him as he lowered her onto the bed.

*   *   *

A slash of lightning shredded the night sky, followed a second later by a cataclysmic boom of thunder. Nell jerked awake and was half out of bed before she realised what had woken her. Gasping for breath, she clutched the covers around her. Outside the window the lightning crackled and a savage wind whipped the branches of the trees, dark tentacles lashing the shadowed greyness of the storm clouds.

She had been having the dream again. The door closed in her face, solid and unyielding to her desperate pounding. She was shut out. Forsaken and afraid.

The room smelled faintly of wood smoke, the beeswax candles, and the lavender of the bedding. It should have been homely and comforting, but Nell felt tiny and lost, and she longed for strong arms to hold her.

'Charles,' she whispered into the darkness. 'Charles.'

*   *   *

Tutty wriggled up to Buckingham, and he obligingly scratched the dog's ears before seating himself. Nell settled herself heavily as Bridget brought in coffee and cakes.

'You're looking well,' Buckingham said.

'You're a liar, Your Grace. I'm looking as big as a frigging house,' she snorted.

'In a good cause. The king loves his children, loves your little Charlie.' He seemed about to say something else, but instead tasted his coffee, added a spoon of sugar to his cup, and drank again.

'Well, George,' said Nell. 'You're my chronicle these days, as I am not fit to show myself in society. What's the new news?'

'The usual. Barbara has moved on from Dryden and taken William Wycherley to her bed, they say.'

The reference to beds hung heavy in the air.

'And Louise?'

Buckingham sighed. 'Yes, she's finally given the king her maidenhead, if that's what you mean.'

Tutty nosed at Nell's knee, and she hoisted the dog onto her lap and nestled her cheek against his, stroking the soft fur.

'Oh. I thought she was still dreaming of a crown.'

Buckingham shrugged. 'I think she knows now

that will never be. Louis sent her to influence Charles on behalf of France, and that she cannot do if he loses patience with her.'

Nell felt a dart of cold fear in the pit of her stomach. 'And what am I to do?'

Buckingham smiled gently at her. 'All will be well. She's led him a longer dance than most, but in the end she'll be no more than just another passing fancy.'

Nell hugged the dog's face to her cheek. 'She's already more than that.' She glanced around the room. The rich wooden panelling of the walls, the fine hangings, the sumptuous Turkey carpet, her clothes, the very coffee and cakes on the table were paid for by Charles. And if she lost him?

She looked at Buckingham, and followed his glance out of the window. They watched the progress of a young wench pushing a heavy barrow of oysters before her. The dart of fear clenched into a knot in her stomach.

'Help me, George. The enemy is at the gates. And like this'—she gestured helplessly to her belly—'I can do nothing. I cannot hope to compete against her beauty. I cannot even be at court.'

'I don't think you'll lose him. You have his child; you have another soon to come. At the very worst he would provide for them, and for you. What you must do is carry on. When he's here, make your company a joy. Make him comfortable and happy. Provide a refuge. As you always do. On no account act jealously or shrewishly. He'll tire of her. She's like some dainty sweet—compelling, but not food to live on. You are that to him. I know it. You must remember it.'

When he rose and kissed Nell goodbye, she

300

impulsively took his hands. 'Thank you, George. I will heed your advice, as always.'

'Good. And take heart—you must be brought to bed very soon now, and can reenter the lists.'

'Not soon enough. Six weeks or more.'

'Oh.' He glanced at her belly. 'I had thought you were further along than that.'

*   *   *

Before dawn on Christmas Day, Nell's labour began. It was harder than her first, and when the baby finally came and she was assured that he was whole and healthy, she fell gratefully into an exhausted sleep, leaving the tiny dark-haired boy in the capable care of Rose, Bridget, and the midwife. She woke in the dark of the night to find Bridget dozing in a chair by her bedside, and the baby asleep in his cradle. Bridget woke as Nell stirred, and brought the baby to her. As Nell nursed him, his eyes closed tight and his cheeks working, she thought that he was worth whatever pain and sorrow his coming had cost.

Charles cooed over his newest son and was pleased with Nell's wish to name the child James, in honour of his brother. He joined Nell for a cosy supper in her bedroom and was solicitous of her health and happiness to a degree that relieved her of her fears. He stayed into the evening, kissing her tenderly when he took his leave, and promising to return the next day.

The Duke of York called to admire his namesake, bearing lavish gifts, and his uncharacteristic warmth made Nell feel more fondly towards him than she would have thought

301

possible. Even so, within a few days the baby had come to be called Jemmy, and when his half brother the Duke of Monmouth visited, Nell whispered to him that it was really he for whom little Jemmy had been named.

*   *   *

Little Charlie toddled across the carpet to Rose, who held baby Jemmy in her arms, and stood holding on to her skirts.

'That's a brave little man!' Rose cried, leaning down to kiss him. 'Nell, they are the most beautiful boys. Perhaps a sweet girl next time, eh?'

Nell shook her head. 'No next time for me. Mademoiselle Buttock shows no signs of retreat, and I cannot compete for Charles's affections while I'm shut away with a great belly and a swollen face. I'll not take that chance again.'

*   *   *

At the end of January 1672, the Theatre Royal burned beyond repair, along with all its scenery and costumes. Worse, an actor died in the fire. Nell had acted with Richard Bell in *Tyrannick Love* and *The Conquest of Granada* and he had been well-liked among the company.

Nell wept at the news. The playhouse had been her true home for so long, the place where her life had been transformed, that it felt like a part of herself had been lost. She kept recalling details—the green leather of the benches in the pit, the narrow stairs to the tiring rooms, the board in the stage floor just off left that squeaked, the

302

comforting smell of paint and sawdust, the little cubby where Orange Moll had kept her wares, and where the fire was supposed to have started. Impossible that it should all be gone.

Nell thought of the actors, suddenly out of work. Recalling her fear and uncertainty during the theatre's long closure because of the plague and the fire, she sent to ask Hart to visit her. He was limping slightly when he arrived but waved away her concern.

'Gout, that's all,' he said. 'I'm turning into an old man, Nell.'

'That you can never be. You're as handsome as ever, Hart. No matter how old we may be, I'll always think of you as I first saw you. Took my breath away, you did, that night in Lewkenor's Lane.'

'What a tiny little mite you were then. Little did I think you'd steal my heart.'

'What will you do?' Nell asked as they settled before the fire. 'What's to become of the company?'

'We'll rebuild,' Hart said. 'Killigrew's already talking to Christopher Wren about the designs. And in the meantime, it looks as if we'll move back to Lincoln's Inn Fields. You know the Duke's Company has just moved to their new theatre, so the Portugal Street place stands empty. We should be able to get a show open in a month or so.'

'Have you seen the new playhouse?' Nell asked.

'Oh, yes. Magnificent. There's nothing they can't do with scenery or effects there, and it's right on the river, you know. Once again they've got us scrambling to keep up.'

'Take this,' Nell said, handing him a purse. 'That none of the actors shall be hard-pressed until they

303

can play again.'

Hart hefted the bag in his hand. 'Jesu, Nell, how much is in here?'

'A hundred pounds. Is it enough to pay the company's wages for a few weeks?'

'And then some,' Hart said, looking in disbelief at the gold that glinted in the bag.

'Good,' said Nell. 'No need to tell anyone where it came from. Just let them know they'll not go hungry.'

'Nell,' Hart said, 'there's another problem you ought to know of. Dicky One-Shank. He soldiers on, does the best he can, but he's growing too old to work. I haven't the heart to turn him out, but the company can't afford to keep him idle, either.'

'Send him to me,' Nell said. 'I'll give him a comfortable berth, as he'd say, and truly I'd welcome his company.'

'He's a proud old goat. He won't want charity.'

'Very well, I'll give him enough work that he feels he's earning his keep. He can feed and groom that poxed donkey that Charles got for Charlie.'

*   *   *

'Will the king really come?' Rose asked again.

'Of course,' Nell said. 'He said there's nothing he'd like better than to have my birthday supper with us.'

'But what shall we have to eat?' Rose worried. 'He's used to having everything so grand.'

'Pigeon pie is his favourite,' Nell said. 'Give him plenty of that and some wine, and he'll be well pleased.'

On Candlemas night, Nell's twenty-second

birthday, Charles arrived alone on foot at the little house that Nell had taken for Rose not far from her own. He embraced Rose and greeted her husband, John, before seating himself near the fire with Charlie on his knee and Jemmy in the crook of an arm.

'What happiness,' he grinned. 'To be here with you, and away from all those glavering busybodies at court.'

There was a knock at the door, and John went to see to it. Nell could hear his voice growing increasingly agitated, and then he came back into the room, red in the face and looking more ill at ease than she had ever seen him.

'Sorry, Nell, I didn't know what to do.' A cloaked woman stepped into the room behind him, her shabby clothes exuding the smell of strong spirits. She pushed her hood back from her face, and Nell felt as though she would faint from the surprise.

'Charles,' she said finally, 'this is my mother.'

*   *   *

'By all means you should take her in,' Charles said. 'She's your mother, for better or worse. The house is big enough, and it's probably best to keep her there than have her getting into mischief elsewhere.'

Nell tried to imagine her mother conversing with Buckingham or Rochester or Aphra and failed to conjure any picture that didn't make her cringe.

'And while we're about it,' Charles said, 'I've a mind to give a pension to Rose and her man. Perhaps it'll lessen the odds that I chance to encounter him in his professional capacity some dark night on Hounslow Heath.'

So Eleanor was moved into a room of her own in Nell's house.

'It's so fine,' she said, looking in awe at the carpets, the billowing bedcovers, the view to St. James's Park.

'I'm happy to be able to provide for you,' Nell answered. 'But it must be understood—this is my house. You give no orders to the servants, and you cause no trouble. And if I ever hear that you have so much as raised a hand to one of my boys, out you go.'

'Oh, I won't,' Eleanor hastened to agree. 'I see now there was much I did badly when you were a little thing, and I'd like to do differently, since you're giving me the chance.'

Charlie and Jemmy were stunned to discover that they had a grandmother, and were cautiously interested. Freed of the need to scratch out a living and the terror of finding herself on the streets, Eleanor seemed to relax and to drop the hard armour she had been accustomed to wear. Nell was amazed to enter the nursery one afternoon and find Jemmy perched on Eleanor's knee and Charlie seated at her feet as she told them a story of her childhood days. The boys smiled happily at her and turned their attention back to Eleanor.

'And then what happened?' Charlie prompted.

'Why, then my mam found that I'd stuck my finger into the pie, and she sent me to bed without supper, and it learned me to ask before taking,' Eleanor said.

Chapter Twenty-one

February, 1673

'All three of them?' Nell slammed down her cup of chocolate and the liquid sloshed over the rim and into the delicate porcelain saucer. She stared in horror at Monmouth. 'How could all three of them be having his babies?'

'Well, I rather think—' he began.

'Hell and death.' Nell jumped up, eyes blazing. 'That Louise is breeding is no surprise. He bedded her practically before the eyes of the court at Newmarket. But Barbara? I thought he'd forsaken her bed long ago. And Moll Davis, too? When did he find the time?'

Monmouth came to her side near the window. 'If Barbara's child is even his—which I much doubt; it's almost surely John Churchill's—it was probably a matter of trying to pacify her about the flow of gifts and favours to Louise. The Weeping Willow's got twenty-four rooms at the palace now and another sixteen for her servants. Better to quiet Barbara with his pillicock than with another outlay of cash, that would be Charles's policy. As for Moll, well, she can't help but have noticed that your boys have improved your position, and she probably wants the same for herself.'

Nell stared across the winter-barren park to the palace. Bastard, she thought. You great poxy goat of a whoremonger. It's not enough that you install that French draggletail in the palace itself, but you must take a flourish with every open arse of an actress or hackney whore that crosses your path, while I sit here with your brats.

She looked at Monmouth beside her, so pretty, so much his father's son. It would serve Charles right if she put a set of horns on him with his own boy. But no. She must bite back her jealousy and anger, never give Charles a moment's doubt about her faithfulness or a hint of a reason to cast her off. But she'd be damned if she'd let him fob her off with less than Louise was getting.

'Squintabella's got twenty-four rooms?' she asked, calmer now. 'What else has she wheedled out of him?'

'Money, of course. He pays her gambling debts, into the thousands of pounds.'

'And?'

'Jewellery.'

'Tell me.'

'She's sporting a pearl necklace and a diamond and telling all who'll listen that the one cost the king four thousand pounds and the other six thousand.'

A further kick to Nell's stomach.

'What else?'

Monmouth dropped his eyes.

'Come,' she said, taking his hand, 'tell me the worst. I'll find out soon enough, and forewarned is forearmed.'

'She's to be made Baroness Petersfield, Countess of Fareham, and Duchess of Portsmouth.'

* * *

Charles had stopped by to visit and he and Nell sat in her garden, the scent of the ripening oranges perfuming the air.

'You made Barbara Baroness Nonsuch, Countess of Southampton, and Duchess of Cleveland,' Nell said. 'You've made Louise Duchess of Portsmouth. Am I not whore enough to be a duchess?'

'Nelly, you know I can't,' Charles protested.

'Why?'

'Don't make me say it,' he said gently. 'You know why. Barbara is a Villiers. Her father and grandfather were viscounts. Louise comes of a noble family, though poor. And though you are their equal—nay, their better—in every way that matters to me, yet I cannot make you a lady.'

Nell looked down at her hands. They were smooth and soft and bejewelled, bearing no trace of the hard labour of her childhood. Her clothes were rich, from the snowy white of her petticoats, with their yards of handmade Belgian lace, to the jewels that dangled from her ears. She was mistress of a grand house and more than a dozen servants. But she would never be a lady, could never be more than plain Nell Gwynn.

She looked to where Charlie and Jemmy and their nursemaids sat in the shade nearby. Both children had Charles's dark hair and eyes, were near copies of the portrait Nell had seen of the king as a young boy.

'And our boys?' she asked. 'They are the sons of a king. Will you not honour that blood, though you cannot honour mine?'

'I do honor you, Nell,' Charles said. 'With my love and with all that is in my power to give. You're right about the boys. I've been distracted and should have considered it sooner. They shall

have allowances of their own. And in a year or two
Charlie shall be—what? Earl of Burford, does that
suit? And when Jemmy is older he shall have a title,
too.'

*　　　*　　　*

The court was a nest of bosom-serpents and
archrogues, Nell thought, for all their money and
titles, and wondered why she wanted to be accepted
there.

'Always pissing up my back, they are, thinking to
work me to get what they want from Charles,' she
confided to Rose one night. 'And Louise. The more
I see of her the less I like her, if such a thing is
possible. At any hint she'll not get what she wants,
she bursts into tears. I truly think Charles would
have packed her off long ago but that it serves him
to keep friendly with the French.'

'Most likely,' Rose agreed.

'It would have made you sick to see her nose
in the air when she told me Charles was making
her boy Duke of Richmond and Lennox, as well
as a whole string of other titles. Never loses an
opportunity to remind everyone what a lofty family
she comes of.'

*　　　*　　　*

The next day, Louise appeared ostentatiously in
mourning, swathed head to toe in black, standing
out among the brightly dressed court like a crow in
a field of daisies. A knot of people gathered around
her.

She has as many tricks as a dancing bear, Nell

310

thought, and sidled closer.

'What's this, Louise?' she asked. 'Don't tell me you've lost some kinsman?'

'Yes,' Louise sighed. 'My dear cousin the Chevalier de Rohan. One of ze most noble of all ze noblemen of France.' She sniffled loudly and lifted her veil to touch a black silk handkerchief to her eyes.

'That's right, duck,' Nell said. 'Let it out. The more you cry the less you'll piss.'

*　　　*　　　*

The following day Nell appeared in deepest mourning. Murmurs and giggles followed in her wake as she made her way to where Louise stood in a tragic pose, one elbow delicately rested on a windowsill and her head bowed in her hand as if in unfathomable grief. At the noise of the approaching crowd, Louise raised her head and took in Nell's dress.

'What eez zis?' she murmured, frowning slightly. ''Ave you also suffered a loss, Mrs. Nelly?'

'Oh, yes,' said Nell. 'The Cham of Tartary.'

Louise blinked at her uncertainly. 'And 'oo is 'ee? Not some relation of yours?'

'Why, yes indeed,' Nell said. 'Oddly enough he was exactly the same relation to me as the Chevalier de Rohan was to you.'

*　　　*　　　*

'Squintabella's got a coach and six!' Nell fumed a week later. 'I know she got it just to wipe my eye. I know it's ridiculous to let her put me out of

311

countenance, yet I cannot help being vexed.'

Aphra shrugged.

'The more showy the equipage, the bigger the whore. That's the only lesson to be learned there.'

'So it is,' Nell said, suddenly brightening. 'And perhaps one I can teach her, too.'

*   *   *

The six oxen shuffled in their traces, rolling their eyes and lowing. They were alarmingly big, their heads at the level of Nell's shoulders, and the team of them stretched almost thirty feet in front of the wagon. All activity in the royal mews had come to a halt while the animals were hitched, and a crowd of farriers, grooms, and stable boys looked on as the wagoner grinned down at Nell, his teeth white against his sun-browned face.

'Ready, madam?' he called. 'Sure and I'd like to see their faces when you go by. The palace has never seen such a sight, I'm sure of that.'

'No,' Nell said. 'Well, let's give them something to talk about, then.'

A groom helped her climb up to the seat beside the wagoner.

'Onward,' Nell said. 'At least we'll have a laugh ourselves.'

The wagon picked up speed as the wagoner urged the oxen along with his whip, and the palace ahead jolted up and down as Nell and her team of six raced toward it. Startled faces sped by in a blur.

'You've a good audience now, madam,' the wagoner shouted as they thundered past the new Horse and Foot Guards buildings. 'I'd say it's now or never!'

312

Nell grasped the whip he offered her, and as he pulled the reins, steering the oxen close to the Banqueting House, she stood, holding tight to him with one hand. With the other she raised the whip, and bellowed, 'Whores to market! Whores to market! Fine fresh whores to market this day!'

A flock of courtiers scattered like chickens, and Nell caught sight of Louise, her mouth a little O of shock; of Barbara, her eyebrows arching in surprise; and of Charles, roaring with laughter. The wagon tore past the palace and out into the park, the wagoner pulling hard on the reins to turn the team and slow them.

'Let them run!' Nell cried, laughing. 'I don't know when I've had such fun in my life.'

Chapter Twenty-two

Test Act?' Nell asked Buckingham. 'What is a Test Act? And why is Charles and everyone so troubled at it?'

They were walking in St. James's Park, with Jemmy and Charlie and their nurses straggling behind.

'Oh, Nell,' Buckingham groaned. 'Do you pay no mind to the business of the kingdom?'

'Not if I can help it,' Nell retorted. She turned to ensure that they were not too far outstripping the boys and their attendants. 'But Charles was in such a taking last night, going on about Lord Shaftesbury and Parliament as if they were devils from hell itself, that he alarmed me extremely. So do please tell me only as much as I need to know to

313

understand his ravings.'

'Very well,' Buckingham agreed. 'Parliament is most discontent that the king has declared war on the Dutch once more and is thus become further allied with France.'

'They fear war with France?' Nell asked.

'They fear France's power and influence, and even more they fear and hate the Roman Catholic church, and anything that smacks of popery. The king tested their patience with his Declaration of Indulgence, allowing his Papist subjects the freedom of their conscience, and now they have put forth the Test Act, which demands that every officeholder under the crown must acknowledge the Church of England and take the sacrament under it, and deny the doctrine of transubstantiation, or lose their position.'

'But the queen is a Papist, and Barbara, and Louise,' Nell said, bewildered. 'And there are many Papists holding offices. The Duke of York himself.'

'And there you have it in a nutshell,' Buckingham said. 'The Duke of York himself, who is like to become king, if God do not grant His Majesty a child. And that is what strikes terror and rage into the heart of Shaftesbury and many others, and why they are now grown so fretful.'

He was about to go on, but a wail set up from behind them, and Nell turned and dashed back to kiss Charlie, who had fallen and scraped his knee.

'You'll have to tell me more another time, George,' she cried. 'I have matters of real importance to attend to, as you can see.'

Over the next months Nell heard far more than she cared to about the king's skirmishes with Parliament.

314

'I have only just managed to exempt the queen's household from the Test Act,' Charles spat, 'but I cannot save James from his own idiocy.' The Duke of York was forced to resign as Lord High Admiral, and the temper of neither king nor Parliament was improved when the duke chose as his new bride the Catholic princess Mary of Modena.

By the end of the year, Charles's battle with Parliament had reached a new pitch of ferocity.

'They defy me at every turn and deny me the money I must needs have, so I have prorogued the whoreson villains,' he announced to Nell one night in bed.

'What does that mean?' she asked anxiously. 'Prorogued?'

'It means, dear heart,' he said, taking her wineglass out of her hand and putting it on the table beside the bed, 'that I have sent the dogs home until I shall fetch them back.'

'And is the hurly-burly now at an end?' she asked, taking hold of his cock and stroking it, but intent on an answer.

'I fear me no,' Charles replied. 'When I dismissed that coxcomb Shaftesbury as Lord Chancellor, he dared to say, 'It is only laying down my gown and girding my sword,' the pompous fool. The battle is just beginning.'

He pulled Nell under him and positioned himself between her legs, but his cock flopped soft against her thighs and he sighed.

'There is nowhere they do not trouble me,' he said, attempting to make a joke of it. But as Nell caressed him with mouth and hands, she reflected that it was not the first time in recent months he had failed to rise, or risen only to fall.

315

A few days into the new year, a grim-faced Buckingham called on Nell. He stood again as soon as he had taken a seat, and paced, leaving his coffee to grow cold. 'The dogs are baying for my blood,' he said finally. 'And truly, I know not what to do.'

'Which dogs?' Nell asked. 'Not Parliament again?'

'It will come to that, too,' Buckingham said. 'As soon as His Majesty had left the House of Lords today, Anna Maria's brother-in-law rose to accuse me on behalf of her son, naming again the death of Lord Shrewsbury.'

'But that was years ago!' Nell cried.

'Yes, years ago,' Buckingham said. 'Years in which I have lived with her though yet I have a wife.'

'And which of them can claim to be without sin?' Nell scoffed.

'None of them.' Buckingham sank into a chair and stared at her in despair. 'But it's a pretext, do you see. They have begged the Lords to take action against me, and my enemies are sure to take the occasion to act.'

'What harm can they cause you? Surely not much?'

Buckingham shook his head.

'There are still ecclesiastical laws against adultery. The House can fine me for all I have. Send me to the Tower with no chance of being let out. Excommunicate me, so that I could not take communion, and so lose my offices. The bastards have got me in a net.'

316

A few days later, Buckingham was back, and Nell was appalled and frightened at the pass he had come to in just a few days. His face was wet with tears.

'Oh, Nell, what am I to do?' he cried again. 'I have met their charges with humble repentance, and it has got me nowhere. Now they accuse me of everything from encouraging popery to attempting the sin of buggery. I would laugh were it not so serious. They have demanded that I be removed from all the employments I hold under His Majesty, and that I be barred from his presence and councils forever.'

'But you have been like a brother to Charles since his birth! Surely he—'

Buckingham cut her off with a wave of his hand. 'The king cannot or will not help me in this. They have left me nowhere to turn. Anna Maria is frighted out of her head. She is making ready to go to a nunnery, and I will then see my love no more.'

A week later, Buckingham's destruction was complete.

'The great axe has fallen,' he announced to Nell, his face haggard and drawn. 'The king has dismissed me from all my places. Anna Maria is gone. None at court will speak to me now, for men ruined by their prince and in disgrace are like places struck with lightning—it's counted unlawful to approach them. I have no will to live, nor even a place to live did I want to.'

'Then you shall lodge with me,' Nell said. 'And we will dare the lightning together. For you have been my true friend, and I am yours, whatever storms may come.'

Chapter Twenty-three

Twenty-sixth of March, 1674

Nell looked around the packed house at the new Theatre Royal. The air was electric with excitement. It had been three years since she had been onstage, and she felt a pang of regret that she sat here, among the audience. She thought of the bustle backstage, the camaraderie and last-minute good wishes, and longed to be a part of it. She wished that it was she, not Michael Mohun, who would speak Dryden's new prologue written especially for this first performance in the new theater.

Beggars' Bush. Nell laughed to herself, recalling that night so long ago at Madam Ross's when Hart had joked that the audience had been waiting since years before the king's return to find out how the play came out. The blustery grey day at the Red Bull came back to her with intense clarity. She recalled waiting eagerly with Rose for the play to begin, remembered the hazelnuts they ate, the cracked shells carpeting the pit, Wat's florid face contorted in a leering grin, the shouts of laughter at his performance as King of the Beggars. Dear Wat Clun. Did his spirit hover somewhere here, wishing he could once more put corporeal feet upon the stage and give voice before an audience?

Lacy had taken over Wat's role, and Hart,

Nicholas Burt, Robert Shatterell, and William Cartwright were still playing their old roles, but many of the faces were new to the company since Nell had left the stage.

The performance over, Nell was loath to leave. She was with Charles in the royal box, along with the queen, Louise, Monmouth, and the Duke and Duchess of York. All those gentry coves, she thought. And me, Nell Gwynn. She had a sudden wave of revolt, almost of revulsion. How had she so lost herself that she sat here, on the wrong side of the curtain? Her spirit ached to belong once more to the tribe gathered in the greenroom, and she started to her feet and threaded her way outward through the bodies.

'I'm going to go around and say hello,' she paused to tell Charles. 'But I'll see you for supper, I hope?'

Four or five of the scenekeepers were gathered at the stage door, laughing and chaffing.

'Evening, lads,' Nell cried. 'Good work today! A good start in the new house.' They snatched off their hats and stood aside to let her pass, their easy grins replaced with formal smiles.

'Thank you, madam,' said Willie Taimes with a nervous nod. 'Wishing your ladyship good health.'

Nell had a sudden memory of him, laughing down at her and joking backstage a few years ago. What show had it been? Oh, yes, *Secret Love*, because he had been bawdily appreciative of her legs in her rhinegraves breeches. And look at him now. He looked as if he expected her to cry 'Off with his head!'

The greenroom rang with laughter and voices. So many actors she didn't know, Nell thought. Cardell

319

Goodman, Joe Haines, and many whose names she could not even call to mind. And the women—only Beck Marshall and Kate Corey were left from the old days, and they must be upstairs.

'Well done, all!' The chatter stopped as faces turned to her.

'Thank you, Mrs. Nelly,' said Marmaduke Watson. 'Much appreciated, I'm sure.' He even bowed.

It was all wrong, Nell thought, all wrong. I'm not a lady, she wanted to shout, I'm one of you. Don't you know me? Don't you remember how we played together? But she had not played with most of those gathered here. Hart, Mohun, and Lacy would be upstairs in the tiring room, she knew, but she was suddenly weary and disheartened. What if they, too, looked at her as though she were a stranger? It was more than she could bear, and she turned back to the stage door, the chatter resuming in her wake.

Nell's coach waited in Bridges Street, her coachman seated on the box. He lifted his head as Nell approached and jumped down to open the door, and she saw that his lip was split and bloody, one of his eyes was blackened, and the front of his coat was torn and streaked with blood and dirt.

'Why, John, whatever has happened to you?' she cried.

'I had a fight, madam.' He jutted his square chin, defying her to question him further.

'A fight? What happened?'

'Well, you see, madam, there was other coachmen waiting, like, for their ladies and gentlemen. And the coachman to the Earl of Shaftesbury—a poxy bastard he is—the coachman, madam, not the earl, begging your pardon—he called me a whore's coachman. So there you have it.'

Nell laughed, her black mood lifted.

'But John, I am a whore! No need to fight because someone says what is only the truth.'

John stared at her, swelling with indignation, and drew a deep breath.

'Well, madam,' he roared, 'you may not mind being called a whore, but I'll be damned if I'll be called a whore's coachman!'

*   *   *

The longtime rivalry between the King's Company and the Duke's continued. The Duke's Company had recently moved into the elegant new Dorset Gardens Theatre, on the riverfront just to the east of Blackfriars, and had been filling the playhouse for days with Thomas Shadwell's new adaptation of *The Tempest*, with singing, dancing, and spectacular stage effects.

Nell was seeing the production for the third time, this time with Aphra, who regarded the Duke's Playhouse as her home, as it had produced her first three plays to great success. The final curtain fell to cheers and ringing applause and Nell looked down at the crowd in the pit, on their feet and heading for the exits.

'A miracle what the show does with scenery and machinery,' she commented. 'No wonder Killigrew is worried. Again.'

'We're worried, too,' Aphra said. 'Opera, that's all the rage now. We make our little effort, as you see, but the French and Italians are taking over the stage.'

'Not like the old days,' Nell agreed. 'Come, will you not join me for a mouthful of something?'

Nell and Aphra drew admiring glances and calls of greeting as they made their way out of the theatre.

'Mistress Nell!' The voice was urgent. Not another fight, Nell hoped.

'Nell!' The voice was familiar but Nell could not at first place the figure who moved towards them. His coat was shabby and his step hesitant. He pulled his hat off as he approached, and Nell saw with a shock that it was her old lover Robbie Duncan. He stared at her for a second and then bowed, hat still in hand.

'Robbie!'

'Aye, it's me.' He stood uncertainly as the theatre crowd swirled around them on the street. 'I'm sorry to disturb you, especially as you're in company, but I don't know where else to turn.' Nell saw that he was on the brink of tears.

'Excuse me for a moment, Aphra. Come here with me, Robbie.' She pulled him out of the centre of the crowd. 'What's happened to you?'

'The Great Fire is what began the troubles,' Robbie said. 'We lost the warehouse with all our stores—my father and brothers and me, you know. All we had, up in flames. And naught has gone right since then. The cloth trade has fallen on hard times, and I cannot seem to put a foot right.'

'Do you need money?' She reached for the purse that dangled at her waist, but Robbie waved her off.

'I'm no beggar, Nell. What I need is work. A new trade so that I can keep myself. And I wondered if you might put in a word for me somewhere. If you're willing, that is.'

322

'Of course I'm willing!' Nell cried. 'You took me out of harm's way and saved me from Jack. It's the least that I can do. Can you come and see me tomorrow afternoon? I live in Pall Mall, a brick house near—'

'I know your house,' Robbie said. 'I'll come. Thank you, Nell. You've as good a heart as always.'

*　　　*　　　*

The sun shone full on the sundial in the Privy Garden. Charles squinted at it and then at the watch in his hand, snapping the watch case shut in satisfaction.

'Saved you, did he?' he mused. 'Then certainly we shall do something for him. Would he do well with a commission in the Guards, do you think?'

'Oh, yes!' cried Nell. 'That would be perfect. You are so good to help him.'

'Not at all,' Charles said. 'My father always taught me never to abandon the protection of my friends under any pretension whatsoever. You are doing right by doing what you can for this Robbie, and for his protection of you when you needed it, I am determined to do all that I can for him.'

He walked on, Nell's arm crooked in his, and stopped to examine the white blooms on a rosebush. His shaggy black dog Gypsy, half greyhound and half spaniel, raced ahead, leaping and snapping at a grasshopper.

'I know I told you I couldn't give you a title,' he said, and Nell's heart skipped. 'But there is something I can do in that line. Would you like to be a maid of honour to the queen?' Nell stopped short and almost laughed.

323

'Will she have me?'

'Oh, yes. She quite likes you, you know.'

'That's very generous of her.'

'She's a kind and loving soul,' Charles said. 'Like you.'

'Thank you.' Nell squeezed his arm, feeling that the sun suddenly shone more brightly on her.

'And I think we can stretch your allowance a bit, as well. Five thousand pounds a year?'

*   *   *

Charles was better than his word, and over the next few months Nell received not only her usual support but occasional showers of additional money.

'But, Nell, can you afford it?' Rose cried when Nell insisted on buying her three pairs of new shoes.

'Yes! Charles has been so generous, he keeps giving me more beyond my allowance! It is such a relief not to feel the constant worry, and there are so many needs crying out. Charlie really is of an age that he needs a tutor, and Dorset recommends his friend Sir Fleetwood Sheppard as learned and honest.'

'A tutor!' Rose marvelled.

'Yes,' Nell said proudly. 'He'll learn Latin and Greek and all that is proper to a gentleman.'

'Who would have thought,' Rose mused, 'when you and I were little kinchins scrabbling in the cinders and hauling barrels of oysters, that your boy would be a great gentleman?'

'And I'm going to get a sedan chair of my own,' Nell said. 'It will save on money, really, for now I have to pay the cost of hiring chair men to carry me.

And I'm going to make some little improvements to the bedchamber, too. If I cannot have an apartment in the palace like Louise, I can at least create a little royal nest of my own for Charles to come to.'

*　　　*　　　*

The French silversmith John Coques presented Nell with a bill of seventeen hundred pounds for his contribution to the little improvements to the bedchamber. Nell could scarce believe how much she had spent—she felt faint when she thought of the amount. But as she stood and admired the newly luxurious room, she decided it was worth it. The bed alone was something the likes of which no one had ever seen. Two thousand two hundred and sixty-five ounces of sterling silver had gone into the making of it. The figure of the king's head alone weighed eleven pounds. An exquisite representation of the rope dancer Jacob Hall—Barbara's latest lover, according to rumour—balanced on a delicate strand of silver rope. Four fat and winged cherubs supported the posts, which were surmounted by four great crowns. Angels flew across the enormous headboard, and under them was a scene of Roman slaves dancing.

To go with the silver bed were silver andirons for the fireplace, silver candelabra, silver side tables. But it was the bed that took Nell's breath away. She traced a finger along the scrolls of a cockleshell on the headboard. Its elaborate carving evoked the frontispiece above the stage of the first Theatre Royal beneath which she had played so many performances, and the rich red curtains were like the playhouse curtains.

'This bed is your stage,' Rochester had said. And finally she had a stage worthy of her role as king's lover. The wall facing the bed was mirrored from floor to ceiling. And that is our audience, she thought. Only ourselves. So you can watch yourself as you enjoy me, see my face, my bubbies bobbling when you are taking me from behind, see me open and wet when I kneel between your legs to worship you, to make you happy as only I can. To keep part of you my own, no matter who else may come.

*　　　*　　　*

When the sedan chair was delivered the following week, Nell could not restrain herself from an outing. Only to visit Rose, which seemed a little silly, but she knew that Rose would enjoy seeing the chair and would not laugh at her for her extravagance.

'Oh, Nell, it's splendid!' Rose cried, running her hand over the soft quilted leather of the interior. 'All these little gold nail heads in such intricate patterns!' She climbed in to try the padded seat. 'Most comfortable. Much better than you muddying your skirts with walking, and surely much better to have your own chair than to have to wait for a hired one to arrive.'

'Take a ride,' Nell urged. 'Tom, take Mrs. Cassells down the road and back.'

Rose leaned out of the window and waved, grinning, as the chair men lifted the chair and set off. 'Imagine me in a sedan chair!' she called back, laughing.

Nell was expecting Charles to supper and did not tarry for a long visit, but took her chair home when Rose came back from her jaunt. She was admiring

326

the cunning way the gilded leather curtains could be hooked into place to cover the windows or held back to provide a view, when her heart dropped into a cold pit.

Jack was standing before her house. He stood side on to her, looking at the house, but there was no mistaking him. The way he held his shoulders, the tilt of his head as he regarded the second-storey windows, the fall of his hair—they were burned into her memory. He turned and his eyes met hers. The briefest moment of surprise flitted across his face before he smiled. A cool, malevolent smile. Nell shouted to Tom as she threw the door of the chair open, but Jack turned and ran, and he was gone almost before her feet were on the cobblestones.

'Did you see that man?' she cried. 'See that he does not come near the door!' The chair men set off the way Jack had gone as she ran for the house and pounded up the stairs to the nursery. The nursemaid, Meg, looked up in alarm as Nell dashed through the door. Charlie and Jemmy were safely at play on the floor, arranging small soldiers in battle.

'You fair gave me a start, madam!' Meg cried.

'I'm sorry,' Nell gasped. 'I saw . . .' She did not want to frighten the boys. 'I missed my honey lambs so much I had to run to kiss them.'

*　　　*　　　*

'He looked straight at me, insolent as you please,' Nell told Charles over supper. 'Oh, Charles, he knows the house. Surely he must know about the boys.'

'I'll post every soldier in England around the house before I'll let him harm you,' Charles

327

promised. 'My men are out there now with your lads. But I'd feel better knowing you had someone closer to hand when I'm not here. What do you think of asking Rose's man to be here nights to keep close watch? We can kill two birds with one stone. I'll pay him enough to keep him from mischief on the roads.'

'That would be wonderful,' Nell agreed. 'I'll ask Rose if they'll move in. I've plenty of room, and I'd be happy having her company as well as feeling safer with Johnny here.'

* * *

Nell was having a restless night. Exhausted though she was, she could not sleep. Worries about Jemmy, about money, about Charles crowded her thoughts. And always at the back of her mind now lurked Jack, though she felt infinitely safer knowing that Rose and John Cassells slept close by. She listened to the church bells toll midnight, then one. Finally, finally, she drifted off. In her dreams, she was being stalked by a large cat. It crept out of the shadows and slunk toward her, its chest close to the floor, its huge paws stealthy in their silence. It crouched, gathering itself to spring. And suddenly Nell was wide awake. She was pinned to her bed by the weight of someone kneeling astride her, and a heavy hand clamped over her nose and mouth kept her silent. It was Jack.

'Mistress Nelly.' His voice was so low she almost could not hear him. 'That's what they call you now, isn't it? Now that you're a fine rich lady. And I mean to take some of those riches, too, for you've robbed me of years of my life.'

328

Nell's mind spun. She had to make a noise, to waken the household. Had to find a way to escape. She tried to lift her arms but they were trapped by her sides under the covers, held in place by Jack's body on top of hers. He leaned close to her, and the reek of his breath brought back her nighttime terrors of all those years ago. She thought her heart would explode within her from fear.

'I've waited so long to pay you this visit,' Jack breathed in her ear. 'So long. I've dreamed about it, Nell, and what I'll do to you.' He reached down, and as his hand came back into Nell's view she saw the glint of a knife blade in the moonlight, and the gleam of his eyes.

'I found His Majesty's guard sleeping below, and he'll never wake now. Then ever so quietly in by the pantry window. You really should speak to the cook about leaving it open so.' Jack caressed Nell's cheek with the blade of his knife, then brought the tip to her throat. She felt the sting as the steel nipped her skin. Jack leaned closer.

'Don't you wonder, Nell, if I've visited your little boys first?'

Nell gave a huge heave, and managed to throw him off balance for a moment. She cried out and almost succeeded in escaping, but he caught himself before he went over, and pushed her back down onto the bed, pressing his hand over her face so hard that she wondered if her neck would break.

'I think I'll just let you wonder about that, you little whore. While I entertain myself with you for a bit.' He thrust himself against her as he brought the blade of the knife to her throat. 'Haven't you missed me, honey? Never fear, we've got all night.'

The next moments happened in a blur—an

explosion of sounds in the shadowed dark. The door to the room flew open and Nell thanked God that John Cassells had somehow heard and come to her rescue. There was a brilliant flash and tremendous roar as his pistol discharged, a heavy thud as Jack fell to the floor, grunts as John heaved himself across the room and onto Jack and they rolled and struggled. A sharp gasp of pain. Running footsteps in the hallway, the children's cries of alarm, a cataclysmic sound of breaking glass, shouts from outside.

Nell freed herself from the bedclothes and ran to the window, crying out at the streaks of blood on the shattered panes. In the moonlight she saw Jack sprawled on the cobblestones. He struggled to his feet and staggered away.

Rose's scream made Nell turn back to the room, now crowded with her steward, Groundes; the two porters; four footmen; and two pages. Rose and Eleanor knelt next to where John lay on the floor, and in the flickering candlelight Nell could see that his shirt was dark with blood and it was spreading across the carpet and floor.

'Fetch a doctor!' Nell shouted, and one of the porters turned and ran, as the others stooped to help John. His face was ghastly white, and blood bubbled at his lips as he tried to speak to Rose, who clutched him to her.

'Don't speak, love, all will be well,' she crooned, rocking him, her hand trying to staunch the bleeding. But John shuddered and then lay still and silent in her arms, his pistol on the floor beside him. A trail of blood led to the window, and blood smeared the shattered window casement.

Charles had surveyed the damage, stationed soldiers at Nell's house, and offered his condolences and a generous lifelong pension to the inconsolable Rose and promised her that justice would be done, that Jack would be found and brought to punishment. But in the cold light of the afternoon, as night approached again, and Nell and Rose sat huddled by the fire in Nell's room, none of it seemed to matter. John was dead, and Jack was out there somewhere. As long as he still lived and went free, Nell would always be in terror that he would return.

Bridget appeared to take away the remains of supper and spoke in a low voice to Nell.

'Madam, Harry Killigrew is below and requests most urgently that he might speak to you and Mrs. Cassells.'

Nell looked to Rose.

'Yes,' Rose said. 'Ask him to come up.'

Harry, swathed in a dark cloak, threw his hat aside as he came into the room, and stooped swiftly to Rose.

'I know the king has put out a watch for the murderer, but if you give the word, Rose, my friends and I can work in other ways.'

'What do you mean?' Nell asked.

'Better not to ask,' Harry said, glancing at her. 'Rose knows. Would you have it so, darling?'

Rose lifted her head, and Nell had never seen a look of such black intensity in her eyes.

'Yes,' Rose whispered. 'Find him, Harry. Find him.'

''Fore God, Rose,' Nell gasped, when Harry had gone. 'What was that about?'

'The Mohocks,' Rose said. 'The Ballers. Have you not heard of them?'

'Yes, I've heard that the Ballers are a crew of dissolute gents who gather at Mrs. Bennett's to watch her strumpets dance naked,' Nell said. 'And Sam Pepys told me how people cleared the paths at Vauxhall when Harry and his mates were there, so drunk and swaggering they were.'

'Yes,' Rose said. 'But they do more than that when occasion offers. When justice needs to be meted out and the law cannot come at the miscreants, the Mohocks have their ways of finding them out, and seeing that vengeance is served.'

Nell felt the hair rise on the back of her neck at the thought of Harry and his friends asking quiet questions in the right quarters, giving coin for information, calling in favours owed, and closing in on Jack, wherever he might be hiding, with no mercy in their hearts.

Two days later Harry reappeared at the house once dark had fallen. He nodded at Rose in response to the question in her eyes.

'Aye, we found him. We made it clear to him before he died that we knew not only of this crime, but of what he had done to you, Nell, long past. And took from him the weapon he used against you.' He brought a leather bag from beneath his cloak, and Nell could see that it was steeped in blood. 'Would you see? His cock and stones.'

Nell's gorge rose and she clapped a napkin to her mouth to prevent herself from vomiting.

'No,' she gasped. 'Merciful God, no.'

Chapter Twenty-four

Jack's invasion of the house and John's death threw Nell's household into grief and confusion. Rose sobbed in her room for hours at a time. The children had loved and admired John, who had seemed the very epitome of dashing manhood, and were fretful and frightened. And no wonder, Nell thought. If you cannot feel that you are safe in your own bed, where is there hope of safety? She was determined to spare them the terrors of her own childhood, and despaired that brutality and bloodshed had come so vividly into their lives. The servants were jumpy. Meals were late, errands were forgotten, and the other tasks of keeping the household running were performed erratically or not at all. And Eleanor, whose presence had been no more than an occasional annoyance to Nell, was drinking heavily, erupting into rages at whoever crossed her path, and causing constant turmoil.

This, Nell thought, was the final straw.

The little donkey, Louise, stood in the drawing room. She raised her tail and let fall a mushy turd onto the Turkey carpet.

'But how did she get in?' Nell demanded again. The stable boy knelt with a pan and shovel to clean up the mess, ducking his head to avoid Nell's eyes. Bridget stepped forward, her hands working in her apron.

'It was your mother, madam. She said she was trying to cheer little Jemmy up as he was feeling so poorly, and she thought he'd brighten to have the creature's company.'

333

Nell was so stunned she couldn't speak. Eleanor had been the cause of little domestic flurries and skirmishes since her arrival, but this raised things to a new level. Dicky One-Shank stumped toward them and silently took the donkey's bridle. Nell shook her head in disbelief as the donkey was led away in disgrace, then turned back to Bridget.

'Was she drunk? Come, I'll not be angry.' Bridget met her eyes, and Nell saw sympathy there.

'Aye, deep cut, madam, and flying the flag of defiance.'

*　　　　*　　　　*

'Fling her out,' Rose said when Nell sought her advice. 'You've done more for her than she had any call to expect, and none could blame you.'

'I can't just put her onto the streets,' Nell objected.

Rose shrugged. 'Then move her somewhere else. We've all enough trouble without her making more.'

Rose's practicality helped make up Nell's mind, and she felt a great weight had been lifted from her shoulders once she had settled her mother in a house in Chelsea. It was far enough away that Eleanor could not easily make inconvenient scenes, yet close enough to salve her conscience. She could still make visits with the boys, limiting the time she spent with her mother to what was bearable.

She little needed the additional pressure of her mother's disagreeable nature, she thought. The year had gone from bad to worse, quite apart from the goings-on in her household. The spring and autumn meetings of Parliament had been fraught with dissension, with the members urging Charles to enforce penal laws against Catholics and to make war on France. He had lost patience in November, and once more prorogued Parliament, so the Earl of Shaftesbury's Green Ribbon Club met and plotted in the coffeehouses.

And Jemmy was sick again. Nell sat by the side of the bed, consumed with worry. He was sleeping now, and the flush of the fever seemed to have broken. He didn't lack for care—at the first sign of his illness she had dispatched a coach to fetch the king's surgeons, and she had hired a nurse to sit with him, though she rarely left the room herself. What was wrong with him? It was not that any particular illness he had was serious in itself, but that he seemed perpetually delicate. His little cheeks worked and his dark eyelashes twitched as he dreamed. Nell laid a hand on his forehead and was relieved to find that it felt cool. His fever had broken. Be safe, my angel child, she thought. You are my life and happiness.

December, 1675

The wits had gathered for supper at Nell's house on a chill winter evening, and the main topic of conversation was the advent in London the previous day of the famous Hortense Mancini, Duchess of Mazarin.

'I saw her arrival at St. James's Palace,' Buckingham said. 'Astride a black stallion and dressed in men's travelling clothes, cloak and boots, and spattered with the mud of the road, with only a manservant to accompany her. Looked like a

335

messenger.'

'Ah,' said Rochester, with a wicked glint in his eyes, 'but the message she brings, beneath that rough apparel, is carnality itself.'

'Still as handsome as ever, is she?' Dorset asked, leaning forward eagerly, wineglass in hand.

'Still the Roman Eagle,' Buckingham nodded. 'Fierce and proud, and daring any man to tame her.'

Nell looked around the table with annoyance. Every man there seemed inflamed at the thought of Hortense.

'She left her husband, didn't she?' she asked, trying to flounder onto more solid ground.

'That she did,' crowed Fleetwood Sheppard. 'Mad bugger he is, too. Practically kept her behind bars, I've heard, so jealous he was.'

'And she's been eight years on the run,' Rochester drawled. 'Ranging over France and Italy, putting in with whatever lover and provider she can find.'

'But her latest bit of luck has run out,' Dorset explained to Nell. 'The Duke de Savoy died, and his widow sent the pulchritudinous Hortense packing.'

Nell strove to keep her voice even. 'And what does she want here?'

The men exchanged leering glances.

'Not much mystery there,' Rochester said. 'The story is she's come to visit the Duchess of York, who's some kin to her. I'm sorry, Nell, but I'd lay all I have that what she's really after is a place in the royal bed, at least long enough to get herself a child and some cash from our Charlie.'

'He knows her, then?' Nell asked, her stomach churning.

'Knows her?' Buckingham laughed. 'He wanted to marry her sixteen years ago, when she was just a girl. But her uncle Mazarin didn't like his prospects, for at the time he was penniless, without a crown or a kingdom.'

'Mayhap she thinks there's still a chance for her?' Sheppard laughed.

Not again, Nell thought. Not again.

*   *   *

Nell's first view of Hortense some days later at court did nothing to allay her concerns. The newcomer, dressed in a gown of cloth of silver, was lushly voluptuous, with hair that fell in heavy black waves and flashing eyes that seemed to change from steely slate grey to ocean blue. Every man in her presence seemed enthralled.

After supper, Hortense took up a guitar and played her own accompaniment while performing a dance from Spain. Her heels clicked rapidly on the marble floor and she moved with a sinuous grace. It was easy enough for Nell to picture Hortense writhing in abandon in a rumpled bed, and from the look on Charles's face, it was clear his mind ran deeply in the same thoughts.

Nell glanced around the company. The queen's face was perhaps set a little more determinedly than usual. Barbara's lips were pursed in contained fury, her eyes like fire. And Louise was looking like a fat baby who fears her sweet will be snatched from her hands. No mistaking, Nell thought, this Hortense blows an ill wind for all.

By May, it had become clear exactly how much trouble Hortense was. Louise, after weeks of tearful squalls and tantrums had failed to draw Charles's attention, departed to take the waters at Bath.

'I've heard it's because the king has given her a dose of the pox,' Rochester said over supper at Nell's, downing the remains of his wine and holding the empty glass up to the firelight. 'These glasses of yours are really rather stunning, George. Far superior to anything we've had in England before.'

'Yes, they are,' Buckingham said shortly. 'It could be true he's Frenchified her—or maybe one can't say that when the wench herself is French? But it could be that's only a convenient excuse to take herself away from court so the king's utter neglect of her is not so apparent.'

'That would fit,' Rochester agreed, pulling the wine bottle towards him. 'And what about you, dear Nell? Is the Royal Charles docking in the famous Gwynn quim these nights?'

'Hell and death, Johnny,' Nell said. 'Is there nothing you won't ask?'

'Nothing,' Rochester agreed cheerfully. 'Well?'

Rochester, Buckingham, and Dorset looked expectantly at her.

'He sups with me quite frequently. But he hasn't shared my bed in some weeks.'

'Harry Killigrew is on as groom of the bedchamber this fortnight,' Dorset commented. 'He tells me that the king retires to bed with all ceremony, then rises, puts on his clothes, and steals away to spend the night with Hortense.'

'Well, it's certainly seized the public imagination,' Buckingham said. 'Have you heard Waller's satire? 'Triple Combat,' he calls it.' He dug in his pocket, drew forth a crumpled broadsheet, and read, to the delight of the others,

'"Such killing looks! So thick the arrows fly!
That 'tis unsafe to be a stander-by.
Poets approaching to describe the fight,
Are by their wounds instructed how to write.'

'It's rather good, really,' he chuckled, looking up from the poem. 'Here's you, Nell, as Chloris:

'"Her matchless form made all the English glad,
And foreign beauties less assurance had."'

'Fine for you to enjoy it,' Nell snorted. 'It's not you being held up for mockery for all the country to hear.'

'Don't take it to heart,' Buckingham advised. 'You know you have the love of the people, and they'd back you in any fight.'

'So true,' Rochester agreed. 'The darling strumpet of the crowd.'

'Besides,' Buckingham said, 'Louise is on the run. That's where you want her, isn't it?'

'It is.'

'So laugh and make the best of it,' Buckingham said. 'By this point you should know that Charles will always return to you no matter where he wanders. Take that shining new coach and four of yours out for a drive. You know the people calling out to you always cheers you up.'

What Buckingham said was true, Nell reflected that night as she sat at her dressing table brushing her hair. Charles might be bewitched by Hortense, and spending less time in her own bed just now, but his affection for her did not seem to have dimmed,

339

and when he came to sup with her and the boys she still felt that he was securely attached to the little family that they were.

She looked at herself in the mirror. She was twenty-six, but younger at that than Barbara, Louise, and Hortense. Her skin was still fair and smooth, unblemished by wrinkles, and her body was still taut and slim beneath the fine linen of her nightgown. She did not doubt that Charles still took pleasure in sharing her bed, and did not doubt that he would return to her bed when his ardour for Hortense had cooled. It was so much better just to accept, she thought, than to allow herself to live in terror, as poor Louise did. But then Louise feared losing her power and influence, and Nell cared nothing for those, only for Charles's love.

*   *   *

Nell had increasingly come to love the newly fashionable games of basset but found that she feared them as well. The stakes were frequently enormous, which increased both her exhilaration, her sense that anything might happen with the turn of a card, and her terror for the same reason. Anything might happen. With the turn of a card. She had grown less cautious with her betting, and the previous night she had won five hundred pounds and had scarce been able to sleep for the excitement of it. It had been her first venture as *talliere*, or banker, though she had previously been urged that she ought to bank, as that position had a greater chance of winning than the punters, or those who only bet upon their hands.

On this night the table was the presentation of

Charles's harem—or his current stable, as Barbara had departed for France. To Nell's left sat Louise, in a sea of carnation ribbons, and to her right, her dark eyes ablaze, was Hortense. An eager crowd watched, while Charles was across the room in conversation with his chief minister, Lord Danby, and the new French ambassador, Honoré de Courtin.

Luck had sat with Nell throughout the evening, and she had taken hand after hand, so that now she was six hundred pounds to the good. Six hundred pounds. Stacks of gold coins lay before her. She pushed aside the thought of where she would stand had the cards not been in her favour so many times.

'Your turn to act as *talliere*, Mrs. Nelly,' Hortense said. 'I take it you shall pass again?'

'No,' Nell said. 'I think I'll take my turn now. I'm feeling lucky tonight.'

'Ah! Then we shall have to be careful,' Louise simpered.

Nell dealt Hortense and Louise their hands of thirteen cards, and after consideration and consultation with onlookers, they laid their bets. Nell turned up the *fasse*—the first card. It was the queen of hearts, and there was laughter.

'Are you sure you're not a fortune-telling Romany, Nell?' Rochester laughed.

'Not sure at all, Johnny,' she winked. 'But it's a good card to start, ain't it?' It was, as she was entitled to collect the stakes that the players had laid on any other queens, and as it happened Louise had the queen of diamonds and Hortense the queen of spades. Louise sucked in her breath and gave a histrionic little moue as Nell scooped up their money.

'Dear me, a hundred pounds already,' Nell smiled. 'Sure you don't want to take back some of your rhino, Louise?'

Louise flashed a poisonous little smile and shook her head tightly.

'Right,' said Nell. 'Then onward.' She dealt two more cards before her and won money on the first, but Louise won on the second and hastily gathered her winnings, murmuring, 'The pay, *s'il vous plaît.*' One of Hortense's cards had won, but she left her money where it was.

'On to the *paroli,*' Hortense smiled, crooking a corner of each of her cards to indicate that she would let her bets ride. 'And the *masse.*' With that, she doubled her wagers.

Nell turned up the next pair of cards. She took money from both Louise and Hortense again on the first card, but Hortense won with one of the cards on which she had doubled her bet, the ace of spades. She scooped her winnings from the ace toward her. Her hand hovered above the king of spades, with its hundred pounds in gold, but instead of collecting her winnings, she crooked another corner of the card, gave Nell an enigmatic smile, and said, *'Sept-et-le-va.'*

There was a gasp from the bystanders. If the next card dealt favored Hortense, she would earn seven times what she had staked.

'Very well.' Nell dealt two more cards, a ten and the king of clubs. The crowd cried out in disbelief. Hortense had won, and Nell now owed her seven hundred pounds on the king of spades. Louise hemmed and stalled, and finally laid down another fifty pounds.

'Well?' Nell smiled at Hortense. 'Happy with

342

your winnings?'

'Yes,' Hortense said slowly. 'But yet I am in a gamesome mood, somehow.' She crooked a third corner of the king. *'Quinze-et-le-va.'*

Nell's stomach went cold. If Hortense should win the next hand, her card would be worth fifteen hundred pounds. She turned over the next pair of cards. The room exhaled. No king had come up. But Hortense now crooked a fourth corner of the king of spades.

'Trente-et-le-va.'

Nell did not know exactly how much in gold was stacked beside her, but it was nowhere near the three thousand pounds she would owe if Hortense should win again. Waves of panic rose at the back of her mind, and she wanted to run.

Rochester leaned over Nell's shoulder and whispered to her. 'You can stop, you know. Pull your money off the table and make an end of it.'

Nell glanced around. She thought she saw mocking behind Louise's smile, as though Louise had heard Rochester's words, could see into the terror that gripped Nell's stomach. Louise, who from the day of her arrival had managed to cry and wheedle and manipulate far more money out of Charles than Nell had ever received. Did Louise know that? Surely she did, and disdained Nell for it. And Hortense? She, too, had won gifts and support from Charles as soon as she had appeared at court. Nell's gut twisted cold with fear, but she smiled up at Rochester and whispered back.

'She can't possibly win again, Johnny.'

She dealt again and blinked. The king of clubs. She could scarce believe it. Hortense had won once more. There were shocked murmurs.

'Unholy bad luck,' someone muttered.

Nell held her breath. Surely now Hortense would act with reason, take what she had won. Hortense surveyed the table. Slowly, she pulled her stakes off her cards one by one, and Nell began to breathe again. But Hortense left her bet on the black king and smiled at Nell from beneath her eyelashes.

'*Soixante-et-le-va.*' In all the games Nell had observed or in which she had played, she had never seen anyone push to this final level of risk. Sixty times the original bet now lay at stake. If Hortense lost, she would owe Nell six thousand pounds. And if she won, Nell would owe her that much.

Nell's head swam. Six thousand pounds. More than her annual allowance from Charles. Enough to buy and furnish a grand house, to build a theatre, to equip and feed an army, to pay off a ship's company for a two-year voyage, to keep her safe and sound for the rest of her life, come to that, if the need arose.

'Nell.' Rochester's whisper was urgent in her ear.

Nell's heart pounded. It was madness. But there was no way out. Not without the humiliation of exposing herself as the impoverished orphan among the king's mistresses.

She turned over her card. There was a groan from around the table. The king of hearts. She had lost. She felt the blood drain from her face. She had a sudden flash of memory—her own bare feet, cold and numb as she made her way down Cheapside on a winter's morning long ago. Not Hortense or Louise or any of them had known that feeling, had ever lacked for a meal. Who did she think she was, playing such games, gambling as much as her soul was worth, with them? She steadied herself, willing

344

her voice not to shake as she met Hortense's eyes. Nell could feel Charles's eyes on her, too, but she dared not look at him, dared not expose her shame and fear.

'I'll have to—I haven't the—I'll make it good.'

'Of course,' Hortense said carelessly. 'Of course. When quite convenient.'

*　　　*　　　*

That night Nell lay awake until the wee hours, haunted by the enormity of her folly, and when she finally fell asleep, she was tormented by her old nightmare of creeping terrified and cold toward safety only to have the great door slam, condemning her to face the overwhelming darkness alone.

*　　　*　　　*

'You didn't have to hold on to the bitter end,' Charles said gently the next evening, kissing the back of Nell's neck.

'I know,' she said, rolling over in bed to face him and burying her face against his shoulder. 'It was foolish. But I couldn't stand the way they were looking at me.'

'Ah, yes. I know that look.'

'You do?' Nell pulled back to look at Charles's face, shadowed in the darkness of his bedroom.

'Yes. I felt that look many and many a time during my years away. When we were at the French court, someone presented me with a pack of hunting dogs. There was an audience watching, oohing and aahing over the magnificence of the gift. And all I could think was that I couldn't afford

345

to feed them. I couldn't even afford to feed myself.'

'I can sell my silver,' Nell murmured.

'No, sweetheart, don't do that. I'll find money in the Secret Service accounts somewhere. But don't get yourself backed into a corner next time.'

'I won't,' Nell promised. 'Oh, Charles, thank you. I swear I've learned my lesson.'

Chapter Twenty-five

December, 1676

So much to do before the party. But it would be worth it. Nell looked with satisfaction at the army of silver that ranged across the kitchen table, waiting to be polished. Plates, flagons, bowls, cups, great wine cisterns, salt cellars, spoons, forks, knives, and platters. Fourteen thousand ounces in all, and all of it would be rubbed to gleaming perfection.

She always enjoyed her birthday parties for Jemmy, coming as they did at Christmas, when everyone was in a festive mood, but this year, celebrating the fifth anniversary of his birth, she was particularly happy. Rose was keeping company with a new man, Guy Foster, one of the soldiers who had been set to keep watch on the house. It was true that Hortense was much in Charles's company, but he dined with Nell two or three times a week and came to her bed with increasing frequency, and she no longer feared that she would lose him or be cast adrift to make her own way.

Nell's steward, Thomas Groundes, appeared at

her elbow.

'If you've time now, Mrs. Nelly, we must go over the orders for tomorrow.'

They sat by the fire in his little pantry office, and Groundes read to her from his lists.

'From the poulterers, a swan, three geese, and two dozen pigeons, all for two pounds tuppence. From the butcher's, one lamb at ten shillings, and a leg of beef, sixpence. From the fishmonger, a dozen each of lobsters and crabs, and eels for a pie. Oysters are cheap just now, only two pounds for three barrels. Now as for cheese ...'

Nell's mind drifted away from the present. Two pounds for oysters. She thought back to when it had taken her a week of selling oysters to earn five shillings, to the day when Charles had come back to London and how a penny had made the difference between hunger and comfort. And here she was to spend twenty pounds for the supper for her party. She thanked what power there might be listening that her Jemmy and Charlie would never know hunger or want.

'Most excellent, Thomas. Thank you.' She stood and made to go. Snow was falling outside the window, and she turned back to Groundes, bent over his books. 'And Thomas—when the fishmonger comes, give him ten shillings and bid him give them to ten oyster wenches who lack clothes enough to keep them warm.'

*   *   *

The next night, Nell's house was crowded with guests, the rooms ablaze with candles and hung with holly and ivy. Charles had not yet arrived, but

347

she knew he would come—he had hinted at some mysterious surprise the previous day. A crowd had gathered in the snowy street outside to watch the guests arriving and share in the festive mood, and Nell sent Dicky One-Shank and the kitchen maids and pages out with spiced wine to warm them. She heard cheers that were louder than could be accounted for by the drink, and knew that Charles must have arrived.

He made his way beaming to where she stood with the boys, Monmouth following in his wake. Charles was carrying two long wood and leather boxes of the kind that were made to hold important documents, and an expectant murmur swept through the party.

The boys made their bows and then rushed into Charles's arms as he stooped to greet them. His eyes met Nell's above their heads and he grinned.

'It's a special birthday for you, Jemmy, deserving of a special gift,' he said. 'But we cannot leave your brother out, so there is something for him, too. Charlie, will you read this to your brother?' He opened one of the boxes to show a scroll of vellum within. Charlie unfurled it, revealing red wax seals, dangling ribbons, and Charles's bold signature, and read.

'"I, Charles the Second of that name, do on this date bestow upon my son James, born upon Christmas Day in the year of Our Lord 1671, the title of Lord James Beauclerk, with the place and precedence of the oldest son of an earl."' Jemmy's eyes shone as he turned to Nell with a smile of pure joy. Applause and cries of 'God keep Lord James Beauclerk' rang out as Charles proffered the second box. Charlie reverentially removed the scroll, his eyes alight.

'What does it say, Charlie?' Nell prompted, and he held it up for her to see, grinning proudly. 'It says I am made Baron Hedington and Earl of Burford, Mother.'

Nell tried to find the words to thank Charles, but was too choked with tears of joy to speak.

'There's more,' Charles said, receiving another two long cases from Monmouth. 'You open these, Nell.'

They contained scrolls with coats of arms for the boys, the same as Charles's royal arms, but each with a different heraldic mark indicating that the bearers were the king's natural children. Charlie's shield was depicted as being supported by a white antelope on one side and a white greyhound on the other and was topped with an earl's coronet.

'The antelope shows that you are descended collaterally from King Henry the Fourth,' Charles explained, 'and the greyhound that your five-times-great-grandfather was King Henry the Seventh. Happy Christmas, sons.'

Chapter Twenty-six

March, 1677

The Tower rose grim and grey, and though Nell was only there to visit Buckingham, she could not help a shudder of fear as her boat pulled to the dock, thinking how many poor wretches had entered this way, never to leave.

Buckingham was as comfortable as he could be

under the circumstances, not in a cell but in the home of one of the yeoman warders, with a fire burning in the grate, a real bed, a table and chair, books and writing materials, and light to read by. It was his own political machinations that had got him here, she thought, but the relief on his face at the sight of her overcame her exasperation.

'You look like you have a cold, George, are you warm enough? Here—heated brandy and food. And a letter from Dorset.'

'Oh, Nell,' he said, cupping the stoneware bottle in his hands and inhaling its scent, 'you can't think how grateful I am that you've come. It's all a silly misunderstanding, you know.'

'George, why can you not keep from quarreling with Parliament?' she asked, and then regretted it as he drew breath for what would surely be a lengthy and impassioned self-defence. 'Never mind, don't tell me. I'm doing what I can, and so are Dorset and Rochester and all your friends, and I'm sure the king will let you out, but really, you must stop from picking fights.'

'I will, Nelly. Tell His Majesty so. Oh, this is good cheer.' Buckingham threw down the bone from the chicken leg he had just gobbled, wiped his hand on his breeches, and gave closer attention to Dorset's letter.

'"The best woman in the world brings you this paper,' he says, and so you are, Nell. 'Resign your understanding and your interest wholly to her conduct.' And I will, Nell. Truly I will, if only you can get me out of this dog hole.' He coughed, and Nell was alarmed by its harsh rattle, and how drawn and drained he appeared when the spasm was over. The handkerchief with which he wiped his lips

350

came near to having more colour than he did, she thought.

* * *

'He's truly ill,' Nell pleaded to Charles in her bed that night. 'He has a churchyard cough would make your heart bleed to hear it.' Charles lay with his back to her so that she could not read his face, but she heard the resignation in his sigh, and knew she had won.

'Very well,' Charles said. 'But on one condition. He must stay with you for now. And you must do your utmost to keep him out of trouble. He'll listen to you, Nell, above anyone in the world. Tell him he has my love, as always, but he must stop his games for good and all.'

* * *

Hortense's downfall began soon after Buckingham's release from the Tower.

'Apparently,' Sam Pepys chortled to Nell over coffee one afternoon, 'she has formed a friendship with Anne, Countess of Sussex, the daughter of the king and Lady Castlemaine, who is now with child, and frequently visits her ladyship in her Whitehall apartments.'

'Which makes it convenient for the king to see Hortense,' Buckingham commented. 'No one can fault him for visiting his own daughter, after all.'

'Quite,' Sam agreed. 'But the other day, His Majesty entered the countess's apartments and found the two ladies in bed, unclothed, and kissing.'

'Really?' Nell could think of nothing else to say,

351

so lurid were the layers of intrigue presented by the idea of Charles's current lover and formerly almost-wife Hortense carnally entwined with the pregnant daughter of Charles and his longtime consort Barbara.

'He was at a loss for words,' Sam said. 'At first. But later he regained his composure to the extent of ordering Anne to France, to the keeping of her mother.'

Shortly after Hortense was deprived of Anne's company, Nell heard rumours of other lovers—men again. And all the court heard Charles's royal roar of indignation when he discovered that Hortense had cuckolded him with the visiting Prince of Monaco.

'And thus has she forfeited his favor,' Buckingham smiled. 'I told you she'd not last.'

*　　　*　　　*

Buckingham had lost some of his gravelike pallor in the days since he had been released to Nell's care, but at her insistence he was bundled in shawls and blankets and sat nearest the fire in the drawing room. Nell, Rochester, and Dorset sat close by, the room cheerfully bright in contrast to the snowy grey sky outside the window.

'You really are the best-loved wench in the king's eyes, Nell,' Buckingham said. 'And do you know why? Because you've followed my advice all these years.'

'Is that so?' Nell asked, annoyance fighting with amusement at his earnestness.

'Your advice, George?' said Rochester. 'It's my counsel has kept her in the royal bed so long.'

Dorset chuckled. 'I think Nell would have managed fine without any of us, you know. She's not only kept her feet on the ground and her sweet cunt in the king's mind, but she's beloved of the people, as well.'

'Exactly,' said Buckingham. 'Because that's what I taught her to do. Keep Old Rowley happy, make no demands, and ride out the storms. The storms are what Charles cannot abide.'

'Speaking of storms,' Rochester said, 'have you heard that no sooner did Barbara arrive in Paris but she began a bit of jockumcloy with Ralph Montagu?'

'Well, he is the ambassador,' Buckingham put in. 'Perhaps he considers it no more than his duty to welcome a newly arrived English lady with all the warmth at his disposal.'

'And further to the matter of royal buttock,' Rochester said, when the laughter had died down, 'I have a new little piece I'm rather proud of. I'll give you only a taste:

'That pattern of virtue her Grace of Cleveland
Has swallowed more pricks than the ocean has
sand,
But by rubbing and scrubbing so large it does grow
It is fit for just nothing but Signor Dildo.

'Good, isn't it? I'm going to send it to the king.'

'God's arsehole, Johnny,' Nell cried, 'he's only just forgiven you for destroying his favourite sundial. Are you longing for a stay in the Tower?'

'What possessed you to do that, anyway, Johnny?' Dorset asked. 'Beat down the sundial, I mean?'

353

'I could not abide to see it there,' Rochester said, drinking. 'Standing there like some great stone prick, fucking the sky, fucking time. It had to be laid low.'

'You were drunk, I suppose?' Nell asked.

'Drunk?' Rochester blinked at her. 'I've been drunk for five years.'

'And see where it's got you! Why do you do it?' she demanded.

'"If all be true that I do think,' Rochester declaimed,

'There are five reasons we should drink:
Good beer, a friend, or being dry,
Or lest we should be, by and by,
Or any other reason why."'

'Excellent!' cried Dorset. 'Yours?'

'No, Aldrich.' Rochester waved his hand. 'But the sentiments are much my own. Do you know, George, of the three businesses of this age— women, politics, and drinking—the last is the only exercise at which you and I have not proved ourselves arrant fumblers.'

'Speaking of women,' Dorset said. 'Are the rumours of your impending fatherhood true, Johnny?'

'Yes.' Rochester looked glumly into the fireplace.

'A son and heir?' Buckingham grinned.

'Alas, no,' Rochester said. 'It's not my wife but Betty Barry who's shortly to be brought to bed. You'll have noticed she's been absent from the stage of late?'

'I hope you intend to provide well for her and

354

the child?' Nell demanded. 'Because if you have any thought of playing her a dog trick, you'll answer to me.'

'Good girl,' Dorset applauded.

'And upon that score,' Nell continued, 'I had to dismiss Fleetwood Sheppard. He got one of the maids with child, you know.'

'Really?' said Rochester. 'How very ambitious of him.'

'Don't make light of it, Johnny,' Nell chided. 'It's a poor example for the boys, and now I'm at a loss to know what to do.'

'Well, why not give Thomas Otway a try if you're in the market for another tutor?' Rochester said. 'You're little Charlie's trustee, Charlie, what do you say?'

'Yes, good thought,' Dorset agreed. 'He's not finding much of a market for his plays at the moment and would probably be glad of a position.'

*   *   *

'Guy has asked me to marry him.' Rose's eyes sparkled and her cheeks were flushed, and Nell was relieved to see her looking so happy.

'That's wonderful, Rose. He's a good man, and you deserve much joy after all the hardship you have suffered. It would give me pleasure if you would let me give you the wedding here at the house.'

Rose hugged Nell. 'Nothing would make me happier. You are the dearest sister I could imagine having, sweetheart.'

The wedding took place at Christmas, and Nell reflected that the year had ended on a good note. Rose was happy, the children were healthy, and Eleanor was behaving as well as could be expected. Charles had forgiven Buckingham, and Buckingham was once more contentedly waging war against his enemies in Charles's cabinet and in Parliament. The Duke of York's fifteen-year-old daughter Mary had been married with great ceremony to the reassuringly Protestant William of Orange, which seemed to have mollified even the most rabidly anti-Papist intriguers. Charles had been able to use the excuse of the threat of war to increase the size of the standing army, and because he breathed easier, all around him did as well.

January, 1678

The new year began badly. Nell returned home from a visit to her mother to find the house in an uproar because of a burglary. Dozens of pieces of her prized silver table service were gone, and advertising for their return produced no results.

Sick at heart, Nell was struck down by blinding headaches and nausea and lay for days in her darkened bedroom, unable to eat or to sleep comfortably. She was grateful that Rose spent much time sitting with her and keeping company with the children, but was frightened at how ill she felt and how long the malady continued. No sooner would the headaches dissipate and she would begin to believe she was well again, than they would return with greater vengeance.

Little Jemmy took to crawling into bed with her in the afternoons, lying still and quiet so he would not disturb her, and she was comforted by feeling the small warm body against her, and smelling the sweet scent of his hair. When her headaches were not too bad, Charlie read to her from his lessons, and she praised him, full of unfeigned admiration for his learning.

*   *   *

By August, Nell was feeling much better and accompanied Charles first to Windsor and then to Newmarket for a week of relaxation and entertainments. The air of the country and getting away from London refreshed her spirits. Charles was in good humour, putting on his oldest coat and taking Jemmy and Charlie with him for an early morning visit to the stables to see his horses that would race that day and to watch the training gallops, and they returned for breakfast ravenous and full of prattle.

'Father's going to ride Flat-Foot himself today!' Jemmy cried, his eyes bright with wonder.

'I know, poppet, he's a man of rare talents, your da is!' Nell laughed, pushing back the mop of dark curls from his forehead.

'The trainers let me sit astride Rowley,' Charlie bragged. 'They said he usually stands still for no one but Father, but he stood gentle as a little pony for me!'

'That's my brave boy,' Nell smiled. 'You'll be old enough to ride in the races soon yourself.' Charlie beamed at her praise, and she laughed to see his resemblance to Charles as he drew himself up straighter in his chair and thrust out a little booted leg in a posture of exaggerated masculine repose.

In the afternoon, Charles rode Flat-Foot to

357

victory, beating a field that included the best horses put forth by the dukes of York, Monmouth, and Buckingham. The boys, beside themselves with excitement, screamed themselves hoarse as Charles thundered to the finish line, and rushed to greet him. He laughingly pulled them up into the saddle with him and let them hold the great silver flagon he had won, and looked as proud of them as they were of him.

'I hope I shall have your company at night, shall I?' Nell called to him happily.

'Assuredly, Nelly. And if you can contrive to serve me some pigeon pie for supper, my day will be complete!'

*   *   *

The dukes of York, Monmouth, and Buckingham joined Charles and Nell for supper at the Newmarket house Charles had taken for Nell. The children had at last gone to bed, exhausted by the excitements of the afternoon, and the grown-ups lingered around the table over wine. It had been a perfect evening to end a perfect day, and no one wanted to stir and break up the gathering.

The pounding at the door was unexpected and insistent, and Nell's porter, Joe, came into the dining room followed by a young messenger who brought a cloud of dust and sweat-scented air with him.

'The council summons you back to London, Your Majesty,' he said, handing Charles a sealed letter as he rose from his bow. Charles scanned the paper and twitched it onto the table in irritation.

'I thought this was handled long since?' he

358

demanded. 'Surely it can wait?'

'What is it, Charles?' Nell asked before the stammering messenger could answer.

'The lot of old grandams that form my council are in a fuddle because of some groundless story of a plot to kill me. I know I told you.'

'I know you didn't,' Nell retorted, on her feet now, as were the others.

'This matter of Christopher Kirby?' asked Buckingham, looking grim.

'Yes,' said Charles.

'Charles, tell me!' Nell cried, feeling her blood running cold at the look on the men's faces.

'Just before we came to Windsor,' Charles said, 'this Kirby came to me in the park, said there was a plan afoot to assassinate me. Then and there it might happen, he said. I took my walk as usual, and no harm came to me, of course, and I told Danby to look into it. Now he writes of some new witness, with wild tales of a vast conspiracy of Papists, and declares nothing will do but I must haste me back and hear the man myself.'

'You should have a greater care for your life, Charles.' The Duke of York had that prim look on his face that Nell knew Charles found so annoying, and sure enough, he threw a withering glance at his brother.

'I am sure, James,' he said, 'that no man in England will take away my life to make you king.' The Duke of York looked as though he had been slapped, and the others looked away in embarrassment.

'And who is it, this new witness?' Buckingham asked. Charles took up the letter again and thrust it at him.

'Someone by the name of Titus Oates. It will come to nothing, you will see. A storm in a cream bowl.'

*   *   *

But the storm swirling in London could not be contained in a cream bowl. When Nell returned to her house in Pall Mall the next day, the servants were in a panic.

'It's a great plot by Jesuits, madam.' Meg's hoarse voice was urgent. 'My sister heard it from the baker's boy, who had it from his uncle, madam. Priests—ten at least, all in black and abroad at midnight, with knives as long as your arm, right there in Cheapside and making for the palace!'

'I heard the same and more from the butcher's man this morning,' Bridget agreed. 'He heard it from Mrs. Knight's cook, who heard it from the porter. And the French are behind it, too. We'll all be murdered in our beds.'

'Nonsense,' Nell declared.

But when Sir Edmund Godfrey Bury, who had taken Titus Oates's deposition, was found murdered on Primrose Hill in October, even people who were not usually credulous began to listen uneasily to the rumours that swept from one house to another.

'My Lady Clifford says she'll not stir out of the house without she carries a pistol in her muff,' Sam Pepys told Nell, biting with appreciation into an almond cake. 'Sir Christopher Wren is searching the Houses of Parliament, looking for gunpowder and another Guy Fawkes. And the Duke of York's own secretary has been taken up for questioning.

And that's just the start.'

'Is it all true?' Nell demanded of Charles, no sooner was he in the door that night. 'Should you not leave town again?' He shook his head wearily.

'Lord Arundell of Wardour is arrested, along with his wife,' he said, 'and four other Papist peers, all of them aged and surely harmless. I cannot think it true that they would plot against my life, but they must be questioned. Poor old man, Arundell. I recall him at the palace when I was a boy—a good friend to my father. And now this.'

The climate in the streets was uneasy, and Nell found herself wanting to remain shut in at home with her family gathered around her. Jemmy was sick again, and worried as she was about him, caring for him distracted her from the troubles bubbling around her. Rose was happily pregnant, but as Guy was spending more time on duty and she was nervous to be home alone, she spent many of her days and nights at Nell's house, and the household became a little island of determined calm.

Guy Fawkes Night arrived with special vengeance. As Nell's chair carried her to Whitehall, Pall Mall was thronged with crowds howling around a burning effigy of the Pope. The flames curled around the grotesque white face and rouged lips and tore through the straw wig that dressed the figure of the prelate as the Whore of Babylon. An ungodly shriek rent the night, curdling Nell's blood. She cried out and Tom, her chair man, looked back at her in alarm as she leaned out of the window.

'What is it, Tom?' she begged him. 'For the love of heaven, what noise is that?'

'Cats, madam. Live cats put inside, to make it

361

more real-like, do you see, when the whoreson Pope is burning.'

*   *   *

Christmas came, but did nothing to quell the torrent of panic, terror, and recrimination. There had been three eclipses of the sun and two of the moon that year, bad portents, and all were anxious to see the end of 1678. On the second-to-last night of the year, Charles supped with Nell. He drank heavily and though he attempted good humour for the sake of the boys, Nell could see that his bleak mood infected his very soul.

'Come to bed,' she cajoled after the boys had gone to sleep, her fingers working at the knots in his neck. 'Put it all out of your mind, until tomorrow at least.'

'You're right, sweetheart,' he muttered, downing the last of his wine and staggering to his feet. 'Come and see can you not make me forget what a hell has come to me here on earth.' He pulled her to him, his mouth on hers hard and insistent, as though he could lose himself within her.

A heavy knock sounded at the door. Charles and Nell froze as Groundes's footsteps hurried through the hallway. Charles relaxed only fractionally when they heard Buckingham's voice.

'Come in, George,' he called.

Buckingham entered, his face set as though against a coming storm.

'Your Majesty. Sorry, Nell, it couldn't wait.'

'What now?' Charles's voice was weary beyond Nell's believing, and she hovered at his side.

'The whispers have become shouts. Shaftesbury

is claiming that the queen is involved in the conspiracy and has tried to poison you, and he is demanding that she be banished from court.'

There was a moment's pause, pregnant with pent-up energy as the instant before a clap of thunder, and then Charles kicked over the chair from which he had risen, picked it up, and hurled it into the fireplace, shattering its legs and making it prey to the voracious flames that instantly danced up the cane seat.

'No! No, no, by God and all that's holy, no! I have banished Papists from Parliament and from London and kept them barred up at home like common thieves. I have cast out my own brother from the Privy Council and the Foreign Affairs Council, I have watched while they hounded poor Louise in terror from her home, I have stood by while that wretched whoremaster Montagu stirs the Commons to bay for Danby's blood. I have agreed to subject all to oaths of supremacy and to speak against their own conscience for fear of their lives. I have sent men to their deaths. I have smiled while the dogs have sought to make me disband the army and put the militia under their control, putting myself at their mercy as did my father, but by Satan's thunderous ass, this is a step too far!'

Nell had never seen Buckingham at a loss for words, but he appeared so now in the face of Charles's wrath, and they exchanged a hasty glance of horrified amazement as Charles paused for breath.

'No,' he repeated. 'No.' He grasped Buckingham by the front of his coat and pulled him close.

'Hie you back to those bastards. Tell them that from this moment, Parliament is no more. It is prorogued. Until the pleasure of the king should be otherwise. Tell them that. And tell them to get them home to their wives and beds, and God help them if they but cross my shadow once the New Year is come.'

*   *   *

January came and the spectre of rebellion, chaos, and murder still stalked the land. Three conspirators were hanged, and then three more. Louise, in an effort to mitigate the rising hatred against her, had dismissed her Catholic servants. But at the Duke's Theatre, she was booed so ferociously that she retreated in terror before the play began, then fled to France. Charles sent the Duke of York away for a three-year term as High Commissioner of Scotland, both fearing for his safety and hoping his absence might help to quell the storm.

Public opinion stood against Parliament, and Charles's minister Lord Danby persuaded him to dissolve it and to hold new elections, hoping that a more malleable and friendly house might result.

'Perhaps,' he said, glancing nervously at the king, 'there may be a chance, can we but find men to stand who will defeat those now in power.'

Charles emitted a bitter laugh. 'A dog would be elected,' he said, 'if it stood against a courtier.'

But the new house that assembled in early March was, if anything, more hostile. Charles's new and expanded council, designed to keep his enemies within view, wrangled and hissed in contention and resentment. Charles refused to receive Buckingham or his letters.

'Why should I?' he retorted to Nell's expressions

of dismay. 'He supported the election of men who would cut my throat. I must look to myself now, and trust none.'

Parliament focused its rage on Danby, furious that he had succeeded in excluding the Duke of York from the act barring Catholics from official positions, and resentful at the marriage of his daughter to the king's son by Catherine Pegge, called Don Carlo. His downfall came when Ralph Montagu, ambassador to France, revealed Danby's intrigues with the French king, Louis, nearly implicating Charles himself.

Danby resigned and, heeding Charles's warning, fled to avoid arrest. But he could not run forever and the king could do little to protect him; in April Danby surrendered. A flood of Papists were removed from their positions at court. Summer came, with the execution of five Jesuit priests convicted of treason, but still there was no sense of calm or resolution. Nell had never seen Charles so grim faced and exhausted.

'Let us to Windsor,' he said. 'I can stomach no more of this blood.'

*   *   *

Windsor was an oasis of green and peace. The hundreds of trees that Charles had had planted when he came to the throne had grown tall and strong, and the old trees, pruned and well tended now, had regained their health and strength. Nell held Charles's arm as they walked in silence through the royal park, the whisper of the summer breeze in the leaves like the distant sound of water. The boys ran ahead, the pack of spaniels tumbling

365

around them.

'You need a proper house here,' Charles said. 'That little place is not enough now that the boys are so big. Hard to believe that Charlie's nine, and little Jemmy nearly eight, isn't it? You shall have the new house near the church. And the continuation of your five thousand pounds a year.'

*   *   *

Nell loved her house in Pall Mall, but the new house in Windsor was truly grand. It stood near the castle, three storeys of rich red brick, surrounded by gardens and orchards, with the royal mews between it and the town. She stood looking out of a window on the third story. The royal park stretched away to the south and east, and to the west lay the river, meandering through the countryside toward London. There was more than enough room for her growing household—the boys, their tutors and nurses, the dogs and the ponies, and the small army of servants she now employed.

Charles came to her side.

'I've always loved this view. When I was a boy I liked to think that I was Robin Hood and the park was Sherwood Forest.'

'And did you rob from the rich and give to the poor?'

'I tried. I took George's favourite ball and gave it to one of the stable boys, but George found me out and pummelled me.' Nell laughed, imagining the youthful Buckingham administering a brotherly beating to the heir to the throne.

'I told him he'd be sorry when I was king,' Charles said, 'but that threat never seemed to have much effect on George.'

*   *   *

Aphra visited Nell at Windsor. She was popular with Charlie and Jemmy, and after they had made their bows to her, they hovered impatiently on either side of her while Nell showed her the house. When the tour had stretched to ten minutes, Charlie could stand it no more.

'Come and see our ponies, I pray you!' he cried.

'Fie,' Nell scolded him. 'Let poor Mrs. Behn have some refreshment first.'

'It's fine, Nell,' Aphra laughed. 'Come, boys, let us see these noble beasts of yours.' The boys each took hold of one of her hands and tugged her out to the stables, chattering happily over each other, Nell following in their wake.

'Fine animals,' Aphra pronounced solemnly, 'and I doubt not but that you are both very fine riders.' The boys squirmed happily at the praise and raced off to find the groom while Nell and Aphra retired inside.

'It's a truly beautiful house, Nell,' Aphra said, turning to admire the grand hall. 'You well deserve such a place of peace and sanctuary.'

'I need it, too,' Nell said. 'The world has had a sight more ups and downs this year than is comfortable. I'm so glad you're here. As much as I like men, I don't get enough of the company of women. I miss Betsy Knepp. She's left her husband and gone to Edinburgh, you know, with some of the other players.'

They sat, turning their attention to the tea and cakes that Bridget had brought in.

367

'I've brought you a copy of *The Feigned Courtesan*,' Aphra said. 'Just printed. Would you like me to read you the dedication?'

'I am doubly honoured,' Nell said. 'First that you think well enough of me to do me the kindness of dedicating the play to me, and second that you offer to read it to me in your own dear voice, so that I can hold the happy memory of it in my head.'

The dedication was long, and by the time Aphra had finished reading, Nell was in tears.

'You are too kind, really, Aphra,' she said. 'I shall have to get it all by memory, so that when I am feeling lower than a pauper's grave I can remind myself that you have regard for me, if no one else does.'

'Surely you don't doubt how many people love you?'

'I do,' Nell said, looking down at her hands. 'It's a fault, I know, but I do.'

'Then remember just this much,' Aphra said, '"You never appear but you gladden the hearts of all that have the happy fortune to see you, as if you were made on purpose to put the whole world in a good humour."'

'Oh, Aphra,' Nell said. 'Truly more praise than I deserve.'

Nell and Aphra looked up as Bridget bustled in, her face red.

'I'm sorry to interrupt, Mrs. Nelly, but Joe says there's a messenger at the door. From your mother's house, and asking to speak with you urgent.'

*   *   *

368

Nell stared at the lumpen mass of wet clothes, the stark white face tinged with blue, the unblinking eyes filmed over with the glaze of death.

Alas, then she is drowned. The line from *Hamlet* floated into her mind, though there was nothing poetic about the sodden corpse on the table, the earthly remains of her mother, Eleanor Gwynn.

'She was drunk?' she asked, and the constable looked at his feet.

'So it would appear, madam. A bottle of brandy lay broken on the bank of the stream.'

'And when did they find her?'

'About six of the morning, madam. She was last seen at supper, and it seems likely she slipped in the dark last night.'

Nell thought of her mother, floundering in the black water, her tangled skirts weighing her down.

Her clothes spread wide, and mermaid-like a while they bore her up. . . .

Why did such poetry come to mind, Nell wondered in some back region of her brain. Had Ophelia looked even thus?

Her garments, heavy with their drink, pulled the poor wretch . . . to muddy death.

Nell turned to the man, who stood a few steps off, head bowed.

'See to having her made ready, please, and bring her to town.' She handed him a purse and turned back to the sunlight.

*   *   *

Eleanor's body was laid out in her bedroom at the house on Pall Mall, and Nell and Rose sat up with her on the night before the funeral.

369

'I can scarce believe she's gone,' Rose said again.

'Nor I,' Nell agreed. 'She looks so small, doesn't she?'

'Aye. It was all the battle in her made her seem so big to us, I reckon.'

They sat in silence for a while in the flickering candlelight.

'I haven't cried,' Nell said at length. 'Does it make me wicked, do you think?'

'No. You took her in, Nell, which is more than she had a right to expect after how she treated you. It was more than I could have done.'

'I couldn't not do it,' Nell said. 'She was my mam, for all the pain she gave me.'

*   *   *

The circumstances of Eleanor's death had provided fodder for the ballad makers, and Rose's husband Guy looked up from the broadsheet in his hands, his face grim.

'Are you sure you want me to read it?'

'Yes,' said Nell. 'We'll hear it soon enough, and I'd rather hear it from you.'

'Very well.' With a self-conscious cough, he read.

'*"Here lies the victim of a cruel fate*
Whom too much element did ruinate.
'Tis something strange, but yet most wondrous true,
That what we live by, should our lives undo.
She that so oft had powerful waters tried,
At last with silence, in a fish pond died.
Fate was unjust, for had he proved but kind,
To make it brandy he had pleased her mind."'

'Oh, poor Mam,' Rose said. 'To be so sorely mocked when she's hardly cold.'

'It's the way of the world,' Nell said, squaring her shoulders. 'I'm sure I'll not fare any better when I'm gone.'

The Church of St. Martin-in-the-Fields was packed. Eleanor Gwynn lay in her coffin, and the great and the good of London had come to see her off. Jemmy sat to Nell's left, his little face sombre, and Rose and Guy beyond him. Charles sat on Nell's right, with Charlie beside him, proud in his new mourning clothes, a copy of his father's.

Nell, out of long habit, found herself counting the house, and reckoned it to be close on three hundred mourners. Buckingham, Dorset, Rochester, Sedley, George Etherege, Henry Savile, Fleetwood Sheppard—all the Wits were there, the Merry Gang sober at least in demeanor and dress. Court and theatre were well represented, and the back of the church was filled with Nell's household, all in black, and with crowds of people who had known Eleanor, or perhaps had not known her and were come only to stare.

'It's the best I could do for you, Mam,' Nell whispered. 'Go to your rest now. God knows you deserve it.'

August, 1679

Windsor was hot, but it was cooler on the riverbank where Nell walked hand in hand with Charles. She watched a line of ducks paddling on the smooth water, making their way to the shade beneath a spreading oak. Hard to believe it had been more than a year now since the first stirrings of the Popish Plot, a year of nightmare and strife. She glanced at Charles and was relieved to see him smile back at her as he drew her arm into the crook of his elbow. Finally the strains and tension of the past months seemed to be losing their grip upon him. As usual, he found release in activity, and already that day he had played tennis and then gone hawking, losing himself in the passion of the moment, finding freedom in the country air, the wind and sun upon his face.

'Will you sup with me and the boys this evening?' she asked.

'Gladly. That will put a cap upon a fine day.'

*   *   *

But at Nell's house that evening, the door opened to reveal not Charles, but a grim-faced Buckingham.

'The king has fallen ill.'

'Ill? Of what?' Nell cried.

'A fever. Quite suddenly come upon him and quite bad.'

'I'll go to him at once.' Nell started for the door.

'No. Best not. I'm sorry, Nell, but you can't help him and you wouldn't be admitted. Come, I'll sit with you.'

Buckingham returned to the castle late in the evening, promising to return if the king's condition changed. Nell sat in her nightgown at her bedroom window, wondering how many lonely and terror-filled nights she had spent—there seemed to be so many. The bright moon in the warm sky brought her no comfort, and only telling herself that the lack of news meant nothing worse had happened kept her from wild panic.

*   *   *

In the morning, the Duke of Monmouth arrived, the dust of the road upon him.

'Thank God you've come,' Nell said, clasping him to her. 'How is he?'

'Very ill,' he said.

'I wanted to go this morning but Buckingham sent word there was no change and I would still not be admitted.' Her words broke off as her throat tightened with a sob.

'Come, sit,' said Monmouth, taking her hand. 'You'll be more comfortable.'

'Yes, of course, you're right,' Nell said. They went into the parlour and Nell sat, but Monmouth paced.

'Tell me,' Nell said.

'He has a high fever and has been delirious at intervals. Bleeding and cataplasms have done little to bring him to himself. They've given him a sleeping draught so that he may rest.' Bridget came in with food and drink, and Monmouth held his tongue until she left, then poured wine for Nell and himself.

'Nell, the Duke of York has been sent for from Scotland.' His voice was even, but Nell felt a clutch of fear at the pit of her stomach. She pushed back her terror and willed herself to remain outwardly calm.

'They fear for his life then?'

'Aye. I wish I could tell you otherwise.' He resumed his pacing and stared out the window.

373

'I'm being watched, Nell. My enemies fear me. For they know the time may be near when the king will finally speak, might finally say . . .' He stopped and turned to her.

'Jemmy, how great a fool can you be?' Nell cried. 'Charles will not make you his heir! You know he's signed a statement that he was never married to your mother. Every time those rumours have arisen he has denied them. Every time there is talk of procuring a divorce from the queen, he has put it down. The Duke of York will succeed him on the throne.'

'So he has always said.' Monmouth came to Nell's side, and she was frightened by the fervour burning in his eyes. 'But it's only a sham. He loves me, and I am his firstborn. When he knows he's dying, then he will say what is in his heart—that I am to be king.'

'For the love of Christ, keep your voice down,' Nell hissed, clutching his arm. 'It's treason you're speaking. If you are being watched, don't give them the misstep they're hoping for. I beg you, put this madness from your mind.'

*   *   *

The following day, Nell was allowed to see Charles. He had come through the worst of his illness, and his life was no longer in danger, but as she sat at his bedside she was alarmed at how thin and weary looking he had become in only a few days.

'I was so frightened,' she murmured, holding his hand to her cheek.

'You were not alone, sweetheart, though most of them more feared having my brother upon the

374

throne than the loss of my presence among the living.'

'Not so,' she said. 'You know how the people love you.' Charles gave a snort of laughter, and it turned into a wracking cough.

'They'd love me a sight more if I'd provided a son got on the right side of the blanket and they did not face the prospect of a Papist king when I'm gone. Why the devil James had to stir sleeping dogs by declaring his faith in the Romish church I'll never understand. It's already cost him the Admiralty.'

'You've always said he's stubborn as one of the army mules.' Nell smiled, but she knew Charles was right. The prospect of a King of England subject to the sway of the Pope was enough to rouse a mob to rage.

'Is there no other way?' she asked. 'Other than your brother coming to the throne?'

Charles stared at her. 'Not you, too, Nell! You know I couldn't make your boys—'

'I didn't mean that!' She was embarrassed that he would think she would presume so far. 'I meant—what about Jemmy? Monmouth.'

'I'll see him hanged at Tyburn before I see him on the throne,' Charles spat.

Nell stared at him, appalled.

'Don't say such a thing, even in jest. He is your son.'

'He is,' Charles agreed, punching the pillows behind him into a more comfortable arrangement before sinking back against them. 'There was good sport at his making, and I loved his mother well.' He stopped, his mind clearly gone back to Jersey and Lucy Walter, so long ago. The rumours that he

375

had married the girl had been so persistent over the years that Nell longed to ask him if it was true. But even if it were, he could not tell her. Could not tell anyone. Ever.

'He'd bring the country to its knees,' Charles said, coming back to the present. 'Oh, aye, I know there are those who think I pay little heed to business. But Jemmy, much as I love him, truly has no head for kingship. He'd be overrun by Parliament before I was cold. No, when I'm gone, it'll be Dismal Jimmy sitting in the chair, and the devil take the hindmost.'

December, 1679

Christmas. Little Jemmy had turned eight, and he was leaving in a few days for Paris, in the company of Henry Savile, Charles's envoy extraordinary to France. He had been delighted by Charles's gifts of accoutrement for his travels—a great black gelding, a fine saddle trimmed in silver, travelling cases for his clothes and goods, even a pair of pistols.

'It'll be good for him,' Charles said again, as they watched Jemmy solemnly hoist a pistol in both hands. 'He'll meet his French cousins, learn dancing and some French. The countryside is beautiful, and he'll appreciate that. He's always been a soulful little thing. God knows where he gets it.'

'But he's so small,' Nell said. 'And he's had so many colds this past year.'

'It's warmer in France,' Charles said. 'And Henry will take good care of him. Come, it's time he was out of the realm of nursemaids and into the world of men.'

*   *   *

The day of departure had come. Nell looked at Jemmy, surrounded by the mountain of his baggage and the great horses, and thought that no one had ever looked less ready for the world of men than her baby, his soft cheeks flushed as he stood bundled against the cold. She stooped and pulled his cap more firmly down over his ears and kissed him again. She had sworn to herself that she would not cry at their parting, but she couldn't help herself. She gathered him into her arms and pulled him close, as if she could plant him within her very heart.

'Do you know how much I love you, my brave little one?' she asked, stroking his cheek, memorising his face so that she would have a picture to hold in her mind during the months of his absence. 'More than food and sun and air, more than life itself.'

'And I love you, Mother,' he whispered, clasping her around the neck, heedless of the overwhelming masculine presence around them—Savile and the servants, grooms, and stable lads.

'You can look at the moon every night,' Nell said, 'and know that I am looking at it, too, and thinking of my sweet Jemmy. Will you promise me you'll do that?'

He nodded solemnly.

'And if you are ever lonely or homesick,' Nell whispered, 'you must call to me. I'll hear you, though you be far away, and send you special love. I will be sending you my love always and counting the

377

days until I can see my boy again and hear of your great adventures.'

'We should be off, Nell,' Savile said. 'So we do not miss the tide.'

'I know.' She stood and watched while a groom helped Jemmy up into the saddle, the enormous black horse dwarfing him. She reached up and kissed him once more, breathing in the sweet scent of his hair. The party set off down Pall Mall, and Jemmy turned to wave as they rounded the corner and she could see him no more.

*   *   *

'The kiss of Judas,' Charles murmured again into his wineglass. 'My own son, in league against me with that misbegotten whoreson Shaftesbury.'

'But the bill didn't pass, did it?' Nell asked, moving closer to him in the bed and stroking his forehead.

'It passed the Commons,' Charles said. 'And would have passed the Lords if Monmouth had his way.'

'I still don't understand,' she ventured. 'How can Parliament claim they should decide who is to succeed you? Surely that is beyond their power.'

'It should be,' Charles agreed, kneading her thigh absently. 'But such is the pass we are come to. My idiot brother James was not content to follow his conscience in private, but must parade his Papist beliefs for all to see, and now Parliament will do all it can to ensure that he does not come to the throne, even if it means that Monmouth, bastard though he is, becomes king.' He sighed deeply and drained his glass. 'At least juries are beginning to return acquittals for some of those poor wretches accused by Oates.'

'But you closed Parliament for the session, did you not?' Nell murmured, pouring him more wine. 'Perhaps next year will be better.'

'Perhaps.' There was not much enthusiasm in his response.

'I had a letter from Jemmy today,' Nell said, hoping to get his mind on happier thoughts. 'He says the French countryside is pretty, but 'not a patch on England.'''

'Does he so?' Charles chuckled. 'The little imp. I shall be glad to have him home again, though no doubt it's good for him to have this time abroad.'

'I miss him most desperately,' Nell said, tearing up. 'The sight of his handwriting, so careful and fine, made me weep for longing to hold him again.'

'Soon enough,' Charles said, taking her into his arms and nuzzling her hair. 'Soon enough.'

*   *   *

Rose gave birth to a daughter, Lily, as the winter cold was starting to dissipate. The infant, so perfect and tiny, squalling fretfully in her cradle, waving her fat little hands, reminded Nell of how much she loved babies and almost made her long for another. But no, she thought. She could not face that again— the enforced isolation, the helpless loneliness, the fear that in her absence Charles would find another bed he preferred to hers. Though in truth it had been long since she had worried now. Maybe the battles with Louise, Hortense, and Barbara had worn him out. Maybe he could no longer be bothered with the hunt. As often as not when he

379

came to her bed he was content to hold her, and when they did couple, it was with tenderness and ease, not the fire of earlier years.

Chapter Twenty-seven

May, 1680

Nell was exhausted. She felt that she had never been well since the start of the year, and now it was spring and she was sick again. She opened her eyes at the sound of a knock at her bedroom door, and Buckingham came in.

'Feeling any better?' he asked, sitting at her bedside.

'A bit. My God, we're old, George.'

'Is that what it is? I thought it was just a broken heart, and being tired and disappointed.' The loss of Anna Maria, now married to George Bridges and mother of a child, had shaken Buckingham to his core, Nell thought, and she doubted he would ever truly recover.

'I can scarce believe I'm thirty now,' she said, sorry she had raised a subject that dispirited him.

'Ah, best take care, then. A wench is good flesh when she's fresh, but she's fish when she's stale.' He gave her a mischievous smirk, and she tossed a pillow at him, knocking his wig askew.

'When was that wig last combed, George? It looks as though rats have nested in it.' He pulled it off and regarded it sadly, scratching the grizzled stubble on his head, and then set it back on, still crooked.

'Never mind,' Nell said. 'Help me to get Lord Ormonde to wring some money from my Irish properties and I'll buy you a new one. And some shoes. Afore God, what a stink those ones let off! Have you stepped in something?'

'Very likely,' Buckingham said. 'Or perhaps it's just my stockings. They're probably due for a wash.'

'What did the boys have to say?' Nell asked. She had wanted to see Dorset and Sedley but hadn't felt up to the task of making herself presentable. 'Anything good?'

'Oh, they were full of some brangle and brawl at the Duke's Playhouse. Charles Deering and a Mr. Vaughan quarreled, and presently took to the stage with swords in hand.'

'That must have brought the show to a standstill.'

'Yes, but the crowd got their money's worth all the same. Deering was dangerously wounded and Vaughan was held and taken away by the bailiffs lest the injury should prove mortal.'

'The poor actors,' Nell said. 'Hard to carry on after that.'

'Oh, and word has come that Johnny's very poorly,' Buckingham continued. Nell thought of Rochester, at home with his wife in Adderbury.

'Poor Johnny,' Nell said. 'So far from London. He hates the country so much. What ails him?'

'The drink,' Buckingham said. 'What else? He's been drinking hard these many years.'

'Aye,' said Nell. 'Drinking with a purpose. As if he wanted it to kill him.'

'He'll soon get his wish, then. The Charlies say Bishop Burnet is visiting him, and he's making his peace with God.'

'Hell and death,' Nell said. 'He must be bad off.

381

I'd go to see him did I not feel like I'm ready to be put to bed with a shovel myself.'

* * *

Nell lay stretched luxuriously on a chaise in the dappled shade of the terrace at the back of the house, the afternoon sun playing on the trees of the orangery. She had woken that morning feeling stronger than she had in weeks, and longing to get out of the house. She did not yet feel well enough to want to venture to the palace, to the playhouse, to see friends. But this was perfect. She loved her garden, especially at this time of year. The heavy sweet scent of orange blossoms wafted on the warm breeze. Butterflies danced and flitted over the green grass that stretched away to the far wall of the grounds. The sky overhead was a sharp and clear blue, with a few sheeplike clouds far overhead. She closed her eyes, enjoying the sunshine's gentle warmth.

She became aware of voices coming from the house and wondered vaguely who it could be—she was not expecting anyone. She opened her eyes as she heard footsteps coming across the terrace and was surprised to see Buckingham making his way toward her with Thomas Otway behind him, and with them, another man. Henry Savile. At the sight of Savile, Nell felt at first confusion, followed instantly by dread. Savile was in Paris with little Jemmy. How could he be here, and no Jemmy at his side?

The expressions on the men's faces did nothing to allay Nell's sudden fear. Buckingham looked grim, Otway shaken, and Savile like a man going

382

to the gallows. And he was dressed for travelling; indeed, the mud-spattered high boots and dusty cloak spoke of hard riding.

Nell pulled herself upright as the trio arrived in front of her. Buckingham stooped to one knee, took her hands in his. Nell willed him not to speak, to turn and go, to leave her in the sunlight, taking away the black fear that clutched her heart.

'Nell, I'm sorry,' Buckingham began, and Nell heard herself crying 'No!' even before he continued.

'Jemmy was taken ill. He had a sore leg, which seemed at first no great matter. But he grew rapidly worse. He—he died three nights since.'

Nell found herself senselessly trying to recall what she had been doing three nights ago, as if the knowledge could summon back that time, could give her the power to prevent what had happened, to call Jemmy in from the night and danger to warmth and safety.

She gaped at Buckingham, at Otway, at Savile, hearing as if at a distance her own cries and sobs. The men exchanged agonised and helpless glances, and Savile knelt before her, knelt as one in penance, in supplication, in prayer, the tears cutting clean rivulets through the grime on his cheeks.

'I swear to you I did all that I could.' His voice was urgent, pleading, and he grasped her hands, kissed them, held them to his chest. 'I beg of you to believe me. He had the best of doctors. The fever came on of a sudden and consumed him like a fire. By the time it was clear how serious his condition was, there was no time to send word.'

'No,' Nell cried, and again, 'No,' as if the word could repel him, could refute the truth she saw in his eyes. She was shaking, couldn't breathe, was suddenly conscious of her stays binding her and cutting off the breath. She raised her fists to flail at Savile, to beat him away, and then she fell, fainting forward onto him.

*   *   *

Nell lay on her stomach, her face pressed against the pillow wet from her tears. She had not known that she could cry so much, that anyone could cry so much. Vast salt oceans had been emptied in service of her grief, and still the tears came. Her head ached and her throat was raw with the sobbing. Her nose ran and yet was so stopped that she could barely breathe.

She clutched to her a little shirt that Jemmy had outgrown. His scent clung to it still, and she buried her nose in it, inhaled, as if by smothering herself in his smell she could recall him to her.

Outside her bedroom window, the sun still shone on the beautiful summer evening. The endless day seemed a mockery. Was it possible that all she had felt had passed and that it was still the same day, that night had not yet come to blot out the glaring light? And yet, what difference if and when night came? The night would bring its own terrors, and it would be followed by another day. And another. Endless days and nights, stretching into eternity. Endless pain and sorrow.

She had cried out for little Charlie as soon as she had recovered consciousness, had tried to be brave and comforting for his sake, but in the end could do nothing but hold him to her, telling him over and over that she loved him. He had cried for little

Jemmy, but she knew he was also crying for her, that the intensity of her suffering frightened him, and she had been grateful when Rose had taken him gently by the hand and led him off to where they could grieve together.

Bridget sat just outside the door, ready if she should call. Buckingham had been there for hours, with Otway and Savile. Other friends had come, word of the terrible news having spread fast. Even now she could hear low voices outside her door. And yet she felt utterly alone.

For the hundredth time, she pictured little Jemmy in his final moments, fevered, frightened, far from home. Had he called for her? How could she not have heard, even from the distance of Paris?

She rolled onto her back and pressed the pillow into her eyes, wishing for oblivion. For the thousandth time she told herself that she should never have let him go, he was too young, Paris was too far, Savile was not the man to have entrusted him to. Charlie, even at that age, had been more intrepid, stronger, had thrown off her motherly concerns. But her little Jemmy had always been more frail, more fearful. Had he wanted not to go? Had he wished to remain at home, and stifled the plea, not wanting to disappoint, to be thought unmanly? The thought of his gentle eyes, the baby cheeks, and lips set in determination, broke her heart anew. Hot tears came from some place within, and she gave herself up to them once more.

When would Charles come? She longed for the comfort of his arms. He was hunting in Richmond Park, and though someone had ridden out immediately, it could be hours before he heard the news. And then what? Would he come? Or would she have to bear the pain alone, as she had borne so many other pains?

Swift and heavy footsteps sounded outside, the door opened, and Charles rushed across the room, casting off his hat as he took her into his arms.

Nell clung to him and sobbed, and she could hear that he, too, was weeping. His hair fell over her face as he cradled her, and the scent of him, the solid familiarity of his arms and body, were a rock of salvation to which she could cling in the heaving ocean of her grief.

* * *

The days passed in blackness. Nell awoke each morning to a new shock of pain and loss, a new awareness of raw agony, as if a limb had been lopped off in the night and she woke each day to find herself drenched in blood and straining to make herself whole again. Her body felt heavy, as if she were filled with sand, the slightest movement an overwhelming effort.

Out of the deep pain there began to creep tentacles of anger. Why had Charles insisted that the poor child be sent so far away? Why had she agreed? Why had Savile not done more? Why had the doctors failed her child? And a new thought gnawed at her mind. What if his death was more than accident or illness? If someone wished her ill, what better way to strike at her than to take from her her precious baby? Who bore her malice and had the means to plot against her?

Louise.

Nell's mind fastened on Louise, recently come

back from France, and the more she thought, the greater became her certainty. Louise hated her for Charles's easy affection to her, for the love and admiration the people showed for her, in contrast to the sneering disdain they held for the French interloper. Louise had many friends in France, collected favours owed to her and hoarded them up like apples for a cold winter. What would be easier than for her to induce someone to poison poor Jemmy's food?

Nell knew it was madness even as she acted, but she could not help herself, was driven onward by white-hot fury. She dressed, summoned her sedan chair, gave orders to be carried to the palace, and made her way to Louise's apartments, her face a mask of cold vengeance. She would gouge Louise's eyes from her head, tear the pouting baby lips from her fat face, pull her guts from her belly with bare hands and eat her beating heart.

'Why, Mrs. Nelly!' Louise was surprised to see Nell but rose to greet her.

'You killed him!' Nell shrieked, advancing.

'Killed?' Louise stammered, her maids backing away from Nell as though from a rabid dog. 'Killed who?'

'My boy! My Jemmy!' Nell cried. 'I know it was you, you venomous bitch!' She rushed at Louise, but her voice had summoned sentries, and hands held her back. She clawed to get free, kicking, scratching, intent on mayhem and death.

'Oh, no!' Louise cried. 'No, *mon dieu*! Let her go, I pray you.'

Released, Nell collapsed to the floor, sobs wracking her, and Louise knelt beside her and took her face in her hands.

'Madame, please. Nell. I beg of you, listen to me.' Nell grasped Louise's arms, but for support now, and listened.

'Yes, we have our differences, you and I, and it is true we do not like each other much. But on my soul, and as a mother, I ask you to believe me. I did not harm your sweet boy. I could not. I tell you truly that if you were to disappear from this earth, I would do all within my power to care for your boy as my own. I swear to you.'

Nell saw the truth in Louise's eyes. What a fool she had made of herself. It was a ridiculous thought to have had. Why had she not made inquiries, gone the subtle way about things, as any sane person would have done?

'Forgive me, madam.' She struggled to rise, but Louise stayed her.

'There is nothing to forgive. If I thought someone had wanted to harm my boy I would have done the same, I assure you. Nelly, would not things be easier for both of us if we ceased our enmity? Perhaps we shall never love one another, but can we not make a new start?'

'Yes,' Nell murmured. 'You are right, and you are kind to understand.'

'Then here,' Louise said, proffering an embroidered silk handkerchief. 'Will you not blow your nose, my friend, and have a cup of tea?'

July, 1680

Nell had come to understand why Charles loved Windsor. She felt safe there, as he did. Not because of the impenetrable walls of the castle or the soldiers who could be stationed to guard it against attack. But because Burford House, as it had become known, was her haven, the emblem of Charles's love for her, the more so now that he had given it to her outright instead of as a leasehold, and encouraged her to assuage her grief by losing herself in decorating the house and making it comfortable and beautiful, a nest where she could live and die, come what might.

Potevine, her London upholsterer, had been busy for weeks with his crew, hanging panels of tapestry, laying carpets, painting and staining and furnishing. Antonio Verrio, the Italian painter who had done so much work on the castle's restoration over the past few years and was in such high demand, had put off all other work and was even now turning the ceilings into sweeping scenes of nymphs and cherubs.

At the thought of the cherubs, Nell's heart lurched, Jemmy's angelic face and chubby baby form drifting once more to her mind. She looked out of the window of her bedroom, her soul calmed as always by the sight of the royal parkland rolling off into the distance, the verdant scene giving off a sense of harmony that soothed her. Charles was finding his peace that day in fishing, as he did so frequently that he worried his doctors. He had shrugged them off the day before, despite their tutting that he would fish on a day when a dog would not be abroad.

Footsteps sounded in the hallway and Nell turned with irritation. Why couldn't she be left to herself for a few minutes?

'Madam.' Bridget's voice was tentative, strained.

'I'm sorry, madam. There's a messenger just come from town. The Earl of Rochester is dead.'

* * *

Nell lay staring into the dark. The funeral had been almost more than she could bear, but at least there had been company there; sound and noise. Now she was alone. Flashes of memory kept flaming into her mind. Rochester's laugh, as he pulled her on top of him in bed, crying 'Come, the dragon upon St. George now!' The feel of his hands on her breasts, his fingers on her nipples squeezing fiery desire into her. His lazy smile at her from the pit as she met his eyes during some prologue delivered long ago. The sneer that tried but could not quite cover the pain that lay beneath.

And now he was gone. Poor Johnny. A satyr, a wizard, a scholar, a dangerous hellion, and a lost little boy. All perished from the earth. And gone to where? To somewhere he had found peace, Nell hoped. She tried to pray, but gave up. Surely any god who could hold his place in the heavens would laugh at any prayer from a whore for the soul of a libertine.

Chapter Twenty-eight

March, 1681

Throughout the autumn and winter, the drumbeats of trouble had grown louder again. There were increasingly strident calls for Charles to exclude his brother James from the succession, and after an exhausting series of arguments with Shaftesbury and his party, and with a new infusion of money from France, he had prorogued Parliament in January and announced that the new Parliament would be summoned in March in Oxford, that bastion of Royalist support that had been his father's headquarters during the war.

Oxford welcomed the king with open arms, and Nell's spirits were buoyed to see the cheering crowds that lined the roads as the royal cavalcade entered the town and to hear the cries of 'God save the king!' and the bells ringing in celebration. People pressed forward, straining for a glimpse of the king. One burly man, waving his hat in the air, bellowed, 'Let the king live, and the devil hang up all Roundheads!'

At Nell's side, Charles smiled broadly, leaning out of the window to wave, and she had a vision of him as a ship in full sail with the wind at his back, not battling head down into a storm as he had done for so long.

Shaftesbury blustered into town and holed up at Balliol College. With his arrival, and the anticipation of the renewed fight over the Exclusion Bill, came restive crowds of partisans. Proponents of both sides stalked the town, wearing the red ribbons of the royalist Tories or the violet of the rebellious Whigs. Shouting matches and scuffles broke out. The Duke of Monmouth moved through the streets in a sedan chair, preceded by a band of ruffians with leaden flails, daring anyone to make trouble. Louise came, and set up a rival camp to Nell's.

Oxford took on a carnival atmosphere. Ballad singers and the sellers of broadsheets drew raucous crowds, pressing to buy the latest parody, which presented Nell and Louise as battling little dogs, Tutty and Snapshort, snarling and tussling over the favours of the king and trying who should wield the greater influence. Nell laughed it off when Buckingham read it to her.

'You know I have never tried to meddle in all that, which is why Charles finds my company a pleasure instead of a burden. That broadsheet that was put around lately got it right:

'*"All matters of state from her soul she does hate*
And leaves to the politic bitches.
The whore's in the right, for 'tis her delight
To be scratching just where it itches."'

Charles was determined to enjoy himself in the fortnight before Parliament met. Nell accompanied him hawking on Burford Downs, and to the racing—the contest for the King's Plate had been moved from Newmarket. Many of Charles's racehorses had been brought there, and gentlemen from around the country had sent theirs. The players of the Theatre Royal descended, and put on *Tamerlaine the Great* at Christ Church. Charles

392

strode into the great hall with Nell on one arm and Louise on the other.

As Nell's coach made its way back to her lodgings after the play, its progress became slower and she could hear the voices of an angry crowd.

'Here, give way!' The coachman's raised voice was hoarse with anger, tinged with a note of panic. The shouts grew louder and closer, and the coach lurched to a halt.

'Whore!'

'Filthy jade!'

'Get you back to France, you impertinent Popish piece!'

Nell thrust aside the leather covering from the window and ducked back, just missing a hurled piece of what smelled to be dog shit.

They think I'm Louise, she realised. And they'll kill me without realising their mistake. She stood so that she could lean her head and shoulders out of the narrow window of the coach and raised her voice to be heard above the mob.

'Pray, good people, be civil! I am the Protestant whore!'

After a moment of confused babble, a laugh went up, and then a cheer.

'It's Nelly! Our lass! Make way!'

Nell waved, smiling, as the crowds parted to let her pass, and the coach lurched forward. She found she was shaking and hoped despite herself that Louise had arrived safely back from the theatre.

*   *   *

Charles opened Parliament on the twenty-first of March. The Commons convened at the Geometry

School, and that night he returned to Nell with a grimly smug smile on his face.

'How did it go?' she ventured.

'Splendidly. They set up a—caterwauling—'No Papist! No York!' Shaftesbury had the audacity to demand that Monmouth be made legitimate. I met their cries with what is only the truth—that the legitimacy of the crown is their only guarantee of freedom. But I assured them that though James would succeed me, he would be king in name only.'

Nell was astonished and looked closely at Charles's guarded face.

'And do you mean to make it so?'

'They're looking for a fight. They'll get one, too, for they have pushed too far. Parliament will meet, as planned. But I will not lie down like the vile dog they take me for—I shall stand like a lion against them. And when we are done here in Oxford, Parliament will not meet again as long as I sit on the throne. And we'll see whose arse is blackest come judgment day.'

A week later came the day appointed for the introduction of the third Exclusion Bill. Charles walked to the convening of the House of Lords in Christ Church Hall. Behind him by a few paces followed a sedan chair, with no occupant visible. The king took his place among the Lords and ordered that the members of the Commons be called from where they had gathered at the Sheldonian Theatre. Then he retired to a back room.

There was a gasp as the first members passed through the narrow entrance into the hall, and curses and shoves as the first ranks of them staggered to a halt where they stood and those behind stumbled on the steps. The king sat enthroned, resplendent in full regalia—velvet and ermine robe, crowned and armed with his truncheonlike gold sceptre. The members had no choice now but to come forward into the room and to bow before their monarch. The silence roared.

The king spoke.

'All the world may see to what a point we are come, that we are not like to have a good end when the divisions at the beginning are such. You had better have one king than five hundred.' Not a button could have dropped but the sound of it would have echoed in the room.

'Lord Chancellor.' Charles's voice rose, as that of a commander on the battlefield. 'I hereby decree that this Parliament is now dissolved.'

He stood and made his way through the rows of men, still bent in helpless obeisance, and swept from the room, the doors booming shut behind him.

*   *   *

Charles swung Nell into his arms and onto the bed.

'Pernicious dogs, I have sent them to the kennel. I'll go to hell and back on my knees before I summon them again, and I'll be troubled with them no more. Come, wench! What's for supper? I have suddenly a great appetite upon me. Supper, bed, and then to Windsor.'

*   *   *

Nell and Charles journeyed back to London from Windsor in August. As usual, the court composer

Henry Purcell had composed a song to celebrate the return of the monarch. This one, 'Swifter, Isis, Swifter Flow,' was a flowery appeal to the river to bear its royal burden speedily to the capital, and Nell thought with irony that the trip would be shortened if they could only sit down and be home instead of having to listen to the singers. But finally it was over, and king and court straggled into the palace to settle down once more, with the sense of battle-weary survivors.

September, 1681

Nell was glad to be back in London near her friends after the long summer, and she found it comforting to be sitting with John Lacy in his house near the theatre. She had spent so many happy hours there as he taught her for the stage, and the books on their shelf, his parts carefully stowed in pigeonholes above the desk, the sunlight spilling across the carpet, made her feel safe and at home. She smiled at him and took his hand across the little table.

'You look tired, John.'

He nodded. 'Aye. I keep wondering why I haven't the energy I used to, and realising with surprise that it's because I'm old. Sixty. What an age. Everything about me aches and creaks.'

'Do you miss being on the stage?' Nell wondered.

'I miss the old days,' Lacy said. 'Playing with Charlie Hart and Mick Mohun and Wat Clun and Kate Corey. But these last years I've found little pleasure in the theatre. Too much squabbling amongst the company and with Killigrew, too much of a struggle to fill the playhouse, too many worries

396

over money. When Hart said he was calling it a day it seemed time for me to go, too. It's not like it was when you were with us.'

'I don't think I'd relish it myself, now,' said Nell. 'The women's roles they're writing now call for nothing more than baring your bosom and being subjected to torture, rape, and terror. And all in verse. Not like Florimel and Mirida. There was joy in those parts. Did you hear about poor Betsy Knepp, by the way? Died in childbirth with Joe Haines's child.'

'I did. Another stab to the heart. Oh, Nell, it's good to see you,' Lacy smiled. 'Tell me something good, something pleasant to warm the cockles of an old man's heart. How is your young Charlie?'

Nell beamed. 'I'm that proud of him, John. He's being brought up as a true gentleman. I'm trying, leastways. Otway got one of the maids with child, same as Fleetwood Sheppard did, so now I've to find someone else to teach Charlie. Serves me right for letting Rochester pick his tutors.'

'Are you happy?' Lacy asked. 'Does the king care for you well?'

'He does. He told me he'd give me as much of Sherwood Forest as I could ride around before breakfast.' Nell laughed. 'It was more than I could do, but he gave me Bestwood Park—used to belong to Edward the Third, you know. The old lad must be rolling in his grave. And he's given me more land around Burford House.'

'Quite the wealthy lady,' Lacy laughed.

'Never as wealthy as Louise, though. And no matter how much I get, my expenses always seem to outstrip my revenue. But I haven't taken to highway robbery yet.'

397

When Nell took her leave, Lacy hugged her to him and then stepped back to study her face.

'"He falls to such perusal of my face as he would draw it,"' Nell quoted.

'Just taking a careful look. So that I can have your smile firm in my memory.'

'No need for that,' Nell said, kissing him. 'I'll see you soon.' But she turned to look up at Lacy watching from the window and waved before she stepped into her sedan chair, and when news of his death came only a fortnight later, she wondered if he had felt the shadow creeping up on him and had known he would not see her face again.

*　　　*　　　*

Hart came to visit Nell a few months after Lacy's death.

'You look as tired as I feel, my Hart,' she smiled, offering him a cup of chocolate.

'And you look as beautiful as always,' he said, wincing as he propped his leg on a footstool, and fondling Tutty, who snuffled his hand in search of treats.

'What's the new news?' Nell asked.

'None good,' Hart shook his head. 'I fear the end of the King's Company has come. There's been so much strife, and the money troubles just get worse and worse. Davenant's son will take over, and run both companies as one. It's been coming for a long time, but still it hurts like the loss of an old friend.'

'And will it harm you?' Nell asked.

'No,' Hart said. 'I can live on my pension, and I still have money put by from the good days.'

'What of the playhouse?' Nell asked.

398

'Oh, they'll use it.' Hart shrugged. 'Charlie Davenant says he'll use Dorset Gardens for operas and such, and Bridges Street for the plays that don't need such grand effects.'

'Our plays,' Nell said.

'Yes,' Hart agreed. 'Our plays. The ones that needed only Hart and Nell to make the people crowd the pit, not gods on clouds and flaming castles.'

'It was a grand time,' Nell said, taking his hand. 'And I'll always be grateful to you for it.'

That night she cried, recalling her first thrilling day selling oranges, her hopes and dreams, her friendships with Betsy Knepp, Wat Clun, Lacy and so many others now gone. After Hart and Mohun had gone from the stage, the last of the other old actors had retired, exhausted and disheartened. And now the King's Company was no more, and the world of the theatre she had known was vanished, as surely as if it had been swept into the sea.

March, 1683

The court's springtime retreat to Newmarket was not a restful one for Nell. Word came that Tom Killigrew had died. She fretted about whether to return to London for the funeral, but the path was made clear when Charles's Newmarket house caught fire three days later. No one was killed or seriously injured, but the house was severely damaged.

'Let's just creep quietly back to London,' Charles said. 'We'll go to Killigrew's funeral. I'm tired anyway. The house will be repaired by the autumn,

399

and we'll have a better time then.' He looked worn out, and Nell worried about him, but was glad of the chance to honour Killigrew and see old friends from the playhouse once more.

It was only when they had been back in London for a day or two that they learned that the early departure from Newmarket had likely saved Charles's life and that of the Duke of York.

'The plotters knew when the court would leave,' Buckingham told Nell. 'They were lying in wait at Rye House, which stands at a narrow point on the Newmarket Road, and planned to assassinate the king and duke as they made their way to London.'

'Who is it now? Not more Papists hiding in the closets?'

'No,' said Buckingham. 'It's worse this time. It looks as if the Duke of Monmouth may have been involved.'

*   *   *

'God's blood, why can the blockhead never learn?' Charles roared. 'He will not be king! I have told him so flat out—to think of it no more—and now this!' He slumped into a chair, his anger depleted, and Nell saw that he was near tears. She knelt in front of him and took his hands in hers.

'Jemmy is a fool. But he loves you. I'm quite sure he would have nothing to do with a plot to kill you.'

'Then where is he? If he's innocent, why has he fled when the conspiracy is discovered?'

'He's afraid,' Nell said. And so was she. There was nothing ambiguous in the plot that had been uncovered to kill the king and the Duke of York and put Monmouth on the throne. It was true that

Monmouth loved Charles. But for the first time, she wondered if it was possible that his ambitions had been whipped to such a frenzy that they would eclipse his loyalty to his father.

*   *   *

The mood in London was ugly. Fear and anger fuelled the swiftness with which the conspirators were convicted, and even the preparations for the wedding of the Duke of York's daughter Anne to Princc George of Denmark and the gathering of Europc's royalty for the occasion did not slow the dispensing of brutal justice. The executions took place the day after the wedding, and Charles fled to Windsor, once more seeking to find peace there from thoughts of blood and danger.

Nell's anguish over Charles's pain and her fear of where Monmouth's folly would lead him added to her sense that the world had slipped sideways somehow and would not soon right itself.

*   *   *

By August, Monmouth had sworn his loyalty to Charles and begged forgiveness, and this day, as Nell rode with Charles to view the new palace being built at Winchester, he was in better spirits than she had seen him in months. The midday sunlight slanted across the red bricks marking out the foundations. Sir Christopher Wren reined up beside Charles, smiling at the king's evident satisfaction.

'The hunting house will be finished by next autumn, Your Majesty, in time for you to enjoy some sport before winter.'

'What do you think, Nelly?' Charles asked, turning to her.

'I think that anything that will make you take your ease is a very good thing,' she said, trying to keep her horse from dancing in circles. 'You work too hard, and are too much among people you dislike.'

'That's the idea of this place,' Charles laughed, 'isn't it, Wren? Far enough from London that I can escape, and room enough only for those I want with me. Perhaps we can spend next Christmas here, everyone's getting along so well. You and Louise, the queen, as many of the children as will come. Perhaps I can even persuade Monmouth to join us.' Nell saw the hope behind his eyes, the shadow pass over his face at the thought of his eldest son.

'I'm sure he'll come,' she said.

*   *   *

The day after Nell returned to Windsor from Winchester, Sam Pepys called at Burford House.

'Mistress Nell,' he said, bowing over her hand as he entered. 'Such a pleasure to see you, as always. Allow me to offer you my condolences on the loss of your friend.'

'My friend?' Nell's mind ran over the losses of the previous year, none so recent that they were news. Pepys's face sagged with pain and alarm.

'I—I thought you would have heard or I should have spoken more carefully. I am so sorry to tell you. Charles Hart died this morning.'

*   *   *

402

Every actor in London was at Hart's funeral and Nell thought first how gratified he would be, and then in her mind's eye saw him turning up the corner of his mouth in a wry smile and shaking his head. 'I'd be a sight more gratified to be standing up to greet them than to meet them lying down,' he'd have said.

Mick Mohun, old Will Cartwright, Theo Bird, Kate Corey, and Anne and Beck Marshall were there from the old King's Company, and the whole glittering complement from the Duke's Company—Thomas and Mary Betterton, Elizabeth Barry, Henry Harris, along with the surviving Killigrews and Davenants. It felt almost like being at home to be with theatre folk again, Nell thought, and she considered for one wild moment what it would be like to return to the stage. But no. Her world was gone, and she would not fit into the new one.

*   *   *

Hart's death undid something inside Nell. She thought she had been bearing up well, but now, a few days after the funeral, she was again suffering from blinding headaches and nausea, and even rolling over in bed made her miserable. She could not stop weeping for Hart, for her youth, for the past. For Jemmy and Rochester and Lacy, for Killigrew and her mother, for the future and what further losses it would bring.

Rose sat with her in her darkened bedroom, stroking her forehead.

'I just want to die,' Nell whispered.

'No, no,' Rose murmured. 'What would I do without you? And little Charlie, and the king? We

403

need you, honey.'

'But it hurts so much,' Nell cried, her eyes filling with tears again. 'More than I can stand.'

'You've been through a lot, sweetheart.' Rose dipped a cloth in cool water, wrung it out, and placed it on Nell's forehead. 'More than your share, I'd say.'

'And it will only continue,' Nell said. 'How did you stand Johnny's death? Senseless. Needless.'

'I don't know, truly,' Rose said. 'I suppose I believe that somehow things will get better, that there is a purpose to it all, though I can't see it.'

'I wish I felt that. How did you come to think so?'

'I don't know,' Rose answered. 'I only know that despite it all, I have hope.'

'Hope,' said Nell, wondering if she could ever feel it again.

'Yes,' said Rose. 'Hope cleaveth to the bottom of the box, and is not easily shaken out.'

*   *   *

Nell's illness continued for weeks. She did not have the strength of body or spirit to go out of the house. She feared perhaps she was dying, and then almost hoped she was dying, to be put out of her misery. She could not recall when she had felt well, and life abroad in public seemed like a distant dream.

Rose was with her constantly. Charles visited every day. Young Charlie frequently had his supper with her in her room. Buckingham and Dorset brought amusing stories of events at court and in town, and Aphra brought her news from the theatre.

'I hate for you to see me like this,' Nell said,

taking Aphra's hand.

'Don't be silly, Nell. We're far too old friends for you to worry about putting on a brave face.' She sat in the chair at Nell's bedside. 'I've brought some books. I thought perhaps you would like me to read to you.'

'I would, very much. But not just yet. It's so good just to see you, to sit and talk. You're almost all that's left of the old days now.'

'Yes,' Aphra said. 'I was so sad to hear of Hart. I never knew him as you did, of course. I can't think what a loss it must be to you—so many old friends.'

'I feel as though the earth has rocked beneath my feet,' Nell said. 'He was always there, Hart. I can't believe he's gone. And I've been so ill that I scarce have the strength to sit up in bed, even. It really feels as though it's more than I can bear.' She began to weep, ashamed to succumb to her grief, but too worn out to restrain herself.

'No need to stop your tears on my account,' Aphra said, putting her arms around Nell.

Her head on Aphra's shoulder, Nell noted the sweet warm scent of her hair and found it comforting. At length her tears ceased.

'What does Dr. Lower say?' Aphra asked, handing Nell a handkerchief.

'Nothing useful,' Nell said, wiping her eyes and nose. 'I fight him when he wants to bleed or cup me, for I'm sure that would only make me weaker. And instead I take the counsel of Rose and Bridget, who advise hot soup and possets and warming pans at my feet.'

'Quite right,' Aphra smiled. 'Take only the treatments that rally your spirits and nourish your soul.'

Bridget came in with a covered cup on a plate, and Nell did feel stronger as she sipped the steaming broth and held the warm cup to her chest.

'And how is young Charlie?' Aphra asked. 'Is he cheering you as he ought?'

'Oh, yes,' Nell smiled. 'He is forever the bright spot in my life, you know. Did I tell you that Charles is going to make him Duke of St. Albans, and give him his own apartments at Whitehall?'

'Really!' Aphra cried. 'Oh, Nell, I am so happy for you and for him. A well-deserved honour for a fine boy and his fine mother.'

* * *

When Nell had been shut in the house for two months, Sam Pepys called. He insisted on opening a window.

'What you need,' he said briskly, 'is fresh air. Fresh sea air. A little cruise would do you the world of good.'

'Cruise?' Nell laughed weakly. 'I can scarce get out of bed to piss, Sam; how am I to go a-cruising?'

'It gave me the will to live when I lost my poor wife. But give me leave and I shall arrange it,' he urged, and Nell, encouraged by his optimism, gave in.

Sam put the full force of the Navy Board behind the project of Nell's convalescence, and he arrived a few days later with four sailors and a litter to carry Nell down to a coach, which took her to Whitehall Stairs and a waiting yacht. The sailors took her aboard and set her gently on a daybed that had been lashed to the rail, where she sat propped against a bank of pillows.

'I feel like an old grandam,' Nell laughed as Sam tucked a cover up around her chin.

'The prettiest grandam I've e'er seen,' he assured her.

Nell had never been further downriver than the royal dockyards at Woolwich, and was excited as the yacht sailed out of the mouth of the river and onto the open sea. White crests topped the aquamarine waves, and billowing clouds scudded across the bright sky. A fresh breeze made the yacht's sails belly out and her pendants ripple high atop the masts.

'Oh, Sam.' Nell grinned, breathing in the tang of the salt air. 'You were right. I thank you. You've saved my life.'

April, 1684

The winter had been long and bitter. The Thames had frozen, but Nell had been too ill to visit the ice fair with Charles. By Easter, she finally felt strong enough to take the short ride to the palace, and, sitting in the chapel, she could barely keep from weeping with pride and happiness as she looked at young Charlie, standing beside Charles to take communion. He was fourteen, nearly a man, already showing that he would have his father's height and build. Two of his half brothers, Barbara's son George, the seventeen-year-old Duke of Northumberland, and Louise's eleven-year-old son Charles, the Duke of Richmond, stood beside him. They were handsome boys all, Nell thought, but Charlie far outshone them in appearance and manner. He looked like a prince. Straight and

407

proud, with Charles's dark, curling hair. And yet she could see her own face in his features as well— the lush eyelashes that framed his hazel eyes, and the full mouth. A man for women to swoon over, he would be.

After the service, young Charlie came and kissed her. 'You mustn't wear yourself out with standing, Mother. Go home, and I'll come to see you this afternoon.' He spoke the words with pride. He had his own apartment at the palace now, his own household of servants and retainers. Yes, he was truly a gentleman, her son was, Nell thought as he returned to his brothers.

Charles came to her side.

'Fine boys,' he said. Though it had been almost four years since his death, the shadow of little Jemmy lay between them, the pain in the heart that never went away. 'Our Jemmy would have been so, too,' he said, taking her hand. They watched the three young dukes laughing together and then tearing out into the sunshine.

'It's time Charlie was betrothed,' Charles said, walking Nell outside. She was startled, had not thought of Charlie marrying.

'But he's so young.' They were outside now, and Charles motioned for Nell's sedan chair to be brought.

'The wedding can wait until they're older,' he said. 'But I've found him a bride I think you'll be pleased with, and there's nothing to be lost by making the match now, if you're agreed.' Shock rolled through Nell. This was more than a conceit, it was already a reality. How long had Charles been thinking on this? Why had he said nothing sooner? What if she said she did not agree? Would he pay her any mind?

Charles handed her into her chair and she was grateful for the seat under her, the comfort of the enclosed space.

'Who?' Nell asked. Who could be good enough for her Charlie? Two of Charles's older sons had made great marriages. Catherine Pegge's son, called Don Carlo, had married Lord Danby's daughter, and Barbara's son Henry had wed the daughter of Henry Bennet, Earl of Arlington, who had been one of Charles's 'Cabal ministry.' But their mothers were ladies.

'Lady Diana de Vere,' Charles said, smiling. 'The eldest living daughter of the Earl of Oxford. They're one of the oldest of the great families of England, Nell.'

Nell almost laughed. Aubrey de Vere, the twentieth Earl of Oxford, was the same man who had fathered a child with the actress Hester Davenport many years earlier, after having carried out what poor Hester soon discovered was a sham marriage.

'Aye, that was an ill trick,' Charles said, as if reading her mind. 'But Diana is his rightly gotten daughter. This is no plot to fob Charlie off on another noble bastard. An Earl of Oxford signed the Magna Carta, you know, and the De Veres have held the earldom for five hundred years and more.'

'Truly?' Nell asked, awed.

'Truly,' Charles said. ''Tis a very good match.'

'Then I thank you, my love,' she said. 'For you know that Charlie's happiness and success is all my care.'

*   *   *

Charlie's betrothal to Diana took place a few weeks later at Windsor Castle. She was a sweet-looking girl of ten, golden curled and pink cheeked, shining in the reflected glory and adoration of her parents. Nell could not help but remember her own self at ten years old, her circumstances a world away from those of this happy child. She was pleased to see how Diana looked shyly up at Charlie and blushed happily as he took her hand. Charlie stood radiant in her admiration. They would be happy, Nell thought. Another miracle wrought.

Chapter Twenty-nine

August, 1684

The oarsmen pulled smoothly, their rhythm practised and steady, the regular splash of their oars in the water gentle and hypnotic. The river was calm and the tide on the ebb, which made the barge's progress eastwards serene.

Nell was not sure why Charles had asked her to accompany him on a visit to the royal dockyards at Deptford and Woolwich this afternoon, but she had readily agreed. He loved the sea, ships, and seamen, and was happy stumping around the muddy dockyards examining spars and rope and masts and inspecting the progress of the newest ships for his navy. And he always enjoyed the company of Sam Pepys, as she did, and Pepys would be their guide today.

The face of the river was dotted with traffic—

wherries and other small boats carrying passengers across the river or up- or downstream, the sunburned faces of the watermen shining with sweat as they pulled; fishing boats bobbing placidly in the afternoon sun; and the long length of the Pool of London choked with innumerable ships anchored and waiting to be unloaded, their vast bulks towering impossibly over the water and the myriad smaller craft.

On the quays hundreds of men were hard at the work that never ceased—heavy loads were lowered on rope whips or trundled down rattling gangplanks to the docks, and the army of dockers, customs officials, naval officers, sailors, merchants, and investors swirled and eddied around huge piles of bales, barrels, bags, and bundles of all kinds. In that small area was everything that came into England from the rest of the world—food, silk, spices, gold—and even timber, coal, and wool from other parts of the realm.

Nell looked over at Charles, who was watching with lazy interest a dispute on the near bank between a waterman and his fare. The dark curls of his wig fluttered gently in the summer breeze, and he absently took off his hat and fanned his face against the muggy heat. Nell smiled, overwhelmed with a wave of fondness for him, enjoying seeing him at his ease and for the moment untroubled by worry. He turned his head, caught her glance, and smiled back, then tilted his head back and closed his eyes, letting the dappled sun and shadow provided by the canopy overhead play over his face. A trickle of sweat ran down his right temple and lost itself in the faint stubble of beard on his jaw.

Nell tugged at the front of her bodice in a vain

411

effort to let some air between the prison of her stays and her damp body, then waved her fan in front of her, the blue ostrich feathers wafting some of the river's damp breath onto her face.

Above, a heavy cover of cloud suddenly obscured the sun, and the sky stood in a billowing gray arc. The great panorama of London lay to their left and behind them, the spires of Wren's new churches standing proud, the clean bright grey of their stones standing out against the darker hues of the City. Nell noticed with wonder the variety of sounds that reached across the water—hawkers' cries, the high-pitched shouts of boys, the low rumble of heavy cart wheels over cobbled streets, the sudden bark of a dog, the almost inaudible keen of a bagpipe's drone carried momentarily on the wind to her ears and then lost again in the gentle slapping of the water against the boat's sides and the splash of the oars' entry into the deep green water.

The barge was abreast of Greenwich now. The old palace, where King Henry VIII and his daughter Queen Elizabeth had been born and where Henry had signed the death warrant for Anne Boleyn, had fallen into disrepair during the war, and the first building of Charles's new palace had risen among its ruins on the waterfront.

'We'll stop here first, I think,' Charles said. 'I want to make a visit to the observatory. You don't mind, do you, Nell?'

'No, of course not, my love,' she said. 'Where you lead, I will follow.'

The barge was already making for the wharf below the palace, and Nell was surprised to see Sam Pepys waiting there, resplendent in a new-looking suit and wig, his almost-perpetual smile beaming his welcome. He stepped forward as the boat came alongside the stairs and took Nell's hand as she alit, lifting her skirts so that they would not drag on the slippery green of the seaweed-covered stone steps.

'Your Majesty,' he bowed. 'And Nelly, how happy it makes me to see you looking so well.'

A carriage took them up through the royal park to the top of the hill, where the new red brick observatory sat, but to Nell's surprise, Charles did not make his way indoors, but instead led her to the terrace.

Nell had always loved the sweeping view from the top of the hill, the park rolling down to the Queen's House, that dollhouse abode that had been built for Charles's mother, and on to the riverbank and the meadows of the Isle of Dogs beyond. From this height she could see the busy dockyards, the ships in the Pool, the Tower, and the City, laid out far below like a child's toys.

'I do love Greenwich,' she mused, taking Charles's arm.

'I know you do,' he said, smiling down at her. 'That's why I thought that you might perchance like it if you were to become Countess of Greenwich.'

Nell stared at him speechless. Was he in jest?

He shook his head, as if reading her mind. 'No, I am in earnest. We'll wait a bit yet, but we will do it, and if the world doesn't like it, why, they may go to the devil.'

'Oh, Charles.' Nell couldn't think of anything to say that could express the depth of her surprise and gratitude. 'Thank you. Thank you, my love, thank you.'

*   *   *

413

Nell's happiness at the title she would receive was dimmed some weeks later with the news of Michael Mohun's death. Looking around the mourners at the funeral, she thought back to the night at Madam Ross's so long ago when she had met the actors of the King's Company on the night of their return to the stage. Charles Hart, John Lacy, Walter Clun, Michael Mohun, Richard Baxter, old Theo Bird, and the rest. Of the older men, only old Will Cartwright was yet alive. The thought felt like another nail in her own coffin, and with a sick lurch to her stomach, she knew that another headache was coming on.

By the time the service was over and she was in her coach, the pain was blinding. She could not wait to get home and lie down, and was dismayed when the coach clattered to a stop too soon to have reached her house. Agitated voices rang out, and angry shouts. She rolled up the gilded leather flap covering the window next to her. A black-coated parson, looking as though the hounds of hell were after him, faced three burly bailiffs, and a small crowd had gathered to hear the confrontation.

'What is it, John?' Nell called up to her coachman.

'Don't know, madam. I'll find out.' He jumped down from the box and strode to the fringes of the crowd. Fingers pointed at the clergyman and the bailiffs, and voices rose in indignant pitch as bystanders explained. John scratched his head and returned to the coach.

'The bandogs are trying to arrest the clergyman for debt, madam. He's fallen on hard times, tells them that if they take him in he'll have no way of paying the debts, but they're having none of it. Shall I clear out the lot of them so we can pass?' He hefted his whip in his hand.

'No,' said Nell. 'Help me out. Let me have a word.'

John lowered the step of the coach and handed her out, and she gathered her shawl around her and made her way to the growing crowd. At the sight of the well-dressed lady, the onlookers fell back to let her through.

'But I tell you, I haven't got it!' The clergyman's eyes were wild, like an animal hunted into a corner.

'What is the sum that is owed?'

The bailiffs swung to face Nell.

'And what business is it of yours?' one of them demanded. 'Madam,' he added, at a nudge from one of his fellows. At the sound of his voice, Nell nearly fell backward with shock, for it was the guard who had flung her to the cobblestones at Newgate so many years before. A world away, an eon away. He had so terrified her then, but now she looked full upon the man and stepped close to him. She looked into his eyes, the top of her head barely reaching his barrel chest.

'It's my business because I choose to make it my business. Now tell me, what is the amount that the gentleman owes?' It was gratifying to see the man drop his eyes and wipe his running nose uncertainly in the face of her anger. He exchanged glances with his fellows, unsure whether they would lose face by backing down before the crowd or win approbation for courteous behaviour. The youngest of the three, a dark-haired lad who towered above the grey-haired parson, made up his mind and stepped forward.

415

'Two pounds, eight shillings, and sixpence.'

'Is that all? And for that you're taking him to prison?' Nell asked. She reached into her purse and counted out the coins. 'Here. His debt is paid. Now leave him be.'

The young bailiff closed his hand around the coins, doffed his hat to Nell, and lumbered off, followed by the others. The clergyman, overcome by his sudden rescue, sank to the ground, gasping.

'Help him, John,' Nell said, taking the man's other arm as her coachman hoisted him to his feet. 'Sir, you must let me deliver you home.'

'No, no, I am well.' The man struggled, but could barely stand.

'You are not well, sir. My house stands but there. Please come to rest and take of some refreshment until you feel stronger.'

* * *

A few days after Nell's rescue of the clergyman, Groundes announced a new visitor to her house.

'Dr. Thomas Tenison, madam, the vicar of the Church of St. Martin-in-the-Fields.' The man looked like a golden-haired giant, Nell thought as he bowed. He was well over six feet tall, taller even than Charles, with the broad-shouldered build of a warrior. But he was in the sober black clothes of a priest, and there was an air of profound peace and gravity about him.

Nell was unused to entertaining clerics, but felt instantly at ease with Dr. Tenison as they settled in the parlour over cakes and chocolate.

'I am deeply grateful for the care you gave to my brother of the clergy yesterday and wanted to thank you in person.' His grey eyes seemed pools of serenity.

'Of course,' Nell said. 'It was a small enough thing to do, to get the bandogs off his tail. To make the bailiffs leave him alone, I mean.'

Dr. Tenison smiled. 'It was an act of kindness that may have been small enough to you, but which meant a great deal to him and no doubt to the course of his life. Not everyone would have intervened as you did. I would be happy to repay you the money that you laid out on his behalf, Mistress Gwynn.'

'Oh, no need, Doctor. I'd give a great deal more if it would help to keep poor wretches from being sent to prison for debts, where they cannot pay what they owe nor do anyone any good. And call me Nell, please, everyone does.'

'Nell, then. Thank you. Is there some other way that I can thank you?'

Jemmy's face came into Nell's mind, accompanied as always by the great wrenching pain in her heart that was never truly gone.

'My boy,' she said, 'my little Jemmy.' She was haunted by his loss, her failure to save him somehow from his lonely end so far from home, and more and more the notion came to her that perhaps his death was a punishment to her. Tears flowed, tears that she dammed behind a wall much of the time because to release them threatened to sweep her away, to make her lost forever in a torrent of grief and guilt.

'Tell me.' Dr. Tenison's voice was gentle.

'I sent him to France. He was too young.' Nell's words came out between sobs. 'I should never have let him go, and now it is too late to save him and

417

protect him.'

Dr. Tenison listened, probed gently. Nell told him all, and when he left an hour later, her heart felt lighter than it had since Jemmy's death, and he had promised to come again soon.

Chapter Thirty

First of February, 1685

The king's chambers were alight with candles, chasing away the dark night outside. A young French singer with an angelic face and voice warbled love songs to the accompaniment of a lute. It was the evening before Nell's birthday—thirty-five she would be, tomorrow—and she felt at peace, optimistic. Charles had not been able to attend her New Year's party, suffering from an ulcer in his leg that had been troubling him greatly, keeping him from his usual walks and exercise, and making him fitful and irritable. But tonight he was feeling better and in buoyant spirits.

Nell looked around the card table. Louise, Hortense, and Barbara were examining their cards, and at least for that moment, they were serene. Charles had made his peace with Barbara and Hortense, and even among the four ladies, there were no flashes of hostility or jealousy. Miraculously, Nell thought, each of them had settled into her place in Charles's life, secure that she held some unique corner of his heart that was hers alone and which the others did not threaten. Barbara caught Nell's eye and smiled, and Nell had a vision of her first sight of Barbara, in the window of the Banqueting House on that night so long ago. Then Barbara Palmer had seemed as far above Nell as a goddess above a goatherd, and yet here they sat in domestic tranquility. Equals.

Charles was in conversation with Monmouth near the fire. Not king and his potential usurper, but father and son. The Duke of York sat with his wife, Buckingham near them. Only the two brothers and their near-brother remained of that family that had been sundered by war and loss.

Charles looked over at Nell and blew her a kiss, and she thought of the first time he had done so, him on his dancing horse amid the cheering crowds, she bouncing in excitement in the window above the street. And here he was, her Charles, her love. He appeared at her side.

'You haven't told me what you want for your birthday, Nelly.'

She smiled up at him. 'Your company is all I want, Charles. Will you have supper with me tomorrow?'

'Of course, of course. And I suppose I shall just have to think of a gift myself, and surprise you, since you will not tell me.'

*   *   *

It was before dawn, and the heavy knocking on the door downstairs was insistent. Nell sat up in the darkness, and heard Groundes's footsteps in the hallway and urgent voices. Fear seized her. She did not move. Perhaps it was only a problem with one of the servants, or a dog got loose, or perhaps . . . no. There was a knock at her chamber door. She opened it to find Groundes with a page in royal livery.

'I'm sorry, madam,' Groundes began, and Nell willed away the rest of his speech. How many times had she heard these words, each time the preface to more sorrow than her heart could bear?

'The king has collapsed, madam. The doctors are sent for, and his condition is very grave.'

*   *   *

'You cannot see him, madam.' The guard stood implacable at the door to the king's bedchamber.

'But I—' Nell was stunned. Was this the same guard who had welcomed her daily for so long?

'No one is to be admitted, madam. No one. By order of the Duke of York.'

'When will I be allowed to see him?' she persisted, and the guard shifted uneasily at the note of desperation in her voice.

'Madam, I don't know. His Grace—'

'Yes, I know, His Grace, the Duke of York, says I must be kept out.'

'Not just you, madam, but all his—' He stopped, embarrassed.

'All his whores? Is that what your orders were?' The guard looked down. Nell felt the sobs rising in her throat and turned to go, not wanting to shame herself before him. She gathered her skirts and swept out of the door, but before she had gone ten yards she stopped. Charles. He might be dying, this minute. She had to try again.

She ran back into the privy chamber. The door to the king's bedchamber was open, doctors coming out, doctors going in. She darted for the door. It slammed shut, and the guard watched in dismay as she sank to the floor, then knelt to help her. She threw him off, beat on the door, her blows resounding in deep thuds. She had heard those thuds in her dreams so many times over the years. And here she was, in life. Was this life? Was she waking, or was this a return to nightmare? She cried out, screaming, sobbing, feeling as if the very air was being cut off from her lungs. She could not breathe. She could not live, without him.

*   *   *

That night Nell tossed in her bed. This was so like that other time, she thought. When had it been? Oh, yes, when Jemmy had died, when the sun had been blotted out, when her world had come to a shuddering stop. And now it was happening again. Charles was dying. All of England knew it now, and held its breath, praying for a miracle, or failing that, that he should go quickly and without pain. The doctors were doing all they knew how, with purges and bleeding and plasters and mixtures that made up for their lack of effect by their noxiousness. The queen had sat by his bed without sleep, distraught and unwilling to leave his side until she had been removed almost by force so that she should get some rest. The Duke of York paced and hovered, the kingship that had loomed on the horizon for so long now almost come upon him. Charlie and Charles's other sons had been called to their father's bedside. And Nell curled alone in her bed, paralysed by fear and grief. She wanted only to cease to feel and drained off the tincture that Dr. Lower had prepared for her, hoping for release

421

into oblivion.

*　　*　　*

Nell pounded on the door, grappled for some hold on its smooth surface, but it would not yield. She cried out, and woke herself with the crying. This time she knew the nightmare had been only that, but it was worse, having lived its embodiment earlier in the day. Had all the times the dream had reoccurred since her childhood been leading to this night, when the door would be shut in her face with such finality?

Charles. She knew he would want to see her. And she must see him, must tell him once more she loved him, all that he meant to her.

*　　*　　*

The streets were black in the winter darkness, but light shone from many windows in the palace. A sharp and bitter wind came off the river, and Nell's teeth chattered with fear and cold. The way through the warren of gardens and passages at the palace seemed endless.

At last she reached the outer rooms of the king's chambers. By a miracle no crowd was gathered there. Only Will Chiffinch, the keeper of the king's privy closet, stood outside with the guards, and just as she arrived, the door to Charles's bedchamber opened, and the Duke of York came out with the earls of Bath and Feversham and a Papist priest who she recognized as Father John Huddleston, who had helped Charles during his escape after the Battle of Worcester.

422

Nell knew that she must look wild and frantic, and that word of her earlier appearance had surely spread. With an effort she slowed her footsteps and restrained herself from crying out as she approached the Duke of York.

'Your Grace,' she began, but her voice caught in her throat and she stopped, desperate to suppress the sobs that filled her chest. 'Your Grace—' But again she could get no further. She bowed her head helplessly to hide her loss of control, then sank to her knees.

'I beg of you. Do but let me see him for a few minutes. I cannot lose him.' She grasped his hand and clung to him. She knew even as she cried that she might be hurting her case, that the last thing he and the doctors wanted was hysteria in Charles's presence. And yet she could not stop. The pain of the impending loss was too great.

She raised her streaming eyes to the duke and saw that there were tears in his grey eyes. The pain and sympathy she saw in his face gave her encouragement and allowed her to speak more calmly.

'I will not distress him, I give you my word. I would not for the world cause him any pain. I love him. More than—more than . . .'

The duke nodded, and stooped to her.

'I know you do. As do I. You may see him. But not for long. Hush your crying now.' He pulled a handkerchief from his sleeve and blotted her tears away, then helped her to her feet. At a gesture from him, the guards opened the door into the king's bedchamber.

The fire roared high in the fireplace and the heat in the room was stifling. Only a few candles burned and the bed stood in deep shadows, dimly lit by the orange flickering of the candle flames and the hearth.

Nell approached the bed. Charles's eyes were closed, and his breathing was shallow and ragged. She could see the irregular pulse beat in the vein at the side of his neck. To see the familiar face once more, each detail of which she had looked at she did not know how many times, was both everything she had longed for and more than she could bear.

'Charles.' She spoke his name softly, and touched the hand that lay limply on the bed coverings. He exhaled slightly, and his eyes flickered open. Nell clasped his hand to her mouth and kissed it.

'Nell.' His voice rasped weakly, but there was a faint smile on his ravaged face.

'I'll be outside,' the Duke of York said, and she heard the door close quietly behind him. She sank into the chair beside the bed and gazed at Charles, taking in every precious detail of the well-loved face.

'Oh, Charles,' Nell said, and stroked his cheek.

'I'm afeared I will die owing you a birthday present,' Charles said, squeezing her hand in his. 'Can you forgive me?'

'I would forgive you anything, had you ever done anything to wrong me,' Nell said. 'But you have not.'

Charles's mouth twitched in a wry smile, his eyes closed again.

'Then you are surely the only person in the wide world who bears me no grudge.'

'Oh, no,' Nell breathed. 'Do you not know how well you are loved?'

'Am I?' Charles asked, and was seized by a fit

of coughing that shook his body. Nell watched in alarm.

'Shall I call the doctor?'

'For the love of God, no,' Charles grimaced. 'They have done all they can to help me on my way. I would rather die now with none but you here than let that pack of ravens try more of their futile tortures.'

'Can you not live?' Nell pleaded, holding his hand to her cheek.

Eyes still closed, Charles shook his head. 'No, sweetheart. I hear the beating of the wings of the angel of death, and I am aweary of the fight.'

Nell wept softly, and Charles turned his head on the pillow to look at her.

'I would I could go with you,' she cried. 'What shall I do without you?'

'All will be well, my love,' Charles said, reaching to stroke her cheek. 'Never fear. All is as it is meant to be, and all will be well.'

They sat in silence for some moments, the crackling of the fire and Nell's sniffling the only sounds.

'What is the hour?' Charles asked.

Nell peered at one of the many clocks in the room. 'Just gone seven,' she said.

'The sun will be up soon,' Charles said. 'I would like to see it one more time. Help me, Nell. Take me to the window.'

Nell pulled the covers from Charles and helped him to sit. He rested for a moment, then, struggling, swung his feet to the side of the bed. Nell leaned down so that she could get a shoulder under his arm and, using her other arm to steady him, helped him to his feet. He panted with the effort, and swayed, but took a step toward the eastward-facing window, and Nell guided him to it.

The starry sky rose black and endless above them. But straight ahead, there was an almost imperceptible lightening. It grew, moment by moment, so that soon there was a glimmer of pale light in the east, and the dark and undulating river shone silver before them.

After but a few minutes more, a sudden sharp sliver of gold appeared on the horizon, growing steadily. Now pink rays emanated from the glowing ball, colouring the slate of the clouds to flaming glory.

'A miracle,' said Charles softly into Nell's ear. 'A new day upon the earth. But I will not see its close.'

'You will!' Nell cried. She wrapped her arms around him and buried her face against his chest, as if holding onto him would keep him from going.

'No,' he said gently. 'But you will. And many a day more. And when you see the sun, the glorious sun, remember me, and this morning we had together. And then I will not be sorry to go.'

'You will be with me with every rising and setting of the sun,' Nell promised. 'And with every rainfall and summer breeze. And every time I look into the face of our beloved son.'

'And he is another miracle,' said Charles.

He turned again to the window. The sun was full above the horizon now, the sky turning a clear blue. He faltered, and she clutched him harder, supporting him.

'Help me back to bed now.'

The steps back to the bed were a struggle, and Nell was relieved to get Charles back under the covers. He shivered there, even in the heat of the

426

fire, and she drew the bedclothes up close under his chin.

'You must go now,' Charles said, watching her, and she thought how much he looked like young Charlie and little Jemmy when she had tucked them up in bed of a night. They had always been comforted when she put them to sleep with a kiss and the assurance that she would be near.

'Good night, my love,' she said softly, bending to kiss Charles on the forehead. 'I love you with all my heart. And I'll be by. Always. Sweet dreams, sweet boy.'

Charles's chest rose and fell in shallow breaths. His eyes were closed again, and the effort of getting to the window had exhausted the last strength he had, but his face looked at peace, and a soft smile lingered on his lips.

With one last look, Nell turned and left the room.

*   *   *

The lead coffin of King Charles stood on trestles in the Henry VII Chapel in Westminster Abbey, the small space crowded by mourners. By tradition, his nearest relative, King James, was not present. His nephew-in-law, Prince George of Denmark, stood as chief mourner, with the dukes of Somerset and Beaufort, assisted by sixteen earls.

Charles's mistresses were not among those welcome at the burial. So Nell stood in a shadowed corner, cloaked and hooded, pulling the heavy wool close against herself, trying to dispel the chill in her bones and in her heart. She shivered, and wiggled her toes in an effort to regain some feeling in her feet. If she had been crying, the tears would have frozen as they coursed down her face. But her sense of loss was so profound that it had shocked her into a state of numbness.

She had cried, at home alone, as she had cried for Jemmy. No, not the same. Each loss, she discovered, had a flavour of its own, a unique grief that took hold of her in some new way. Hart. Lacy. Rochester. She told over those deaths and how each had cast her into a new abyss, one which should have been familiar, should have offered some path, some road to peace and hope. But no, each of them had shaken her anew. Hart, who had seemed as eternal as the sky. Lacy. How was it possible that such an electric presence and booming voice could simply cease to exist? And Rochester. What a bitter loss that had been. A waste of so much promise, so much brilliance, so much—what? So much of whatever it was that quickened the flesh in which we all walk, making the difference between life and so many pounds of cold meat.

Nell could not see the coffin, or the Archbishop of Canterbury, but she could hear his voice ringing in the cold. The flames of the candles guttered and winced at the draughts that swirled among the stones. Nell had not been in the abbey since the funeral for Buckingham's poor baby, now sleeping beneath the floor of this same chapel. How the grey stones had echoed and mocked Anna Maria's sobs, showing how few there were to mourn that tiny bundle. If voices cried today their sound was lost, deadened by the bodies standing shoulder to shoulder around the coffin, still in the winter darkness.

At long last it was over. Nell faded behind a tall

428

candelabra, melting into the shadows there. For she had one last goodbye to take.

Finally the abbey was empty, with only a solitary guard beside the coffin. Nell knew him—Prather, his name was, a man who had served the king for many years, first in the wars and then in the household guards. He looked up at the sound as Nell moved from behind the candelabra, hand going to the hilt of his sword. When she dropped her hood he saw who she was and nodded—not quite a bow.

In silence Nell went forward to the coffin. Was it possible that this dull box could really contain all that had been Charles? She put her hand on the coffin, as if hoping to feel warmth, a breath, some sign. There was a scuttling sound in a distant corner, a rat, no doubt, and she was glad that Prather stood guard, his lamp casting a circle of golden light around the coffin as the candles in the abbey burned low and the realm of shadows advanced.

She drew from within her cloak the flowers she had gone to such lengths to find—snowdrops, the first blooms to break the winter ground. She laid them on the coffin, and their waxy white brought unbidden to her mind the face of her mother as she had lain still and pale. But the flowers' scent rose sweet, the scent of life and hope amidst the panoply of death.

Nell bent to kiss the coffin. 'Goodbye, my love,' she whispered. 'I think I'll join you soon.'

Chapter Thirty-one

Nell's sedan chair halted before the palace doors. The guards were the same, the great rambling pile of stone that was Whitehall was the same, the same birds landed on the same bare branches. Yet all had changed in the space of a few days, and Nell felt that the light had gone out in the world as she made her way to the privy chamber.

The Duke of York, now King James, sat at his desk, heaps of paper before him, a pen in his hand. His eyes were tired as he looked up at Nell, as though he had not slept since Charles's death. *Heavy lies the head that wears the crown*, she thought. She dropped into a low curtsy, and he gave her his hand and guided her to a chair.

'With almost his last breath, Charles spoke of you,' he said, a sad smile wreathing his lips. '"Let not poor Nelly starve,' he said. He knew you truly cared for him. And so do I.'

'Thank you, Your Majesty,' Nell said. 'For knowing that to be true.'

'It will take me some time to sort through all that must be dealt with,' he said, waving a vague hand at the cluttered desk, the scrolls that tumbled onto the floor. 'But,' he said, and the word was freighted with portent, 'you know that things cannot be as they have been.'

Nell's heart raced and her stomach dropped. Here it was, the moment she had run from all her life. Abandoned, bereft, alone in a cold world. James saw the fear in her eyes and raised his hands, as though to tamp down her terror.

'I would not see you in hardship. I will send you five hundred pounds directly, to keep the wolf from the door. But I pray you spend it with care until I see what else may be done.'

'Thank you, Your Majesty. I thank you with all my heart.'

*　　　*　　　*

It had been three months since Charles's death. Spring was almost come, and the days were growing longer. Nell sat with Groundes in his little office, forcing herself to listen to the numbers he recited. But all she knew was that he was telling her she needed money, money she did not have. She could sell some of her remaining silver plate. But the money would only go so far.

She thought of her pearls. They had cost Charles four thousand pounds. That amount of money would keep her household for months, yet her heart ached at parting from them. She could see his smile as he had given them to her, his pleasure at her cry of joy, the touch of his fingers as he fastened them around her neck. She stifled a sob before it erupted.

'I'll sell my pearls.'

Groundes silently noted the pain.

'What of the other houses, madam? Are they yours to sell? To mortgage?'

'I don't know. Dorset and Buckingham and others have acted as my factors, and I don't know the true state of things.'

'Something must be done, madam,' Groundes said gently. 'Perhaps it's time we found out where we stand? To write to the king and seek to find our feet at the bottom of the mire.'

*　　　*　　　*

'Read the letter over to me,' Nell said, twisting her handkerchief in her hands. Groundes shuffled the pages, cleared his throat, and read.

'"Sir, the honour Your Majesty has done me has given me great comfort, not by the present you sent me to relieve me out of the last extremity, but by the kind expressions from you of your kindness to me, which is above all things in this world, having, God knows, never loved your brother or yourself because you have it in your power to do me good, but as to your persons.

'"Had he lived, he told me before he died that the world should see by what he did for me that he had both love and value for me. He was my friend, and allowed me to tell him all my griefs, and did like a friend advise me, and told me who was my friend and who was not.

'"I beseech you not to do anything to the settling of my business til I speak with you. God make you as happy as my soul prays you may be,

'"Yours, Eleanor Gwynn."'

*　　　*　　　*

The trees in the royal park in Windsor were in full leaf, butterflies and birds fluttering in the greenery under the summer sun. Nell was tired, as she always seemed to be these days, but the core of ice at her centre had finally thawed, and she felt once more that she was among the living.

King James had affirmed that the Pall Mall

432

house and Burford House were hers, should not be taken from her, and would pass to Charlie after she had gone. He had paid the mortgage on Bestwood Park and her other debts and settled on her an annual allowance of fifteen hundred pounds, to be paid to her for life. She would not starve. She would not live as grandly as she had, but in truth she had no wish to. Her pleasure came in quiet company— Rose and Guy and Lily, Charlie, Buckingham, Aphra.

The very air in Windsor still seemed to hold Charles's presence, and she felt at peace there. She walked alone under the green canopy of the great oaks, Tutty racing ahead and then dashing back to hurry Nell along, his little laughing face looking up before he darted off again. The little dog was getting old, but seemed infused with new energy today. The church bells rang noon. Buckingham would arrive soon. She must remember to have a fire lit in his room. No matter the warmth of the weather, he had always a chill in his bones.

Nell heard voices and looked back toward the house. It was Buckingham, wig awry, waving off a servant and making his way toward her. He moved heavily and his face was not lit in greeting but dark with worry. Not more bad news, Nell thought. Who else is there to go?

'It's Monmouth,' he panted, as he reached her. Monmouth was in France. France, as Jemmy had been . . .

'Dead?' she cried.

'No, worse.' He ran a hand over his brow as though he could wipe away the lines there. 'He landed with an army, headed for London to kill the king and take the throne.'

'Dear God, no.'

'The king's forces met him at Sedgemoor. Of course he was defeated, and taken, and now sits in the Tower. He begged the king for mercy, swore he would become a Papist, but the king's hands are tied. He cannot pardon such treason. It will mean Monmouth's death.'

'The poor pretty fool.' Tears ran down Nell's cheeks. 'Why, why, why?'

'Because,' Buckingham sighed, 'he has lived ever as if the world were made only for him.'

* * *

The day of execution came swiftly. The ballad sellers hawked new-minted broadsheets, Monmouth's likeness in blocky black woodcuts printed at the head of mournful verses. Nell thought back to that first awful day of executions after Charles's return, the jostling crowds around the scaffold, their noses keen for the scent of blood. Though Monmouth had been convicted of treason, King James in his mercy had ordered that he should be spared the horrors of a common traitor's death, and instead would lose his head at the stroke of an axe. But it would be on Tower Hill, where a crowd could gather to see him die.

Dr. Tenison had gone to see Monmouth at the Tower that morning and would attend him on the scaffold. Nell could imagine his deep calm voice, giving what comfort he could. If Monmouth believed in a God and forgiveness, surely he would die in as much peace as he could, with Dr. Tenison at his side.

A bell tolled in the distance, and Nell knew that

the hour of death had come. She tried to pray for Monmouth, but nothing came. No words that could convey her thoughts, no sense of a God who was listening. She sat and waited, each moment an eternity, and finally heard Dr. Tenison's voice at the door and then his footsteps on the stair.

Nell stood in shock at the sight of him as he entered the room. His white stockings were splashed with bright blood, his eyes stark with horror. Nell stared. She had never seen him less than self-possessed.

'Forgive me, the state I'm in—the—the blood. I wanted to come before anyone else should bear the news.' He came to her silently and knelt before her, taking her hand in his, and Nell stared at him, uncomprehending.

'The news? Is he not dead, then?'

'Yes, he is dead.' Dr. Tenison bowed his head, and Nell saw that he was shaking with sobs. 'The headsman did not know his business, or I know not what.' He faltered, and Nell's stomach turned over.

'What? I pray you, tell me, what?'

'Oh, Nell. It took five strokes of the axe, and still he was not—the work was not complete. The headsman finished him with a knife. God help us all, what butchery was there.'

Nell thought of Monmouth's beautiful face, his bright curls matted in blood, his soft mouth contorted in a wordless shriek, and she found it was her own voice that was screaming as she fainted.

March, 1687

London was lonely. Charles had been gone for two years, and every street and park, every room in Nell's house echoed with the voices of those no longer living, taunted her with memories of happy times now gone. The April sky was bleak, holding out little promise yet of spring. Rain beat upon the windows and wind rattled the shutters. So empty, Nell thought, looking from her bedchamber window out over the barren branches of the trees below. And so cold. Will I never feel warm again? She longed suddenly for company. How few of her loved ones remained. Charlie was in Belgrade, newly installed as colonel in a regiment of horse in the Imperial Army of Holy Roman Emperor Leopold. Buckingham was off hunting somewhere in the Yorkshire countryside, and she had thought he would have been back by now, but had heard no news. Maybe Rose would come, she thought, and then felt pathetic and foolish. She could not always run to Rose when she was feeling alone. She shook herself. What could she do to pass the evening? Invite some other friends for cards or supper? But who? Somehow the thought of dressing herself for company, of putting on makeup and fixing her hair, seemed more than she could face. She longed for old and comfortable friends, with whom she didn't have to pretend or make an effort.

A knock and voices at the door below. A twinge of hope. Perhaps someone had come to visit, maybe Rose or Aphra.

But it was Buckingham's page who appeared with Groundes, with that look of fear and loss that

436

Nell knew too well, had seen too many times.

'George.' His name caught in her throat. 'He's . . .' She could say no more.

'Dead, Mrs. Nelly. My master's dead. Caught cold hunting and was out of his head with fever by the night.'

'Where? Who was with him?'

'In an inn in Helmsley, a mean place not fit for his lordship. They was kind, did what they could. But—I'm sorry, madam.'

'George.' The word was a whisper this time. Nell found herself reaching out her hands, grasping for support, grasping for someone or something that wasn't there, falling, falling, as greyness flooded her mind.

*   *   *

Nell opened her eyes. She was in her bed, but did not recall how she had come to be there. It was dark. Dr. Lower stood over her, and Rose and Bridget were behind him. Nell tried to sit up and found that she could not. Something felt amiss, in a way she could not quite discern.

'Don't try to stir, pet.' Rose was at her side then, her hand cool on Nell's forehead.

'Whaah? Whuh?' Nell tried to form words but they came out wrong.

'You've had an apoplexy, Mrs. Nell.' Dr. Lower's voice was steady and calm.

'Baah.' Nell tried again. What an odd sensation. The words seemed to be right there in her head but somehow her tongue could not find them.

'Best just to rest for now,' Rose said.

Rest. Nell shut her eyes. Yes. That was all she

could manage, anyway.

Over the next days, Nell drifted in and out of a haze. So tired. She was so tired. Her face and body felt heavy, and movement seemed impossible. Whenever she opened her eyes someone sat nearby—Rose or Bridget or Meg. Dr. Lower came and went, and then Dr. Lister and Dr. Harrell and Dr. Lefebure. The entire court staff of physicians, Nell thought. The flock who had attended on Charles over his last days. All that effort, all that pain he had suffered at their hands, and to what effect? He had gone just the same.

Finally, the fog seemed to clear from Nell's head. Rose helped her to sit, propping her against a bank of pillows, pulling the covers up to her chest, adjusting the woollen nightcap that swaddled her head. The sky outside the window was streaked with pink. It was evening, it seemed. Or perhaps it was dawn. Hard to tell. But it didn't seem to matter. Nell struggled to speak and somehow the words came, slurred but clear enough for Rose to understand.

'What's amiss with me?'

'The pox, most like.' Rose looked down at Nell's hand, which she held in hers and stroked. 'It's a long while coming on sometimes, you know. But eventually . . . and then the shock over poor Buckingham.'

*   *   *

Dr. Lower came to Nell every day. She begged him not to bleed her, not to torment her with plasters and clysters and poultices and cupping.

'If that's the price of recovering, I'd rather not,'

438

she said, managing a smile.

'Very well.' He shook his head. 'You shall have your way for now. But if we see no improvement in you . . .'

'Why, I'm better already.' Nell smiled at him. 'You see how I can sit and speak? Here, sit with me, and I'll tell you a story about the Weeping Willow and how she grew.' Dr. Lower laughed despite himself and sat beside the bed.

*　　　*　　　*

Summer came. Nell felt just strong enough to venture to her bedroom window. Her garden was in bloom, the trees spreading their green canopies, and in St. James's Park beyond, she could see courtiers, the breeze catching their gaily coloured silks so that they seemed like sails.

'What a glorious day,' she said, turning to Rose. 'I'm so glad to be alive.' And suddenly something was wrong, and blackness filled her head.

*　　　*　　　*

When Nell awoke, the sun had gone. She tried to sit and found herself squirming helplessly like a caterpillar. Something was horribly amiss. Rose was at her side instantly, and Nell could see the truth in her face.

'I'm dying?'

Rose hesitated.

'Yes?' Nell prompted.

'Yes.'

The world seemed to have contracted to this room, the small space between the walls. Nothing

439

lay beyond it, or nothing of substance.

'Don't leave me?'

'Never,' said Rose. 'Never.'

*　　*　　*

'I have lived a wicked life. And for this, God has
punished me. He took my little Jemmy, made him
suffer for my sins, and now he has stricken me
down.' Nell heard her words hang in the air. The
speaking of them had been hard, but once they
were out, she felt a weight lifted from her, the
weight of the secret fear that had been crushing her
heart. She lifted her eyes and met the soft slate grey
of Dr. Tenison's gaze.

'How have you been wicked?' His voice was
gentle, almost curious.

'Why, I have been whore to the king and borne
him two bastards. And whore to many men before
that.'

'Yes.'

Outside the bedroom window, Nell could hear
the rumble of a wagon's wheels in the street and the
driver shouting at some obstruction in his way.

'Tell me,' Dr. Tenison asked, 'would you have
married the king had you been able?'

'Of course,' Nell said.

'And were you true to him?'

'I was.'

'And did you bear him malice in your heart?'

'I would like to have killed him on a few
occasions,' Nell admitted, and was relieved to see
Dr. Tenison's smile.

'I think I should have trouble finding a wife who
could not say the same of her husband.'

440

'And he had a wife,' Nell said. 'The queen.'

'That is true. And your relations with him were grievous sin. But you have shown that you have a Christian heart, by many deeds in the time that I have known you. And I have no doubt that there were many more in your life before that. You have shown charity for the poor, the sick, those who could not of their own accord make their lives better or more comfortable. And I know that you have done it out of concern for them, admonishing me frequently that no one should know the source of their help.'

'I felt embarrassed,' Nell said. 'Lest any should think I was playing the grand lady.'

'But it shows that your actions were pure of pride and vainglory. You have been a true and loving friend. To Monmouth, to the poor Earl of Rochester, to many others. You have loved your boys with an unstinting heart.'

'But Jemmy...' The tears came hot now in Nell's eyes and ran down her cheeks. Tutty came snuffling up to her, his wet nose nudging her hand, his limpid eyes gazing up at her in concern, and she stroked his head, pulling the silky ears gently.

'Jemmy's death was not because of anything you did. I am sure of that,' Dr. Tenison said. 'I know you would gladly have laid down your life if it would have spared his.'

'But how could God have let such a thing happen?' Nell said. 'My poor little boy, gentle and good, and dying alone so far from home, when I had sent him off like that.'

'I don't know. We cannot know. We can only seek to find some good in whatever may befall.'

'What good could there be in the death of a

441

blameless child?' Nell demanded, sobs shaking her. 'Tell me that.'

'It has brought you to think about your life, and the life to come,' Dr. Tenison said. 'That you may repent your sins, and be forgiven, and find peace through God's infinite goodness and mercy.'

'And how am I to repent?' Nell thought he might as well have bade her walk upon the moon.

'If you allow me, I will help you find your way.'

Nell wanted peace, ached for relief. But it seemed impossible. She shook her head, doubt and shame taking hold of her once more.

'I fear God will shut his ears to me.'

'Speak to Him even if you doubt, and He will listen.'

*   *   *

Charlie came home from Belgrade. He could not stay long, Nell knew, but it was enough to see him again, to hold him to her. She was amazed at the sight of him as he came into her bedroom. He was seventeen now, and in his absence he had suddenly become a man. Her heart ached with joy and pride and sadness all at once to see how much he looked like Charles. He leaned down to kiss her and pulled a chair close to the side of her bed. She ran a hand through his dark curls, stroked the fair cheeks, fresh-shaven smooth.

'My joy.' She took his hand in hers. 'If I have done one thing right in all of my life, it was to bear you. And if there is one thing that has made my stay upon this earth worth the living, it is to see you now, handsome and strong and smart and good, and with a fine life before you.'

442

'Mother.' His eyes were swimming with tears. 'You'll get better, I know.'

Nell smiled and shook her head. 'I fear I won't, my love. But I don't mourn it. Of all those that have been dear to me, there are precious few left. The world's a different place now, without them, and with you gone so far away.'

'I'll stay if you like, you know.'

'No,' she said. 'You must go and live your life. I know you'll be thinking of me.'

'Every day.'

*　　*　　*

Dr. Tenison's visits were daily now, and Nell looked forward to his presence as she had to no one's since Charles's death. She smiled at him over her cup of chocolate.

'I have been praying each day, as you told me,' she said. 'I felt at first as though I were speaking to empty air. I wondered why I bothered. My mind would not cease its jangling. And as Claudius said, 'Words without thoughts never to heaven go.' Then it came to me that I have been battling to understand. And perhaps I can never understand. But I can believe anyway. That's what you've been telling me, isn't it?'

Dr. Tenison nodded.

'And now,' Nell continued, 'all of a sudden, I feel that someone is listening.'

'Tell me.'

'It is the oddest thing, but yesterday when I closed my eyes and bent my head and began to try, there was the smallest breath of air, a tiny breeze that came in at the window. As if a presence had entered the room.'

'Not odd at all.'

'And I had a sudden sense of peace, that I was safe and loved and whole.'

'And so you are,' he said.

'And that I have no reason to fear, no matter what comes.'

'Yes,' said Dr. Tenison. 'He will be with you, and keep you safe. Even in the valley of the shadow of death.'

*   *   *

Nell had made her will in July, but as the days shortened into autumn, she called her secretary James Booth to her to make a codicil.

'I want to leave money in Dr. Tenison's hands, that he might give it to the poor of the parish of St. Martin-in-the-Fields. To those who have need of warm clothes to see them through the winter. And to free those who linger in prison for debt. And tell him that as he has shown me the path of such kindness and mercy, he should see that some of it goes to poor Papists of the parish.'

Booth's pen scratched across the paper, and he looked up as he finished.

'Aught else, madam?'

'Yes.' Nell hesitated. Her hope was great, but so was her fear. 'When I am gone, ask my son to inquire of Dr. Tenison if he would stoop to give my funeral service. Tell him I know I have not deserved it, and will understand—none should blame him if he would not. But my soul should rest easier if he would do me that last kindness.'

Nell could feel Rose's hand holding hers, and the smoothness of Rose's palm against her skin, the gentle grasp of the fingers, made her feel safe. She gave her sister's hand a squeeze. Rose moved her chair closer to Nell's bedside. She stroked Nell's forehead, and Nell opened her eyes to look into her sister's face.

Rose. She had been there always, as long as Nell could remember. Strong, warm, protective, loving. Eternal as the sun and moon.

Rose smiled, but her eyes were full of tears, and Nell wished that her passing would not cause such pain.

'You are always such a comfort to me,' she whispered. 'When I was small. When I ran away and you took me in and sheltered me. When I was afraid of losing Charles. You have always been there, and you have always made things better. I wish I could have done the same.'

'But, Nell, you have,' Rose protested softly. 'You have always taken care of me. Always helped me. Never forgot your sister. Not many would have done that.'

'I wish I could do more,' Nell said. 'Not leave you alone.'

'You do not leave me alone,' Rose said. 'You are always in my heart. You will be always in my heart. Every day you will be with me.'

She brought Nell's hand to her lips and kissed it. Nell closed her eyes. She was so tired. The draught that Dr. Harrell had given her had eased the pain, and she felt somehow as if she had no body, as if her mind floated above the bed, and only her hand in Rose's anchored her to the world. She could hear her own breath, was aware that it was ragged

445

and slowing. But it caused her no distress. All was well. Rose was there, and now she felt little Jemmy's hand slip into hers. Could that be? He'd been gone so long. He spoke. What a joy to hear his sweet voice. She could not quite make out what he was saying, but she could feel the warmth of his love and his welcome. Charles was there beside him now, and his voice, too, was drawing her to him. And she knew the others were there behind him— Charles Hart, Buckingham, Rochester, Monmouth, John Lacy, Wat Clun, Michael Mohun, old Tom Killigrew, her mother and her father, and so many others. They had not gone after all. Nell smiled and sighed.

Rose heard the long exhalation and waited, counting. But no inhalation followed, and the small hand she held was still. She raised it to her cheek, taking a last caress. Nell's eyes were closed, her face finally free from pain, at peace. A tendril of russet hair strayed over her forehead, and for the last time, Rose gently brushed it away.

*   *   *

Rose had sat some time with Nell, and Dr. Harrell had come back, to pronounce what anyone could see—that Nell was dead. And now Meg and Bridget were washing her and laying her out in the soft candlelight.

One of Nell's hands was at her side, closed around something. Bridget uncurled the fingers. In her palm lay a small knot of ribbons, its blue and gold streamers flattened and faded.

'What's that?' asked Meg.

Bridget shook her head. 'Some penny fairing, it

446

looks like. Who knows? We'll leave it with her. It must have meant something to her. Mayhap it will give her comfort on her path.'

*   *   *

Outside, the word spread through the waiting crowd in a rush of whispers and gasps. Nell was gone.

A tiny red-haired girl among the press of people listened in wonder at the sighs and sobs around her and tugged at her mother's hand.

'Who was she, Mam? Was she a princess?'

'No, poppet, she was one of us.'

The little girl looked upward and watched in awe as a lone firework burst in the night sky, a shower of bright sparks exploding in a corona and then fading gently into the blanket of stars.

Acknowledgments

There are so many people to thank for their help on Nell's long journey to print . . .

My wonderful agent, Kevan Lyon, who has shepherded me and the book along since before I had a complete first draft.

My Avon U.K. editors, Kate Bradley and Helen Bolton, along with all the team at HarperCollins.

My U.S. editor, Kate Seaver.

Elise Capron, the first agent to read part of the manuscript, who liked it, wanted to see more of it, liked that, and passed me on to Kevan Lyon.

My foreign rights agent, Taryn Fagerness, for making sure that Nell would be published in Britain, Turkey, Poland and Hungary! (So far . . .)

Diane McGee of McGee Creative, for her work to bring Nell to the silver screen.

The members of my writing groups, Emily Heebner, Willow Healy, Elizabeth Thurber, Gil Roscoe, Bill Treziak, Carolyn Howard-Johnson, and Uriah Carr, whose thoughtful feedback helped shape Nell's story into something far better than it would have been without their suggestions.

Kerry Madden, whose belief in the book encouraged me to keep writing and whose teaching helped me be a better writer.

The members of Kerry Madden's classes at Vroman's Bookstore in Pasadena, the first people who heard any of the manuscript, who loved Nell and gave me valuable suggestions about telling her story.

My many good friends in London, who gave me

friendship and hospitality, believed in Nell and in me, and accompanied me on research jaunts. Some of the highlights:

Alice Northgreaves wandered around Windsor with me, provided general enthusiasm and many helpful suggestions and ideas, and also read the manuscript with an eye for Americanisms and anything that would strike a British reader as wrong.

Donna Stevens also read the manuscript; made use of her contacts at The Tower to find out where Buckingham would have been held; took me to a luncheon given by the Worshipful Company of Gunmakers, where I really did feel like Nell Gwynn at Whitehall; and who has offered unflagging willingness to portray the third harlot on the left if Nell makes it to the screen.

Alison Guppy drove me to Epsom, where we had a delightful day, including an enormous lunch at the King's Head, where Samuel Pepys stayed in the summer of 1667, when Nell was cavorting next door with Dorset and Sedley.

Laura Manning believed from the beginning, and frequently asked me 'How's the book coming?' when almost no one knew I had started writing it. She and David Lyon rescued me when I had lost my wallet in London, took me to see the dinosaurs at Crystal Palace Park, and found a fax machine on a Bank Holiday evening.

Tim Ross read parts of an early draft and educated and entertained me with his lexicon of twentieth– and twenty-first-century London slang.

Clare Vicary and Alex Laing spent a memorable Bonfire Night with me on Blackheath and on the long tramp into Lewisham to get the bus to

Brockley.

Buck Herron fed me many delicious meals and emotional sustenance.

Laura Tarantino spent a wonderful afternoon with me at Ham House. Fortunately, we didn't know about the ghosts until later.

Jackie Rowe explored Oxford with me, and she and Laura Hewer took me out for a wonderful day at Audlcy End and Saffron Walden.

The habitués (and sons of habitués) of the Lord Nelson Pub and Ferry House Pub on the Isle of Dogs and the many other Londoners who lent their faces and voices to characters in Nell's London.

The Reverend Canon Martin A. Seeley, Principal, Westcott House, Cambridge, who provided patient, thoughtful, and invaluable guidance about Dr. Thomas Tenison's spiritual counselling of Nell, introduced me to the vicar of St. Martin-in-the-Fields, unwittingly served as my model for Dr. Tenison, and gave spiritual care and friendship to my mother and truly heroic support to my family and me in many ways during my mother's long illness.

The Reverend Nicholas Holtam, Vicar of St. Martin-in-the-Fields, who also gave me very helpful comments about Dr. Thomas Tenison's ministering to Nell, provided information about Nell's grave, and introduced me to Malcolm Johnson's book *St. Martin-in-the-Fields* and Edward Carpenter's *Thomas Tenison, Archbishop of Canterbury: His Life and Times.*

Malcolm Johnson, for his very informative book *St. Martin-in-the-Fields* and for information about Nell's grave.

The Venerable Dr. William Jacob, Archdeacon

451

of Charing Cross, who provided me with information about Nell's grave.

My father, who introduced me to Nell many years ago, gave me occasional financial help as I was slaving over a hot computer, and provided suggestions about ballad singers and music.

My sister Rachel Hope Crossman, who provided expert knowledge on pregnancy, childbirth, and babies.

My sister Jennifer Juliet Walker, who designed my gorgeous website.

The very helpful members of staff at the Theatre Archives of the Victoria and Albert Museum, the British Library, the William Clark Davis Library, the Los Angeles Public Library's Central Library, and the Dabney Library at Caltech.

Anne Melo and the staff at the Pasadena Public Library, for their help with my many Interlibrary Loan requests.

Alison Weir, who told me about the existence of Interlibrary Loans.

Hilary Davidson at the Museum of London, for allowing me to view so many beautiful pieces of clothing from Nell's period.

The lovely lady at the National Portrait Gallery in London who in November 1991 took my mother and me down to the basement and pulled out Nell's portrait for us to see.

Diana Gabaldon, for being an inspiration and for her lovely review quote.

C.C. Humphreys, actor and author of the *Jack Absolute* series, for his superb review quote, as well as for the first one, which was as pithy and piquant as it was unprintable.

Leslie Carroll, author of *Royal Affairs* and other

452

wonderful books, for her enthusiastic review quote.

Stephen Jeffreys, whose brilliant play *The Libertine* introduced me to the Earl of Rochester.

Samuel Pepys, whose diary recorded for posterity many scenes of Nell's life on and off stage and left such a vivid picture of her times.

All the wonderful bloggers and reviewers for their help in getting the word out about *The Darling Strumpet*, including Sarah Johnson of *Reading the Past*, Amy Phillips Bruno of *Passages to the Past*, Margaret Bates of *Historical Tapestry*, Anita Davison of *Hoydens and Firebrands*, Marie Burton of *Historical Fiction Connection*, Carlyn Beccia of *The Raucous Royals*, and Helena of *The Misadventures of Moppet*.

Jim Piddock, whose performance in the one-man show *The Boy's Own Story* in San Francisco in 1982 inspired me to begin researching Nell with the thought of putting her life on stage.

Weston DeWalt, who gave me early advice and encouragement.

The late Leonard Michaels, whose class at U.C. Berkeley long ago gave me the confidence that I could write, which stuck with me for the many years when I wasn't writing.

Jane Merrow, an early acting heroine of mine, who made my month with her great compliment, 'I am a born Londoner and you brought old London completely to life.'

David Paul Needles, who has been there when I really needed him so many times.

The late Khin-Kyaw Maung, a life-saving friend for many years.

Sarah Ban Breathnach and Melody Beattie, whose writing helps me every day.

All the authors whose books have given me so much joy.

And finally, much love and gratitude to my three fairy godmothers: Katherine, who took me in from the cold and helped me get my feet under me; Dilys, who rescued me when I had lost my way and led me onto the right path; and Mari, who guided me to the top of the mountain until I could see the sun rising ahead.

Notes on Facts, Truth, and Artistic Licence

Nell has been in my mind and heart for a long time, and I've tried to tell the story of her life as fully and as truthfully as possible. When I knew the facts, I used them. When I didn't, I surmised what was likely. Occasionally, I invented, based on what seemed possible and in keeping with Nell's life and times.

Almost all of the major characters and many of the minor ones were real people in Nell's world. Dicky One-Shank is my creation, but there were sailors who worked as stagehands, and Nell surely knew some of them. Jack and everything to do with him are my invention. He began as a fairly minor character, but kept shoving his way onstage, and the members of my writing group thought he was such a great villain that they urged me to make him a bigger part of the story and not let him drift away once Nell left Madam Ross's.

Readers with detailed knowledge of the period may notice that I have given Charles Sackville his earldom and other titles a few years early. When Nell first knew him, he was Lord Buckhurst, but my writing group found they got confused between Buckhurst and Buckingham, so Buckhurst became Dorset.

I have taken a few minor liberties with the timing of events in the interest of making the story flow. The biggest change was moving up Moll Davis's pregnancy by about a year so it came at the same time as Louise's and Barbara's, but those two ladies actually did give birth within two weeks of each other.

Dr. Tenison did give Nell's funeral sermon, as she had hoped, and saw to it that she was buried in the vicar's vault at St. Martin-in-the-Fields. The crypt now houses a nice café, and when I went looking for Nell's grave some years ago, I was told that it might be under the ovens. According to several sources, many graves were obliterated when the church was rebuilt in the 1720s. Vicar Holtam of SMTF told me that Nell's burial was 'so recent and significant' that she might have been reburied, though no one now knows where. I'm sure Nell would be pleased to know the good vicar considers her significant. But wherever her bones may lie, she lives in beloved memory.

With young Nell in the forefront of my mind, I was particularly moved when I read about a book called *Half the Sky* and the authors' efforts to effect real change in the lives of young girls forced into prostitution.

I visited their website, and hope you'll take a look . . .

http://www.halftheskymovement.org

'Half the Sky lays out an agenda for the world's women and three major abuses: sex trafficking and forced prostitution; gender-based violence including honor killings and mass rape; maternal mortality, which needlessly claims one woman a minute. We know there are many worthy causes competing for attention in the world. We focus on this one because this kind of oppression feels transcendent—and so does the opportunity. Outsiders can truly make a difference.'